JAPANESE LITERATURE REVIEWED

DONALD RICHIE

WITH AN INTRODUCTION BY J. THOMAS RIMER

JAPANESE LITERATURE REVIEWED

DONALD RICHIE

WITH AN INTRODUCTION BY J. THOMAS RIMER

ICG Muse, Inc.
New York, Tokyo, Osaka & London

Published by ICG Muse, Inc.
420 West 42nd Street, #35B, New York, N.Y. 10036

Distributed by Yohan, Inc.
Striped House Building 2F, Roppongi 5, 10-33 Minato-ku,
Tokyo 106-0032

ISBN 4-925080-78-4

These reviews, originally appearing in *Newsweek*, *Harper's Magazine*, the *Asian Wall Street Journal*, *The Japan Quarterly*, *The Far East Economic Review*, the *Atlantic Monthly*, *The Nation* and *The Japan Times*, are reprinted here with permission. The word order of Japanese names follows current usage family name first. I would also like to thank Alisa Freedman for her meticulous editing and checking of my final manuscript.

Cover Design by Rie Ito

Contents

Introduction

This is the kind of book that readers of Japanese literature, until now, could only dream about. Dream, I say, because this collection of essays is first of its kind, one that is truly intended for those general readers, whatever their background, who take an interest in Japanese literature and culture.

There are many writers who have issued in book form their collected essays on American, British or French literature. Think of John Updike, perhaps, or all those "Letters from Paris" in *The New Yorker* over the years. In the field of Japanese literature, however, there are very few if any writers who have attempted to aim their comments in the direction of a more general public and, furthermore, who are comfortable presenting their views and observations without the need of any elaborate scholarly structures or theoretical axes of one sort or another to grind—or at least to sharpen. Academic commentators do have their place, of course, but in the case of Japan, such wise and accessible writing remains rare and is badly needed.

This is not to say that Donald Richie comes to his task—one he has obviously enjoyed—without adequate preparation. As even a casual reader will soon discover (if he or she did not already know the author's formidable reputation) Mr. Richie has long known Japan and Japanese culture extraordinarily well, and he is erudite as well in his knowledge and affection for European and American literature, which he often uses to create telling comparisons.

His knowledge of Japanese and European film is also brought to bear in a manner that can shed light both on the work of literature he is in the process of discussing, while comparing the original with the film version as well.

Written over the space of several decades, these reviews provide a virtual cornucopia of observation and comment on the entire range of Japanese literature, prose, drama, and poetry alike, from the very beginnings until the most recent times. Mr. Richie, however, would be the first to say that he had no intention of writing a history of Japanese literature and indeed the book is organized along principles of taste and conviction, rather than on any purely historical considerations. Nevertheless, adding piece by piece, year after year as translations became available to him for review, he has constructed a kind of sturdy mansion of Japanese letters, with startling windows and occasionally peculiar corridors.

The collection can be dipped into or read straight through, but in either case the sense of a larger whole will always be present somewhere in the background. And those who read carefully will be rewarded with reviews of a number of books in English translation which, because they are not available in American editions, are often unknown to readers here.

The collection is also a kind of cornucopia because Mr. Richie has included not only works of literary ambition but novels for popular entertainment as well. Both shed considerable light on the linking layers of Japanese literary and artistic culture, and he has a sufficiently sure and catholic taste to locate and appreciate the virtues of what he reads, whatever this might be.

The reader will also discover that the majority of the reviews included are favorable. Mr. Richie once told me that he only reviewed what he enjoyed. There are occasional grumbles, to be sure, sometimes strikingly articulated.

And in the case of either praise or blame, frequent textual analyses help explain his conclusions.

And of course, Mr. Richie has his particular heroes—or, more often than not, heroines, since he seems to indicate that, on the whole, Japanese women in all periods are superior writers to their male counterparts. Among writers he particularly enjoys, I was gratified to read his high praise for the work of Inoue Yasushi, one of the greatest of twentieth-century Japanese novelists, whose austere and thoughtful stance has made his works less popular in English-speaking countries than they should be. And, although he enjoys much popular literature as entertainment, he cannot resist some discerning and disdainful remarks about that blockbuster of Yoshikawa Eiji, *Musashi*.

Above and beyond, the reviews themselves are surprisingly consistent, given the fact that they were written in no particular order and over such a span of years. I think that those who read through this collection will be astonished to discover how much Japanese literature by now has, in fact, been made available in English. A number of enthusiastic and gifted translators have risen in recent decades, and it is possible to have an overview of the accomplishments of Japanese literature in both the classic and modern periods which would have been considered impossible even twenty years ago.

There is, therefore, much to be thankful for. And in terms of directing a reader to find and read the books that prove his point, I know of no more sophisticated or persuasive guide than Donald Richie. Read, enjoy, and then seek out some of the works he so generously describes.

J. Thomas Rimer

Preface

I have written quite a few book reviews (usually about one a week from 1975 onwards), and I am still at it. Soon there will be fifteen hundred or so. So when it comes time to collect some of them, the problem is what to leave out. I finally decided to include only the reviews of literature, dropping those on film, art, sociology, anthropology, history, politics, economics. One of the reasons for confining myself to literary reviews was that there was enough of them so that, together, they gave some idea of Japanese literature itself. Though each review is discrete, linked they could approximate a narrative. This is why I have arranged them chronologically.

My first draft of this collection was over six hundred printed pages, far too long for a paperback manuscript. So out went that section which dealt with books about Japanese literature, those excellent multi-volume histories of Kato Shuichi and Donald Keene included. Out, just as regretfully, went books about individual authors, including Ito Ken and Anthony Chambers on Tanizaki, Edward Seidensticker on Nagai Kafu.

There are other omissions as well. One can review only what one can get a copy of. Also, I usually only review a book I like. If I don't like it and still review it, this is usually only to warn. Consequently there are whole sections of the Japanese literary canon unrepresented.

Since the order is chronological, I start with the early literature, on to Edo literature, and further into Meiji plus modern literature. This last is the largest of the groupings and I label it that only because I could not find the dividing line between Meiji on one hand and modern on the other.

It will become apparent through this collection that I am perhaps a scholar but am not an academic, that I am a generalist and not a specialist, that I am in many respects an informed amateur. Here lies, I think, my value.

Donald Richie

Early Literature

Classical Japanese Prose: An Anthology

Helen Craig McCullough's *Classical Japanese Prose: An Anthology* is the most comprehensive selection of Japanese prose since Donald Keene's 1953 *Anthology of Japanese Literature*. Unlike the earlier collection, this one confines itself to "classical" prose (defined as 9th to 17th-century) and contents itself with excerpts.

This it must do since the majority of works in the period are long. Two of them—the *Genji* and the *Heike*—are so long that they cannot be included at all. The result is a collection of bits and pieces. Just what these are is not indicated in the table of contents nor in the general introduction. For the interested reader here is my listing of what is included and what is not.

Three sections of the *Taketori Monogatari* (there is a also complete translation by Donald Keene, 1978, published elsewhere); 39 of the 125 sections of *The Tales of Ise*, taken from McCullough's complete 1968 translation; *The Tosa Diary*, complete; the first book of the *Kagero Nikki* (published complete in the 1964 Seidensticker translation as *The Gossamer Years*); 21 of the 320 sections of Sei Shonagon's *Pillow Book* (complete, Ivan Morris' 1971 translation); excerpts from McCullough's complete translation of the *Eiga Monogatari*; three of the 10 tales in the *Tsutsumi Chunagon Monogatari* (complete in the 1985 Backus translation, *The Riverside Counselor's Stories*).

There are also four from the thousand tales in the *Konjaku Monogatari* (62 are included in the 1979 Ury translation); four from the 197 tales in the *Uji Shui Monogatari*, (complete translation, Mills, 1970); the first of five books from *The Confessions of Lady Nijo* (complete in the 1982 Brazell translation); the *Izayoi Nikki*, complete; the *Hojoki*, complete; 60 of the 243 parts of the *Tsurezuregusa* (complete in Keene's *Essays in Idleness*, 1967); the *Tokan Kiko*, complete; one of the six books of the *Masukagami*; and six of the 40 sections of the *Taiheiki*, from McCullough's complete 1959 translation. The selection concludes with two *otogi-zoshi*, complete: "Little One-Inch" and "Akimichi" and two Basho travel diaries, complete: *The Journey of 1684* and a well known work that McCullough renders as *The Narrow Road of the Interior*.

It is apparent that the selection is wide. It is also apparent that most of the works have been translated before. What is not so apparent is that all this new translation is McCullough's. She is listed as compiler and editor though not as translator. It argues for a devotion to anthologies that one of the finest of translators from the classical Japanese would give her talent and her time to works that had already been adequately (and even brilliantly) translated.

The bibliography is selective and gives no indication of the wealth of translated material among which the reader may choose. Not listed—at least not in its proper place—is the Sadler translation of the *Hojoki*, and the F.V. Dickins' translation of the same work is not mentioned; neither the Sargent and Porter complete translations of the *The Tosa Diary* are listed; likewise not indicated is the George Sansom translation of the *Tsurezuregusa*, the Waley translation of Sei Shonagon, and many more.

It might also be argued that equally valuable would have been translations of works as yet untranslated for there are many. Here, however, the anthologist might counter that this is just what she has also done. Indeed, so far as I can determine, this is the first English appearance of the *Masukagami*, and I can find no alternate translation of the *Izayoi Nikki* either.

As to these translations, a quality of variability is to be expected. I much admire McCullough's work. Her industry and accuracy have made available many a classical work. At the same time one single translator cannot do everything equally well, though I confine this opinion to the question of an appropriate English style.

For purposes of comparison here are three different English versions of the famous opening passage from the *Hojoki*:

> The waters of a flowing stream are ever present but never the same; the bubbles in a quiet pool disappear and foam but never endure for long. So it is with men and their dwellings in the world.

> The flow of the river is ceaseless and its water is never the same. The bubbles that float in the pools, now vanishing, now forming, are not of long duration: so in the world are man and his dwellings.

> Ceaselessly the river flows, and yet the water is never the same, while in the still pools the shifting foam gathers and is gone, never staying for a moment. Even so is man and his habitation.

The first is McCullough's, the second is Keene's, the third is that of the late and neglected A. L. Sadler. (His 1928 complete translation of the *Heike Monogatari* has never been made generally available except in excerpts. More may now be known about the Heike texts, but no one, I think, understood them better.)

As to the purpose of this project, and as to anthologies in general, several attitudes are possible. My own will have become apparent. I question such an assemblage of bleeding parts. Surely, the way to read a work is to read it complete. Certainly, this is the only way to fully experience it. But an anthology is not interested in the reader's experience of a work. Its aims are more modest: it seeks to acquaint with, to introduce, to give a superficial knowledge.

When this anthology says that both the *Genji* and the *Heike* are omitted because "they deserve to be read in their entirety," I am sure that no one thinks that other works included are not equally deserving. Yet such is the suggestion in the act of anthologization itself.

The intention of this anthology is, I think, to make a text. It is a potpourri for class instruction. As such it will serve its purpose well: judiciously chosen sections sturdily translated. The more serious reader, however, might better turn to those complete translations listed above.

Classical Japanese Prose: An Anthology, compiled and edited by Helen Craig McCullough. Stanford: Stanford University Press, 1990.

The *Man'yoshu*

The largest and oldest collection of Japanese lyric poetry, the *Man'yoshu* was compiled probably in the second half of the 8th-century. The last specifically dated poem was composed in 759.

This very large work is comprised of 4,516 poems in 20 books. They represent over 400 named poets, and hundreds of others who composed the anonymous verse which makes up over half of the collection.

The variety within the work is enormous, ranging from aristocratic banquet verse to rustic ditties in provincial dialect, from poems of courtiers to the lyrics of frontier guardsmen. Though a variety of poetic forms are included the largest number, some 4,200, are *waka*.

Though the compilers of this vast work are unknown, the mode of classification seems to have followed the divisions used for Chinese poetry. By content the poems can be divided in three categories: *zoka*, miscellaneous poems about legends, banquets, travel, etc; *somonka*, which are love poems; and *banka*, or elegies.

The poems themselves are written in what is known as *man'yogana*, the Japanese language recorded with Chinese characters which are sometimes simply phonetic renderings of Japanese syllables, but at other times have an actual meaning. Just what this meaning is remains in some cases doubtful, and modern scholarly opinion is not at all unanimous regarding some of the verse.

This is a problem for those who would render this important collection into another language. Brushing aside the well known (and probably true) observation that, in any event, poetry cannot by its nature be translated, one is still left with the fact that assumptions regarding poetry change. An 1882 translation cannot satisfy the expectations of 1982 because the very conception of poetry was quite different one hundred years ago from what it is today.

We can read, say, Tennyson, and make due allowances, but we cannot read a translation of, say, the *Man'yoshu* made by a contemporary of that poet and make like adjustments. Tennyson is reflecting the world of the late 19th-century in his poems, but the translator of the *Man'yoshu* is reflecting 8th-century Japan through the assumptions of 19th-century England. It is, for this reason, that new translations of earlier literature are continually necessary if the work is to be kept alive in translation at all.

In the introduction to his excellent translation of the *Man'yoshu* (the first ten books, a second and concluding volume to be issued later), Ian Hideo Levy has redefined the work in completely contemporary terms: "*The Ten Thousand Leaves* [Levy's rendering of the title] is a chorus of lyrical voices born out of a tradition of ritual verbal art that stretches back into Japan's pre-literate centuries, back into myth itself."

The assumptions, already, are quite different from those of earlier translators. Basil Hall Chamberlain said, "The work is invaluable to the philogist, the archaeologist, the historian, the student of curious manners which have disappeared ... we may add that there are some clever and many pretty things in it." This tone, so infuriating to modern sensibilities, is well reflected in *Man'yoshu* translations of the period (and some modern ones as well) and precludes all contemporary appreciation.

A modern translation (Seidensticker's *Genji*, for example) thus opens an ancient classic for the contemporary reader. The assumptions of the reader are already those of the translator in that they share an assumption as to what a novel or a poetry collection (in the case of the *Man'yoshu*) is. And these assumptions change quite rapidly. In due time, I suppose, it is possible that Levy's fine work will be considered limited but, for the time being, his *Man'yoshu* is startling in its apparent rightness.

To give some examples: some years ago the Nippon Gakujutsu Shinkokai translated (in its complete rendering of the work) one of the farewell poems of Prince Otsu as: "Today, taking my last sight of the mallards/Crying on the pond of Iware,/Must I vanish into the clouds!" Levy's translation is "The duck that cries/in Iware Pond, where the vines/crawl on the rocks: will I see it just today,/and tomorrow be hidden in the clouds?"

Both are obviously modern translations but already the rightness (from our point of view) of the Levy translation becomes apparent. Not only does he include the poem complete (completeness, no matter what, is a fairly modern invention in the field of translation), but he prefers the common "duck" to the poetic "mallard" and (properly) turns the exclamation into a question. Levy's assumption (one he shares with all of us) is that accuracy of detail and naturalness of diction renders much more feeling (after all,

Otsu wrote this shortly before his execution) than does heightened language ("mallard") and strained ("must" instead of "will") expression.

Prince Arima, off to the execution grounds in 658, seems to have had yet some hope. He tied together some pine branches in a prayer for safety. An early translation (found in Kato Shuichi's *A History of Japanese Literature*) goes: "If fortune favours me,/I may come back/And see the knot again." Levy's translation has it: "I draw and tie together/branches of the pine/on the beach at Iwashiro,/ If all goes well/I shall return to see them again." An equally modern translation, that of Sato Hiroaki, renders it: "At Iwashiro I tie together branches of a beach pine; if I'm lucky, I'll return and see them again."

The latter two are very much of our time, Sato's is even colloquial ("I'm/I'll"). Also, they are the more accurate. It is the branches which the unfortunate prince hopes to see again, not (for heaven's sake) the knot. Also the fact that all this occurred at a distinct place (Iwashiro) is of importance to the modern translator though not, obviously, to an earlier.

Levy's new translation of the *Man'yoshu* thus makes available to us, on our own terms, as it were, one of the glories of Japanese poetry. His work is so well done, so right, so lacking in anything approaching affectation on one hand or pedantry on the other that we will find the translation definitive and impatiently await the second and concluding volume.

Man'yoshu, translated with an introduction by Ian Hideo Levy. Tokyo: University of Tokyo Press, 1981.

Otomo no Yakamochi

Born near the beginning of the 8th-century, and dead near its close, Otomo no Yakamochi, an important government official and even more important poet, is thought to have helped compile the *Man'yoshu* anthology. In any event, nearly five hundred of his own poems are included.

Consequently, treating the poetry as biography, and taking advantage of the mass of scholarship that has grown around this important anthology, a great deal is known of Yakamochi and the world in which he lived. So much so that a full accounting of his life and times becomes possible, and one has indeed just now appeared.

Such a biography of a poet who lived well over a thousand years ago would be possible perhaps only in Japan where records are kept and the past is, to an extent, treasured. Certainly a biography of any equivalent poet, say that of the Northumbrian who was just completing *Beowulf* when Yakamochi had already begun his poetic journal, would be quite impossible. In any event, quite enough is known about the life of the so-called Nara Period, and Yakamochi's life within it that a very plausible accounting is possible. Also, there is the poetry.

It has been said (by Kato Shuichi) that there is in Yakamochi's poetry "little individuality either in vocabulary or expression of emotion." Further, it has been stated that the poet's view (his emphasis upon the lineage of the Otomo family, for example) indicates a somewhat anachronistic view. The poet's merits lie in "his polished sentiments expressed toward the world of nature." Indeed, the poet was a "disillusioned aristocratic intellectual" (all these quotes are from Kato, an authority of which the present biographer does not avail herself) who was perhaps the first to feel, or at least record, that sadness which was so soon to be identified as Japan's major poetic refrain. In the poetry of Yakamochi "the *mono no aware* of the Heian Period was not far away."

The emphasis of the present biography is slightly different, but it is perhaps just this absence of individuality which, paradoxically makes a biography based mainly on poetry. That is to say, the personality of the poet is reflected in the conventions of his verse and these, in turn, tell us much about the times in which the poet lives. At the same time, his concerns show a definite personality, but one which is more than commonly shaped by his times. I cannot imagine a biography of, say, Kakinomoto no Hitomaro, unquestionably the greatest poet of the *Man'yoshu* collection, because his excellence is unique to himself.

One might then say that Yakamochi is, in this sense, representative. Yet, at the same time, his *mono-no-aware*sque awareness makes him definite, unique, and (given our hindsight) appreciable. Indeed, of all the poets in the *Man'yoshu*, he is, I feel, the proper candidate for biography.

In conceiving, researching and writing this biography, Paula Doe has, on one hand, a surprising wealth of information. On the other hand, however, she has but a single tactical possibility—conjecture. This, however, is also one of the strongest (and most poetic) of biographical tools. One infers, draws conclusions, hesitates among possibilities and then chooses. It is the lack of sound biographical data that makes the use of conjecture imperative, and, at the same time, it is use of conjecture which gives such biographies their peculiar persuasiveness.

One thinks of like books. Helen Waddell wanted to do a life of Abelard (1079–1142), materials for which are slight indeed. Consequently her book became a treatise in the proper use of conjecture. Marguerite Yourcenar wanted to write a biography (in this case an autobiography) of the Emperor Hadrian (76–138), materials for which were entirely fragmentary. Using conjecture and imaginative reconstruction, she created a life which must rank as one of the finest historical biographies ever written.

Paula Doe does not allow herself anything like the latitude allowed by Yourcenar, but her methodology resembles that of the author of *The Memoirs of Hadrian* in that imaginative conjecture cannot but play a part. And it is to this part that, I think, the strengths of her book are owed.

What I am saying is that, in general, scholarship is admirable but not interesting. What is interesting is the conjectural connection between subject and biographer. This is based upon an emotional understanding of the subject and his times, something which all the biographical facts in the world cannot create but which, sometimes, a lack of facts can. Doe's scholarly historiography seems impeccable, but it is not for that reason that one values her book.

The reason one values it is that a 20th-century scholar meets an 8th-century scholar-poet and an understanding occurs. The result is illuminating, interesting and, in human terms, quite touching. Yakamochi, ambitious, unhappy, turning away from the world of men and toward the world of nature, comes again alive and the poetry (most of his five hundred verses are used) becomes, in this context of the poet's life, again vivid. Other than some feeling against the title, I have nothing but praise for this meticulous, scholarly, and human work.

A Warbler's Song in the Dusk: The Life and Work of Otomo no Yakamochi, by Paula Doe. Berkeley: University of California Press, 1982.

The *Kokinshu*

The *Kokinshu*, well over a thousand poems gathered at the end of the 10th-century, remains in many ways the most innovative of these early poetry collections.

It was the first to arrange the poems not by single authors but by topics. Seasonal poems and love poems (by far the largest categories) are given their own sections, as are later groups of elegies, laments, etc.

The *Kokinshu* was also the first to arrange poems within a genre into a meaningful sequence. Thus the seasonal poems follow the calendar of court rites, and the love poems follow a course from infatuation through disillusion or renewal.

Finally, this collection marks the beginnings of Japanese poetics, at least in any systematic sense. Basing itself upon earlier Chinese aesthetic writings, the preface to the *Kokinshu* posits three major poetic concepts: *kokoro* (heart/mind), *kotoba* (words) and *sama* (style), all combining harmoniously to a total effect (*sugata*).

As Earl Miner has elsewhere noted: "This accounted for poet, world, reader, and expression—as any full poetics must—and was so sound that the later introduction of valued prose narrative and drama only modified without overturning it."

There have been many Japanese editions of the *Kokinshu* and one in French (that of Georges Bonneau, 1933–35), but until now no complete English edition—though there have been many partial translations. Among them: those of Robert Brower and Earl Miner in *Japanese Court Poetry* (1961) and of Sato Hiroaki and Burton Watson in *From the Country of Eight Islands* (1981).

This new edition is certainly complete. All of the 1,111 poems and their annotations are translated, as are both the original Japanese and Chinese prefaces. In addition, each poem (*romaji* and English) is annotated by the translators, and there are references to Japanese, Chinese and Western-language sources. There is an author index and biographical entries for the poets involved, an appendix on the Chinese influence on the prefaces, and both a first-line and a subject index, as well as a comprehensive general introduction.

There is obviously much here of scholarly and antiquarian interest. Is there anything else? In the *Kokinshu*, we are reading poetry which was written about the time of the Carolingian revival of learning. Can Theodulf, the Visigothic poet, be now read with pleasure by the casual reader? I do not know since I have not read him. But I suspect that the pleasure might partially come from knowing something about the civilization of Charlemagne's court.

In the same way, reflections upon Heian court life a thousand years ago might give body. "Already they say spring is here/but as for me/while yet there is no song from the mountain thrush/I cannot believe spring has come." This nicely bucolic lyric of Mibu no Tadamine gains considerably when one allows it the context of the Heian court with its very poetic formulae and, at the same time, its very human and inchoate outpourings of emotion. The language of nature was codified (The song of the mountain thrush would announce the arrival of spring, it was decreed), but at the same time the responses to this language were not.

Of a consequence, there is a tension in Heian poetry—emotional impulse, formal restraint. When the form is stronger, the interest is (for us, not for them) less. When the impulse seems stronger, then contemporary us respond the more.

For example, the following—adjacent poems, both of which are about the moon. The one I would think more conventional goes: "In the end I find/my pleasure in the bright moon/is tinged with sadness—/for every wax and wane/numbers the months of our lives." So what else is new? This is just a formal response that the poem takes toward its material, not a vital one.

In contrast, then: "How late is the long/awaited moon to emerge from/behind the rugged mountain crests/how the other side must long to hold it back." Though the former poem is by the well known Ariwara no Narihira and though this one is humbly anonymous, I would maintain that, for the lay reader, at any rate, the latter poem is the more deeply felt.

That one can venture this, of course, indicates that at least some of this poetry has an abiding interest, one which in the historical context of its time can move the reader yet. As Ki no Tsurayuki says in his preface: "The seeds of ... poetry lie in the human heart and grow into leaves of ten thousand words."

Kokinshu: A Collection of Poems Ancient and Modern, translated and annotated by Laurel Rasplica Rodd and Mary Catherine Henkenius. Princeton: Princeton University Press, 1984.

The *Kokinshu* was the first in a series of such anthologies compiled by royal dictate (that of the Emperor Daigo) and was so ordered "that many matters should not be consigned to oblivion and an interest be maintained in the things of long ago." Its aims were, like many such collections in many countries, antiquarian, and its four poet—bureaucrat compilers wished to stress the genealogy of native verse, as it were, and perhaps also that poignant connection between then and now which is so much a part of antiquarian interest.

The poems themselves were chosen from three groups: anonymous poems from older (and more recent) times;

poems from the so-called *rokkasen* (six-sages) period; and poems by contemporaries and by the compilers themselves. These included their own work in ample measure, their poems making up almost one-fourth of the whole.

Perhaps wishing to render the past immediate, or perhaps for other reasons, the poems were not arranged chronologically nor by single authors. About ordering patterns in this work, there is an excellent chapter called "*Kokinshu* as Literary Entity" included in the work under review. About such patterns in Japanese (early) literature in general there is an extraordinary chapter, "The Collective and the Individual," by Earl Miner in *The Principles of Classical Japanese Literature*, which must be read by anyone interested in the subject.

What we, a thousand years later, make of the collection depends a lot on the kind of readers we are. Masaoka Shiki, the haiku poet, as early as 1898 began attacking what he pleased to call its "triviality." And among the Japanese sages and *sensei*, it has been pro and con ever since. Indeed, the later *Shin Kokinshu* (ca. 1205) is sometimes professed preferred, the reason given being its "profundity," an apparent antidote to the presumed "triviality" of the former.

Actually, however, the *Kokinshu* is the more original and more responsive to life back then. Its immediacy is still felt. I can respond more immediately to this 10th-century Japanese poetry than I can to Orosius, Boethius or the *Anglo-Saxon Chronicle*, all roughly contemporary to the *Kokinshu*. Provided the translation is good.

This new translation, by Helen Craig McCullough, is very good indeed. I cannot compare it with the original (though this is a bilingual edition, *romaji* and English on facing pages), but the resulting English poetry seems right. The translator has preserved the Japanese syllable-count, and she also respects the integrity of the original line(s).

McCullough's is the best of several which have appeared. That of Earl Miner and Robert Brower (found in *Japanese Court Poetry*, 1961) is excellent but incomplete—by design to be sure. That of Rodd/Henkenius sometimes appears peculiar and reads more like a translation pony than poetry.

McCullough's is not only complete, it also includes, in addition to the poems in the basic text, the Chinese and Japanese prefaces, the 11 so-called "deleted" poems, and the 29 poems that appear in one or another of the variant textual lines.

(In addition, two works by Ki no Tsurayuki, the principal *Kokinshu* compiler, have been included: the *Tosa Nikki* and the first translation in any language of the *Shinsen Waka*—and here McCullough is up against competition: Miner's translation of the *Tosa Nikki* (found in *The Japanese Poetic Diaries*).

Along with this complete translation (which contains, as well, appendices on the authors and their poems, on the *Shinsen Waka*, and an index of first lines) the publisher has issued a companion volume, a nearly 600-page study by McCullough on the *Kokinshu*, the first full-scale such in English. Called *Brocade by Night* and subtitled "*Kokin Wakashu* and the Court Style in Japanese Classical Poetry," it is a complete commentary about the work and its times.

Brocade by Night: "Kokin Wakashu" and the Court Style in Japanese Classical Poetry, translated and annotated by Helen Craig McCullough. Stanford: Stanford University Press, 1985.

The *Tosa Nikki*

One day in late January 935, the ex-governor of Tosa boarded the boat to return to the capital, Kyoto. He was Ki no Tsurayuki, a celebrated poet, one of the compilers of the *Kokinshu* anthology. He also contributed more poems than any other (nearly five hundred) to the imperial anthologies, became known as the most representative *waka* poet of his time and exerted much poetic influence on later generations.

On this January day, however, though still grieving for the loss of a little daughter, dead in Tosa, he was pleased at the prospect of the return to Kyoto, the pleasant voyage ahead, and being able to leave behind the cares and responsibilities of a provincial governorship.

He also had a small plan. He would keep a diary of the voyage. Further, for what reasons are not now known, he would write it, not in Chinese characters, but in the *kana* syllabary. Finally, as a conceit to explain this mode of communication, he would pretend that the writer was a woman, since women (went the belief) knew only *kana*. Thus his diary begins: "It is generally a man who writes what is called a diary, but now a woman will see what she can do."

The resulting *Tosa Nikki* is not only the first of the many later *kana* diaries, mostly indeed written by women, but also might be called the first novel, in that narrator hides his identity (referring to himself often as "a certain personage") and takes the point of view of an anonymous but well-born lady who takes a lively interest in what is going on about her.

It was an uneventful voyage (except for a pirate scare) which eventually became, it would seem, quite uncomfortable. For one thing, after all the good-byes were said, the boat remained in port a number of days before the weather permitted departure. For another, there were numerous storms which necessitated lengthy stays on uninhabitable islands. And, finally, when Osaka was reached and the river entered, it was discovered that there was so little water in that the boat had to be pulled upstream, bumping and scraping until, at last, the capital was thankfully reached. In all, the 300-kilometer journey took 55 long days.

During all of this time, the "lady" remained collected, recording her *waka* in the diary (and poems by others of the passengers, perhaps also actually written by herself) and jotting down what had happened that day. Or what had not, as the voyage became more and more obstructed: "February 8. In the same place. I wonder if the wind and waves had a tender feeling for him [the governor], as they seemed to wish to delay him for some time? He certainly had no tender feeling for them!" Or after "he" had written some poetry: "People who hear this will say to themselves that this kind of stuff is very poor. But [he] produced it with a good deal of difficulty and thought it pretty good; so they should stop whispering such cruel things about it. But suddenly the wind and waves got up, and so they had to stop talking."

Soon many were violently seasick and so conversation further ceased. Still, after a period, the verse-making (apparently the principal occupation of the passengers) went on. On March 13 an old lady from Awaji, who had been very ill indeed, suddenly spouted forth a poem: "Everybody was astonished when she came out with this so unexpectedly; and among them ['he'], who was also feeling unwell, praised it very highly, and said it was not what he had expected from one with such a sea-sick countenance." Later "he" tried his hand at capping hers: "But they are not so good as the one by [the lady from Awaji] and, feeling jealous of her, he regretted having made them; so, as the night was drawing on, he retired to sleep."

Eventually, bumping and scraping, (no one apparently thought of getting out and walking, surely a faster means of locomotion than sitting in a boat being pulled up a dry river bed), they reached Kyoto's Yamasaki Bridge and, as we can well believe, "there was no limit to their delight . . . ." The governor remembers the poor little girl, dead and buried in far Tosa, never again to see the Kyoto of her birth, and this short work ends with the admonition, "well, well—this [diary] must be torn up at once."

But it was not, and it has delighted and instructed down the ages. Though it has sometimes been criticized because the author did not take much interest in the lands through which he was passing (as had the earlier Ennin travel diary, *Nitto-guho-junrei-koki*), it could be argued that the lands through which Tsurayuki was passing were not very interesting. He has also been scolded by scholars because his diary is not (in contrast to Michizane's *One Hundred Couplets on My Thoughts*) at all deep. But being profound about a highly uncomfortable and protracted provincial journey would certainly have been inappropriate.

Like much casual (in contrast to official) literature, it imparts an atmosphere, a reality in the depiction of which weightier works (since they do not so aim) fail. The *Tosa Diary* is read now for its charm and its simplicity and for the lively picture of 10th-century Japan which it gives.

It was early translated into English, and this is a reissue of the 1912 edition. Though the book was later several times retranslated (most notably by G. W. Sargent), the original William N. Porter version remains (as perhaps the extracts above have indicated) highly satisfactory. Porter's style, apparently (not actually) artless, reminds one of early English-language diaries (that which Defoe wrote on a journey to Wales, for example), and this combination of the earnest and the *fausse-naïf* serves Ki no Tsurayuki very well indeed. Also, Porter's is the only version which gives the original (in *romaji*) on facing pages.

The Tosa Diary, translated by William N. Porter. Tokyo: Charles E. Tuttle Company, 1981.

The *Yamato Monogatari*

The *Yamato Monogatari* was written during the middle years of the 10th-century. Perhaps compiled rather than written, this collection of poems and anecdotes about poems seems to have been gathered from a number of sources, the major one being court gossip of the period.

It is typical of this interesting era in Japanese history that it was poetry which was gossiped about. The works of the ladies Murasaki and Shonagon are also concerned with such literary chit-chat, though both in their own ways rise above its limitations. The *Yamato Monogatari* was indeed written during the time that Murasaki describes in her *Genji*; and during this same period Shonagon's *Pillow Book* is full of indications that writing and talking about poetry was something of a fulltime Heian occupation.

It was a period when the first fine enthusiasm for things Chinese had somewhat faded, and the latest novelty was the native language. *Yamato kotoba* (as used in the title, however, the word refers to the province) were all the rage, as was the *waka*. Courtiers vied with each other in poetic expertise and the many ambiguities of these *kotoba* helped create the need for explication which the *Yamato Monogatari* provides.

Whoever wrote or compiled the book (tradition says it was a Heian courtier with a special interest in such poem-tales) knew all about the old poems and stories included in the *Man'yoshu* and the *Kokinshu*. Later, interested parties kept adding to it (up through the Muromachi Period) with the result that, in the first half of the work, we have an interesting evocation of the Heian literary world (and no other seems to have been recorded), while in the second we have a more romantic view of some distant golden age when everyone who counted was a poet.

Though the work has considerable literary importance (and it is surprising that it has had to wait this long for a full translation), its main interest for the contemporary reader is more sociological (or even anthropological) than it is literary. Over a hundred historical figures ranging from emperors to courtesans appear, and all are shown as animated by a love (perhaps not too strong a word) of literature and an absolutely dazzling skill at literary one-upmanship. What a curious civilization, that of the Heian aristocracy—no wonder the Minamotos finally took over.

Though sections of the *Yamato Monogatari* have been translated before, this is—as I above noted—the first complete rendering into English. It is a very good one, too. The poems (given in *romaji* and English) seem sensibly translated, the anecdotes are rendered into graceful but straightforward language, and there are several excellent appendices, including one on early Heian literature which is the best short, concise introduction to the subject that I have read. Though the translation was originally a doctoral dissertation, it does not read like one: the scholarship is sound and invisible, and the notes are full and discreet.

Tales of Yamato: A 10th-Century Poem-Tale, translated by Mildred M. Tahara, foreword by Donald Keene. Honolulu: University of Hawaii Press, 1980.

The *Utsuho Monogatari*

Often called Japan's first novel, the *Utsuho Monogatari* is a very long (20 volume) work, the date of which is uncertain. The first part, however, was probably written around 980, say some scholars, and the authorship has been variously attributed to Minamoto no Shitago and to Murasaki Shikibu's father. This latter establishes the *Genji* connection, which has given this particular *monogatari* some added luster. Murasaki is supposed to have read the *Utsuho* and been impressed by it. Her own *Genji Monogatari* is therefore thought to have been at least partially inspired by it.

Such is the contention of Professor Uraki Ziro, whose English rendering of the complete *Utsuho* is here under review. "There is a lot of evidence that Lady Murasaki read [it] with great pleasure and gained many hints for the writing of the *Tale of Genji*." Other scholars are not all that certain. Kato Shuichi says flat out: "It is not permissible to see the *Utsuho Monogatari* ... as simply a stage on the road toward the *Genji*.... It was not the *Genji* but the *Konjaku Monogatari* which took up [the influence]."

Rather then, the *Utsuho* should be regarded as an important work on its own. It is not only the longest fictional work to have until then appeared, it was also the first to have some inner structure. Also, in its four sections, it showed some concern in reflecting early Heian reality.

Included are portraits of people not only from aristocratic and official life but also from the gentry as well—the first and last time in Heian Period novels that such folks were fictionalized. Also, it is maintained, the *Utsuho* portrays more of the political concerns of the period than do the later novels.

The importance of children born to important parents, for example. The big conflict in this *monogatari* is not concerned with love or sensibility but on the question of which child of the two wives involved becomes the crown prince. (The story of this large work is, incidentally, easily told. The heroine, much courted, is finally married to the proper prince. The hero, most successful at court because he plays the koto so well, ends up with the emperor's daughter. The koto theme—in the first and last of the four parts—is what binds the novel together, to the extent that it is.)

The scholarly history of the *Utsuho* continues. Though apparently popular enough before *Genji* appeared, it shortly—in face perhaps of the incomparably greater work—disappeared, and the existing manuscripts remained uncollated until the end of the 19th-century when Hosoi Sadao's edition appeared. The first translation into modern Japanese, that of Professor Uraki, our present English translator, came only in 1976. And only now is the English translation appearing complete, though there have been prior translations of parts of it.

Going into all of this scholarly endeavor would perhaps not be necessary if there were anything else to say about the *Utsuho Monogatari*. But there is not. As the late Ivan Morris has written of it: "It is immensely long ... and, for most modern readers, extremely dull." Antiquarian interest is the only one which may be expected.

It is, of course, possible to take a fairly distant book and translate it so well, to so beautifully present its context, that it glows with new life. This is what, for example, Edward Seidensticker does for the *Kagero Nikki* in his *The Gossamer Years*. But Professor Uraki, no matter how well he knows Heian Period Japanese, is not a like master of modern English.

This translation is of interest because it is the first complete one. It is also a labor of love, and it is on those terms that it should be respected. Otherwise, it is filled with such phrases as "Sanetada wept at heart ..." and "Princess Inumiya has grown up so finely." And there is also the matter of the English title. Every reference calls it *The Tale of the Hollow Tree*. Professor Uraki alone calls it *The Tale of the Cavern*. I do not know his reasons and cannot imagine his sources.

The Tale of the Cavern, translated by Uraki Ziro. Tokyo: Shinozaki Shorin, 1984.

The *Kagero Nikki*

The *Kagero Nikki* is the diary of a court lady who lived in the 10th-century and is known only as the mother of Fujiwara no Michitsuna, a courtier under whose guidance the Fujiwara hegemony was at its strongest.

The diary covers twenty-one years, from 954 through 974 and is mostly concerned with her unhappy marriage. Though a son brought satisfaction, the husband brought only unhappiness. By the end, the couple was completely estranged.

But from this unhappiness was born something like literature. The lady herself describes her artistic aims: to tell what had happened so that her readers would know what life was like for such a well-born but unfortunate lady. As such it was a bold and unprecedented undertaking, this chronicling of her 15 *kagero* years.

The word can mean several things, all pointing to the ephemerality of existence, which is the reason that Edward Seidensticker named his 1964 translation *The Gossamer Years*. The term implies the insubstantiality of life remembered and one must agree with Seidensticker that if hers is perhaps not an unprejudiced description, it is certainly a vivid one.

Indeed, as Earl Miner has suggested, it is difficult to decide whether she is the most realistic of major diarists or simply the one most tortured by ordinary human realities. In any event, "it comes as a shock to recall that Murasaki Shikibu's *Genji Monogatari* makes of these same years something of a golden era."

But, as Sonja Arntzen, author of this new translation, reminds us, of all the famous women writers of the period, only the author of the *Kagero Diary* did not serve at court. "Thus, her voice is the only one we have for the secluded married woman."

This voice, Arntzen admits, may seem "like one long, self-indulgent whine." However, there are other perspectives, and it is with this apprehension that this new translation is concerned. "We grow unconsciously," says the translator in her closely reasoned introduction, "into what it is possible to think and say within our culture, our gender, and our position in the world. We do not often reflect upon the fact that we are all caught in the discourse of our time and place."

It is just this upon which Arntzen has reflected in her translation, the recovery of the original timbre of the author's voice; a tone which attempts to suggest the unexamined certitudes, the unstated assumptions of this existence separated from us by a thousand years.

In so doing, she explains much that has been hitherto ignored. In speaking of *aware*, for example, she notes that the love poetry is almost exclusively that of yearning after "the thrill is gone." She here purposely uses a phrase from a blues lyric because in both Heian verse and the lyrics of Billie Holiday (my example, not hers) "pain expressed is pain released."

"If one imagines removing the music and the timbre of the singer's voice from a blues song and paraphrasing its lyrics, one would be left with repetitive whining and grating complaint." It is this which she feels earlier translations (Waley's, Seidensticker's, McCullough's) have unwittingly transmitted. "We had the content of her complaining but not its style, not the artistry of its expression."

This artistry is what Arntzen wishes to disclose, and her translation indeed reveals a woman who is certainly more than the sum of her complaints. The text unfolds in psychological time, moving by association from memory to thought to conversation. This thought slips between past and present, and, as the translator has noted, "emotional states are given more weight and attention than events."

All the poetry in the original is included, and the text is now as disjunctive as was intended, the narrative being constantly interrupted (and enriched) by the poems, the quotation of others, and the intrusion of the author's own voice. The linear conventionality of Western thought (an assumption of Western languages) has not prevailed, and a consequence is a new apprehension.

But, as Arntzen is well aware, "there is no such thing as a transparent translation." One may allow the original to shape the translation so radically that the style may appear alien to the reader; or one may make the translation conform so closely to stylistic norms of contemporary English that all difference is effaced.

With this knowledge, she has given us a reading which returns to the original much of its original intention. It is, says Arntzen, merely "one of the many possible versions of the *Kagero Diary*," but it is also one which speaks most clearly to us right now.

The Kagero Diary, translated with an introduction and notes by Sonja Arntzen. Ann Arbor: Center for Japanese Studies, University of Michigan, 1997.

The *Konjaku Monogatari*

The *Konjaku Monogatarishu* is a Japanese anthology of tales, stories and fables originally collected during the early 12th-century. The compiler is unknown, but there is evidence that the material (much of it from earlier sources) was systematically arranged rather than merely gathered. The thousand or so stories are arranged under headings ("Tales of India," "Tales of China," "Secular Tales of Japan," etc.), and their order suggests that some kind of cumulative effect was intended, though whether the stories themselves were intended to be read, recited or even (one theory) accompanied by pictures, *kami-shibai*-style, is not definitely known.

Despite its considerable merits, the collection has not traditionally inspired any widespread critical interest. Its title is not mentioned until 1451, and there is only one pre-modern printed edition, that of 1720. The modern editions were compiled from various manuscript and printed editions, and since the original was apparently never fully completed, there is no telling how much of this original has been retrieved.

Popular interest in the work began to be evidenced only in this century. (Lafcadio Hearn, who would have loved it—as well as mined it extensively—apparently knew nothing about it.) The interest was occasioned by Akutagawa Ryunosuke's discovering a copy, being delighted with it, and rewriting a number of the tales. Several of these formed the basis of the famous film *Rashomon*.

At about the same time, Tanizaki Jun'ichiro also discovered the old collection (using probably the Haga edition, 1921, a pioneer printing of the complete text, together with variants and possible sources). These two famous modern writers, in effect, popularized the collection. Today it is very well known indeed, and it is included (right after the *Genji Monogatari*) in the high-school curriculum.

It is also beginning to be translated into foreign languages. The earliest was probably the Robert Brower translation of 75 stories (1952), followed by the S. W. Jones translation, 37 stories (1959). There has been an excellent French translation (Bernard Frank, 1968) of 58 of the stories, and there is a German edition (Schuster/Mueller) of 23 of the stories as well. This new translation contains the greatest number of stories (62), the best general introduction, illustrations from the 1720 edition, and excellent notes. In addition, the translation itself seems to be extremely fine.

The book is intended for the general reader ("Although," writes Marian Ury, the translator-editor, "I would hope that this translation might be of some use to scholars, the readers whom I have principally in mind are simply all those who, like myself, are fond of stories and are interested in how they are told."), and it reads extremely well. (An ogress, disguised as a benevolent old lady, is heard to murmur while regarding the newborn child of her house guest, "Only a mouthful, but my how delicious!") In addition the stories themselves are lively and diverting.

Though originally written (or at least collected) with didactic intent, once we are past the Buddhist tales, the educational aspects of the various strange happenings are pleasantly neglected, and we are invited to revel in story for its own sake. In addition, though there are some attempts at moralism, the compiler seems to be pleasantly undoctrinaire, as well as perhaps unsure as to precisely what the moral should be. What is singled out for moral consideration is quite often refreshingly beside any conceivable point. This obviously lends, if not credibility (the stories are patently incredible), a kind of belief in the integrity of the storyteller: we are not being told this for any underhanded moralistic, religious, or propagandistic reason; we are told this because it is interesting. Perhaps, consequently, we find it so.

Though some of the recent work on the *Konjaku Monogatarishu* is so recondite that one would never guess that the stories were interesting (I have in mind Kobayashi Hiroko's *The Human Comedy of Heian Japan*), this new translation properly places emphasis upon the sheer interest of the material. "I can only ask my readers to learn from the stories themselves, as the original audience did," writes Ury. By giving us the stories whole and by respecting the intentions of the original compiler, she has given us, intact, a view of medieval Japan.

Tales of Times Now Past, translated and edited by Marian Ury. Berkeley: University of California Press, 1979.

The *Genji Monogatari*

"Not much can be said with certainty about *The Tale of Genji* except that it is a very long romance, running to fifty-four chapters and describing the court life of Heian Japan, from the 10th-century into the 11th." Thus begins Edward Seidensticker in the introduction to his new and superlative translation of the complete work.

The happenings in the *Genji Monogatari* form a picture of aristocratic Heian civilization, a complete rendering of a society, with a decided emphasis upon the romantic attachments formed among its members. The world's first novel, it is also, in both senses of the word, a romance. It is a series of love stories and, at the same time, it is an historical romance, in that it begins in the generation before that of the author. There may have been some original intention to end the book in the author's own time, but this does not occur. Rather, as the translator observes: "All that can be said is that a vaguely nostalgic air hangs over the narrative and that the setting is vaguely antiquarian. One of the things the *Genji* means is that the good days are in the past."

While one reads and admires the novel for many reasons—its historical interest, the compulsion of a story line which is always the same and always varied, its picture of a way of life so different and yet so like our own—it is this "vaguely nostalgic air" which, if examined, gives the novel its peculiar power.

This feeling for nostalgia, this appreciation of the evanescent, this approval of the transient—this is the authentic Japanese tone. It pervades much of the major art from the earliest scrolls through the latest films; it is discernible in the literature from early court diaries to contemporary novels and poetry. It suggests a closed and poignant world, full of sad wisdom, a somber place only in that the truth about the world, about life, about the vagaries of being human are not hidden, but expressed, and even celebrated.

It is this quality which makes the *Genji* a timeless work of art and one which especially endears it to our harassed century. Murasaki is honest about life in a way that few writers are. Existence is not affirmed; it is described. Nothing is sacrificed to the optimistic or pessimistic demands of plot—there is no plot; form is not allowed to moralize—there is little form, and the author has no thesis to present, no agenda to satisfy.

My so stressing this aspect of the work may surprise those who know it only in Arthur Waley's translation—a gorgeous, beautifully tinted rendering, in which a bright, lively, really adorable world is revealed. The more sober aspect of the work now revealed surprised me as well. Until I read the Seidensticker translation I did not know that the darkness, the sadness, the acceptance was so strong, so pervasive, so totally the work itself.

There are many reasons for the differences between these two translations. First, the Seidensticker is complete and the Waley is not. The latter omits one fairly important chapter (the 38th), several sections of others (the concert scene in the second part of "Wakana," for example), and many, many smaller sections within the work itself. Thus, in the Seidensticker version, Murasaki's book appears for the first time complete in another language. Waley's is an abridgment.

At the same time, the Waley, with all of its cuts, is longer than the Seidensticker. This is because the earlier translator so embroidered, so explained, added so much of himself that his work became not only an abridgment but also a gloss.

As an example of these differences and as a way of explaining the dissimilarities in both content and tone (and even intent), I will compare the two translations of a single passage and attempt some generalizations.

Seidensticker (on page 615 of his translation) writes: "It was very dark. Wanting to see her face even dimly, he pushed open a shutter. 'This cruelty is driving me mad. If you wish to still the madness, then say you pity me.' She did want to say something. She wanted to say that his conduct was outrageous. But she was trembling like a frightened child. It was growing lighter."

Waley (already on page 660 of his version) writes: "The house was still quite dark. But midnight must by now be long past; and thinking that out of doors there might already be a little light, he gently raised the shutter, and turning round caught (as he had hoped to) a clearer view of her form and face. 'I cannot think, I cannot move,' he cried, looking at her desperately. 'If you wish me to recover my sense, to be calm, to leave you, let me hear you say one word. Speak, though it be only in pity....' Never had she seen anyone behave like this; what could it matter to him whether she spoke or not? At this point, however, she did try to say something; but so violently was she trembling that the words turned into meaningless jangle of sound. The room was growing lighter every moment."

Here one can see the differences between the two translations. Waley is prolix, he dramatizes; Seidensticker is laconic, he understates. Waley conventionalizes; Seidensticker allows himself conventions similar only to those Murasaki herself employed. And, among other differences, there is that of tone. This depends upon the kind and quality of language used, and the choice of word depends upon the context in which an author or translator sees his work, this context in turn being based upon what models he—knowingly or not—has before him.

Waley sees the work somewhat conventionally. His hero cries in a well known cadence, "I cannot think, I cannot move ..." and quite prepares one for his "looking at her desperately." He also stresses the picturesque, the archaic, with such poetic effects as his saying that her words "turned into meaningless jangle of sounds." This last is Wordsworth through Yeats, the absence of an article hinting directly as the "special" effect toward which he aspired and which, in fact, he nearly always achieved.

Waley's language (as a whole and not just in the short quote abstracted above) suggests a vision of Japan which came not so much from the country itself (he never went there, and, in fact, once said he never wanted to lest he be disappointed) but from reflections of Japan—particularly those of the French (the Goncourt brothers, Gauthier, Remy de Gourmont) and the England of "The Yellow Book," of the decidedly Japanese l'art Nouveau, and of the Symbolist poets. His translation reveals something more *japonoisserie* than Japanese.

To say this is not to question Waley's worth, only to define it. I do not want to suggest that he is to the Japanese as Constance Garnett is to the Russian. Nor do I wish to affirm the Seidensticker by denigrating the Waley—something the latter does not deserve nor the former need. Waley's is a remarkable achievement precisely in that it is a recasting, a rethinking of the original. It is a work in its own right and will continue to live on its own merits.

Turning to Seidensticker and using his above quote, one notices shorter sentences, plainer statements; there is no embroidery, no poetic effects. One also notices a kind of irony which is missing from Waley's heightened rendering of the passage but is presumably present in Murasaki. "She did want to say something. She wanted to say that his conduct was outrageous." The first sentence leaves open the possibility of her behaving as Waley had her—confused, distraught, prey to emotions. And so she also is in the Seidensticker, but the second sentence defines precisely how she would behave if she could. There is a suggestion of common sense, no matter her trembling, which acts as an antidote to high emotionalism.

Too, one notices how Seidensticker handles a convention. If she wishes to cure his madness, "then say you pity me." This is quite a different thing from Waley's "speak, though it be only in pity." Seidensticker is availing himself of a convention which translates "pity me" as "go to bed with me," a convention which surely parallels that of Murasaki and her time.

Seidensticker's language as a whole suggests a model (consciously held or not) very close in circumstances and sensibility to Murasaki herself. In translating the work of a worldly and detached woman, who lived within the strict and often petty confines of her station and her age, who had no interest in the world outside these, who acutely and ironically observed, and who made use of earlier conventions, often to make gentle fun of them, but who did not believe in the sensibility of her own age and was drawn to the sense of earlier times, one of the possibilities which might have suggested itself to Seidensticker was the surprisingly close parallel Murasaki shows in this regard to Jane Austen.

Take the following passage, for example: "He continued to reprove her in silence and she to suffer agonies of guilt; and that the silence did nothing to relieve the agonies was perhaps another mark of her immaturity, which had been the cause of it all. Innocence can be a virtue, but when it suggests a want of prudence and caution, it does not inspire confidence."

I do not mean to suggest a precise parallel (though I am emboldened in these observations by knowing of Seidensticker's appreciation of and fondness for Jane Austen), but I do mean to say that in translating Murasaki he has found a style extremely well suited to her, one which includes her straightforwardness, her detachment, and her occasional irony and her rejection of modern modes. It also, and perhaps this is most important, sounds as though the writer is a Japanese writing about other real Japanese—which is to say that these qualities of celebrating the mundane yet pining for a past are those which Seidensticker's models also share.

The result is as near a perfect translation as any this century has offered. For parallel achievement I can think only of the C. K. Scott-Moncrieff translation of Proust. While I am in no position to compare Seidensticker's *Genji* with Murasaki's original, his translation is so stylistically coherent, so completely of a piece, so right for the story it tells and the woman who told it, that I can only presume the correspondence to be extraordinarily close.

The difficulties Seidensticker faced in expressing in a modern language a work written almost a thousand years ago in a classical language must have been formidable. He himself speaks of some of them—that Murasaki did not, properly speaking, name her characters, that the work abounds in allusions and puns, that the pronoun use is—to put it mildly—confusing. There are others as well: there is no paragraphing in the original, no punctuation in any modern sense, nor is the dialogue, strictly speaking, quoted. Then there is the poetry: the *Genji* contains almost eight hundred poems, and the problem of what to do about them.

And on and on—each passage bringing more puzzles and more new answers to be discovered. Seidensticker's too is a rendering (all translations must be) but one so remarkable in tone and feeling that it reveals to us a "new" work. It is a work which is lighter in texture and darker in import—the laconic leads to truth and truth is dark. Murasaki's world is less gorgeous, less densely hued, and less sentimental—though fuller than we knew of true sentiment. It is emotionally far more complicated, much less clear-cut and much less conventional. This new beauty is more melancholy and more accepting—and it is the more ravishing because it is true.

The Tale of Genji, by Murasaki Shikibu, translated with an introduction by Edward G. Seidensticker. New York: Alfred A. Knopf, 1976.

During the years that Edward Seidensticker was making his translation of The *Tale of Genji*—1959 to 1975—he was also keeping a journal. Here he wrote about the day's labors and pleasures and relieved the varied strains of having to be the Lady Murasaki all day long by unbuttoning and being thoroughly himself at night. *Genji* finally finished, he has made a selection from the diaries—covering "the period of earnestness," 1970 to 1974—and it is this which is here presented.

And a thoroughly captivating mixture it is. One learns a great deal about the *Genji*, about translation, about Murasaki as a writer, and about Seidensticker both as a great translator and as a person.

Of the many difficulties of rendering the *Genji* into English (characters with no proper names, pronoun trouble, a general lack of punctuation, etc.) one learns a good deal. How each is finally dealt with is shown in the daily detail, and, at the same time, the journal forms a running criticism of the novel itself. "How very different is Murasaki's story from anything in the *Ise [Monogatari]*. Her narrative has flesh and blood. It is as if she were writing a story the plot for which the author or authors of the *Ise* had but sketched in. He avers (or they aver); she demonstrates."

As the work progresses, the general fitness of the Japanese language for such purposes is considered, and this leads to interesting observations. "But why does he [Tamakazura] not express himself more clearly? It is really very difficult to believe that Ukon understands all these instructions so deviously given and amounting in the end to something like an order to do nothing at all. One suspects that Ukon, and Murasaki's original audience as well, merely caught the general drift and really did not wish things to be too explicit. So too with the poems. It was enough to know that this was a poem of frustration, that a cry of longing, the other a twitting for an insensitive failure to catch the signals."

Some months later the topic is brought up again but now (and typically) in contemporary context. "There is a transcript of one of the Nixon tapes in the *Times* this morning, a conversation between Nixon and Dean. It is next to incomprehensible. Through the densest vapors one senses a vague intimation of meaning. And yet it was a matter very important to them, and they must have understood each other—through tone of voice, facial expression, gesture, it must have been. I kept thinking, as I forced my way through it: even such is the prose of *The Tale of Genji*, and perhaps it was through such extra-verbal devices that meaning was conveyed."

The observation of vagueness leads to frequent collisions with Arthur Waley, who refused to observe it, and would rewrite if he had to. "A big difference between my *Genji* and Waley's will have to do with his Yugiri, a stuffed shirt largely of his creating, and mine, the incarnation of sunny common sense. Mine is surely the nearer to Murasaki Shikibu." And "I kept wondering why Waley translated the whole of this chapter [Maboroshi] when he so boldly abridged much better chapters. Probably there is no real explanation. Just caprice, and the matter of what came easily."

At the same time, the author is afraid of Arthur Waley (called Art when he goes too far), and when the time comes to compare Ed's first drafts with Art's final, there is an amount of procrastination (all of it cheerfully admitted) and some dread. Scrupulous as ever, however, Seidensticker impartially compares, finds himself rebuked on some small points, but reassured (and rightly, I think) on all the larger.

These journals are, in a way, very like Heian diaries and one of the many pleasures of reading them is not only the Genji information but also the Genji attitude which more and more informed Professor Seidensticker's days. The entries are, for example, full of flowers and the blossoms of Ann Arbor are in no way inferior to those of the old Heian-cho. ("They certainly are in noisy bloom, magentas and reds screaming at one another. It is not a good idea to plant several varieties of azalea side by side. They do not get along.")

The journals are also very Sei Shonagon-like in both their skillful use of non sequitur and their purposeful lack of the expected consequential. Out of nowhere and in answer to a self-directed query as to why the author was reminded of something: "Well, because it was there that I was so shaken when Katharine poured her tomato juice in the lampshade." Nothing more, no mere explanation—and it is only in context that one realizes that the lady in question was perhaps Katharine Sanson. Or (again like *The Pillow Book*) the sudden and unexplained illnesses (Seidensticker's are mainly those of ears and teeth). "Whatever it is," he writes, and this is the last we hear of it, "it is much worse when I am reclining than when I am rampant."

Only Seidensticker would have used that last word, and its combination of absolutely rightness and ambiguous aura, is typical of the delights of his style. Indeed, if style is the man, then we here have Seidensticker, warts and all. These latter may, for some readers, loom large when he takes up arms against some of the most popular and agreed-upon ideas of our day. I refer in particular to his basic and obvious disagreement with the liberal cant of our times—particularly its mindless adulation of the young, its long overdue but even now yet false "concern" for ethnic minorities, and its suspicious denigration of that distinctive quality which it chooses to define by use of the horrid "elitist."

Professor Seidensticker wades right in, with no compunctions at all, and presents his heresies with the smiling candor with which he also reveals his pleasures and predilections. For example, his work at hand: "That is what scholarship is about: getting utterly lost in the pursuit of buried fact. They may tell you, they who do it, that it is the pursuit of truth; but the real point is getting utterly lost and forgetting all about such illusory matters as the passage of time."

While reading this admirable journal, I kept wondering what it was it reminded me of. Not having any obliging Katharine to pour tomato juice into the lampshade, I was left to my own devices and finally remembered. Gibbon's diaries—that's what they remind me of. It is not a question of imitation, and, in any event, the style is quite different. It is rather a matter of tone. Both are learned and reclusive men, both are intimately concerned with an earlier age, and both take up cudgels against their own. Men of erudition, of sensitivity, and also of a quiet bravery, they hold aloft (without even seeming to notice that they do so) the banner of excellence in accommodating times. Honesty—as both aver and then demonstrate—is the mark of real scholarship and real life.

Genji Days, by Edward G. Seidensticker. Tokyo: Kodansha International, 1977.

There seems to be something of a *Genji* boom going on right now. Liza Dalby has the author writing her memoirs in *The Tale of Murasaki*; Ichinohe Saeko has a full-length modern-dance version in the works; Tomita Isao has written a *Genji* symphony, and Miki Minoru, a three-hour *Genji* opera. In addition, an Australian expert on Japan recently told a group of American business executives to skip all those books on how corporations work. Rather, *The Tale of Genji* could provide with a unique glimpse "into the life, indeed the soul, of another nation."

The most popular comic-book version has received new printings, the *anime* is again in the spool-shops, there is a *Genji* computer game, an American media producing group is planning an ambitious film which will "re-interpret and re-present" the *Genji* story, and a new English translation of the entire work is being completed.

This indicates an uncommon interest in this thousand-year-old novel, one which has been called the very first. The awareness of the millennium might have something to do with it (*Beowulf* has also seen a major revival), also the success of *The Geisha*, a novel which Stephan Spielberg is still rumored to be tinkering into a film version. Gold's novel has nothing do with *Genji*, but to the great unwashed mind, one Japanese female entertainer is much like another.

Perhaps another reason for the *Genji* revival, if one may so term it, is that the work has always been convenient to Japan in its "identity- building" phases. One such was during the Meiji Period. Interest in the *Genji* was suddenly everywhere. It was the first novel, it was a truly "Japanese" chronicle, it inculcated ancient virtues, it proved history—it did all sorts of things that Murasaki has never intended it to do. Out of print for two centuries, there were suddenly new editions and a number of translations into colloquial Japanese.

Among these the most influential have been those of Yosano Akiko. (Others include Tanizaki Jun'ichiro's, Enchi Fumiko's during the postwar identity-building phrase and—during this one—literary nun and TV *talento* Setouchi Jakucho) It was Yosano's, however, that has had the greatest initial impact.

Again, the reasons had little to do with the *Genji* itself. Yosano had early published a collection of *tanka* entitled in its English translation *Tangled Hair*. These lightly erotic poems branded her as a "new woman." This term, in 1901, unlike now, indicated an ambivalent position. Still, immoral though she might have been perceived, the new woman was undeniably new, and this was something that the late Meiji Period was interested in—a new identity for modern Japan.

So when a liberated modern woman took to translating into modern language the work of Japan's first woman liberated enough to sit down and write a book, the press (and consequently the reader) took notice.

Yosano's first rendering of the work (1913) was not only a translation but also a popularization. Like Arthur Waley, she shortened or left out and sometimes substituted précis for text. A contemporary watched the "pen race across the page" as she took in the original at a glance and with barely a pause recast what she had read into modern Japanese. The process was not so much "'translation' as simultaneous interpretation."

No looking up anything in the dictionary, no pause to ponder, Yosano bum rushed Murasaki into the 20th-century and the arms of a new generation of admirers. She explained her method at the end of yet another translation of the work. Her approach to the translation process, she said, was that of "painting group beginners [who] may venture free renditions in order to emulate masterpieces from earlier ages. I eliminated those fine points which, being alien to modern life, we have no sympathy with nor interest in, and the excessive nicety which needlessly puts [readers] off."

Fashions in translation do change, it is true, but Yosano's work we must call popularization. It is psychologically interesting but, like the *manga* and *anime* versions this *Genji*, it is not what is presently called translation.

Tanizaki's are translations (despite its mutilation of the first at the hands of the military censors in 1939), but it is Yosano's which captured the pubic imagination. She once wrote: "I am sure that a hundred years hence there will come a time when I will be recognized by all those of good sense." And sure enough, indicative of good sense or not, her *Genji* is again at the top of the local popularity pile.

The phenomenon can only grow. For those many in the media who are now in the *Genji* business, I might helpfully call attention to some forgotten items. There is Yoshimura Kozaburo's 1951 film version which had the Heian court ladies following Genji through the polished corridors like so many postwar groupies, and there is a TV series, made in Seventies, part of which was directed by Ichikawa Kon, and all of which starred the late Itami Juzo as our hero. And this is but the tip of the iceberg.

Yosano Akiko and The Tale of Genji, by G.G. Rowley. Ann Arbor: Center for Japanese Studies, University of Michigan, 2000.

Besides writing *The Tale of Genji*, Murasaki Shikibu

also penned a collection of poems and left behind the *Murasaki Shikibu Nikki*, considered one of the four major Heian Period diaries though it is the least diary-like. It does not use daily entries, part of it seems to be drafts for letters, and the period covered is relatively short—from the early autumn of 1008 to the beginning of 1010. It also was originally somewhat longer. The *Eiga Monogatari* indicates that other parts once existed though of what these consisted is not known.

The period during which the diary was kept found Murasaki in the service of one of the consorts of the emperor (Ichijo), and the first and longest part of the diary is about the birth of a prince, the resulting delight of the court, and the child's grandfather (Fujiwara Michinaga), now assured of continuing power.

It also contains passages of personal reflection and offers some criticism of life at court. It is thus not as autobiographical as the *Kagero Nikki*, nor as fictional as the *Izumi Shikubu Nikki*. It has, rather, been often compared to the *Makura no Soshi* of Sei Shonagon. Indeed, as Bowring states, "It shares a love of description and anecdote together with a willingness to criticize fellow ladies-in-waiting."

Such a comparison would not have pleased Shonagon who has some critical things to say about the learned and pedantic author of the *Genji*. Nor would it have pleased Murasaki who here writes of Shonagon in retrospect, "[she] was dreadfully conceited. She thought herself so clever and littered her writings with Chinese characters; but if you examined them closely, they left a great deal to be desired."

Murasaki, of course (like Shonagon and all the other women at court) wrote *kana* rather than *kanji*, this being thought the language proper to women, but she had more than a smattering of such Chinese learning.

Another of the court ladies, upon hearing that the

emperor was listening to someone reading *The Tale of Genji* aloud, sarcastically observed that the author "seems very learned ... she must have read *The Chronicles of Japan*."

Thus, says Murasaki, she "spread it abroad among the senior courtiers that I was flaunting my learning. She gave me the nickname Lady Chronicle. How very comical. Would I, who hesitate to show my learning even in front of the servants ... ever dream of doing so at court?"

The rivalries of court life loom large in all of the extant diaries of the period, but none of them reveal the reasons so clearly as does that of Murasaki. All of these women were, in effect, prisoners. They were required to attend this or that, their quarters were arbitrarily moved about, and they were expected to continually adulate their betters. As in any constrained society, this led to in-fighting, intrigue, gossip.

Murasaki wonders about young girls exposed to this life. "And with all those young nobles around and the girls not allowed so much as a fan to hide behind in broad daylight. I felt somehow concerned for them, convinced that, although they may have been able to deal with the situation both in terms of rank and intelligence, they must surely have found the pressures of constant rivalry daunting—silly of me, perhaps."

And she is almost alone in criticizing the system. Watching the emperor grandly approaching by boat (across the palace pond) she notes that the bearers, all of low rank, had to kneel face down, very difficult when hoisting a palanquin. "'Are we really that different?' I thought to myself as I watched. Even those of us who mix with nobility are bound by rank. How very difficult."

Such moments are rare, however. Usually the criticism is more oblique—complaints of the awful boredom of court life, or evidence (much description of clothing) that the endless rites and rituals were really there to ensure control.

Successfully, it would seem. Even Murasaki, intelligent and aware though she is, plays the well-bred lady, head full of court propriety. She commiserates with some court dancers who had to pass into the full light of torches. "All I could think of was what a dreadful ordeal it must be for them. The same misfortune had been visited on us as well, or course, but at least we had been spared the torches and the direct stares of the senior courtiers … in general, however, we must have presented a similar spectacle. I shudder to recall it."

She was already a well known author, and she may well have been still completing her famous book while writing her diary. Sections were being read at court, and one of the senior courtiers looked into the ladies quarter and asked, "Would our little Murasaki be in attendance by any chance?"

It is perhaps this incident that gave the authoress the only name we now know her by. He had made a reference to one of the characters in her book. This she quite understood, and her response was "I cannot see the likes of Genji here, so how could she be present?" But present she was and so stuck in courtly tedium that it alone might account for her losing herself in the composition of her novel.

The boredom—and an enterprising spirit which even now shines from the pages of novel and diary alike. "Why should I hesitate to say what I want to?" she asks herself. And she realizes that, indeed, there is no reason. Thus she still stands here before us, her readers, as the preeminent writer of her time.

The Diary of Lady Murasaki, translated and introduced by Richard Bowring. London: Penguin Books, 1996.

Here is a new edition of the *Genji* which is indeed fully

illustrated, so much so that there is no longer room for the text. It is a comic book version of the novel, a *manga*. As such, it is defended by Professor Konaka Yotaro, one of its editors, who avers that "the reader will be quite literally rewarded with a picture of the Heian Period unavailable to those who limit themselves only to printed literature."

He establishes precedent by saying that the work has appeared in "pictorial form" since the 12th-century and that this version thus "rests squarely on that 800-year-old tradition."

The *Genji* scrolls to which he refers, however, merely supplemented the text. His edition supplants it. Even suppresses it. The original *Genji* is made up of 54 chapters but I can find only 36 in this comic-book version. Also, a number of characters seem to be missing. On the other hand, some have been added—or at least been given new names.

I searched in vain, for example, for anyone in any other edition named the Emperor Kiritsubo and a consort also named Kiritsubo. Yet, here they are on the opening page. "Look," says a court lady, "Kiritsubo is heading for the Emperor's quarters again tonight."

It could be argued that an occasional missing character is compensated for by the arrival of some truly new ones. For example, not only is the Chinese cat given much space, but a puppy (unmentioned by Murasaki Shikibu, author of the original) is awarded a close-up. And when Genji has prayers said for the pregnant Aoi, the Shinto medium gets a big close-up, too, because she is bare-breasted.

The text, what remains of it, certainly becomes more immediate in modern, colloquial form. The Lady Fujitsubo when meeting Genji for the first time, says: "I'm so glad to meet you, Shining Prince." The Minister of the Right at one point says: "That was certainly awful weather last night." When Lady Rokujo's carriage is struck, one of the retainers shouts: "Hey, this is no carriage to be so rude to." The

Central Minister, hearing that "Yugiri and Kumoinokari were sweet on each other," comments, "That Yugiri!"

One addition I found particularly piquant occurs when Genji wakes after a dream. Just over his head is a small cloud inscribed "Poof!" I looked in vain for that "poof" in both the Waley and the Seidensticker translations, but they have failed to include it. Perhaps this is one of the rewards mentioned by Konaka available to those who refuse to limit themselves to printed literature.

A picture of Genji and Tamakazura resting their heads on a koto is accompanied by saying that they are doing just that. How uncomfortable, I thought, head on the strings, and how bad for the instrument, getting it all oily. Imagine lying there with your hair getting tangled up with the koto strings—here is a picture of the Heian Period which, in the words of Konaka "quite literally rewards."

Thinking this odd behavior, I looked up the passage in the Seidensticker translation where I found that "they lay down side by side with their heads pillowed against the koto." Well, perhaps this translation is the more authentic, but it is certainly the less exciting.

Concerning the treatment of the text, Konaka has more wise words. "To make the text come across in English," he writes, "the translator, upon consultation with the editors, had to take many liberties. I have no doubt that his bold approach will add to this volume's distinctiveness." He is correct. The volume is not only distinctive, it is singular.

Problems are instantly overcome. For example, the original *Genji* is related largely in indirect discourse while this edition is largely in direct. New, if minor, characters constantly talk to sustain the narrative, which deprives it of much of its tone. The editors, however, imply that this is a good thing as it makes the story move faster. Any complaint that the *Genji* has been reduced to its story alone is not seen as justified—the intelligences at work in this edition recognize only the power of narrative and eschew any other literary means.

The fact that the story of *Genji* is not as such very interesting is triumphantly turned to advantage. The narrative can with little difficulty be rendered as Heian home-drama, which is of course, a definite advantage, one much appreciated by those who do not limit themselves only to printed literature.

Another simplification is that the characters, in the manner of *manga*, all look alike, perhaps because in the original Murasaki always has someone saying "she reminds me somehow of someone." The people all have the high nose, long legs and big eyes of *manga* which has nothing to do with the Heian ideal and everything to do with Harajuku.

Konaka remarks that his edition is "a far easier read" than the original. "Who knows," he adds, "the present version may be easier for Japanese to comprehend than some of the modern Japanese translations!"

Prescient professor! As I write, the staff of the late Tezuka Osamu, "overseen by the Vatican" as one daily puts it, is completing a 26-episode *manga* version of The Bible for TV. And cartoonist Ishinomori Shotaro is making "a record of Japanese history in cartoon form"—48 hardback volumes of 225 pages each, from Jomon to right now. Ishinomori, assisted by a team of "professors" from Tokyo University, says "I have to blend ... facts with my imagination. I call this 'faction,' a mixture of fact and fiction." Perhaps so, but remember, folks, you saw it first in *The Illustrated Tale of Genji.*

The Illustrated Tale of Genji, adapted and illustrated by Tsuboi Koh, edited by Shimizu Yoshiko and Konaka Yotaro, translated by Alan Tansman. Tokyo: Shin-Jinbutsu Orai-sha, 1989.

The *Okagami*

The *Okagami* (The Great Mirror) is a *rekishi monogatari* (historical tale) written sometime between 1085 and 1125, and covering events from 850 to 1025. The events are those relevant to the rise of the Fujiwara family, leading up to the life and career of Fujiwara Michinaga (966–1027), its ablest or at least its most consistently politically successful member.

In five sections (or six, by some countings), it begins with a narrative of the various imperial reigns leading up to the emperor under whom Michinaga served, continues with chapters on the various ministers of the Fujiwara family, and ends with a long account of Michinaga himself. This is followed by a section of stories about the Fujiwara, more about Michinaga, and finally a collection of "stories from ancient times," which has little or nothing to do with what went before.

There are two complete translations of the work. The first is that of Joseph Yamagiwa, originally published in 1967; the second is this one (1980) by Helen McCullough. The major difference between the two lies in the edition used for translation.

There are many copies and versions of this work. These are usually divided into two categories: the *kohon* (which McCullough calls "old texts" and Yamagiwa, "ancient texts") and *rufubon* (which McCullough calls "vulgate texts" and Yamagiwa, "texts currently circulated," i.e., later copies with additions and emendations). Yamagiwa translated a later *rufubon*, and McCullough translates the earliest complete version, the composition date (it is a copy, of course) of which scholars have decided is around 1275.

Yamagiwa gives his reasons for translating a late edition: he was quite familiar with the earlier ones but thought that the later ones gave more information—which they do. McCullough is quite familiar with the later editions but feels that the earliest edition is the real one. (She also refers to the Yamagiwa edition as one "that can be said to have outlived its usefulness." This is not so. His is the only translation of an important *rufubon*—though McCullough gives some *rufubon* variants in one of her appendices—and the *Okagami* is such a mess anyway that both *kohon* and *rufubon* translations are certainly desirable.)

The work itself is a grab-bag—though McCullough makes a specific claim for its not being one. It is a collection of old stories and anecdotes (*setsuwa*) the aim of which is to present Michinaga in the best possible light. One of the narrators in the work states and often repeats his primary concern: "I have only one thing of importance on my mind, and that is to describe Lord Michinaga's successes."

One of the sources was the earlier *Eiga Monogatari*, a work extremely flattering to Michinaga. (There are other sources as well, fully indicated in both this and Yamagiwa's edition.) Since the *Okagami* is less openly adulatory, some Japanese historians have seen it as revisionist history, an exposure of the man behind the power. This theory does not hold up. As McCullough has noted, the latter work, far from being censorious, is nearly as adulatory as the latter.

"The difference between the *Eiga Monogatari* and the *Okagami* is not that one praises and the other blames but that one describes and the other explains." The explanation lies in the long chapters on the emperors and the Fujiwara ministers. The implication is that, after all this gestation, we have one perfect bloom: Michinaga himself, a beau ideal of Heian culture. It is a *rekishi monogatari* in that the history is all a little shaky—as, indeed, it would have to be since it takes the shape of an apotheosis. Yamagiwa makes a case for its not being a *rekishi shosetsu* or historical novel, implying that there is too much history in the work to permit that term. I wonder.

Since both scholars are deeply immersed in the work the question of why one should read it at all does not occur—though McCullough does give some reasons. She speaks of its "sheer entertainment value," which she finds "considerable," says that it is the best study ever done of Michinaga, and is of the opinion that "its treatment of the sources of Fujiwara power is still useful and instructive." One might add that it is one of the few works which give the flavor of Heian culture and present, in no matter what fragmentary form, the civilization of that period.

Another question which both scholars might have asked but did not is why the *Okagami* was written. To be sure, this kind of thing was being written back then, often in imitation of Chinese models. But if we allow political motivation to other early works (for example, the *Kojiki* and the *Nihongi*), then later works such as the *Okagami* should be allowed their share of such motives as well.

McCullough notes that there is "an apparent reluctance to dwell on the shortcoming of the Fujiwara leaders," and there is a reluctance bordering on refusal when the emperors are written about. One would never guess from the account in the *Okagami* that the Emperor Yozei (the 57th, reigning for the eight years following 876, but living to a ripe old age) was criminally insane, given to tying up young girls and throwing them into ponds. (But then one never learns from historians, Japanese or otherwise, about the afflictions of a ruler even as late as the Emperor Taisho.) Certainly the treatment of Michinaga is so partial and so favorable to its subject that one ought, I think, at least expect some kind of political motivation at work. (One should also add that a much more balanced account of our hero is given by McCullough in one of the appendices of her edition.)

The *Okagami* was written well over a century after the events described. The span is roughly equivalent to that between our time and that of Abraham Lincoln. We have a number of hagiological works about the Great Commoner, and an amount of apocrypha has grown up around him—the figure of Honest Abe and the like. Yet the political aims of such works are apparent. The Lincoln boom did not occur until America became involved in two world wars and there was a political necessity for "affirming America's greatness"—from 1917 on, the very time when adulatory Lincoln biographies began appearing.

I suspect something like this occasioned the *Okagami* but I know nothing of the period and less (if possible) of the sources. Both Yamagiwa and McCullough, however, know all there is to know. I think, nonetheless, that the extent of political motivation in the composition of the *Okagami* is an important one and not like to see it so completely disregarded.

Okagami, The Great Mirror: A Study and Translation by Helen Craig McCullough. Princeton: Princeton University Press, 1980.

The *Matsura no Miya Monogatari*

The *Matsura no Miya Monogatari* was written about 1190 and is usually attributed to one of Japan's earliest and finest poets, Fujiwara Teika. The reputation of the poet is so great—the late Robert Brower called him "the single most important influence in the entire history of classical poetry"—that anything he wrote deserves attention.

In a way, however, this towering repute has worked against what translator Wayne Lammers calls Teika's "experiment in fiction." *The Tale of Matsura* stands outside the canon of his work (as a sole surviving example of sustained prose) and, as the translator says, "it cannot be considered a resounding success." This would seem to be so. Unlike earlier *monogatari*, it is not realistic in intent, it is fragmentary, it is highly conventional and it is a historical romance.

Set even before Nara was capital, it is about the precocious hero, Ujitada, a paragon among men, who falls in love, loses the girl, and is sent to China as ambassador. There, he goes to Mount Shang where he is instructed by divine sages but, nonetheless, falls in love with a beautiful princess. She dies, however, as does the emperor.

Ujitada, a loyalist, attempts to protect the infant successor, fleeing from the troops, and with the help of Sumiyoshi, visiting Japanese deity, he does so. Now homesick, he wishes to return to his country, but love calls once again. The new beloved, however, turns out to be an incarnation of the empress, or perhaps a diety.

In any event, Teika—or whoever wrote the book—at this point decided to stop. The end of the story, says Lammers is a rapid decline "with obvious signs that Teika had lost interest in it." The putative author himself writes that the rest is lost and adds some comments supposed to be by later commentators. This Nabokov-like indication of a highly unreliable narrator has persuaded some scholars that the book was really written in the 9th-century and is not by Teika at all.

Lammers, however, thinks that "we may be as certain of his authorship ... as we are of Murasaki Shikibu's authorship of the *Genji Monogatari*." In the notes and appendices of the book, just as interesting as Teika's text, the translator indicates why he thinks so. The plight of the infant emperor, for example, was plainly modeled on the flight of the Emperor Antoku, an event which occurred in 1183.

Also in the ending, both the lacunae and the various colophons indicate that Teika was trying to forge an "ancient tale," and made heavy use of *Man'yo* diction in the poetry of the early part. The lacunae are quite counterfeit and a true forgery, for whatever playful purpose, was apparently intended.

Perhaps it amused earlier readers. For us at this late date the work is opaque. As Lammers says, "the tale presumes a vast knowledge of prior Japanese and Chinese literature on the part of the reader, and it cannot be appreciated in its full complexity, even by the specialist, without supplementary information."

This he has lavishly provided, and it is in his expert unraveling of the history of this curious work that the present-day reader's interest lies.

The Tale of Matsura, by Fujiwara Teika, translated with an introduction and notes by Wayne P. Lammers. Ann Arbor: Center for Japanese Studies, University of Michigan, 1992.

The *Ryojin-hisho*

The *Ryojin-hisho* is a late Heian Period collection of popular songs of the day, lyrics called *imayo* which are now regarded as one of the masterpieces of early folk art. We owe their preservation to the enthusiasm of Emperor Goshirakawa (1127–1192), a ruler whose reputation is otherwise not of the best. A contemporary, Kujo Kanezane, said that "he could not tell black from white," and the redoubtable Yoritomo said that he was the "number one scoundrel in Japan."

Nonetheless, Goshirakawa was a music lover. He was particularly fond of the *imayo*, which he had heard sung and recited by the local lowlife—the strolling players and prostitutes of the period. David Jenkins has said that he was "something of a Prince Hal," and so he may well have been.

He must have been genuinely fond of these lyrics. Even when they were long out of fashion, he kept collecting and eventually had gathered thousands of them. Of these only 566 survive, part of volume one and most of volume two out of the original ten volumes. Barely survive at that. They were missing for over 700 years and only discovered by accident in a Tokyo used bookstore in 1911.

By 1169, the date usually given, the collection was fairly complete, and Goshirakawa was talking about it. Though he said "ever since my teens I have loved *imayo*," in his later years he saw them as a means of "salvation." Perhaps ingenuously he remarked that if the common people could expect salvation merely by repeating a formula (a current Buddhist belief), why not the emperor, too, since he had rescued an entire repertoire. "If I were to sing *imayo* now, why should I not be taken to the Lotus Seat?"

Why not? So far as history is concerned, the collection has all but rehabilitated him. It has its moments of religiosity, but, in the main, the lyrics are insouciant, pleasantly frivolous and surprisingly sophisticated. Some are in the form of categories, a genre with which Sei Shonagon was more than familiar: "things I can't stand," "things that are especially fleet," "things you find around the frightful mountain monks."

There are lessons for ladies on holding the line: "And even if he's come to say he's sorry/yes, even if he repents/turn your eyes away/for a while." It was a songs like these that perhaps enlivened the long afternoons in *The Tale of Genji*, in which *imayo* recitation is reported to have caused great amusement.

There are glimpses into the local lowlife itself: "A little louse is playing in my hair./He likes to head/for the scruff of my neck/to eat." And some of the lyrics are sophisticated indeed: "You know/I do believe/that shrine-maid/over there/really is/a male dancer/from Hakata."

The originals are usually in four lines with various 7/5 syllable patterns. They are also, it is said, marked by a freshness and simplicity of rhythm which inspired many a modern poet, including Saito Mokichi and Kitahara Hakushu.

So how do you translate into English these light, charming and evanescent lyrics? Well, in the case of this collection, very well indeed. Moriguchi and Jenkins are language teachers and know both their own and each other's languages. They also have that relatively rare ability to provide an appropriate and consistent tone for their work.

It is this voice which both sustains and approximates a translation. It runs parallel to the original, as it were, and both reflects the images and the reverberations. Take the following, for example: "When I see some lovely girl/I long to be a vine, from top to toe entwined with her./You could try to hack me down/but we'd be bound/never more to come apart."

I do not know the original but believe this translation must come very close to conveying the poem's impression. I think so because of the consistency of the vocabulary and the playful assonances of both word and meaning—"but we'd be bound" has both literal and figurative meanings; "never more to come apart" reflects a common sentiment ("never more to part") rendered surprising and literal by the playful but honest "come."

The Dance of the Dust on the Rafters, translated by Moriguchi Yasuhiko and David Jenkins. Seattle: Broken Moon Press, 1990.

Japanese Tales and Legends

W. H. Auden once wrote that in the folk tale "situation and character are hardly separable; a man reveals what he is in what he does, or what happens to him as a revelation of what he is." This being so one ought to be able to reconstruct a man (a nation, a race) from the folk tales of the culture. In this way some differences in culture might be noticed.

In this new annotated collection of 347 Japanese folk tales by Fanny Hagin Mayer, there are many interesting differences from European tales. Take rats, for example. In Grimm (Auden was writing about the Grimm Brothers), a grateful rat is unknown. Grateful dogs, foxes, wolves, yes—but grateful rats, no. In Japan, however, there is many a grateful rat.

I do not know the reason for this. Certainly rodents are even now not regarded with the aversion usual in the West. I have been told that this is because one had to have attained a degree of prosperity before the rodent was attracted. Rat-infestation meant being well-off.

In the same way we notice in Japan (in the folk tale and otherwise) that the plump person is not considered unattractive, and even a remark such as "you've put on some weight," is considered more a compliment than anything else. Certainly it is not the insult it would be among diet-conscious Westerners. Rather, it implies that you are prosperous enough to have become fat. This remark could then be considered a folk relic from Japan's more poverty-stricken periods.

In the same way, (situation being character, character being a national trait) we find no Cinderella-type stories where something nice happens to a girl or a woman. Boys and men, yes. Also, while there are many stories about brothers, there are few about sisters. Just what one would expected in an officially male-oriented society where male-bonding is an accepted social norm.

The taboos are different as well. All folk tales contain much violence, but in the Western form, the bad people all have to be fittingly punished. In addition, the taboo against sex and the natural functions is so great (as befits Christian nations) that the folk tale often appears bowdlerized, or the sexual references are so hidden away that only the folk-lore expert can ferret them out.

Not so, the Japanese folk tale. Here natural man is naturally presented, with diverting and often amusing results. One tale in this collection, charming and funny, cannot be repeated in a family publication, hence I will content myself with merely offering its final line: "The girl had been two badgers disguised."

As one might expect from a culture greatly concerned about ritual pollution, much is made of breaking wind and falling into rural toilets. If Grimm, for example, uses child murder to call attention to a taboo by breaking it, so the more humane Japanese tale directs the intelligence to the forbidden by making fun of it.

Auden continued his thoughts on the folk tale by writing that "the defect of primitive literature is the defect of primitive man, a fatalistic lack of hope which is akin to a lack of imagination." (And, being a very fair writer, he went on to add: "The danger for modern literature and modern man is a paralysis of action through excess of imagination.")

While these remarks on primitive literature are certainly true of its Western examples (fatalistically doom-ridden as many of them are), they do not apply to the primitive literature of Japan—that very human recounting of resourcefulness, pluck, craftiness, and just plain good (or bad) luck.

This collection of folk tales, more than half of which

have never before been translated, has been derived from a number of sources—the standard-Japanese reference work (the *Meii*) and from the files of some ninety of the early Japanese collections.

Arranged by subject-matter and broken into two categories (stories in their entireties and derived stories), these are cross-referenced with the variations appearing in the standard sources, the Yanagida Kunio and Seki Keigo collections, and with variations already translated.

One of the interesting facts about folklore is that once a story has been collected and becomes known in written form, the oral version often dies. This has occurred to many Japanese folk tales including the popular "Urashima Taro," not a single oral variant of which survived collection (though there are a number of other Dragon Palace stories.) The first story in this present collection is an oral "Momotaro" quite different from the official version.

(The "official" version, incidentally, seems an early Meiji invention, propagating perhaps unconsciously a vindication of imperialistic ways—for what other than colonizing is little Taro doing, not only with the *oni* but with his little-brown-brother animal helpers as well).

Thus much of the material in this collection (all of it quite "alive" until the earlier years of this century) will be new to the general reader. As the editor-translator has written, these folk tales bring us a Japan which "through the centuries has known little of the religious and literary innovations instituted by the elite of the land." The stories are truly folk, and an authentic voice is heard in them.

Ancient Tales in Modern Japan: An Anthology of Japanese Folk Tales, selected and translated by Fanny Hagin Mayer. Bloomington: Indiana University Press, 1984.

Royall Tyler has excellently translated and edited a

collection of 220 stories taken from the major Japanese collections, some 18 in all, including such sources as the *Konjaku Monogatari* (which contributes 111 tales) and some, the *Heike Monogatari* (one tale), not usually considered a repository of such.

He includes a lot which has not been collected before or has else remained little known in obscure Japanese collections—from the *Tamon-in Nikki*, for example, a collection of medieval monkish diaries at Kofukuji. When he includes something fairly well known (those taken from Yoshida Kenko's *Tsurezuregusa* (*Essays in Idleness*), his colloquial translation makes them like new.

Tyler has chosen his tales in main from collections originally put together between 1100 and 1350, though his earliest is from the 700s and his latest is 1578. Most tell about things occurring, or purported to occur, between 850 and 1050. This collection consequently gives a real indication of how early Japanese thought of themselves. It is a view which is quite down to earth, unlike that in some of the other literature of the period. There is much rutting and farting and falling down, lots of superstition and not much aspiration.

In his introduction, Royall Tyler explains and indicates the connection between life and tale, using the latter to explain how people thought and lived in medieval Japan. For example, on the difficulties of marriage in the Heian Period, he mentions the general darkness of the bed chamber, then continues: "On the third night, he stays in bed with her on into the morning, for her parents and household, and in fact for her, to see."

Likewise distinguished is the translation of these tales. Tyler has, as he says, simplified—mostly in the matter of story titles and titles of office. "I have called everyone a monk unless he is obviously ministering to the laity, then I have called him a priest. I have left out all ecclesiastical titles."

He has also, in one instance, combined stories and has unified the style. "Classified Chinese produces a very different effect from pure conversational Japanese," but "I have tried to blend all these variations into about the same sort of English." Also, he found that he had "to change the order of statements in the narration so as to make a story sound natural in English." This being his aim, he had occasionally to sacrifice Japanese-style narrative. "The medieval Japanese did not value forward movement in a story as much as we do."

Japanese Tales, selected, edited and translated by Royall Tyler. New York: Pantheon Books, 1987.

Under the graceless title of *Tales of Tears and Laughter* lies an elegant and interesting translation of thirteen narratives of medieval Japan. They are from that vast repository of short fiction (some 500 have now been recovered) called *otogi-zoshi*.

Though this generic term is from time to time deemed too large to be of any value (some scholars breaking it up into "medieval novellas" and "short stories of the Muromachi Period") it has become a common category—one, it is true, often confused with *otogi-banashi* (children stories) partially because the genres share such narratives as the ones about Urashima Taro and Issun-boshi.

The interested Japanese reader is familiar with the large thirteen-volume collection *Muromachi Jidai Monogatari Taisei*, and the reader of English is offered various uncollected translations as well as Marian Ury's *Tales of Times Now Past* and Royall Tyler's *Japanese Tales*. And now this excellent new translation.

As Virginia Skord points out in her introduction, these narratives have checkered histories. They have been copied, added to, had sections removed and bear the marks of many hands. "Rendering the myriad nuances of Japanese literature into readable, engaging English is never an easy task, but the translation of *otogi-zoshi* presents the additional challenge of recreating an interesting story in English without destroying the conventions of the original text."

Translation problems are compounded in that "these texts have been transcribed into print from original printed or manuscript sources, with lacunae, corruptions, and miscopying preserved intact. In preparing the translations, it was necessary first to annotate the Japanese text: to parse the long strings of unpunctuated prose, supply Chinese characters where appropriate, identify possible textual errors, puzzle out lacunae and track down allusions."

Some of the stories display an amount of patchwork. *Dojoji monogatari* (*The Tale of Dojoji*) is multipart and contains much more than the portion we know from the noh and kabuki versions of the text. Yet at the same time, it is likely that the third and latest section of the story was written by someone who had seen a dramatization of the original legend.

Some are plainly variants. "The Little Man" is a variation on the same source which gave us the familiar tale about Issun-boshi. It also probably contributed, says the translator, to another of these texts she translates: "Lazy Taro." Other of the stories are combinations. "The Mirror Man" is a blending of a folktale with a *kyogen*. And the various fabricators of "A Tale of Brief Slumbers" weave in references to the *Genji Monogatari*.

All are interesting. Though Barbara Ruch, an authority on this literary genre, finds that the literary value of the so-called *otogi-zoshi* (an "enigmatic term") has often been questioned, there are at least several which would qualify as literature. She has elsewhere identified these as being the *chigo monogatari*, those stories dealing with "the pleasures and agonies of homosexual love in medieval temples," works such as the "Tale of the Priest Gemmu" or the "Long Tale for an Autumn Night." These are not translated by Skord (portions, however, appear in a 1980 issue of *Monumenta Nipponica* (35:2) translated by Margaret Childs).

Tales of Tears and Laughter, translated by Virginia Skord. Honolulu: University of Hawaii Press, 1991.

The *Poetic Memoirs of the Lady Daibu*

Sometime between 1213 and 1219, a court lady, now older and retired, sat down and wrote her memoirs. Though scholars disagree as to just when this occurred, she had them all ready when she was asked to contribute to an imperial anthology in 1232. Several of the poems from her work (memoirs in those days were composed of alternative poetry and prose) were included. Perhaps this called further attention to the memoirs themselves. Before that time they were probably shown to very few people, mainly friends and acquaintances. By 1260, however, at least several copies had been made for more general circulation, and it is one of these, in the collection of Kyushu University, which is used as the basis for most later scholar editions.

The Lady Daibu or, to give her full title, the Kenreimon-in Ukyo no Daibu, lived during one of the most momentous periods in Japan's history, that which saw the defeat of the Heike and the rise of the Minamoto, the transfer of power from Kyoto to Kamakura, the last of the old Heian civilization and the beginnings of the military feudalism of the Kamakura Shogunates.

When she wrote her memoirs, however, she remembered little of that or, to be more precise, she remembered it only in how it affected her. In this she followed the tradition of such court diaries as hers, but it must also be said that her memoirs lack the social observations of the Murasaki Shikibu diaries and the characterization of the *Kagero Nikki*, to name but two works written within a century of hers.

Whether not including what she had never intended to include can be considered a lack is debatable—though we may consider this lack our loss. She was—more than many literary court ladies—concerned exclusively with her own emotions and those events which created them.

The main event which created them, however, happens to be of the greatest interest to us, reading her work hundreds of years later. This is her unhappy love affair (the burden of the memoirs) and the death of her lover. Our interest lies in his identity. It was Taira no Sukemori, a grandson of Kiyomori, and one of the characters in the *Heike Monogatari*. Familiar with him and his family from this great prose work, no reader will fail to feel the frisson occasioned by his suddenly walking (in the flesh as it were) into these memoirs. It is somewhat as though Lancelot, say, known to readers through Chrétien de Troyes and many later works, should suddenly appear, alive and well, in a contemporary diary.

Sukemori was killed, or he killed himself, during the battle of Dannoura which signaled the final defeat of the Heike clan, and the Lady Daibu never recovered from the event. Her memoirs are filled with his memory. Or, to be more precise, filled with her memory of this memory because she is almost excessively concerned with her own emotions.

When Joan Crawford does this we have a derogatory term for it. Yet, though one occasionally does indeed want to slap some sense into the Lady Daibu, it will do no good to apply such standards here. She came from (and was very much a product of) a civilization which considered showing sorrow the most seemly female occupation. All of these court diaries heave and sigh to various degrees but some dramatize the pervasive sorrow and at least describe the prevailing gloom.

The Lady Daibu does this only occasionally. She is truly pathetic when she discovers some old letters and tells what she did with them, and she reaches (tentatively) literature when she, for once, manages to stand back from her emotion and allows it to be expressed rather than merely stated. "I glanced outside," runs the passage, "and saw a spotted dog scampering round the base of one of the bamboo clumps. It looked just like a dog that had lived in the Emperor's apartments in the old days. Whenever I had gone there on an errand, I had called it to me and draped my sleeves over it. It had always recognized me and used to frisk about wagging its tail. Now, at the sight of this new dog, a vague sorrow came over me."

This is the departure for a poem (there are over 300 in the work), this being the main way in those days through which emotions were codified and communicated: "This dog is, after all,/the very image/of the one I knew;/but people's faces bear no likeness/to what once they were."

From our point of view she has spoiled her effect, but our point of view cannot profitably be brought into it. From her point of view (which is pre-literary) she was recording in the only way available and allowable to her. Since her poetry isn't really very good (and we have the translator/editor's word on this), we must read the memoirs as a kind of history. Our pleasure therefore takes the very real form of reading a letter from the past, considerably augmented in this case by the cameo-appearances, as it were, not only of Sukemori, but of other characters from the *Heike*.

The Poetic Memoirs of Lady Daibu, translated with an introduction by Phillip Tudor Harries. Stanford: Stanford University Press, 1980.

The *Torikaebaya Monogatari*

One of the curiosities of early Japanese literature is the *Torikaebaya Monogatari*, a 12th-century romance of unknown authorship. It is among the few surviving *giko monogatari*, those narratives written in imitation of the classical tales, the most famous of which is the *Genji Monogatari*. It is also an oddity in that its narrative is so peculiar.

It is, as its new translation says, "the story of a brother and sister whose natural inclinations lead them to live as members of the opposite sex. Their difficulties in concealing certain physical attributes and the complications they face in their sexual encounters are fully chronicled. Eventually the hero and heroine take each other's place in society and thus return to their true sexes."

The sister, dressed as a man, becomes one of the luminaries of the Heian court, admired by all. Of her, the author, earlier adopting the pronoun which she would have preferred, says, "While the boy was still young he did not understand much about his body. Satisfied that there were surely others like him, he continued to conduct himself as he chose. Gradually, however, he learned about other people and after much thought came to realize that he was different.... He strained himself, kept his distance from the other men, and was somber. His reticence when mingling in society was admirable."

Perhaps only in Heian society would the girl's innate feelings be regarded as masculine virtues. But, as the *Genji* and other literature of the period indicates, the manly ideal was, by contemporary standards, effeminate. The kind of sensibility we now, rightly or wrongly, call feminine, was expected in men, at least among courtiers.

The girl turned man is, indeed, well thought of in court. In particular by other men. One of them, Saisho, found him "radiantly beautiful," was "flooded with tenderness for him," even "wept profusely, as was fashionable in those days." And eventually Saisho desires to get even closer to our heroine, who is using the masculine name of Chunagon.

"In the grip of his passion he seized Chunagon. 'What are you doing? Have you lost your mind?' snapped Chunagon in disgust, but Saisho paid no heed. Though Chunagon treated his pursuer coldly and though his determined appearance certainly was manly, he could do nothing when Saisho seized him, and his heart grew weak. 'What is happening?' he wondered. He wept tears of shame." In the meantime, "Saisho was amazed at what he had discovered...."

It will be noticed that there is a certain amount of ambiguity, due almost entirely to the author's decision to give his brother and sister opposite pronouns. There are consequently references to his menstrual periods and sentences such as "Chunagon was embarrassed to reveal his pregnancy...." Later, when the pair change sex again, this time, to their original sexes, the author complicates things further by having them exchange names so that we must constantly bear in mind not only the sex of the person but the person him/herself. "And with Naishi no Kami (the brother, hitherto a woman) now an indescribably refined and elegant man, neither felt the other was real."

Indeed, that is one of the problems of this work—nothing feels quite real. On the other hand, this very quality may well have been one of its attractions for earlier readers. The *giko monogatari* prized an atmosphere where nothing is for certain, where all is ephemeral and fleeting, where the only reality is often the literary tags and allusions which stud the script.

Perhaps our feeling of unreality is such that we no longer know what to do with a story like this which is not, at the same time, a satire. Our tradition of transvestite-romance has a dissident edge. Society's sexual pronouncements are questioned, and, along with them, much else in society is rendered suspect. This is as true of Charley's aunt as it is of *Tootsie*. It is not true, however, of much Japanese transvestism. It is not true of the kabuki's Benten Kozo, and it is not true of the *Torikaebaya Monogatari*.

Here the masquerade has no social purpose. We are not invited to find irony and humor. Benten Kozo impersonates for sound business reasons; Chunagon, because he was born that way. The edge of a thoroughly subversive essay into the transvestite—the Marquis de Sade's Augustine de Villeblanche, for example, an even-now breathtakingly audacious swipe at marriage, family, society—this edge is simply not there.

Nor is there any humor, a lack which is a sure indication that intentions are all ostensible. Sometimes, to be sure, we of the West may be amused, but I do not believe that amusement was among the writer's intentions. "Even when Naishi no Kami was like a man, gallant and strong, she had been unable to escape when Saisho took her. So she was all the more vulnerable now that she was an ordinary woman. She did not want to appear inconsiderate; but the Emperor would not yield even to coldness, and she was as unable as ever to extricate herself. There was nothing she could do about this act of violation. It was embarrassing and painful." As for the Emperor: " 'Oh, god! What is this?' he cried, realizing that Naishi no Kami was apparently not a virgin, and a sense of disappointment mingled with his other feelings."

Perhaps we find this funny because we might otherwise find it uncomfortable—one disarms a presumed threat by laughing at it. The translator makes something of a case for the author and his/her early readers also finding several passages amusing. I wonder. It all seems so straight-forward, so singularly lacking in attitude.

This being so, it seems unfortunate that so innocent a book has been so castigated by the Japanese themselves. After the reign Meiji had begun and the various social and financial incentives to a subscription to Western-style mores had become evident, literary pundits turned against this particular tale, finding it indecent, etc. It is, of course, nothing of the sort. At the same time, however, it is difficult to say just what it is.

In the event, with this English translation interested readers may themselves decide. It is published with full notes, a good introduction, textual variants, and later passages. Indeed, the only criticism I might have of it is the English title it has been given. Did no one look up the meaning of "changeling" before it was applied? It simply does not mean what it is here implied.

The Changelings: A Classical Court Tale, translated with an introduction and notes by Rosette F. Willig. Stanford: Stanford University Press, 1983.

The *Heike Monogatari*

Here is the first complete English translation of the *Heike Monogatari*, that famous account of the events which led to the downfall of Heike clan and the ascendancy of the Genji.

It covers the 90 years between 1131 and 1331, but is mainly concerned with the 18 years between the premiership of Kiyomori, head of the Heike, and the destruction of that clan at the battle of Dan-no-ura. These events are presented in great detail, and there is an abundance of violent action, but the work—read more as literature than as history—is most distinguished by its tone.

This is frankly elegiac. We view the events from a distance, morality is allowed to intrude from time to time, the fall of the Heike is seen with an ethical eye, and the lesson of the eternal evanescence of all things is detected in many an incident.

The work then is not history, as are the roughly contemporary *Chronicles* of Froissart. Rather, as in the exactly contemporary Chrétien de Troyes, past events are reviewed and interpreted and an element of romance, notably missing in real history, is added. There are several reasons for this.

First, like Homer, the Heike story was originally oral literature. It was a kind of ballad-chronicle chanted by *biwa*-playing storytellers. It was not until the early 14th-century that it was transcribed, and even that original work has not survived. What is now regarded as the most authoritative text dates from 1371, a revision of this transcription.

The storytellers were concerned with entertainment and education. Thus legends and supernatural happenings are included, a real villain—in the person of Kiyomori—is created, morals are drawn, and the great lesson of *shoja hissui* (those who flourish are destined to fall) is tirelessly repeated.

By the 14th-century, Japan was becoming somewhat self-conscious about its literature. Feeling the need for a proper history, it had already created its own official version in the *Kojiki*. Now, perhaps, the need for an epic poem was similarly felt. The Heike happenings were at hand, and the result should have been a real epic. It still passes as one and the popularizations (Yoshikawa Eiji's *The Heike Story* is the most famous contemporary example), films and TV shows which reuse this material all insist upon the epic aspect. The work itself, however, is lyrical, not epic. In this regard, it is much closer to the romantic Virgil than it is to the action-packed Homer.

One of the reasons for this is that the model for the transcribed work may have been the various Chinese dynastic histories which were known at the time. These "basic annals," though perhaps epic in intent, are more concerned with reinterpreting history according to accepted theory rather than actual authenticity. The Chinese annals are all, in their way, success stories, with an amount of favorable publicity given each reign. The Japanese "annals" are different only in that they are not concerned with the successful and the triumphant. They are, in typical Japanese fashion, concerned with the failures. In either case, however, it is history as it was which is sacrificed to the ideal of history as we want to see it.

There is certainly an amount of kowtowing to China in the text itself. We read, over and over again: "If we examine the history of ancient China, we see that …" This constant reverting to the mainland was doubtless *à la mode* at the time, but to us there is a quality essentially uncertain in this constant reverting to Chinese parallels, as though some kind of authority was necessary not only for action but for emotion as well. It makes for a curiously tentative "epic."

More purely Japanese is the interest in emotion itself. The story stops, time and again, not only to tell us what the characters are wearing but to observe how many times they wet their sleeves, how many times they complain about "this present degenerate age."

It was surely a curious one, that age, a remarkable combination of sensitivity and brutality. Poems were endlessly penned and heads were paraded in the streets; conversations on style turned into learned debates and, at the same time, the most ferocious tortures were common. Bloody civil wars were endemic, but it is the losers who are most mourned.

In these details lie, I think, the strengths of the work. The uncertainty not only of war but of life itself is emphasized. There are no false heroics, only the sad details of lives wastefully lost. The evanescence of all things is the real burden, and moments of beauty are all the stronger when we realize that they too are to pass.

It is here that *The Tale of the Heike* enters the mainstream of Japanese literature. The lyric regard for the tragic detail assumes not only a knowledge of the transient. It also invites a quiet celebration of that fact. If all things pass, it is because all things must, and since all things must and this is what is, then it is good. This tragic sense of life has illuminated much of Japanese literature, and in the *Heike Monogatari* is seen in one of its earliest forms.

That a book this famous has had to wait so long for a full translation is not surprising, given the difficulty of the task. A. L. Sadler's excellent translation, which appeared many years ago, is only partial, and though other works of the period (Helen Craig McCullough's very fine edition of *Yoshitsune*) have been translated from time to time, the *Heike Monogatari* has had to wait.

The present translation is extremely apt. Here is a sample: "Kiyomori came out to receive him and said: 'Your father and I were intimate enough to talk to each other about problems great and small. Since you are his son, I have always valued you. I have sympathized with your long rustication, but because the cloistered emperor has been holding all power in his own hands, I have not been able to help you." The tone is just right—literal, stately, properly stilted, quite fitting.

The Tale of the Heike, translated by Kitagawa Hiroshi and Bruce T. Tsuchida, with a forward by Edward Seidenshcker. Tokyo: University of Tokyo Press, 1975.

The *Heike Monogatari*, the most important (and the most readable) of the Kamakura/Muromachi war tales, has now appeared in a new translation by Helen McCullough. This brings to three the number of English versions of this *gunki monogatari*.

The first was a partial translation by A. L. Sadler. The second was that of Kitagawa Hiroshi and Bruce T. Tsuchida which appeared in 1975. It used (as does the McCullough) the Kakuichi text (1371) edited by Takagi Ichinosuke and others. It also included a translation of the four pages appended to the 10th chapter ("The Imperial Pilgrimage to Mt. Koya"), an anecdote which does not appear in all other Kakuichi texts and, in any event, as McCullough remarks, "is not relevant to the main *Heike* story."

All three translations have their strengths. Sadler's may be vitiated by its choice of text (scholarly Heike texts were not available that early) and by its somewhat period style. At the same time this style has its admirers—as does Arthur Waley's period style in his version of the *Genji Monogatari*. McCullough is one of these and notes in her preface that "from time to time, I have borrowed a felicitous word or phrase from A. L. Sadler's spirited early translation."

The best way to indicate the merits of these various versions is to compare passages. I have chosen a favorite, a section from "The Death of Atsumori," (Chapter XVI, Book 9). Kumagai is standing over the fallen youth.

> "Alas! look there," he exclaimed, the tears running down his face, "though I would spare your life, the

> whole countryside swarms with our men, and you cannot escape them. If you must die, let it be by my hand and I'll see that prayers are said for your rebirth in Bliss." "Indeed it must be," said the young warrior, "so take off my head at once." Then Kumagai, weeping bitterly, and so overcome by his compassion that his eyes swam and his hand trembled so that he could scarcely wield his blade, hardly knowing what he did, at last cut off his head." (A. L. Sadler version).

> He suppressed his tears and said: "Though I wish to spare your life, a band of my fellow warriors is approaching, and there are so many others throughout the countryside that you have no chance of escaping from the Genji. Since you must die now, let it be by my hand rather than by the hand of another, for I will see that prayers for your better fortune in the next world are performed." To this, the young warrior replied simply: "Then take off my head at once!" So pitiable an act was it that Naozane could not wield his blade. His eyes saw nothing but darkness before him. His heart sank. However, unable to keep the boy in this state any longer, he struck off his head." (Kitagawa/Tsuchida version).

> "I would like to spare you," he said, restraining his tears, "but there are Genji warriors everywhere. You cannot pos-sibly escape. It will be better if I kill you than if someone else does it, because I will offer prayers on your behalf." "Just take my head and be quick about it." Overwhelmed by compassion, Naozane could not find a place to strike. His senses reeled, his wits forsook him, and he was scarcely conscious of his surroundings. But matters could not go on like that forever: in tears, he took the head. (McCullough version).

The various virtues of these passages are evident but they have their differences (Sadler and Kitagawa/Tsuchida give the aggressors' name as Kumagai, McCullough as Kumagae; his initial tears are suppressed/restrained in

Kitagawa-Tsuchida and McCullough but run down his face in Sadler), etc., but their very similarities would indicate that they are all trustworthy.

However, the purveying of story-line information is only one of the duties of a translator. Perhaps the most important of these is the creation of a tone which will carry the purport of the text and make it understandable. And here, in my opinion, the new McCullough version is the best.

Sadler was working within the lingual confines of his time and these now, naturally, seem quaint. There are those who would cherish such quaintness, but I am not one of their number. Kitagawa and Tsuchida are two people, and so the translation had to go through an extra step along the way. The direct transmission of an original text to a single interpreter/translator was not possible. A further complication is that only one of them (Bruce Tsuchida) was a native English speaker. At the same time, there is an occasional awkwardness ("unable to keep the boy in this state any longer") and too great a reliance (in this passage at any rate) on expected phrases— "his heart sank."

McCullough has the benefit of a modern text and modern diction. At the same time she is working directly with the "original voice" and is able to do so without making any compromises. She can approximate the pace of the original (notice how much faster her prose moves) and can suggest a reality ("Just take my head and be quick about it,") that decades of pious sentimentality has obscured. And in the midst of reeling senses and wits forsook, there is the hard-boiled reminder that "matters could not go on like that forever."

Also McCullough offers (in addition to the excellent translation itself) two surrounding essays which are of major importance in understanding and enjoying the work.

The first of this is an introduction which in a mere 10 pages recounts the "story" of the *monogatari* (no mean feat, that), the history of the various manuscripts and how they came to be written, notes on performance by the *biwa hoshi* and much else. It is written with the simple elegance that distinguishes the translation itself and is free of any scholarly affectations.

The second is the terminal essay, an important addition to any Heike bibliography, in which the translator considers this *gunki monogatari* as literature. Using the resources of modern scholarship, she sees the *Heike* as a work of its period, separates stereotypes from original observations, notes structural similarities with other literary forms of the period, and ranges widely in finding apposite comparisons.

For example: "... like Trollope, whose Marys, Lucys and Graces are really all the same self-sacrificing paragon, the author brings his stock figures to life through the situations in which he places them." And "Kiyomori, like Milton's Satan, is a towering figure whose greatness is perverted to evil ends." Or "Noritsune ... is a Germanic-style hero who hates a traitor, despises laziness ... fights with spectacular fury, and dies gloriously in a doomed cause."

The Tale of the Heike, translated with an introduction by Helen Craig McCullough. Stanford: Stanford University Press, 1988.

The *Soga Monogatari*

With this new rendering of the *Soga Monogatari*, the last of Japan's war-tale *gunki mono* untranslated now appears in English complete. (A prior translation by Kitagawa Hiroshi was incomplete, only six of the 12 books). Though not the best of the genre (the *Heike Monogatari* is that), it is by far the most popular.

Indeed, as Thomas J. Cogan states in the introduction to his new translation: "The *Soga Monogatari* has served as a major source of themes and motifs for various genres.... The Soga brothers figure more prominently in subsequent plays and stories than anyone else in Japanese history except Yoshitsune." In addition it has, along with *Chushingura*, endured as one of the two most popular Japanese tales of revenge.

The story, though it manages to fill 300-some pages in English, is simple enough. The Genji official, Kudo Suketsune, angry at being deprived of his inheritance by his uncle has his nephew murdered. Finally, eighteen years later, the dead man's two sons exact revenge by killing Suketsune, now a crony of Yoritomo. The elder brother is himself killed, but the younger is captured. Yoritomo, impressed by filial piety, would have had him pardoned, but Suketsune's son demanded the execution and thus ended the Soga *kyodai* and their famous saga.

Just when this narrative got written down is a matter of conjecture. Apparently, like many of the *gunki mono* (including the *Heike Monogatari*), it first appeared in recitation—traveling monks and nuns, balladeers. Later the narrative appeared in *kowaka* ballad dramas and in several noh plays (not to mention later appearances in kabuki, *shimpa*, and *shingeki*). Just when it was written is likewise uncertain, perhaps in the first half of the 14th-century.

In any event, the tale had gone through a good many hands before it achieved any definite written form. One can tell by the amount of debris that it acquired along the way: much didactic religious moralizing, a lot of cautionary Confucianism. In any event, the text now commonly used is excessively preachy and sententious. Indeed—as Cogan is careful to point out—one-fourth of the total work is devoted to digressions taken from Chinese and Buddhist sources.

While this has not apparently limited the popularity of

the story itself, it may account for a limited readership. Indeed, as no lesser authority than Douglas Mills (author of "The *Soga Monogatari*, *Shintoshu* and the *Taketori* legend," *Monumenta Nipponica* 30:1, 1975) has written: "As literature, [the] *Soga Monogatari* is rather tedious, being overloaded with religious propaganda, but," he hastens to add, "its evolution in various literary genres well repays study."

One of the reasons that the work might seem tedious to Western readers is that it was written, or compiled, with none of their expectations in mind. And it is particularly irritating to the Western mind to be thwarted in the matter of story. For example, in Book 5 just as the brothers are going off for a hopefully fatal encounter with Suketsune, the reader is suddenly diverted by digressions which seem cumbersome and inappropriate, particularly at this juncture of the tale.

But this is not only because one does not expect them and takes no interest in them. It is also because the modern reader is prejudiced in favor of the tale itself. One may imagine a reader, however, who is not so hampered. He probably knows the outcome of the story already (it is difficult to imagine a Japanese who doesn't) and enjoys all the edifying discourse along the way—perhaps merely because it has always reassuringly been there.

The *Soga Monogatari* contains some 40 longish episodes from Chinese, Buddhist and earlier Japanese sources, which from the Western viewpoint don't belong there and only get in the way. However, whatever else, the compilers of this *gunki mono* were not engaged in the construction of what the West would call a fully unified and linear narrative.

There are many other kinds of narrative than the merely linear and if that is all the West knows, then it is to its own impoverishment. The agglutinated form the *Soga Monogatari* takes is ideally as capable of giving enjoyment and instruction as any other.

I cannot say that it does, but then I have my prejudices. What it does give, however, is a glimpse into the medieval Japanese mind—this mind-set, to use a particularly unwelcome neologism. Reading this new and very able translation of the *Soga Monogatari*, one may come close to capturing what it must have felt like to have been a reader or a listener in Japan during the late Kamakura Period.

The Tale of the Soga Brothers, translated with an introduction and notes by Thomas J. Cogan. Tokyo: University of Tokyo Press, 1987.

Four Huts

The simple life remains attractive. An existence resting solely upon the essentials, the round of days and months, circumscribed but by what is necessary—such a life seems somehow superior.

It has long seemed so. In the West, Elijah—with some ill-grace to be sure—retired to his hut and was fed by the crows, Marie Antoinette played at being simple in Le Hameau, and in Connecticut, Walden Pond held the hut of sincere and solitary Thoreau. All, in their own ways, were looking for a life simplified and hence appreciable.

The tradition is perhaps even stronger in Asia, and there are many huts to choose among. Burton Watson has chosen four and built this fine book about them. These four texts about four huts encompass the confines of the Asian simple life and offer the reader both comfort and insight.

The four are *The Record of the Thatched Hall on Mount Lu*, a text from 817 by Po Chu-i; Yoshishige no Yasutane's 982 *Record of the Pond Pavilion*; Kamo no Chomei's famous *Record of the Ten-Foot Square Hut*, from 1212; and Basho's 1690 *Record of the Hut of the Phantom Dwelling*.

There a number of similarities among the texts. All four writers are poets, all four are Buddhists, all claim to be quite contented with their simple dwellings and hope to go on living in them, though not all of them actually do so, and all "clearly took pains to clothe their accounts in the most elegant and effective language they could devise."

In addition, the later poets were influenced by those earlier. Yoshishige clearly patterned his piece on Po's, Kamo may not have known Po's account, but he was much influenced by Yoshishige's, and Basho, great reader of the classics, knew all three.

Thus, Watson can give us here not only the four texts in all their authenticity but can also indicate that a literary tradition has grown about the idea of the attractions of the simple life. This has resulted in a degree of idealization and an amount of self-consciousness about the enterprise of the wise poet living in the better sort of hut.

Yoshishige sets the tone. "So, after five decades in the world, I've at last managed to acquire a little house, like a snail at peace in his shell, like a louse happy in the seam of a garment. The quail nests in the small branches and does not yearn for the great forest ... the frog lives in his crooked well and knows nothing of the vastness of the sweeping seas."

The complaiscency is endearing because one feels that it has been earned. Kamo no Chomei certainly feels that it has. "Now that I've reached the age of sixty, when life fades as quickly as dew, I've put together a lodging for my final days. I'm like a traveler who prepares shelter for one night, or an aging silkworm spinning its cocoon."

It is true that the aging poet is living alone in a simple hut, but it is also true that he is aware of his doing so and is to that degree playing the part of the aging poet living alone in a simple hut. He knows he is part of a tradition, and it is this tradition which he upholds.

Thus there no complaints about bugs, leaks and loneliness. The simple life in the solitary hut, being idyllic by definition, is automatically free from those imperfections which would ordinarily send one speeding off the mountain and into the city.

Perhaps it is just this utopian aspect of the simple life that most appeals. How nice it would be if it were possible. Though it is perhaps in our times impossible—the hippies tried and look at them now—it ought somehow to have been possible in ages past.

Hence the consolation which these texts bring with them and, like a soft wind among the pines, the hope. Arcadian simplicity, an idyllic innocence in our man-made world, these are necessary delusions—small beacons of hope in the blackness of man's works.

Both the Po Chu-li and Matsuo Basho translations were published earlier and appear here in revised version. The Yoshishige no Yasutane is being here translated, I believe, for the first time. The Kamo no Chomei *Hojoki* has enjoyed many translations, though it has never, I believe, been better translated than now.

Four Huts: Asian Writings on the Simple Life, translated by Burton Watson. Boston: Shambhala, 1994.

Four Travel Diaries

There are extant some seventy travel diaries from Japan's "medieval" period (12th to 16th-century), most of them still untranslated. These four here published were chosen because the translators believe they best represent the genre's various styles and can thus give an idea of an otherwise unavailable corpus.

The first is a translation of *Takakura-in Itsukushima Goko Ki*, an account by courtier Koga Michichika of the ex-Emperor Takakura's pilgrimage to the Itsukushima Shrine in 1180. Like many another it was a commissioned work. Though not overtly stated in this diary, its ultimate purpose was political.

Itsukushima was a Taira family shrine, and Takakura was the son of ex-Emperor Goshirakawa, accused of having attempted to confiscate Taira-held lands. Michichika's account was intended for the mollified regard of Kiyomori, head of the Taira clan.

Much is made of the inconvenience. Not only was an imperial journey of this distance unprecedented but the head of state worshipping at a military shrine was equally singular. Kiyomori was therefore to appreciate the degree of abnegation, and just in case he didn't the diarist ended his account by remarking that the emperor "had lost weight alarmingly and that the doctors had prescribed moxa treatment for him." In fact, the unhappy Takakura shortly expired, and the busy Michichika penned a full account of this event in the later *Takakura-in Shoka Ki*.

The other three diaries in the volume are all by traveling priests and (unlike that of Michichika) are in the first person. *The Shinsho Hoshi Nikki* written around 1225, finds the Priest Shinsho accounting for his wanderings not only to Kamakura but all the way to snowy Nagano. He had been a retainer, but when his lord was assassinated he forsook this world. His account is thus also somewhat politically motivated in that it is, in part, a vindication of his actions.

The priest Sokyo wrote his *Miyako no Tsuto* in 1367, though not much else is known about it and its author. His, however, is the account most personal among the four. "I had yearned for many years to live under the trees and on the rocks [a phrase used to describe a like desire on the part of the Buddha].... With the thought that there is no place where one can stay forever, I left [Kyushu] and wandered around without destination." And so he did, and we can still read all about it.

The last of the four diaries is by the priest Jokoin Gyoe who wrote his *Zenkoji Kiko* in 1465. Here again there is a sub-text in that the author was a member of a religious organization, the famous mountain priests, the *yama bushi*. What political import remains is mildly propagandistic as he explains the holy rites.

He went to the main hall of the temple to offer prayers and then "spent the night in front of the altar." During this time he also performed that esoteric ritual which consists in part of wandering in complete darkness under the altar and finding by touch alone the holy objects sought. "Realizing that, in truth, I was allowed to do this because of the considerable merit I had accumulated in my previous lives," he opines, "I shed profuse tears of joy...."

Donald Keene has remarked in his *Travelers of a Hundred Ages* (1989) that few of the medieval travel diaries are of major literary importance and that "even when the description of famous places have charm, the charm is apt to be conventional." He quotes, however, an observation of Plitschow's that even so, contemporary European travel diaries did not mention nature at all—at least the Japanese observe that nature exists, unnatural though the form the observation often takes.

All four diaries are, as was the custom, interspersed with poems, and all are distinguished by that lack of individuality one associates with most male writing of the period. In contradistinction to writing by women, which was so realistically individual that reading their works—the diaries of Murasaki Shikibu and Sei Shonagon for example—remains a living experience and not at all an antiquarian exercise.

With the majority of these male diarists, however, time-honored poetic imagery takes the place of any realistic description. Indeed such would seriously disrupt a genre in which authors fitted their observations into traditionally sanctioned forms. As Plutschow has noted: "Consciousness of a place is brought forth only by antecedent, and this makes the travel diaries a tradition-bound, retrospective literature of little interest to an historian."

Most of the diarists subscribed, for example, to the necessity for *utamakura*, the famous place name which would come up dragging behind all sorts of associations—legends, pseudo-history, past poems and prose, indeed anything that could be connected to it. It is through this heavy grid that the real place must be viewed. And sometimes not even then.

As when another of these wandering monks, the Priest Sogi, says in his *Tsukushi Michi no Ki*: "Here, too, the pine forest stretches out into the distance, and though it does not at all seem inferior to that of Hakozaki, and both of these are unsurpassed, this place is of no special renown and therefore I am not much attracted to it."

Yet, all this granted, I do think these antique diaries remain of considerable interest to the contemporary reader, if not the historian. For here, mummified by convention though they are, rise these faint voices from the past. They speak to us, in no matter what peculiar accents, over the centuries.

Four Japanese Travel Diaries of the Middle Ages, translated by Herbert Plutschow and Fukuda Hideichi. Ithaca: Cornell University Press, 1981.

Ippen

Ippen (1239–1289), a priest and founder of the Ji Section of Pure Land Buddhism, is known both as a "wayfaring saint" and a "saint of abandonment." The latter sobriquet refers to his belief in abandoning the self by trusting Buddha through the ecstatic incantation of the deity's name; the former refers to the priest's extensive travels about Japan bringing the good news to the faithful.

In contrast to the teachings of Shinran, the founder of the Jodo Shin Sect which emphasized the believer's faith, Ippen's teaching requires no faith at all since salvation had been decided by Buddha's vow. All one needed to do was trust the promise and keep reminding the deity by repeating the holy name, by chanting and later by dancing.

The Ji sect, as James Kodera has pointed out, created a unique religion, one which combined Pure Land Buddhism, Shingon Buddhism and folk Shinto. As such, it was popular, and this degree of acceptance was intensified since it was one of the easiest of all religions to practice. As Ippen often implied, all one had to do was wait out one's life until the purple clouds rolled up and then climb on and proceed to a promised heavenly throne.

(Other routes, arranged travel-agent-like by other sects, were disapproved of, particularly those popular one-way boat trips to holy Mount Horai, an island in the Western Paradise. The vessels were designed to spring leaks, thus guaranteeing instant acceptance in the midst of holy endeavor—no waiting.)

Ippen was one of the most active of the Jodo priests, and the book under review contains not only a full chronology but also a map illustrating where the holy man went. In fact, his was a mendicant order and was only transformed into a proper sect during the Edo Period.

Perhaps one of the reasons all this took so long was that its very popularity worked against its ecclesiastical elevation.

Popular it certainly was, proper sect or not. One of the reasons was that this was a time when the decay of Buddha's teaching (*mappo*) was judged to have begun and people were troubled about the state of their afterlife. Ippen preached that the name of the Buddha Amida itself contained the attainment of Buddhahood and the salvation of all beings, both united in a single, timeless event.

Thus, the name alone sufficed. One did not have to be pious, let alone meditate. It was to this end that Ippen traveled. He not only chanted and danced, but he also distributed paper talismans (*fuda*) inscribed with the holy name. It was understood that anyone receiving one was automatically saved. The tickets were free, too, merchandizing having yet to achieve its present heights.

Ippen also left a large number of other writings. There is the *Ippen Shonin Goroku* (*The Record of Ippen*), poems in Chinese, his *waka*, a number of letters, and his disciples have left accounts of "words handed down."

The original edition of this book appeared a decade ago. This new edition contains, in addition to some minor revisions and an updated bibliography, plates from the *Ippen Hijiro-e*, the Kamakura Period biographical picture scrolls now divided among Kangikoji, the present headquarters of the Jishu tradition, Shojokoji, and the Tokyo National Museum. This new edition thus contains just about everything there is to know about Ippen.

No Abode: The Record of Ippen, by Dennis Hirota. Honolulu: University of Hawaii Press, 1997.

Zen Monk Poetry

Here is a collection of poetry originally written in Chinese by Japanese Zen monks. Some 16 have been here selected, men who lived between the years of 1278 to 1429, and the 71 poems included indicate the range of this particular liturgical genre.

It has a name—it is called *gozen bungaku*. The term does not refer, however, to either the number or the location of the implied monasteries. Despite accepted opinion, Zen is just as cluttered with administrative guidance as are most religions, and the "five mountains" refers to ranks of the monasteries—big Nanzenji on the top and little Manjuji on the bottom.

Back then, Japanese went to China to study in the same spirit that they later went to Europe and to America. Going to the source, they brought back the real thing. It could then be taken to one of the better temples and adulterated to the Japanese way. And indeed, it was said—by *gozen* priest-poet Kokan Shiren—that Japan was, after all, the true home of both Buddhism and Chinese civilization.

This meant, however, that proper poetry was composed only in Chinese. Like Latin in the West, it became the medium for an exchange of courtesies between men of education. The poetry itself was occasional: congratulations upon promotions, celebration of leave-takings and visits, felicitations for anniversaries, sympathy for sickbeds, also poems on such universal subjects as old age, homesickness, sorrow, and pictorial beauty.

None of the poets apparently doubted the adequacy of Chinese as a medium. It was perhaps thought that only Chinese could encompass the Chinese experience itself; that the native *waka* perhaps could perhaps not. Whatever, as time went on, the specifically liturgical character of the poetry slowly disappeared.

Along with the Chinese language came something of a Chinese attitude. Slowly the spirit of Confucius nudged over that of the Buddha. By the 14th-century, some of the priests had come to look down on the work of the earlier poets as embarrassingly churchly. Though there had been a specific injunction against verse becoming a preoccupation replacing religious striving, this is just what occurred.

As the translator of this collection notes, by the 15th-century, *gozen* poets were Confucian belletrists in monks' clothing. And one of them, Chugan Engetsu, could lie back and write of himself: "I chant leisurely verses, playing the elegant hermit."

This occasioned an amount of criticism and some contrite verse, but as Marian Ury has herself elegantly remarked, "a guilty conscience need by no means be a bad thing for art." The *gozen* poets were indeed producing a kind of lyric poetry.

Just how good was it? This question is seriously considered and the translator notes that in China itself some of it was praised as not being recognizably the work of a foreigner. But such praise, of course, implies an opposite expectation.

Zekkai Chusin, one of the later of the *gozen* poets is usually thought of as being accomplished. His poems are sustained compositions rather than collections of couplets, and his subject matter is (helpfully for lyric effect) entirely secular. Also, amid the ceremonial felicitics, time and again, a personal (and consequently surprisingly modern) tone is heard. Take, for example, the work of Kokan Shiren (1278–1346). It is called "The Earthquake":

> That which is fixed, moves; the hard becomes soft.
> The earth is like waves, my house like a boat.
> A time of dread, but also of charm:
> Wind bells chime without rest, though there's no wind.

To discover the charm of an earthquake argues for an independence of spirit and a degree of sophistication. Just think: seven hundred years ago such a person lived; and brushed just such eloquence in a tongue not his own.

Ury does not translate all of the best poets. Ikkyu, for example, is ignored, but the translator knows why she is ignoring him. He is much translated anyway, and "it should be remembered that Ikkyu stands apart from his period and his time."

This would suggest that those which are chosen do not stand apart, that they are much of their period and their time. And so I suppose they are. Ury is introducing us to a school of poets and a genre of literature.

Poems of the Five Mountains, introduced and translated by Marian Ury. Ann Arbor: Center for Japanese Studies, University of Michigan, 1992.

Shotetsu

Shotetsu (1381–1459) was a poet-priest who wrote a lot (more than 30,000 poems were lost when his house burned down, and he still left behind some 20,000 others), and yet he is not represented in the Imperial anthology of 1439.

The reason for such neglect had nothing to do with the worth of the poetry and much to do with politics. Shotetsu was a great admirer of Fujiwara no Teika, the poetic arbiter of more than a century before—in his *Shotetsu Monogatari*, he said that anyone who presumed to criticize the earlier poet should be punished in the life to come. The officially favored school of poetry, the conservative Ninjo school, did not follow Teika. Their favorite tended to be whichever court poet was currently in favor.

Even within his own Reizei school, which called for a

return to the ideals of the earlier poet, Shotetsu was a controversial figure. He was particularly fond of the master's love poetry (not a popular enthusiasm in official court poetry), and his own style was convoluted and elliptical, making him, said the late Robert Brower, "one of the most difficult of the classical poets."

And, perhaps paradoxically, one of the classical poets who speaks most directly to our time. For example: "No one/remains now/for me to spend my time with—I who/in the past/was known to spurn/the company/of those grown old."

The thought is of a psychological depth that we do not usually associate with writers of Shotetsu's time. Or consider the complexity of: "If one may not think/of what one sees/in one's sleep/as reality/then what use/could there be/in dreams/when one is awake?"

There is a subtlety in some of this poetry which makes it seem practically contemporary. What is surprising about this depth is that these poems are mostly offerings penned at poetry gatherings, in which one person is given a theme and responds. In the above two examples, Shotetsu was responding to "Reminiscing" and "Dream."

This way of writing poetry would seem to cancel inspiration. Sometimes it does. The impossible demand for "Tanabata, Related to 'Animal'" brought forth merely: "If only/they knew that tonight/the clouds make a path/for the stars/to meet—then dogs/would not bark at them/no matter/how late the hour."

Mostly, however, the level of lyric insight is surprisingly high. Or perhaps Carter simply chose his 208 poems with great care. An authority on his subject (with Brower he edited and translated *Conversations with Shotetsu*, 1992) and his period (he compiled the 1991 Stanford anthology of traditional Japanese poetry), Carter finds (and displays) in this poetry "a sense of utter freedom demonstrated within the severest limits."

The translations are (as indicated by the examples above) formally structured to fit the poem. Carter says that he wishes to use the "natural resources" of English to suggest the variety of pauses and stops in the original *uta* form. At the same time, he desires to stick, whenever possible, to the syllable count of the originals, while at the same time attempting to follow in matters of syntax and word order the patterns of the originals.

This is successfully accomplished, (the originals are given in *romaji*), creating a collection which captures and preserves something of what must have been the illuminating lyric contrast, the unexpected merging, which is the objective of all poets.

Of this Shotetsu could be a master—as in his response to a demand for a poem about hail in the forest: "What looked/like rice/left behind/by foresters/taking a break/from gathering/brushwood/turned out instead/to be hail."

Unforgotten Dreams: Poems by the Zen Monk Shotetsu, edited and translated by Steven D. Carter. New York: Columbia University Press, 1997.

Ikkyu

Ikkyu Sojun is one of the most interesting, even most endearing of the early men of Zen. Dead set against the commercialization and bastardization of his church, the Rinzai sect, Ikkyu set himself up as an example of the proper Zen spirit.

At dressy temple, celebrations he wore only tattered robes, and when he finally did wear something decent, he took it off in the middle of the ceremony and tried to "offer" it on the altar. He chose as master a man so eccentrically modest that he had refused his own seal of transmission and could certify none of his pupils, thus ending their church careers.

When Ikkyu had found a new master, he did his best to antagonize him in the interests of Zen. He went up to this master, Kaso, and announced himself a master. Kaso replied: "You are only an adept, not a master." To which Ikkyu replied: "Then I am happy to be an adept. I despise masters." And Kaso, a good master filled with proper Zen, replied: "Now you are a master." And Ikkyu did rise within the church, became an abbot and is credited with rebuilding and revitalizing Kyoto's Daitokuji after the Onin War (1467–77).

At the same time, however, he continued his attractive gadfly activities. He used to stroll about waving a wooden sword at startled passersby to illustrate the difference between the "wooden sword" orthodoxy of the so-called Five Temples of Zen and his own "keen-as-steel" Zen. He would also parade a human skull about and alarm the crowds with this display of the Buddhist doctrine of transience. And he would frequent bars and brothels.

This last is one of his best-remembered attributes. Not only did he like sex, he also wrote most approvingly of it. He was the only one of the Zen masters to do so, and even in his 70s, he was displaying all of the sensual ardor of an adolescent.

Perhaps one of his reasons was to thus display the hypocrisy of the other monks who equally partook and then denied doing so. But certainly another was that, through sex and its open practice, he could break down dualistic misconceptions about the nature of sacred and profane—precisely, he could attack the dualistic principle at the base of such a presumed dialectic.

This was one of the major attributes of Ikkyu's life and work, this continued battle against all forms of dualism, that convenient and dangerous breaking up of the world into black or white, good or bad, sacred or secular. For Ikkyu, life was not either/or but both/and. Beneath any notions of duality was the wholeness of things—this being one of the basic precepts of true Zen.

The dispersal of this truth was one of the "duties" of Ikkyu's life. It was also one of the reasons why his writings took the forms that they did. Didactic in main, they are the opposite of sententious, proceeding as they do (in proper Zen fashion) through indirection. This is particularly true of the poetry.

That in his *Kyounshu* (The Crazy Cloud Anthology) is in classical Chinese (considered not too classic by the Chinese themselves who have found fault with it since the rules of Chinese prosody are bent and broken at will), a tight construction, four lines, each line containing seven characters.

The way in which Ikkyu usually proceeds is to introduce contradictory elements into the final line. This collapses the established frame of reference and also calls into doubt the duality which has been set up. (He often uses analogy to the same effect.) The form is then righted by a reference which returns us to the subject without the duality, and thus the seamless world of Zen is rendered intact. Ikkyu, particularly in his poetry, wanted to deliver the experience of Zen rather than make statements about it.

For example, the three poems (Nos. 69–71) in the *Anthology* which take the scriptures as toilet paper. The poems attack the conventional notion of the distinction between sacred and profane by resorting to the scatological. Thus in one of them "the dog pisses in the sandalwood old Buddha Hall," and in another priest, scripture held, "without ado, he flicks his hand round and wipes himself."

At the same time, however, that the dualistic principle has been exploded, we are taken back to the wholeness of the theme because the allusion is one which the scriptures actually authorize. Turned about, we are sent back the way we came—our round trip expressing to us thus the wholeness and the singleness of all experience since all experience is sacred and profane.

This is most attractive—particularly to us in this questioning and doubting age. Perhaps that is why there has been so much scholarly work on Ikkyu in recent years. One of the earliest in English was Donald Keene's "Portrait of Ikkyu" which is found in *Some Japanese Portraits* (1987); and before that was *Ikkyu Sojun: A Zen Monk and His Poetry* (1973) by Sonja Arntzen, whose new translation of the *Kyounshu* is occasioning this review. There is the work of James Sanford, and Jon Carter Covel's highly imaginative *Zen's Core: Ikkyu's Freedom* (1980).

Ikkyu and the Crazy Cloud Anthology contains translations of 144 of the 880 poems in the original work. In addition, each (poem printed in Chinese and in English translation) is given a very close reading, and a suitable commentary is appended. In addition, there is a long, informative introduction to the poetry, to Ikkyu and to his times. Finally, there are notes, bibliographies, an index to the poems and a glossary-index.

Sonja Arntzen is a scholar who not only knows her subject but can also communicate it, make us experience it. For example, the following: She is discussing *furyu*, an aesthetic term difficult to translate. She points out its various meanings, its evocation of simple rustic life, also its slightly romantic (erotic) tinge, and, finally, its slang effect—for it was also a slang word. "The closest equivalent in English is 'far out'," writes the author, "itself slightly passé slang." It is characteristic of slang that one needs to acquire a feeling for what it means in order to understand it. Also true of slang is what Louis Armstrong said in response to the question, "'What is jazz?' 'If you have to ask, you'll never know.'" Ikkyu would have liked that.

Ikkyu and the Crazy Cloud Anthology, translated with an introduction by Sonja Arntzen, with a foreword by Kato Shuichi. Tokyo: University of Tokyo Press, 1986.

Ikkyu, Zen's most famous priest, born an illegitimate child in 1394 and at 80 made Daitokuji's chief abbot, was forever at odds with the church he represented and forever faithful to the Zen which had illuminated him.

This Zen was that of Rinzai himself, a belief which several hundred years before Ikkyu's birth, the founder had defined by saying: "You have only to be ordinary, with nothing to do but … defecating, urinating, putting on clothes, eating food, and lying down when tired …"

The Zen that Ikkyu found in his own time was much different. He felt he must protest against the travesty. This included corrupt priests, temples tied up with clerical red tape, and many worldly trappings advertising but not practicing personal revelation.

Ikkyu's protest took the form of poetry and other writings, of painting, and most important, of example. He took to wandering and then settled in a hut deep in the mountains. There he practiced what he would have called true Zen.

For him, Zen was the most vital and the most personal thing in life. It was, in fact, life itself. And like life, it was entire and whole. Thus it contained much upon which the Zen church officially frowned. This included—most notoriously—Ikkyu's admission of the passions.

In this, he followed both Rinzai and the Sixth Patriarch, who had written that: "Outside of licentiousness there is no true Buddha nature." This Ikkyu correctly understood to mean that licentiousness has its part in human nature as well. He believed, for example, that his own *satori* was deepened by frequenting brothels, and he demonstrated this to unbelievers.

One may imagine the scandalized attitude of the Zen

church. It is an attitude which even now continues. Ikkyu is still marginalized by being rendered as some quaint Zen saint, a bit mad but mad in a way which Zen officially approves. It is telling that in the official biography, the *Ikkyu Nempu*, there is no mention of the person the most important to him—his mistress, the blind woman named Mori.

He was not mad. He was an iconoclast and, in the Zen tradition, a nihilist. Karaki Junzo (quoted by Donald Keene) defined this as a man who knows that this world is emptiness. Since this is our world it behooves us to demonstrate the truth.

Ikkyu thus compared himself to mere nothingness, called himself a crazy cloud (*kyoun*) and compiled his 1,000-poem *Crazy Cloud Anthology* (*Kyounshu*). In it, he demonstrated his beliefs through a directness which has lasted through the ages.

And been often translated. Collections have been brought out by James Sanford, Sonja Arntzen, Stephen Berg, Jon Carter Covell (with Sobin Yamada) and John Stevens. Ikkyu has had book-length studies devoted to him by Sanford and Covell as well as, more recently, Stevens.

In this collection over one hundred poems are included. Since the translator (also author of *Lust for Enlightenment: Buddhism and Sex*) is celebrating Ikkyu's unfettered Zen life and the joys of sexual intimacy, the selection emphasizes this. As in a poem named "A Woman's Sex":

> It has the original mouth but remains wordless;
> It is surrounded by a magnificent mound of hair.
> Sentient beings get completely lost in it. But it is
> also the birthplace of all the Buddhas of the ten
> thousand worlds.

Some of the poems are amazingly frank given the country and the period. The most explicit are not included in this collection, but a number of those with softer cores are—such as "Lady Mori's Gifted Touch":

> My hand is no match for that of Mori.
> She is the unrivaled master of love play:
> When my jade stalk wilts, she can make it sprout!
> How we enjoy our intimate little circle.

Also included in Steven's collection is the curious prose work *Skeletons* (*Gaikotsu*), a series of sketches written in 1457 when Ikkyu was 63, which describes, under the guise of a dream, the belief that the world is indeed an illusion.

It has had some prior translations—including those of Thomas Cleary, Mori Taikyo and R. H. Blyth, as completed by N. A Waddell. All, however, are out of print, and it is good to have Stevens' new, colloquial translation. The original manuscript apparently had Ikkyu illustrations as well but this has long disappeared. Stevens includes illustrations taken from a 1693 woodblock edition of the work.

He also illustrates his selection from *Ikkyu Banashi*, making his the prettiest, as well as the most portable, and the most colloquially translated of the available editions.

Wild Ways: Zen Poems of Ikkyu, translated by John Stevens. Boston: Shambhala, 1995.

The *Kanginshu*

The *Kanginshu* is a collection of over 300 songs, compiled in 1518. About one-fourth of these came from such public entertainments as the noh and the *kyogen*, and the remainder from songs sung at parties and the like. In this, the collection somewhat resembles the *Ryojinhisho*, the late Heian Period collection of songs of the day brought together by the enthusiasm of the Emperor Goshirakawa (1127–1192). Though the 16th-century collector is an unknown monk, his motivation was the same—saving the past from the savaging of the present.

The title is to be literally translated as *Songs Sung in Tranquility*, indicating that the collector had reached the point in his life when he could regard the past with some serenity. Perhaps the past always appears better, but in Japan there is a definite literary posture for those asserting this.

The Emperor Goshirakawa pensively and visibly regrets the past days of dancing at the palace, and Yoshida Kenko, lamenting the lowered standards of his own time, ca.1330, speaks of the degenerate way they torture these days, complaining that (in Donald Keene's translation): "Today no one knows the shape of the rack nor the manner of attaching the criminal."

These writers had literary precedent for their nostalgia, and it is this which is shared by the anonymous monk who brought together these pages of the past in the *Kanginshu*. He was an antiquarian and, like all antiquarians, wanted to preserve antiquity. There have been several English translations of sections of this long work. Asano Kenji has done large sections of it; Frank Hoff has translated various lyrics (under the engaging title of *Private Music*); and Burton Watson has translated ten *kouta* in *From the Country of Eight Islands*. None of the translations have been complete—nor is this new one by Moriguchi and Jenkins.

Theirs is different, however, in that—like their monkish author—they want to render the past alive, to bring it up-to-date. Here are two renderings of the same poem—the first is by Watson, the second by Moriguchi/Jenkins:

> Behind your fan, staring like that when you know
> I have a husband, saying, shall we try something?
> shall we? shall we?

> You send melting glances from the shadow of
> your fan to me, a married man, you seem to want
> to do it so (so?) so (do it?) so, let's do it!

Besides changing the sex of the writer (perfectly understandable: the original does not specify pronouns), Moriguchi and Jenkins make the urge contemporary ("do it" has a more modern ring than "try something" because of its disdain of euphemism—though both phrases are in common current usage).

Even more contemporary is the Moriguchi/Jenkins use of approximations for dialogue, the parenthetical ejaculations, which attempt to recreate (or create) the biological urgency of the situation:

> Give, cries out the clam from beneath the hard
> rock, go on, man, give me now all the pleasure of
> this world!

Right on, man—not perhaps the diction one expects from the 16th-century but one resolutely contemporary, and in any event, it could be argued that the nameless monk, in making this collage which so cannibalizes the past, was engaged in a very postmodern enterprise.

Further indications of modernity are found in the Moriguchi/Jenkins deconstruction of the purposes of the anonymous monk. No longer is he allowed to be a retired ecclesiastical personage sitting in a known position. Rather, he is a romantic poet who is, on the first page, given props and personality by the translators: "... an elderly man sat down at/a table in his hut,/and in the light of a green-shaded lamp,/began to write."

He constructs a quoted world of woe, which thus

expresses his romantic disappointments. The many love songs in the collection "do not constitute occasional literary conceits ... the themes are returned to again and again and rise in a clamor of outrage."

As for the method of compilation, "the way in which [the] songs are folded into the *Kanginshu* and the subtlety of their meaning shows the anthologist acting much more as a composer and that the exile is occasion for turning over not only the mysteries of love but those of life."

Such sentiments would well suit the English title which has been given the collection. They would also suit the aims of the translators who say that the work "is a continuation of our joint exploration of a certain tradition of Japanese poetry that speaks to and from the heart." Though this is something all poetry does all the time, one can understand their concern.

The Song in the Dream of the Hermit: Selections from the Kanginshu, translated by Moriguchi Yasuhiko and David Jenkins. Seattle: Broken Moon Press, 1995.

Edo Literature

Miyamoto Musashi

One day the celebrated swordsman Bokuden was crossing Lake Biwa in a crowded ferry-barge. Another samurai created a commotion and Bokuden chided him. Furious, the younger man announced himself as master of the *Muteki-ryu*, or Invincible School, and challenged Bokuden to a duel then and there. Observing the crowded condition of the barge, the older man suggested rather a duel upon a small and desolate island they were just then passing, saying that he himself was only a poor adept of the *Mutekatsu-ryu*.

With a cry, the arrogant younger samurai leaped ashore on the islet, calling for the other to follow him. Bokuden seized a barge pole as though he would vault to shore but instead pushed the barge away from the island leaving the stranded samurai to fume. "Did I not tell you I was of the *Mutekatsu-ryu*?" he called.

Just as his was the School of Winning-Without-Hands, so he needed not draw his blade to defeat the blustering samurai. And after that, the barge peacefully proceeded to its destination.

Though Miyamoto Musashi did not know this story (it is from a later Edo Period collection, the *Ho-dan-zo*) he might well have savored it—for it perfectly epitomizes the eventual aims of Japan's most famous swordsman.

Born in 1584, orphaned or abandoned as a child, Musashi had no choice but to defend himself as best he could in a dangerous war-torn world. By the time he was thirteen he had killed his first man—by beating the swordsman over the head with a stick. A *ronin* attached to no lord, a swordsman attached to no school, he fought in a number of campaigns, including the battle of Sekigahara, and observed various methods of sword-fighting, but never aligned himself to faction or discipline.

"I went from province to province," he wrote, "dueling with strategists of various schools and not once failed to win, even though I had as many as sixty encounters.... When I reached thirty, I looked back on my past. The previous victories were not due to my having mastered strategy.... After that I studied morning and evening searching for the principle and came to realize the way of strategy when I was fifty."

In 1645, a few months before his death at the age of sixty-one, Miyamoto set down what he had learned of the art of strategy. Retired, devoting himself to calligraphy, poetry and painting, he wrote the *Gorin no Sho* (*A Book of Five Rings*).

He himself called the work "a guide for men who want to learn strategy" and into it he put what he himself had learned. It is in many ways a surprising work. There is none of the ideological blathering of, say, the *Hagakure*. Rather, the book is a precise description of the techniques and strategies of what later became *kendo*. And there is little of the vagueness which then and now afflicts military manuals; rather, Miyamoto's message is precise and particular. Having lived, as it were, out of his century, the author is immune from the intellectual fashions of his day.

Right off he begins by comparing the art of the swordsman to the art of the carpenter—an amazing comparison for his time, sensible though it seems to ours. Through the carpenter paradigm, Miyamoto can talk about styles, techniques, master-plans, natural rules, in a way which renders the ordinary mystique of swordsmanship transparent.

Another parallel (which must have been resolutely unfashionable in his era, one of renewed Confucian learning) is implicitly in the title of the book. The five rings are those of Buddhism, referring to the five parts of the human body, but this notion of Buddhism itself derived from Taoism. And indeed it is the natural world of the Tao (and of Shinto) which pervades this book.

This means that Miyamoto is never concerned with theory but always with practice; never with the generalized statement but always with the particular item; never in the "why" but always in the "how." And it is this which gives the book its power and value.

The aim is the perfection of technique. As someone once said, doubtless in another context, if you learn enough technique the art will take care of itself. And so, as we read this book, we see that as the technique becomes finer and finer, so, its implications become more and more broad. The way of *kendo*, the way of the brush (painting and poetry), the way of the archer, the way of flowers (*ikebana*) and tea (*chanoyu*) become one.

Midway through his career as swordsman, Miyamoto himself stopped using a sword for *kendo* and began using a bamboo staff; he learned to stop seeing combat as himself vs. the other swordsman and began seeing both as identical; he saw that the swordsman's gaze does not rest upon his own blade, or that of the other, but is an all-embracing look which sees everything at once.

He was proceeding to that final perfection which dissolves opposites, destroys dichotomies, and must lead toward a combat which is won without its having taken place—which is why I think that Miyamoto would have appreciated the *Ho-dan-zo* anecdote with which I began this review. The sword has become no-sword, intention becomes no-intention, and all knowledge is spontaneous knowledge. The last technique is something the body knows without knowing that it knows. In this Zen-like configuration, the first thing learned becomes the highest knowledge.

It is no wonder that the Japanese know Miyamoto as the "Sword Saint" (*Kensei*) and that every *kendo* bibliography must begin with *A Book of Five Rings*. It is both the first and the last word on its subject.

A Book of Five Rings, by Miyamoto Musashi, translated and with an introduction by Victor Harris. Woodstock: The Overlook Press, 1974.

Ihara Saikaku

Despite occasional claims to the contrary, homosexuality in Japan has had a long, involved and—if one allows the term—honorable history. Honorable, because most of the accounts insist upon such qualities as steadfast fidelity, lifelong devotion and often terminal self-sacrifice: honorable qualities all.

Idealized versions of something so personal as sexual inclinations often have political intentions behind them, and in a military society such as Tokugawa-era Japan, it would not have been surprising if the authorities found as many uses for devotion as did those in Plutarch's Sparta or Chrétien de Troyes' Champagne.

Certainly homosexual practice was common early in Japan. Sir George Sansom has mentioned that Francis Xavier complained that the three great sins of the Japanese were "idolatry, sodomy and abortion." The historian also tells how the Jesuit father, preaching the gospel before Lord Ouchi Yoshitaka, described the second of these sins as particularly horrid, averring that "those practicing it were filthier than swine and lower than dogs." At this, "the Daimyo changed color and no doubt because he, in common with many military men and monks in that part of Japan, was given to such habits."

Common then, perhaps tacitly approved by the ruling houses, homosexuality became, to whatever degree, fashionable. At least the best-known writer of his era, Ihara Saikaku (1642–1693), would seem to have so thought. He intended his 1687 *Nanshoku Okagami* (*The Great Mirror of Male Love*) to be a bestseller.

Paul Schalow, to whom we are indebted for this meticulous translation and its brilliant introduction, says that Saikaku chose the topic "because it had the broadest appeal to both the samurai of Edo and the townsmen of Kyoto and Osaka, his regular audience."

"Popular literature in pre-modern Japan," he continues, "did not depict male love as abnormal ... but integrated it into the larger sphere of sexual love as a literary theme." Indeed, "if there had been an audience for it, Saikaku could have written as sympathetically about female sexuality as he did for male homosexuality."

In his *Great Mirror*, Saikaku tells forty stories about homosexual love. The first half are about older and younger samurai and perhaps represent Saikaku's "attempt to ingratiate himself with the government." The second half are about the affairs of townsmen (and some samurai) with pretty boys from the kabuki. The latter, says Schalow, "reflect the cultural assumption that romantic love was to be found not in the institution of marriage but in the realm of prostitution." The motives of the boys varied accordingly. Their roles did not. The assumption was that an adult was the lover of an adolescent. That two grown men might love each other is, indeed, a thought with which no authoritarian government is happy.

Another assumption was that the adult half of the couple came in only two varieties. These were the *shojinzuku*, or connoisseur, a man who also liked women but knew the best about both sexes; and the *onnagirai*, who as the name indicates, knew nothing about women and did not want to learn.

In general, the former were cultured townsmen and the latter were samurai, noted for their "single minded devotion." The *onnagirai* also contributed the often offensively misogynous tone of some of the stories where the charms of women are denigrated the better to boost those of boys.

Another contribution of the *onnagirai* is the sentimentality of the stories. Handsome samurai vows to be faithful to two boys, bites off first joint of each little finger, gives one to each. Handsome page makes handsome samurai stand naked in snow as penance where, not surprisingly, the latter perishes. Handsome page disembowels self. And so on. Many stories have names such as "He Fell in Love When the Mountain Rose Was in Bloom." One recognizes the genre, it is still with us—*shojo manga* (girls' comics)—though the readers are different.

Even though there is much documentary intent—dropping the names of the better-looking pages and boy actors—Saikaku was writing chivalric romance. He was also propagandizing, popularizing and giving the public what he thought it wanted. This he did in a style which, say later critics, was never more laconically elegant.

The resulting work is of great historical and artistic interest, and here Saikaku has been particularly fortunate in his translator, who creates a spare, ironic style which must be close to the author's own.

To appreciate its superiority one need only compare it with those bits of the *Okagami* presently in print—that 1928 travesty known as *Comrade Loves of the Samurai*, by E. Powyes Mathers and based on a partial French translation by Sato Ken. The comparison will indicate that Schalow's translation and its presentation is a vindication of a sometimes bowdlerized and often maligned work.

The Great Mirror of Male Love, by Ihara Saikaku, translated with an introduction by Paul Gordon Schalow. Stanford: Stanford University Press, 1990.

In 1688 Saikaku completed his second collection of stories about samurai, the *Buke Giri Monogatari*. The first, finished the year before, the *Budo Denrai Ki*, had been quite successful. It glorified the institution of the vendetta, those raids of vengeance that kept the samurai busy during a reign of enforced peace. The new collection was, as the title indicates, to glorify that feeling of obligation (*giri*) for a superior or benefactor with which the Tokugawa government was quite successfully attempting to inspire in otherwise idle samurai.

These volumes were not Saikaku's only contribution to establishment literature. In 1687 the prolific novelist had written the *Nanshoku Okagami*, collection which extolled the beauty and benefits of homosexual love, particularly among samurai and served as a subtle compliment to the Shogun Tsunayoshi's well known predilections.

The *Nanshoku* tales, filled with tragedy, *giri* and sentimentality, made the samurai appear a race apart, filled with the most noble considerations and the most undying loyalty. Pederasty was accorded almost the dignity of a caste designation, and the amorous exploits of these superheroes was intended to give the samurai a sheen, indeed a glamour, which they might not otherwise have had.

The two succeeding collections of samurai stories continued the operation. Though the objects of affection were more orthodox (not entirely, however—the most famous of the homosexual stories is actually from the *Buke Giri* collection), the focus was not upon romance as such but upon exploits centering around feelings of obligation and the necessity of vengeance.

If the Japanese were a cynical society, one could say that Saikaku was writing for an establishment which was successfully seeking political control in the most open manner. But Japan is not cynical (or, if it is, is in so grand a manner that a new and different term is called for) and from

Tsunayoshi on down, the only acknowledged concern was for peace, decorum and the greatest good for the greatest number.

Even making allowance for Saikaku's innocence in this matter, however, these later works are not nearly so interesting as those he wrote earlier. In these (*Koshoku Ichidai Otoko*, *Koshoku Gonin Onna*), Saikaku was writing about the merchant class and could say what he wanted, since it enjoyed no official favor. Further, it was the class he had come from and the class he knew. Consequently, these earlier books are filled with the most lively observation, the most life-like of details. Having no ax to grind (except, interestingly, a faintly anti-establishment bias), he could write about things as they were, to which he added his own infectious skepticism and his own particular humor.

By the time the now-famous writer got around to samurai *giri*, however, he was not only writing about a class he could view only from the outside, he was also in a position where it was more profitable to uphold rather than to undermine the Tokugawa establishment.

The West does not think highly of such an accommodating author (though it certainly has its share of them), but in all fairness one must point out that accommodation of this sort can be explained without recourse to current Western notions.

We, full heirs to the still-continuing romantic revolution, prefer our authors to take anti-establishment attitudes, often assessing their worth according to the depth of their dissidence. This, however, is only one way of thinking about it.

It is quite possible to accept an accommodating author on his own terms. If the status quo does indeed afford the greatest good to the greatest number, if due to it there are no wars and a fairly impartial system of justice (for certain classes), then routine unfairness, police-state-like surveillance, and a top layer of samurai-swordsmen who must somehow be controlled are a small price to pay. And, as for integrity ... well, it is all a case of integrity toward whom. Certainly, in this case, *giri* is integrity personified.

Nonetheless, as literature, the samurai stories are not nearly so interesting as the merchant-class stories probably because the characters seem less real. At the same time, any realistic evaluation of Saikaku must include these because he, after all, wrote them. This also is the value of this admirable translation of all six books of the *Buke Giri Monogatari*. Caryl Ann Callahan's English style is right for these stories, her scholarship is impeccable and (properly) nowhere unduly evident, and her introduction is a model of civilized, disinterested presentation.

Tales of Samurai Honor, by Ihara Saikaku, translated by Caryl Ann Callahan. Tokyo: Monumenta Nipponica, Sophia University, 1981.

When he was, in 1689, past his middle years, having already written about courtesans and stage-people; about sex, both homo and hetero; about the family and unfilial children—in short, about anything he could think of, Saikaku turned to more moralizing works, the audience for which was the affluent new bourgeoisie, then as now anxious to be taught.

Among the books turned out was a collection of stories about the judicial procedures—the *Honcho Oin Hiji* (*Tales of Japanese Justice*). The title itself is a variation on that of the Chinese classic *T'ang Ying Pi Shin* (*Trials in the Shade of a Pear Tree*), a collection already well known in Japan. But only one story seems to have been lifted from the Chinese collection itself. The others are Japanese, either fact or folklore.

Many have been traced to the archives of the Itakura

family (two members of which were notable judges of the period) and to other works about this family and about judges in general. One, at least, seems to be from legend. Readers will be surprised to find in "Twins Who Break a Blood Tie," the same situation that Brecht later used in *The Caucasian Chalk Circle*. Both versions have the same Chinese ancestor, long turned to myth.

A sage and venerable figure, the oriental judge: Chinese, Japanese, Burmese or Malay, with chin whiskers and long fingernails or not, he is an impartial dispenser of right; he knows the law but knows the human heart better—he is justice personified.

Though the West has its famous judges as well, the closest to this image of disinterested benevolence is not a judge. He is instead more often an attorney (Perry Mason) or an inspector (from Holmes to Poirot) or a detective (Sam Spade et al.)—someone within the legal machinery but not of it. The West no longer personifies justice itself, though some of the Asiatic patina of the oriental judge has rubbed off onto such Western creations as the all-knowing Charlie Chan and the all-seeing Mr. Moto.

Many Westerners know the oriental judge only through the stories of the late Robert van Gulik, but the figure is found (where van Gulik found it) in many early Chinese collections. And Japanese also, since the concept of the all-knowing, all-seeing, all-understanding judge came to Japan quite early.

Preceded by the magistrate himself. By the 16th-century, the judge was a functioning entity in Japan and a useful one: a presumably unimpeachable individual who stood between the demands of an isolated individual and representatives of a monolithic government.

That the judge did not always and invariably (in life as in literature) opt for the claims of power and influence is the subject of many approving Chinese and Japanese collections. These are devoted indeed to a delineation of his power to scent out truth and give judgment accordingly. The rights of individuals or representatives concerned were not always consulted (since such rights were held only by those, the samurai, already in full power) but the spirit rather than the letter of the law was traditionally observed.

As may be imagined, in the police state of Tokugawa Japan, the existence of such fair-minded individuals was something in which the common populace very much wanted to believe. It was perhaps consequently, in Japan as well as in China, that there rose a kind of sub-literary division which dealt entirely with such cases. Such it was with this collection of stories by Saikaku, a man who wrote about whatever he thought would sell.

Saikaku's stories uphold the infallibility of the oriental judge: it is impossible for him to be wrong; justice is invariably served. This being so, one's interest in reading case after case becomes, despite former popularity, less than compulsive.

Some critics have attempted to vindicate these little stories by calling them Japan's first detective fiction. So they may be but, as Donald Keene has elsewhere written, "they have neither suspense nor excitement and rarely rise above the commonplace."

Another way to look at them, and one chosen by the present translator and editor, is that they do "contain the compressed wit and ironic flashes for which the author is known" —that they are, in fact, "a compendium of wry twists on the trial accounts popular at the time it was written."

This may be true, but such definition seems to imply that Saikaku was in some way sending up the originals. I can find no evidence of this. Certainly, he never once doubts the disinterested benevolence of the Judge himself.

He seems to have only the highest respect for the oriental judge and his works.

As detective fiction (which these stories are admittedly not), the collection falls into the category which finds how-it-got-solved to be more interesting and important than who-did-it. In this, of course, the book is truly oriental since an interest in legal mechanism rather than legal morality has long been in evidence. The collection is also very Japanese in that, to this day, the harmonious and peaceful solution is much more important than any abstract question of rights or even guilt.

Whether this interest is sufficient to arouse the desire to purchase and to peruse is something which each reader must decide. The student of "The Continuing State of Traditional Japanese Ways" (Advanced Course), however (and all of us interested in the local literature are, willy-nilly, taking our Master's in it), the book is interesting ammunition for the pro side of the continuing debate. The oriental judge now is not much different from back then—Saikaku's wise and benevolent magistrates and those now presiding in the country's courts are of a common cut.

Tales of Japanese Justice, by Ihara Saikaku, translated by Thomas M. Kondo and Alfred H. Marks. Honolulu: University of Hawaii Press, 1980.

When Ihara Saikaku died in the early fall of 1693, he left a number of manuscripts. There was some wonder that this popular and prolific writer, who usually published hot from the brush, should have left behind so much. Various theories accounting for this untypical act were evolved. One was that his eyes had gone bad; another was that, consequently, he had taken up writing haiku again since he could dictate these, and a third was that he had grown pessimistic about humanity and no longer wished to mirror it.

Certainly the tone of these posthumously published works is much darker than that of *The Life of an Amorous Man* and the *Five Women Who Loved Love*, both of them fairly early works. At the same time, say some critics, these later works are, perhaps consequently, more realistic. Saikaku, in one of the prefaces to these manuscripts, implied that he was so full of observations of "people's follies" that he could not simply suffer them in silence. Certainly, if depicting the consequences of poverty and stupidity is more realistic than delineating those of wealth and wit, these final works are realistic indeed.

Among these last works, and here receiving its first English translation, was *Some Final Words of Advice* (*Saikaku Oritome*), which was written in 1689. It was to be a series of stories about townspeople, divided into sections, each devoted to one of the five cardinal virtues.

When the manuscript was discovered, apparently uncompleted, among the dead writer's papers, one of his disciples, Hojo Dansui, said that Saikaku had intended its two major portions to constitute a trilogy when appended to the earlier *Japanese Family Storehouse* and that the completed whole was to be read by merchants and craftsmen so that they might "acquire an understanding of daily life and adopt those tales as ideals on which to model their own lives."

Whatever Saikaku's intentions, they are scarcely carried out in the stories themselves which all but approach cynicism. Though diligence sometimes occasions the collection of wealth, just as often it doesn't; prudence sometimes accumulates money, but mostly it is the cause of bankruptcy. Though each chapter has its perfectly proper moral, the various moralities are wildly at variance, and the collection as a whole expresses a moral pessimism.

It consequently makes very interesting reading. The ostensible theme of the collection is stated in various ways, perhaps best in the thirteenth story: "As long as a man sticks to the straight and true and works himself to the bone, he is acting in accordance with divine providence, and there is no way that he can fail in his livelihood." Yet this unexceptionable and not very interesting observation is undermined in every possible way by Saikaku's recounting what horrors occur to those who practice what they preach. This is highly educational and makes one wish to say that here is a most satisfyingly subversive book.

Yet, one cannot. Though I do not believe that Saikaku actually intended these tales "as ideals on which to model lives," neither can I conclude that they are a series of attacks on Confucian and Buddhist morality. Their definition must lie between those two extremes: Saikaku put down what he saw and what interested him and did not worry much about further implications.

We do indeed get passages which certainly read like sarcasm: "Surely there is nothing quite as annoying as when wives fuss over whether their kitchen utensils are better than those of their neighbors, and this practice often leads to a significant drain on our country's resources." Yet, even here, one must hesitate to ascribe. Saikaku was never more dead-pan than in this collection. One knows what he says but doesn't quite know what he means.

"Why, I've been so worn out by my miseries that I know I'm not long for this world. You know that silk jacket I had with that embroidered golden phoenix? I made it into an altar cover and gave it to the temple ... I've had my personal things burned because when you haven't a speck of dust or an ash left in this floating world, then there's nothing to give you any trouble. But since my only child hasn't had smallpox yet, who knows what will become of him?" This very funny and revealing speech is that of a slatternly housewife, one who "does not even prepare a meal that would keep the mice happy." It is both amusing and satirical.

Yet, the context is a sober one. This, the author is saying, is what happens to all townsmen's wives. Try as we may, we all end up this way. People are just no damn good. This conclusion rings oddly with the moralistic prefaces for each tale, yet I do not think any general condemnation was intended. After all, people are interesting because they are no damn good, and hell is a location much more diverting than heaven.

Here, late Saikaku might be compared (and contrasted) with late Mark Twain. This comparison becomes less startling if one recalls that both were highly popular writers interested in nothing but people, yet each was also a moralist; both saw through society's pretenses, and yet both remained to the end fascinated by the diversity of the human scene; both also ventured, in varying degrees, down the road to cynicism and yet, at the same time, kept to the end their abiding interest in human diversity. Twain damns the human race and Saikaku questions it—and neither can turn their eyes from the fascinating spectacle. Both are, in their various and diverse ways, humanists.

This very interesting book, *Some Final Words of Advice*, appears to be a model translation. I have no way of comparing it with the original, but from what I know about Saikaku and what I know about people, the tone seems right. Here is some advice on a poor doctor's necessity for keeping up appearances: "Once a doctor rides in a palanquin, he had better plan on doing so permanently." And here is advice-giving traveling salesman: "These are all household services, but they are definitely not intended for your below-average man." Isn't that precisely the right tone?

Some Final Words of Advice, by Ihara Saikaku, translated and with an introduction by Peter Nosco. Rutland: Charles E. Tuttle Company, 1980.

Matsuo Basho

Matsuo Basho (1644–1694) is usually credited with having raised the haiku from a transient pastime to an enduring literary genre. Certainly, he was among the first to make the haiku a vehicle for feeling, an expression of apprehension. How this occurred and what later developed is the concern of an excellent study of the poet and his methods.

Ueda Makoto, its author, divides his book into six sections. The first, after the preface and a chronology, is devoted to the life; the remainder, to the work. There are sections on the haiku, on the *renku* linked verses, on the prose, including the famous travel journals, on the critical commentaries through which Basho explicated his own poetry and formed that of others, and there is a final section on the permanence of Basho, how Japanese critics and poets have responded to him during the centuries since his death. The work concludes with notes and references, and an index.

Ueda is particularly good in dealing with poetry and the impulse which creates it. His *Literary and Art Theories in Japan* is a very valuable study; his anthology, *Modern Japanese Haiku*, is a pioneer collection and still one of the best. In his Basho study, he is especially informative on the peculiar nature of Japanese poetry itself.

What, he asks, is a haiku?—then answers his question in the most succinct manner, giving in the process one of the best definitions that I know of this poetic form. "What is a haiku?—basic to all seems to be an internal comparison, a comparison between the finite and the infinite which are brought together in one experience, which is the poem." He also divides haiku into a number of forms, naming them for the principles detected in their construction. One such, for example, is synesthesia, or a merging of the senses:

"The sea darkens/And a wild duck's call/Is faintly white."

Ueda is also particularly good at indicating how Basho thought about what he did, and when this is based on evidence, the results are illuminating. Basho went about criticizing the poems of others, and much of it is here translated. The poet Kyorai, for example, writes of the dilemma of Kikaku, one of Basho's disciples—how to end a certain haiku.

Basho had misread a character (read "brushwood gate" rather than "wooden gate"), he thought the poem so negligible that the ending did not much matter. When he discovered his error, however, he stopped production of the anthology on which he was working in order to include "such an excellent poem."

It is perhaps difficult for the foreign reader to comprehend why the choice of an adjective should be responsible for the excellence of a poem, but such are the ways of haiku, and Ueda explains all that is explicable.

At the same time, Ueda occasionally explains when he has no business doing so, there being no proof upon which to rest his ideas. Such procedure has become commonplace in writing about haiku (look at Blyth—conjecture, conjecture, conjecture), but that does not excuse it.

There are two varieties of such explication. One is based upon groundless reconstruction. For example, Basho wrote a haiku about ice tasting bitter in the mouth of a thirsty sewer rat. The reference is to a Taoist classic about a rat's being able to quench his thirst with one small drink from a big river: the moral of which is, happiness is found by living within one's means. Basho is apparently unconcerned with this moral. Indeed, why should ice be bitter?

Here comes groundless reconstruction to the rescue. "On a cold night Basho felt thirsty and wanted a drink of water. He went to the kitchen of his modest hut and finding the water frozen, broke off a piece of ice and put it into his mouth. It was so cold that it tasted bitter, and Basho momentarily thought of the *Chuang-tsu's* dirty rat living in a sewer." Well, perhaps. But, in the words of another major poet: "Who hath measured the ground?"

The other variety of false explication consists of finding a reason within the poem for the conjecture desired. For example: Basho on his travels saw an abandoned child "about two years of age and crying pathetically ... I tossed him some food from my sleeve pocket and mused as I passed by: Poets who sang of a monkey's wailing/How would they feel about this child forsaken/In the autumn wind?" To which the conjecturing commentator adds: "The haiku, consisting of 19 syllables instead of 17, also seems to indicate that the poet's emotions were overflowing."

One must really decline this. First, if the poet's emotions were that overflowing, he would have stopped and done more for the unfortunate than "tossed him some food." Second, if two syllables extra indicate an emotional flood, then I have lost the thread of the author's argument. Third, if the poet, confronted with such human misery, can remember the proper classical quote (a monkey's wailing), and the proper seasonal tag (the autumn wind), and the proper syllable count (approximately), then his emotions are not "overflowing."

However, I should also indicate, that this kind of excess is relatively rare in Ueda's work. Mostly, imagination is put to good use—as, for example, when the author compares the Basho of *The Narrow Road to the Deep North* to the *waki* in the noh drama, "who conjures up bygone persons and events" for the reader. Also, this book is well over ten years old now, and I doubt that the present Ueda Makoto would so conjecture.

This is a reprint of the 1970 original edition, one of the Twayne biographies, that curious series which never seems to be available in any bookstore anywhere. The reprint appears to be complete, and perhaps it is, even though the bibliography mentioned in Ueda's preface is nowhere to be found. The reason why I tend to blame Twayne and not Kodansha for its exclusion is that the former publisher has an absolutely inflexible format for their series. I know of a recent case where they insisted upon dumping one-third of an important new biography because its length did not suit Twayne's predetermined optimum. If a publisher is capable of that, it is certainly capable of lopping off a bibliography here and there.

Since, however, Ueda's is one of the very best of this series, it is very good to have it finally available. Basho has, in general, been well written about by contemporary scholars, but perhaps never has he been so well put together as here.

Matsuo Basho, by Ueda Makoto. Tokyo: Kodansha International, 1983.

As the subtitle indicates, this new Basho publication is a collection of "Literal Translations for Those Who Wish to Read the Original Japanese Text, With Grammatical Analysis and Explanatory Notes."

Oseko Toshiharu, an official with the Japan Travel Bureau, has collected all of the poet's haiku, most of the circumstances surrounding them, a lot of grammatical exegesis, and presented the results to the interested reader.

Each haiku is given in the original Japanese, then in *romaji*, then in an English translation which attempts to be literal. We are thus shown something much closer to Basho's intentions than that which we usually receive—all too often a version of what the translator thought that the poet was trying to say.

While it is true, as Oseko himself stresses, that the translation of poetry from one language to another results in a serious loss, there are, nonetheless, ways in which some of the original may be salvaged. His is one of them.

In his introduction, the translator states his means. He has tried to be as literal as possible and has attempted to retain the original word order since this is closely related to the degree of emphasis desired by the poet and to the effectiveness of his entire composition. In addition, he has followed no traditional English forms, no rhymes, for example. Nor has he translated into the traditional Japanese 5-7-5 syllable count.

At the same time, he has decided to restrict his translations to the three-line form, preferring it to the one-liner of Sato Hiroaki, the two-liners of Chamberlain, and the four-line haiku translations of Yuasa Nobuyuki.

Let us see how this works. I will take one of my favorites from *The Narrow Road to the Deep North*. Written after a sleepless night at Shitomae-no-Seki, it seems to me to be all a haiku ought: a salient shaft of observance, cause and effect, a seasonal sensibility, a taste of the common humors of humanity.

Here is the original: *Nomi shirami uma no shito-suru makuramoto*. Which I might render as: Fleas, lice, a horse pisses near my pillow.

The situation is in no great need of explication. It is obviously summer, obviously the inn is humble, obviously one has trouble sleeping. This is reported, and the result is apprehended as humorous. There is also a subtext, not important to the poem but interesting.

The urinating animal was discovered at Shitomae-no-Seki, which place-name has been rendered as "Passwater Barrier," which offers Basho a local reference and which proves a pleasing parallel unstated within the work. (The reason for this singular place-name is not given by Oseko, and so I will include it for the gratification of the curious reader. Yoshitsune, his wife and newborn babe passed this way during the hero's wanderings. Here is the place the infant first peed.)

Let us now see how this homely verse has fared at the hands of various translators. Here is Yuasa's four-line version:

> Bitten by fleas and lice,
> I slept in a bed,
> A horse urinating all the time
> Close to my pillow.

All sorts of things have been gratuitously added. Here is Dorothy Britton's three-line version:

> Fleas and lice did bite;
> And I'd hear the horse pass water
> Near my bed at night.

A rhyme scheme, some rustification, and a turning of the sense into a pleasing habitual. Here is Donald Keene's version:

> Plagued by fleas and lice I hear the horses staling—
> What a place to sleep!

What a place to sleep, indeed. And here is Oseko's "literal" translation:

> Plagued by fleas and lice,
> Still worse, hearing the horse urinating
> Close by my pillow!

Which from its incorporation of Keene's first line on is not literal at all. At the same time it indicates the difficulty of making an understandable translation even if it cannot provide many of the answers. And this book does offer a means of getting closer to Basho.

It is also a bit slovenly. It is printed in ready-type (which is a euphemism for typewriter) and full of minor mistakes in English spelling and grammar. Also, there are omissions when the Japanese version of a haiku may be missing. But then most labors of love are unkempt.

Basho's Haiku, edited and translated by OsekoToshiharu. Tokyo: Maruzen Company Ltd., 1990.

Kanshi

Poetry written by Japanese in Chinese, *kanshi*, is a product of its time. The Tokugawa shogunate, encouraging the study of Confucianism because of its emphasis upon loyalty to superiors, set up schools for Chinese studies. As a result, a knowledge and appreciation of the language, hitherto restricted to court officials and the Buddhist clergy, became available to samurai and even townsmen.

In time, an ability to turn a tolerable verse in Chinese became a desirable accomplishment, much in the same way that an English gentlemen of conservative and Tory tastes prided himself upon a certain facility with Latin verse.

By the end of the 17th-century, Japanese writers of *kanshi* were under the influence of an earlier Chinese school of poets (the *Kakucho* style), which emphasized diction and the formal elements over any consideration of content or originality. A close imitation of high T'ang Period poetry was recommended. As a result, early 18th-century Japan was attempting to recreate the poetry of 18th-century China.

Later, such proscription was relaxed under the influence of the later Ming style (*Seirei*) which encouraged individuality and innovation. One was to imitate not high T'ang but late Sung. This proved beneficial. No longer did Japanese poets have to strain for style. They could write about the actual scenes and experiences of Japanese life. In the process, a body of interesting and personal work was created.

That we know any of this in English we owe to Burton Watson. In earlier volumes, he translated the Buddhist poets Gensei and Ryokan and the poet-historian Rai San'yo (*Japanese Literature in Chinese*, 1976), more Gensei (*Grass Hill*, 1983), and devoted a single volume to the best known of these earlier poets (*Ryokan: Zen Poet of Japan*, 1977).

Now he presents translations of 119 poems in Chinese by writers not represented in his earlier collections. These include Ishikawa Jozan, Rokunyo, Kashiwagi Jotei, Okubo Shibutsu, and a number of other Edo writers strongly influenced by the *Seirei* tradition.

The spontaneity and freedom exhibited by these poets in what is, after all, a foreign tongue, attests not only a thorough grounding in classical Chinese but also a full awareness of the poetic process.

Metaphors are both classically apt and personal. Jozan writes of a flight of homing crows as being "like a *go* board where the white stones have all been defeated/or a sheet of paper covered with random spatters of ink." Jotei looks at a morning lotus and thinks of "someone up very early/makeup done, she hasn't yet left her mirror."

Jotei's "Rainy Night" is indicative of what *kanshi* can become in capable hands: "She promised, then never came—night drags on/dark windows, the moon hidden, rain like mist/I shut my half-read book, blow out the lamp, amid the sound of steady dripping turn to sleep alone."

That we can now so appreciate this verse is due, of course, to the quality of the translation. Watson has that gift of apprehension which allows him direct insight into the intentions of the author. From these, he can build that parallel construction which is his translation.

He is both confined and strengthened by the many

poetic conventions which defined the *kanshi*, those which faced the Japanese writer of Chinese and which face the translator of the results into English.

In his introduction, Watson entertainingly indicates what is involved, showing us the form, listing the restrictions. He takes a sample Chinese poem, gives us the Chinese pronunciation and then offers a literal translation, one in which the rules on rhyme are observed, and another which follows the syllabic considerations which the Japanese imposed. These lead to an exposition and justification of his own methods.

But the translations are their own justification. At the end of a Jozan poem is the line: "What is there that's not a children's pastime? Confucius Lao Tzu—a handful of sand." And that handful, without a word of explanation, parallels a reference to a Chinese classic as well known to contemporary readers as the Biblical reference is to us.

Or this line, from another Jozan poem: "Full of aches, weary of the long night watches,/and for no reason the stubby torch goes out!" Admirable, the use of the "and" (one more indignity) and the use of (too short, mere remnant, inadequate) "stubby." Delights such as these stud this verse, making this collection one of the best translations of the year.

Kanshi, translated by Burton Watson. San Francisco: North Point Press, 1990.

Arai Hakuseki

Japan was, for various reasons, late (though not as late as China) in producing autobiography. The work commonly regarded as the first did not appear until 1719. This is the famous *Oritaku Shiba no Ki* of Arai Hakuseki (1657–1725), Confucian scholar, administrator, and adviser to the Shogun.

Though comparisons have been made with Cellini's autobiography (a Western first, written between 1558 and 1562, though not published until 1730), the only real comparison is that both were written to vindicate and validate a life. (Though that, come to think of it, is perhaps the real reason behind all autobiography.) By comparison with the Italian, the Japanese biography is less personal, more official and much more straightforward in its plea for attention.

Another comparison sometimes made is with Voltaire. Perhaps this is because Hakuseki was also an encyclopedist. Otherwise there is certainly small similarity. Voltaire was anti-establishment from the first (though he did curry an amount of favor with Louis XIV). Hakuseki was always a member of the establishment. Indeed, in the words of the translator of this edition, "[he] regarded the existing firm basis of the power of the *bakufu* as proof that it was a divinely sanctioned institution which he was bound ... to support and safeguard." It was he also who early observed and, to an extent popularized, that concept of *kokutai*, the "national essence" or "unique nature" of the Japanese. He can, in fact, be viewed as a forerunner of nationalism. Of him, the translator writes he was the kind of man who "saw that the standard of living was rising, but condemned this trend as an undesirable taste for luxury ...."

Not too attractive, this aspect of him. We also learn that, as a child, he stated that he would rather reign in hell than serve in heaven. Later, he himself recounts that during his youthful study he always instructed a servant to bring buckets of cold water to his desk side. When he had studied himself drowsy, he would douche himself with the icy contents and, invigorated, continue with his duties.

Hani Goro in his 1936 book on Hakuseki finds in him

"an expression of passive resistance to feudal repression." This is a statement more hopeful than accurate. On the contrary, Hakuseki was all in favor of feudalism and quite convinced of the necessity for repression.

With one important difference: he wanted the repression to be more fair than it was. Though he was a friend to the feudal bureaucracy (and was himself a member of it), he was opposed to its venality, its dishonesty, and its stupidity. He wanted an ideal dictatorship, a "benevolent government" in the Confucian sense of the term.

He was not against the *bakufu* but against some of its more extreme measures. For example, if a suspect died before being tried (and detention in Tokugawa prisons could go on a very long time), his body was pickled so that, when the courts finally got around to sentencing, they would still have a body to punish. Hakuseki was much against this: "Official acts of this kind can only be called thoroughly unseemly." He was not, however, against a system which imprisoned innocent suspects for whole decades.

The *Oritaku* is thus in the tradition of the Chinese records of public service. These were intended to foster loyalty and to inspire right conduct among descendents. At the same time, however, Hakuseki had another motive, and it is this which makes the book interesting to us now.

Disappointed in his political ambitions, witness to a corruption which grew greater every year, he determined to set down the truth. Specifically, he felt a moral obligation to transmit a true record of the rule of the Shogun Ienobu and his infant successor. He was, he states, the only man alive who knew the whole story, and it is this which he presents.

In so doing, he unavoidably tells us a lot about himself. His report of the great earthquake and fire of 1705, for example, was written to tell how the lord fared and how he himself rushed to the palace to find out what had happened to the lord. Though this is the point of his story, he must, at the same time, tell a lot about the earthquake, and this is fascinating.

"There was a noise like a lot of chopsticks snapping, together with the hum of a swarm of mosquitoes. This must have been the sound of buildings falling and the shouts of men." Later, "my lord came out again and called me over and said, 'It reminds me of the crowds flocking to the flower-viewing at Ueno when I was a child,' and smiled."

And Hakuseki tells a lot about his time, as well. It is this, and not his professions, which make the book so interesting (at least in its first section—the latter two are drier): an eye-witness to 16th-century Japan speaking directly to us. One might wish for more Cellini-like details; one must be grateful for what one is given.

Told Round a Brushwood Fire: The Autobiography of Arai Hakuseki, translated with an introduction and notes by Joyce Ackroyd. Tokyo: University of Tokyo Press, 1979.

Chikamatsu Monzaemon

Though the playwright Chikamatsu Monzaemon (1653–1724) has been inaptly called "the Shakespeare of Japan," he remains the single local dramatist of eminence. His accomplishment was to be, as Charles Dunn has said, the first to create "characters of realistic complexity and show the tragedy and pathos of their entrapment by circumstance."

One of the reasons that he was able to do so was that his best work was done for the *joruri* puppet-play. The dolls (much more primitive in his day) needed all the realistic complexity they could get. It is interesting that when he wrote for the kabuki (real live actors) the results were thought so bad. Donald Keene has written that these works "are inferior in every respect to the *joruri* plays he wrote at the same period."

The characters in the kabuki plays are often stereotypes with no realistic complexity at all since his leading roles were determined solely by the strengths of the actors performing them. Since one of them (Sakata Tojuro) was considered good at playing gentle and amorous young men involved in unhappy circumstances, the playwright was stuck with this wimpy character. In the *joruri* puppet plays, however, he could take the same character and flesh him out with realistic contradictions, and he becomes Tokubei in *The Love Suicides at Sonezaki*.

Though Chikamatsu could not escape many of conventions of the dramaturgy of his time (Keene complains that "his concern with *giri* and *ninjo* deprives his *sewa mono* of some of the variety we expect of a great dramatist,") this more realistic genre managed to make even the hoary conflict between social responsibility and personal inclination something more dramatic than it usually was.

Despite his prowess in the *joruri* and his various difficulties with the kabuki, Chikamatsu often moved between the two stages. After all, Chikamatsu's plays (all one hundred of them) were written under contract for commercial theaters. And toward the end of his career, he moved back to the kabuki.

C. Andrew Gerstle has here chosen five of the late plays (all hitherto untranslated, none represented in the standard repertoire) and gives a cogent and close reasoned request for our attention. (Eleven earlier plays are translated in Donald Keene's *Major Plays of Chikamatsu*, published almost forty years ago.) Among the reasons given for this suggested regard is that realism is not the only criterion for excellence.

Japanese dramaturgy was, until quite recently, unconcerned with realistic means considered necessary in the West. "Like ancient Greek drama or more recent European opera," Gerstle writes, "the action is carried forward by different types of language and presentation, marked by lively, dramatic sections and intense, lyrical moments of high passion."

The *joruri* or *gidayu* narrator-chanter (with whom Chikamatsu always worked in the closest collaboration) was the one who decided whether a line should be sung or declaimed. This heightened lyricism, indeed very opera-like, was something which the actors of the kabuki could not contrive—perhaps another reason for the assumed inferiority of the plays he wrote for them.

Once realism is removed as a favored style, however, it is possible to see new virtues. Chikamatsu himself wrote that *joruri* "is basically a musical form, and the length of the lines recited is therefore determined by the melody." To which Gerstle adds that "as in opera, the essence of human feeling, particularly sadness, is expressed by words in song riding the high notes of the music." Which would also explain why reading Chikamatsu as realistic drama is a difficult business. If you read him as an opera librettist, however, a kind of Japanese Lorenzo da Ponte, then his excellences become evident.

This is the kind of reading that Gerstle would favor and indeed contrives. He includes musical notation in the text to help show how it was traditionally read and performed, how the reader of today may imagine how it once appeared. Original, yet supported by scholarship, this interpretation of late Chikamatsu gives us an alternate view of the dramatist and more closely focuses his accomplishments.

Chikamatsu: Five Late Plays, translated and annotated by C. Andrew Gerstle. New York: Columbia University Press, 2001.

Ogyu Sorai

Ogyu Sorai (1666–1728) was the leading Confucian thinker of the Edo Period. A Chinese scholar at a time when this language was the classical "Latin" of the Japanese scholarly tradition, he concerned himself with philological study. His goal was to return to the Confucian sources and not rely upon *kambun* translations and the bad scholarship of the Neo-Confucians.

In this, as Richard Miner has suggested, Sorai was like Erasmus who called for a return to the sources, studying the New Testament in its Greek original rather than the Latin Vulgate on which the Scholastics (corresponding to the Neo-Confucians) had based their commentaries. And, like Duns Scotus and William of Occam, he effectively battled the Neo-Confucians just as they successfully dissolved the Scholastic synthesis.

Among Sorai's writings was a series of thirty-five letters written sometime between 1720 and, the date of their being published, 1727. These are the responsals of which this edition is the first English translation. They were written in answer to written questions put forward by two young samurai.

What the greatest Confucian authority of his time, in his busy final years, was doing writing to two unformed minor warriors is explained by the theory that the questions were really from their lord who, curious but not wishing to intimidate, used the teen-age correspondents.

Sorai, for whatever reason, readily responded. Neo-Confucianism could not be recommended because of its effect on one's character. Believers are often arrogant and "have wretched personalities." One must go back to the originals. "Not being conversant ... is tantamount to seeing things in terms of our own contemporary customs, and this is truly like being the veritable frog in the well."

When it turns out that one of the young respondents had made his parents stop praying to Buddha because of the Neo-Confucians influence, Sorai admonishes him. He does this, first, because it was those fakes who counseled it; second, because Buddhism is better than nothing. "Remember that Confucius believed that playing draughts was better than being idle," and besides, "the leisured are lonely and do all sorts of untoward things."

This leads Sorai into other problematical statements. "People are far more important than laws," he says, something with which we might now agree. But, he goes on to write: "A law may be bad, for example, but if the person enforcing it is able, it will have some benefit." This is seasoned Sorai.

So is his passage on "eccentrics," who turn out to be underlings difficult to control because they have minds of their own. "An eccentric is like an unruly horse. As long as you fail to quiet it, you will be too nervous to mount it." But "if you broke in an unruly horse, you would realize that there is no need to worry." Therefore, "unless you are willing to be thrown many times, you will never be able to mount unruly steeds."

Much of the advice is expected, though occasionally prescient. "If the root [read agriculture] is slighted and the branch [read commerce] is favored, the province will decline, and the resulting mob of merchants will become the bane of that province." Which is just what occurred. And occasionally the advice is laconic: "As for remonstrating rulers, it is best not done."

What now strikes us most about Sorai is his absolute self-confidence. One feels that his young correspondents were perhaps typical of their age in their elucidation of complete quandary, but he sails above them, sure, certain, not one doubt obscuring his certainty.

It was perhaps this quality (among many others, to be sure) that drew so many post-World War II thinkers back to him. Maruyama Masao gave him pride of place, and both Harry Harootunian and Najita Tetsuo have included him in their influential reassessments of the period and its thought.

Very little of Sorai's writings have been hitherto translated. This book contains the first complete translation of a single work and gives us the sound of the man himself: reasoned, stubborn, occasionally supremely condescending, but never doctrinaire and always curious.

Master Sorai's Responsals: An Annotated Translation of Sorai Sensei Tomonsho, by Samuel Hideo Yamashita. Honolulu: University Press of Hawaii, 1994.

Yamamoto Tsunetomo

The *Hagakure*, more properly, the *Hagakure Kikigaki* (*Notes of What Was Heard in the Shadow of Leaves*) is a manual for samurai consisting of well over a thousand short anecdotes. It was dictated by Yamamoto Tsunetomo, a retainer of the Nabeshima clan in Saga, as an alternative to killing himself upon the death of his lord.

Though he might have preferred the latter, by this time (1700) *seppuku* had been outlawed. Taking the tonsure, he started dictation, and sixteen years later had completed his curious, if long-lasting, work.

He was writing for warriors who were no longer allowed to fight. The profession of samurai had become an anomalous one now that peace lay heavy on the land. Yamamoto's work represented a vindication and a romantic backward look. It also had its political uses in bolstering an institution that had already begun to topple.

Consequently, fealty was stressed. The warrior's

highest duty is to his lord. And this is a duty that only a samurai willing to die at any moment can fully devote himself to. This devotion is an emotional bond. The desire to serve one's lord, Yamamoto declares, should be like the desire to please a lover. Bushido, the way of the warrior, as the author's famous phrase has it, is a way of dying.

Despite all of this expressive vindication, Yamamoto himself was never in a battle, and though he may have wished to kill himself upon the death of his lord, the samurai around him were apparently already a lax lot. All the more reason, he may have thought, for properly instructing them.

This he does at enormous length. "It is ill-manners to yawn in public," though you may prevent this, mysteriously, "by stroking your forehead upward." Be careful, too, because "a forced smile is stupid in men and indecent [sic] in women." Also "you should look into the mirror—most people don't look into the mirror, so they look unkempt." In fact, "it is best that you carry powdered rouge in your sleeve pocket. We sometimes are of bad color when sobering up, lying down or rising. We should touch up with rouge at such times." In any event, "in order to calm yourself, it is important to swallow your saliva. This is a secret."

The *Hagakure* is a profoundly fatuous book in that its entire aim is to seem rather than to simply and truly become. The codes and secrets confided here are only concerned with social approval. All of the counsels are inane because none of them can have any inner reality. They are all based upon appearances.

It is a cautionary work, but it is also fretful because the author is really writing about a period a century before he was born and because he can find no place for himself in his real world. The book is a cry of romantic despair at the world's not being different from what it is.

The cry is somewhat muffled in the number of translations this work has curiously received. None of them, for example, are complete. All of them translate different sections but often duplicate each other. There is the anonymous translation that appeared in various issues of the magazine *Traditions* between 1976 and 1980. In 1979 the William Scott Wilson translation appeared. There is the Kathryn Sparling translation of the Mishima Yukio edition, and there is the Mukoh Takao translation.

Now we have that of Utsuo Kiyoaki. His is a bilingual volume (the first), so the translations can be checked against the original in the Kurihara Koya edition. One of the first things one then notices is that the name of the author is given an alternate reading. Usually Yamamoto's name is read as Tsunetomo. Utsuo reads it as Jocho.

The reader will also notice that the translator treats the book as a local event. He comes from Saga, where Yamamoto came from. "He is proud of what is an important part of local history," says the afterword. Both the translation and the editing of the book are amateur, and this works nicely in cutting the pretensions of the *Hagakure* down to size.

There are also sections that have never been translated before. New to me is the description of the audience the author had in mind. "Among themselves young samurai only talk about money matters, profit and loss, and tidying over difficulties. They discuss fashion and love affairs. They seem to think that if they don't talk about such things, the conversation will lose its liveliness." Doesn't that have a modern tone, though?

The Living Hagakure, by Yamamoto Tsunetomo, translated by Utsuo Kiyoaki, edited by Kurihara Koya. Privately printed, 1991.

Translations of the *Hagakure*, that 18th-century do-it-yourself manual, how to be a samurai in only one thousand easy lessons, continue to appear. Here an earlier one is even reprinted. One wonders at such popularity and then understands why.

A glance at the contents page reveals the purport of the book: Resolve to Die for Your Lord; Stifle a Yawn; Be Kind to Visitors Even When Busy; Appearance; Ever on Guard; Not a Word to Incriminate One's Master, etc.

One thinks of Emily Post. The samurai should not yawn because yawns "more often than not make you look foolish." Neither should a samurai ever be negligent concerning his facial expression: "one's concentrated effort, serene attitude, taciturn air ... gritten teeth [sic] with a piercing look—each of these reveals dignity." One thinks of those Victorian volumes concerning proper deportment for young ladies.

The difference is, of course, a vital one. The young ladies expect to gain husbands and consequently some economic assurance in this world; the samurai expect to gain death and some sort of social standing in both this world and the next. The author is very determined on this point and so, unlike *The Book of Complete Etiquette*, which is all about how to live, his book is all about how to die. Both, however, are also about appearances.

We thus find that Yamamoto seems to be somehow in bed with Ms. Manners in that both are concerned with social appearances. Both are also apt to regret the passing of the old days of good manners. Yamamoto, however, regrets more. He was writing about the virtues of a period at least a century before he was born and wrote this fretful and cautionary book because he could find no place for himself in the real world. The parallel of Mishima Yukio at once suggests itself: indeed, the novelist grasped this book as does the drowning man the straw and even put out his own edition of it—a cry of romantic despair.

The cry is somewhat muffled in this translation—

something perhaps apparent from the quotations above. The translator has a samurai refer to himself as "left here dry without any means of subsistence;" later on another samurai says that "a samurai is duty-bound to give a helping hand to another in diversity," and on and on. One knows, eventually, what is meant, but such errors in such number disconcert.

There remains the question as to why such a silly book as this should merit four translations in as many years. One of the reasons was certainly Mishima's involvement with it; another might have been the postwar martial arts boom; yet another would be the need for discipline, any discipline, in a lax and officially peaceful world. What I don't understand, however, is that now that Emily Post is a joke why there are still readers around who can take the *Hagakure* seriously.

The Hagakure: A Code to the Way of the Samurai, by Yamamoto Tsunetomo, translated by Mukoh Takao. Tokyo: Hokuseido Press, 1980.

Senryu

The haiku is well known in countries other than Japan, but the *senryu* is not. Though cast in a similar form (17 syllables, 5-7-5), this verse tradition has yet to be adopted abroad. Perhaps among the reasons is that *senryu* are not conventionally serious or reassuring, as so many haiku are. Rather, the *senryu* is humorous, satirical, upsetting, seditious.

R. H. Blyth, who has written more in English on the *senryu* than anyone else (including the 1949 *Senryu* and the 1966 *Edo Satirical Verse Anthologies*), says that "*Senryu* are expressions of moments of vision into, not the nature of things, but the nature of man."

And this being so, *senryu* cannot but be about foibles. Take, for example, this one, by Yanagidaru Shui, translated by Blyth: "On a rainy night, the fire-watch-tower-man occasionally pisses over the side." The cause-and-effect of the haiku is here (it is raining so it is all right) and so is the analogous principle (both rain and urine are water), but what a difference!

J. C. Brown, in this new collection, says that "the main difference between *senryu* and haiku is one of tone. The meaning and structure of a haiku can be brilliant, but I personally often find them conventionally serious and sentimental." In *senryu*, too, "the form seems somehow to have escaped the structural restrictions that bind and perhaps limit haiku."

Certainly, the rules are less stringent. No obligatory seasonal reference, no heightened diction, no special poetic techniques other than the 5-7-5 format (which I am disregarding here by putting the *senryu* in a single line). Yet, historically, the *senryu* came from the *tanka* form. Like the *haiku*, it became independent—a section of the longer poem which became paradigmatic of the whole, and eventually took its place and incorporated all of its elements.

Blyth quotes one which he feels does this: "Someone got ahead of him in the lavatory—he praises the moon." This verse, says Blyth, "has everything in it: the 'calls of nature,' the annoyance at not being able to follow them, the desire to camouflage it, the poetic pretense . . . ."

The man deemed responsible for creation of the *senryu* was one Karai Hachiemon, an official in Asakusa, who concocted the form in 1764 and later took the pen name of Karai Senryu. He made a number of collections. These were followed by many more. Now it seems there are as many *senryu* as there are haiku.

Senryu, however, are the result of literati at work (as are the haiku) and are, I believe, not to be thought of as a spontaneous "popular" poetry. These are not "poems of the people," though they may be "poems for the people" in that *senryu* have always been popular. But they are certainly not artless.

Blyth quotes one such: "Till asked, I put the lid on my heart." Then he adds that this is "poetry according to Wordsworth's recipe: tender feelings expressed in the language of ordinary men." He also included another: "She gets up habitually at six, the troublesome hag," and then points out that the onomatopoeia of the Japanese (*Mutsu mutsu okite moteamashi baba*) with its four m's and two b's well expresses "the venom of the daughter-in-law."

Brown in this *senryu* collection includes the original Japanese, a *romaji* transcription and English translation, as well as illustration. He is listed on the title page for "calligraphy and illustrations," but I feel sure that he did the excellent translations as well. Here are some of them:

> Politely listening to the samisen—what a racket.
> Fireworks, variously named, are all just smoke.
> To a crab's eyes all people creep sideways.
> The sick person observes the doctor's nostrils well.

The selection is from the 18th to the early 20th-century, but the authors are simply given by name (the first, above, is by Keisen; the last, by Yasharo; the other two are apparently anonymous), and there is no scholarly apparatus at all.

This is a book compiled by a man who loves *senryu* and wants to share his enthusiasm. He is, in this way, much like the literati of old who made these early collections.

Senryu: Poems of the People, calligraphy and illustrations by J. C. Brown. Tokyo: Charles E. Tuttle Company, 1990.

Though this collection is not, as the jacket intemperately

boasts, "the first comprehensive anthology" of *senryu* (that would be the R.H. Blyth collection of 1949), it is certainly the first to present samples of this curious verse form (over four hundred of them) into a full historical and aesthetic context.

It is also the work of one of the finest scholars of Japanese literature. Ueda Makoto, has created fourteen major works including studies on *waka*, haiku and *tanka*. He is also author of the indispensable *Literary and Art Theories in Japan*. In this new work, he expertly places this seventeen-syllable verse form in its historical setting, the eighteenth and 19th-century amateur poetry circles of the larger cities.

Though, like the haiku, it falls into the 5-7-5 syllable pattern, it observes fewer rules. As Ueda explains, "it draws less on nature than on human nature." Also, while the haiku juxtaposes separate objects and asks the reader to make a connection, a *senryu* offers a situation and expects the reader to see it in the light of reason—or of common sense. The resulting feeling of incongruity, or relief, or simple superiority will lead to laughter—one of the reasons that *senryu* is known as comic verse.

Or, as Ueda phrases it: "A poet moved by the beauty of nature would write a *hokku* [haiku]. A poet wishing to vent a personal emotion would compose a *waka*. Someone with a novelist's eye but without his ability (or patience) to construct a lengthy plot jotted down *senryu*."

For example: "Little by little the mother is helping her son to become a bum," or "For the rest of his life he's resented by the widow—the fugu seller." These are concentrated narratives which could be expanded from their present laconic form.

The point is that they are not. Because they are so brief they can present, like the haiku, an instant of insight. "The ladle seller serves portions of air to display his wares." Or,

"Now that he has a child he knows all the local dogs by name."

Amusing incongruity is a major point in *senryu*. "Starting to kill himself, the actor stops to watch a fight in the audience." This can lead to humorous speculation. "In paradise how cheap they must be—lotus roots." It leads to diverting moral observation as well. "To put it briefly courting is tantamount to begging."

Always implied is criticism, some of it direct. "By his own lies he's moved to tears—that fellow Chikamatsu." It is also implied by parody, as in this reworking of Chiyo's famous haiku: "My well-bucket taken by the morning glory—I borrow water," of which the *senryu* version is "The following year/Chiyo planted the flower/far from the well."

Reading a *senryu* at the end of the 20th-century is different from reading it at the end of the eighteenth. Its entire context is missing, and since humor exists upon what it taken for granted, we need notes. How many we get and how useful they are depends upon the annotator.

Blyth comments on each, and every *senryu* in his collection and the effect is often that of the jokester who explains the joke after he has told it. Burton Watson in his translations (found in the Sato/Watson *From the Country of Eight Islands*) offers not a word of commentary, and his work seems consequently much more *senryu*-like.

Ueda offers commentary sparingly. Sometimes it is needed. "Threatened with a well/and a rope, her parents agree/to take him in" probably needs the note: " 'If you don't approve our marriage I'll either drown or hang myself,' the daughter had said to her parents." But I doubt that " 'My daddy? He's dead right now' says the actor's son" needs the three-line explanation forced upon it.

At the same time, I am reluctant to blame the translator for unnecessary explanations. It is just the kind of thing that zealous but cautious publisher's editors do. In any event, it does not much detract from what is now the best available text on its subject.

Light Verse from the Floating World: An Anthology of Premodern Japanese Senryu, compiled, translated with an introduction by Ueda Makoto. New York: Columbia University Press, 1999.

Ueda Akinari

This is the sixth complete translation of all nine tales in the *Ugetsu Monogatari*, the most famous of Ueda Akinari's supernatural story collections. (The others are Hamada Kenji's, published by the University of Tokyo Press in 1971, Rene Sieffert's French translation, Gallimard, 1956, and one each in Czech, Polish, and Hungarian.) This edition, however, is the first to use as text the original wood-block 1776 printing, and the first to include full and scholarly notes, appendices, etc., as well as a substantial and well-realized general introduction.

There have been many other translations of the individual tales, and it has been perhaps this earlier work which has most contributed to the fame of what Hamada Kenji calls these "gothic" works. Certainly, Lafcadio Hearn's adaptations of several early drew attention to both work and author.

It is fitting that Hearn first introduced Ueda for they shared several traits in common. Both were antiquarian by inclination and romantic by temperament; both were much taken by ghosts and demons, and the grotesque in general; and both were given to recountings of other author's works.

Just as many of Hearn's collections of Japanalia contain retellings of stories by others, so, Ueda's compilations are often recountings of other Japanese—or, more often, Chinese—stories, all the intricacies and attributions of which the translator has painstakingly worked out in this edition.

We also know some of the Ueda material from other sources as well. Upon reaching the conclusion of the most famous of the tales, *Jasei no In* (The Lust of the White Serpent), we also find ourselves not only in the middle of the Chinese opera *Pai Niangtzu*, but also at the beginning of the noh *Dojoji* and in the finale of the kabuki *Musume Dojoji*.

No such sense of familiarity, however, troubled or delighted the readers of the author's time. He was writing for simpler folk—as was America's own Ueda Akinari, Washington Irving, when he assembled various spectral German tales and gave the characters such New-York-sounding names as Rip Van Winkle. Rather, the Edo reader was hearing them mostly for the first time, believed in the supernatural just as strongly as did the author and was mainly interested in what happened next and how frightened he got.

To the late 19th-century (both in Japan and abroad), all of this was quaint and delightful. Just as deeply superstitious but no longer afraid of ghosts and demons, these readers found appealing the idea of a reading population to whom such events were real. Such naive evidence of an irrational supernatural brought many a delighted frisson, more than a few happy shudders, as well as a strong feeling of moral superiority.

This was particularly true in England and America where early publication of the Hearn and Ueda translations and Hokusai's more fantastic sketchbooks created a delightful if tiny kingdom named Japan, peopled with child-like subjects who lived among harmless horrors and enchantingly hideous grotesqueries. Tourists from abroad found what they wanted to find when they flocked to

(Henry Adams' phrase) "Nikko —the only sight worth seeing," where the gingerbread mausolea nestled like toadstools amid the roots of the great forest.

The contemporary reader is now acquainted with far greater horrors than the innocent Ueda ever concocted. One might therefore think that, after the wars and other mass-murders of our century, these tales might once again assume their original power and terror. That they do not is largely because we have accurately located the vengeful ghost and the devastating demon as something within ourselves. We are so horror-sated that we can no longer project, as could Ueda's reader. Rather, we can read such tales only as spiritual allegory if we are to savor any of their original power.

In the middle of *Jasei no In*, the hero learns from the exorcising priest that "because I have failed to be true to my own self, I have allowed [the spirits] to deceive me." Here is a living psychological truth, for every reader of any century. But such moments of illumination are few. Ueda is too taken with the flow of his anecdote, the constraints of his original source, and the conventions of his time to ponder long upon the human meaning of his tales. Consequently, to the contemporary reader the stories must often appear bland, moralistic, too rigidly conceived and too mechanically worked out.

Having said this, however, I should add that as literary curiosities, the stories continue to be perfectly viable. As such they both need and deserve the extensive labors of Dr. Zolbrod, whose introduction, notes, and literary appendices I found, upon several instances, more interesting than the stories themselves.

Ugetsu Monogatari, by Ueda Akinari, translated and edited by Leon M. Zolbrod. London: George Allen & Unwin, Ltd., 1974.

Ryokan

Ryokan (1758–1831) is one of Japan's favorite literary figures. A Zen adept and later a hermit, he wrote about his daily life, celebrated nature, played with the local children and in many ways displayed the most eccentric and likeable character.

Since he lived rather than taught Zen, he never dignified his various jottings as poetry. "Who says my poems are poems?" he asks in one of them. "My poems are not poems. After you know, my poems are not poems, then we can begin to discuss poetry."

These were no self-conscious literary endeavors. (In fact, they are quite free, and many of the rules of literary composition are ignored.) Rather, they were expressions of his way of living and of equal worth, with the games of hide-and-seek which he used to play with the local children.

After one such game, the next morning in fact, the children having long before gotten tired, or given up, Ryokan was found still crouched in the outhouse where he had hidden himself. Asked what he was doing, he whispered: "Be quiet, please, or else the children will find me."

This anecdote is in itself a kind of Ryokan-like poem. All of them represent an action, or an occurrence. None are differentiated. All come from the great wholeness that he was experiencing.

"Standing alone beneath a solitary pine; quickly the time passes. Overhead the endless sky—who can I call to join me on this path?" This emotion is matched and balanced by another. "After spending the day begging in town, I now sit peacefully under a cliff in the evening cool. Alone, with one robe and one bowl—the life of a Zen monk is truly the best!"

Balance—that is what these poems demonstrate. And,

of course, the acceptance through which balance becomes possible. And with this balance, a way to live: "Today's begging is finished; at the crossroads I wander by the side of Hachiman Shrine talking with some children. Last year, a foolish monk; this year, no change!"

This is very attractive. The simplicity of this life and its wholeness, its balance and its unstated certainty all attract. One thinks that Ryokan has found an answer, a superfluous observation since no question has been asked. "Priest Ryokan must fade like this morning's flowers, but his heart will remain behind."

And so it does. It has delighted and inspired thousands of Japanese and now, in John Stevens' sensitive, simple, colloquial translation, it may reach across to others. These poems—a representative collection of Ryokan's verse—direct, declarative, with their apprehension of the seasons, the days, their unique view of the great rim of existence, speak of a peace and a fulfillment, the achievement of which, like its apprehension, lies in an acceptance for which most of us can only hanker.

One Robe, One Bowl: The Zen Poetry of Ryokan, translated and introduced by John Stevens. New York: Weatherhill, 1977.

Poet, calligrapher and Zen monk, Ryokan remains one of the most beloved figures in Japanese Buddhist history. One of the reasons for his popularity is his perceived simplicity. He (unlike his Soto Zen peers) trained no students, presided over no monasteries and produced no recondite treatises.

Rather, he became a mendicant, wrote poems, brushed characters, went about his begging rounds. He admired children's honesty, directness and simplicity. He even emulated them.

Finding bamboo sprouting in the privy, Ryokan tried to burn holes in the roof to encourage its growth and ended up burning the outhouse down. Once, at a tea ceremony, he drank the whole bowl, then, realizing that there was none for the next guest, spat part of it back and passed it over. At another formal occasion, he picked a piece of snot from his nose and, when he saw the other guest did not want him to deposit it on the cushions, stuffed it back into his nostril.

Such traits are endearing in the great, and over the years, Ryokan's reputation has grown from village eccentric to national saint. The fact that he hated the calligraphy of calligraphers and the poems of poets made his own seem the more natural. That he was intensely forgetful (once, we are told, in an incident otherwise unspecified, he even forgot his underwear; later, advised to make a list so that he would not forget, he forgot the list) made him the more lovable.

There is, consequently, a lot of literature about him—and since so little is actually known, much literary embroidery as well. It is the ambition of the present volume to present Ryokan as he probably was.

To this end the biographical sections are based only upon contemporary sources. This includes "Curious Accounts of the Zen Master Ryokan," by Kera Yoshishige, here translated for the first time. Also translated are a number of poems in Chinese, a number of *waka*, extracts from Ryokan's correspondence, and sections of his reflections on Buddhism, which contain his well known criticism of the clergy and the famous "Words of Advice"—including "Things I Can't Abide: People Who Never Stop Talking."

There is a lot to choose among. Ryokan (says Robert Brower) wrote over 400 poems in Chinese, and some 1,400 of his Japanese poems have been preserved. The latter are mostly 31-syllable works, but there are among them 90 long poems and 20 others in nonstandard forms. Among these, the most admired are those in the archaic style, imitative of the language and cadences of the *Man'yoshu*, and about 150 of these exist. Those selected from this volume are representative and are newly translated.

For English readers Ryokan is fortunate in having Burton Watson as his translator. Though there are many good renditions (including those of John Stevens, Yuasa Nobuyuki , and the present authors), it is Watson's work (the 1977 collection, and the later additions) that has defined for the West the poetic excellence of Ryokan—his unassuming rationality, his sincere simplicity.

It is thus a bit disconcerting to discover in the essays that introduce these new translations a will to complicate. This is not so evident in Haskel's biographical essay, which is in the historical humanist mode, as in Abe Ryuichi's "A Poetics of Mendicancy," which contains such passages as "a comparison with the Derridian theory, for example, helps illustrate Ryokan's deconstructive perspective...."

Genuflections to the French, though now as common as were noddings to the Chinese in Ryokan's time, are useful only if they are performed with a like rigor. Structuralist assumptions are beneficial only if they are defined. To simply use terminology unexamined ("Barthes' proposal to understand text as the topos of incessant semantic production") is to promote jargon—something particularly unwelcome in a work on Ryokan.

Great Fool: Zen Master Ryokan—Poems, Letters, and Other Writings, translated with essays by Abe Ryuichi and Peter Haskel. Honolulu: University of Hawaii Press, 1996.

Calligraphy used to be seen as an index of character: A person's integrity visibly appeared in his or her brush strokes. Now, of course, thanks to the advances of modern technology, many have forgotten not only how to shape their *kanji* and *kana* properly but also, often, the *kanji* themselves. And the legible, uniform font of the computer printout naturally offers no index of character at all.

Hence, it is interesting to find scholars concerning themselves with the nearly forgotten moral associations of calligraphy. I know of no other work that has tried to do what Kato Kiichi attempts here: a reading of a single poet's writing as an index of his thought and of his person.

The poet is the well known mendicant monk Ryokan, now a popular figure. There are many editions of his work, many translations, a number of learned biographies, some stage adaptations and at least one (quite bad) movie. This individuality makes Ryokan a good choice for calligraphic investigation. In addition, the poetry itself is ample and excellent.

As the late Robert Brower has said, "His poetry grows from the largely unremarkable incidents of his daily life … his plain, direct style has an effect of immediacy and true-to-life realism for which he has been greatly extolled in modern times."

Sanford Goldstein, one of the present translators, has stated that the *kanshi* Chinese poems are truly superb and that the *tanka* are experiences to which he returns again and again. Of the calligraphy itself, he says that often "the effect is more aesthetic than comprehensible." Ryokan, however, "saw even without thought or plan … the characters that must be small or large, the thickness or thinness of line, some shapes darker, some lighter."

This is also how Kato explains the effect of the calligraphy. He examines 50 examples of Ryokan's writing. On the left-hand page is a reproduction of the work itself; on the right-hand page is a printed rendition (Ryokan is hard to read), a *romaji* translation and an English translation. This is followed by commentary on the calligraphy and an English translation of the commentary.

Some of the commentary is a bit impressionistic. For example, "The character shapes ... sway to the right or left as if butterflies are flitting from flower to flower." But there is also solid detail: "... the haiku is written on the right half of the paper, the left half remaining blank, so that the balance of the whole composition is maintained."

Ryokan's Calligraphy, by Kato Kiichi, translated by Sanford Goldstein and Kitajima Fujisato. Niigata: Kokodo Co., Ltd., 1997.

Rengetsu

In Tomioka Tessai's portrait of his close friend, Rengetsu, he shows her as a pate-shaved and placid old woman in an ecclesiastical kimono, penning away at a *waka*, while beside her sits a small table just waiting for one of her cups or jars (for she was a potter as well as a poet) a person serenely, even noticeably, at last herself.

At last—for she had to work hard to attain this harmony. Born in 1791 from the illegitimate union of a samurai and a geisha, she was earlier given to the care of Otagaki Teruhisa, a lay priest at Chinoji. She took the family name, and, when she was sixteen, a husband.

The children of the union all died, as did the husband. A new marriage proved no more fortunate. Finally, at the age of 33, twice widowed, all her children gone, she suffered the death of her adoptive father and—since she had no official position in Chinoji—expulsion.

Already a nun, she now had to make her own living (pottery, teaching *go*) and initially had a hard time. Yet she made the best of it. There is a famous story of a thief entering her hut one night. Awakened, she lit the lamp so that he could see better and then, thinking he was probably hungry, she insisted on fixing him a bowl of rice and tea. This event was later turned into a poem—though whether in those troubled times, this thief was the same one or not is unknown.

Not a trace
Of the thief
But he left behind
The peaceful stillness
Of the Okazaki hills.

Her kindnesses have become famous. When Tessai was still unknown, and she was already well regarded, she gave him a number of her poems with a note saying: "When times are hard add your paintings to these sheets and sell them."

It is pleasant to learn that Tessai paid his debt to her. When Rengetsu, in her late seventies, was getting ready to die, she placed in her casket a shroud which had on it a painting of a moon and lotus by Tessai. She commemorated this (and the present collection therewith took its title) in her death verse:

How I hope to pass away
While gazing at a round moon
In a cloudless sky that
Shines over lotus flowers
In full bloom.

In this poem, the moon again resumed its place in her inner harmony. It had figured in much of her verse, and good Buddhist as she was, she had sometimes seen through it, as it were:

The autumn moon—
It, too
Can become
A tie to
The floating world.

Yet her beliefs were all devoted to a certain harmony. At her death the moon was back in place. And so were all of her other many activities. She had perhaps been reproached at devoting herself to activities un-nunlike. This she answered in a verse:

From dawn to dusk.
Spending the day
Gathering clay:
Surely Buddha would not
Think this a trifling matter.

Her calligraphy has become as famous as her poetry. It appears in the illustrated poem cards (for she was also a spirited artist) and on her ceramics as well—much of this is illustrated in this volume.

Her line is, like her verse free, unconventional. Of it, Melinda Takeuchi has said that it is "characterized by a relatively unfluctuating line that appears charged with tension." It was perhaps this tension that so distinguishes her work and her life—the mundane imagery drawn from life (legacy of Ozawa Roen, the poet who most influenced her) as contrasted and reconciled by her religion: the common lotus and the celestial moon.

When these two demands coincide we have in their resolution some of her finest poetry. As in:

So quickly!
The willow planted
Three years ago
Now beating against
My windowpane.

Finally in 1875, Rengetsu died. She was 84 and had long redeemed (if that is the word) her life. She had taken her misfortune and forged for herself a new and a better life. Not only was she famous for her good works (and not only toward burglars), but she also left behind a legacy of over 50,000 pieces of art: pottery, hundreds of paintings, thousands of poem-cards.

John Stevens, a Rengetsu scholar—as well as a scholar of much else Japanese—has, in this elegant little pocket-sized book, given us clean and faithful translations of Rengetsu's *waka* (divided, as certainly would have pleased her, into a seasonal pattern) and has in addition written a full introduction.

Lotus Moon: The Poetry of the Buddhist Nun Rengetsu, translated and introduced by John Stevens. New York: Weatherhill, 1994.

Chikamatsu Shigenori

There are many collections of tea-ceremony lore, but this one will be new. It was rediscovered only a decade ago, and this is its first English translation.

In 1739, Chikamatsu Shigenori, Tokugawa retainer in presentday Aichi, compiled a manuscript which he called *Legends of the Tea Ceremony*. It contained 305 stories and anecdotes. When Shigenori died, however, it was still not published. This event occurred only in 1804 when an anonymous compiler selected and revised 129 of the stories and published them under the title of *Stories From a Tearoom Window*. It is this version which is here translated.

Shigenori's purpose, besides his definite antiquarian interest, was through his work somehow to restore to the tea ceremony part of the purity it had, during its long history, lost. In approval, Kimura Toshiatsu wrote in the preface to the 1804 edition: "The essence of the tea ceremony does not lie merely in the satisfaction of the sense of taste, but in the friendly association of strangers, of those of the lower classes with those of the nobility. In the observance of manners in the severe formalities of the tea ceremony, mutual understanding and friendliness are created." This is, presumably, what the earlier, purer tea ceremony was like.

We all know what it turned into, after the powerful and the moneyed got hold of it. "Since Lord Yoshimasa indulged himself in the tea ceremony," soberly writes Shigenori. "It gradually grew into luxurious extravagance." He adds, "a single earthen vessel comes to be more esteemed than a jewel ... this can be called the current evil of the tea ceremony."

Perhaps this vulgarization was what led Sen no Rikyu, most influential of the tea masters, to exercise such extraordinary rigor. ("Rikyu said that the overlapping of the paper strips on the *shoji* frame (in the teahouse) should be as follows: 3 mm is too narrow, while 4.5 mm is a little too wide.") This famous arbiter codified just about everything concerned with the tea ceremony (and much else). We know because of the single exception: "There seems to be no fixed rule as to where to place the oil lampstand. This is said to be a comment made by Rikyu to Lord Nobunaga." And, sure enough, there is no fixed rule, even now.

It was Rikyu who gave the rulers some much needed lessons in taste, and many are the stories ("the single remaining morning glory") where he attempted to teach Nobunaga or Hideyoshi something about the true spirit of the tea ceremony. The latter, for example, tasteless as always, ordered a pure gold basin filled with water and brought in and then told Rikyu to arrange some red plum branches in it. Faced with this impossibility, Rikyu stripped the blossoms from the branches and then scattered them on the surface of the water.

"It looked wonderfully interesting. Hideyoshi had intended to trick Rikyu, but Rikyu was able to resolve the difficulty skillfully, much to the lord's admiration." One wonders about the admiration. One wonders if Hideyoshi was even capable of it. This was, after all, the same man who gave the monster tea-party for the millions with pure gold service, an anti-tea-ceremony event not recorded by our author.

Though Shigenori is concerned for the purity of the earlier tea ceremony, he is not unimpressed by the rise in tea utensil prices once the powerful and monied started interesting themselves. Consequently, much of this collection is taken up with dull stories about how expensive this cup or that tea-container eventually became.

Several of the stories are interesting, however. For some time, the kettles cast at Ashiya had been best for tea. Even the noted Sesshu did designs for them. However, Ashiya kettles suddenly became unpopular. The reason was that a noted criminal was sentenced to death by boiling in a caldron which happened to be cast at the Ashiya works. After that, tea adepts used different kettles.

Shigenori also gives us some fascinating indications of what informed taste was like in 1739. He speaks of the fashion of calligraphy done by Zen monks and its use in the tea room. "Such a mundane custom was [originally] accepted because tea connoisseurs were generally illiterate, while priests alone were literate and therefore highly respected [but] actually, calligraphy by Zen priests is generally unbelievably bad and hardly worthy of appreciation. ... And yet, the tasteless and unreal phrases of such calligraphy are often introduced by ignorant people as if they were invaluable maxims. Such people value only money and neglect true insight."

If what he says is informed (that is, if he is not a reactionary philistine, which also seems to be partially the case), then the *chanoyu* is in an even worse way today with all connoisseurs scrambling for the few remaining Zen-*ga*.

Nonetheless, this provincial and antiquarian accounting of tea ceremony lore is of a certain historical interest, and the author's concern for its present (1739) decadence is touching.

Stories from a Tearoom Window, by Chikamatsu Shigenori, edited by Mori Toshiko, translated by Mori Kozaburo. Rutland: Charles E. Tuttle Company, 1982.

Meiji and Modern Literature

Mori Ogai

Published serially between 1911 and 1913, *The Wild Goose* (*Gan*), one of several autobiographical works of Mori Ogai (1862–1922), examines the tentative attraction between a student soon to go off to Germany (as Ogai was) and the young mistress of a money-lender. In the moral climate of the early 1880's, perhaps nothing could have come of this but, whatever the original anecdote, the experience remained with the author and became the nucleus for this novel.

Attraction was a subject he had been thinking about. He had earlier written about its problems in his 1907 *Vita Sexualis*, a publication which offended officials who ordered the text withdrawn. He had even earlier experienced some of its difficulties.

In Germany in the 1880's, he had felt a strong attraction for a German woman. And she for him—to the extent that she followed him back to Japan. He, convinced by his family that such a marriage would not forward his career, married elsewhere.

So, he knew all about the callow, unfeeling student who could have loved the beautiful mistress of the money-lender but did not. And since this was all that happened, this is all there is to the resulting account—at least so far as action is concerned.

One reads the novel—and it is one of the most popular of Ogai's works—for its insight into its women (the money-lender's mistress and his wife) and for its recreation of 1880 Tokyo—Ueno, the Shinobazu pond (home of the wild goose), and the student quarter of old Nezu. The book is filled with an attractive nostalgia in which the author's memories for a love affair that never occurred is mixed with his recollections of a city that had already vanished.

The book, however, is also a creation of its time and consequently its dicta on woman now read oddly. For example: "A woman, in any matter whatsoever, will hesitate with pitiful irresolution until she has made up her mind. Once having done so, however, she looks neither to right or left, as a man might, but, like a horse with blinders on, plods steadily toward her goal."

Any woman? All women? Such monolithic opinions, however, are also those of the young student (friend to hero) who is narrating the story. So it is he (as well as Ogai, of course) who also piles on the symbolism.

A bad snake gets into the cage where the lonely mistress had kept an innocent little bird. Get it? And at the end of the story, the student accidentally kills the wild goose of the title (another innocent bird) just after he has more or less turned down the waiting woman.

And to make certain we appreciate the connection, Ogai has the hero say: "Some wild geese are just unlucky." This then allows the narrator to say: "Though there was no logical connection, the image of the woman ... flashed through my mind."

At the same time, this novella is often more subtly constructed that this. Its use of metaphor is as telling as its symbolism is obvious. The money-lender "paid little attention to the content of her remarks but listened rather as to a cricket in a cage whose engaging chirps brought a smile to his face." On the next page, the mistress permits herself an untruth, and the author notes that: "Tiny insects that must forever be escaping from the pursuit of more powerful creatures have their protective coloring: women tell lies."

The slightly sententious tone is rendered descriptive—decorative insects are equated in terms of a person we are getting to know. We learn much about her sad existence, and no one has told us it is sad. We are told an awful lot though, nonetheless. And, in addition, since the work was originally serialized, we got recapitulations, filled with what we already know.

And yet, despite all that is obtuse and didactic, despite the generalizations and the platitudes, there is the atmosphere of a real place and a real time. Perhaps it is this which makes *The Wild Goose* a satisfactory book. Its satisfactions are not those of story or even character—they were those of a retrieved reality.

The translation seems perfect. It is the work of Burton Watson, and it has had the benefits of long consideration. Sections of it were completed forty years ago, and one of them was published in the Grove anthology, *Modern Japanese Literature*, in 1956. In 1959 another translation appeared, that of Ochiai Kingo and Sanford Goldstein. Now, Watson has completely revised the original translation and filled in passages previously omitted. The result is the definitive version of a strange and limited but captivating novel.

The Wild Goose, by Mori Ogai, translated with an introduction by Burton Watson. Ann Arbor: Center for Japanese Studies, University of Michigan, 1995.

In 1916 Mori Ogai began publishing his *Shibue Chusai*, a biography of a scholar–doctor who lived (1805–1858) at the end of the Tokugawa Period. This account became "one of the most admired, though by no means most read, works in modern Japanese literature."

Ogai's life had been full of change, and toward the end of it, he began interesting himself in Tokugawa history—particularly in trying to discover the reality of the samurai class as it experienced the end of one age and the beginning of another.

In his studies Ogai relied on Tokugawa genealogies of the samurai peerage and discovered references to a physician named Shibue. He had found his hero.

In more senses than one. In his book he compares himself to Chusai, to his own disadvantage: "His career resembled mine strangely. The only difference is that one man lived in the past and the other in the present, and that our lives have not overlapped. No, that is not all. There is a more important difference: Chusai had reached the highest position in the fields of philosophy and literature that a scholar could make for himself, but I have been unable to advance beyond the realm of confused dilettantism. I cannot help but feel ashamed before Chusai."

In the words of Donald Keene (who also translated the above): "The passage is revelatory of Ogai's attitude; he was able to identify himself so completely with an obscure figure of the past that his account at times verged on autobiography."

Now, some 70 years after Ogai began serializing this biography the distinguished scholar-translator Edwin McClellan has given us his own, personal version of Shibue Chusai—one which translates portions of and augments Ogai's account. And McClellan's concern is much the same as Ogai's—understanding what happened in history, making it come once more alive. What the later author writes of the former and his work ("It is a book written by a modern Japanese in his later years for whom the past has become terribly important.") is in large part true of himself.

While Ogai identified with Chusai, it is his wife Io that McClellan most admires—so much so that his book (using the same sources that the earlier author used, as well as Ogai's work itself) is a full biography in which the life of the wife can well stand alongside that of the husband.

As McClellan says at the end of his very interesting account of this woman and her times: "Io was not in the ordinary sense a distinguished or famous person; so that had it not been for Ogai's chance encounter with her, we would never have known about this remarkable woman, so brave and so proud."

She carried a dagger in those threatening times in which she lived and routed louts and robbers; at one point (apparently surprised in the bath) she confronted some intruders unclothed except for her dagger (though Ogai in his account generously gives her an *okoshimaki*.)

She was also of a most inquiring mind and even taught herself English. And she knew what she wanted. When she settled on the older Chusai (already both widowed and divorced) she persuaded an acquaintance to act as her go-between. ("It is to Ogai's credit," writes McClellan, "that he does not find this shockingly unfeminine.")

In writing his biography of Io, the American author found not only that his focus is different from that of the Japanese but also that Ogai occasionally got things wrong. Using the same sources, McClellan can state, for example, that "the dialogue that ends the ... passage is mostly Ogai's invention, and it makes one slightly uneasy ... it is clumsily done."

Most of the time, however, the two authors get along admirably. Certainly one of the reasons is their regard for the past and the dead who once lived. Both are concerned with concrete, telling details, and completely unconcerned with the stereotypes of most history books. As McClellan puts it: "Our preconceptions about Japan in 'feudal' times are such that we sometimes are unable to realize how free social life in Edo could be in the first half of the 19th-century ... we see in Chusai's circle a tolerance for eccentricity, indeed sometimes for outright impropriety, that is very attractive."

Ogai saw it, too. He willingly recounts that his hero is afraid of thunder. "Whenever he heard its rumblings, he would have his mosquito net hung, sit inside it, and have sake brought him." He was also fond of concocting things, one of which was eel-sake. Mori even gives the recipe.

(For the curious, it is: put a piece of broiled eel in a bowl and pour a small amount of drippings over it, then fill the bowl with hot sake, place the lid over the bowl and let contents stand for a while before drinking it.)

McClellan quite shares Ogai's eye for the human detail, and like the older author, he has not only respect but also affection for these long dead folk. In writing of one of these who had become embittered, a terrible scold, he adds: "But, of course, the fact is that she was given little chance to be anything else." About another: "He was, one gathers, a quiet and decent person and not half so interesting as his [completely reprehensible] younger half-brother."

His is a most engaging style. A certain doctor, Sakuma, "was known by the nickname of 'Pigeon Doctor' (was he fond of pigeons or did he look like one? Ogai does not tell us)."

And his is a most engaging book. Seeing Shibue Io through the various lenses of her husband, her son, Tamotsu (from whom much information was gleaned), the novelist Ogai and the biographer McClellan is an interesting, moving, disarming experience.

I do not know of another historical biography constructed as is this one. And the experiment, if so it is, is most successful. These lens do not endistance—rather, they bring closer. In McClellan as in Ogai, the past lives once again.

Woman in the Crested Kimono: The Life of Shibue Io and Her Family Drawn from Mori Ogai's Shibue Chose, by Edwin McClellan. New Haven: Yale University Press, 1985.

Toward the end of his life, Mori Ogai wrote a series of nine interconnected works which even now continue to occasion an amount of critical disagreement.

Ranging from nine pages in length to 371 pages, they were all *shiden* (historical biographies), set in the late Tokugawa Period and concerned with the careers of Confucian literati.

Serialized in the *Nichinichi Shimbun* in both Tokyo and Osaka editions (1916–1921), they made odd newspaper fare and some readers responded with protests, using such words as "pointless" and "maddening."

Marvin Marcus, who has devoted this full-length study to these works, has remarked that Ogai persisted "in administering daily doses of documentary minutiae to the nation's readers, thus challenging their values by trying their patience."

Eventually, the newspaper itself suspended publication. No attempt was made to editorially stand up for the author. They had only asked the eminent Ogai to contribute because the *Asahi Shimbun* had gotten Natsume Soseki.

Since their troubled reception these *shiden* have had a difficult critical life. Detractors brand the works "inhuman, obsessive, and unreadable," while the admirers insist on "the transcendental ineffable quality of the Ogai style."

One contemporary critic called them "masterpieces of modern Japanese literature," while another says that they are not "even up to the standards of second-rate biography."

Marcus in this study of these manifestly misunderstood works is concerned to place them within the genre of which they form a part and to indicate what it was that Ogai accomplished, and in so doing what he contributed to the art of biography as it was understood in Japan.

Before Ogai, much biography was a "vehicle of state-sponsored hagiography." In this, Japan followed the Chinese example and political biographies, such as those found in the *Dai Nihonshi*, were considered unexceptionable. And still are—as in the numerous current biographies issued by various captains of industry.

Japan also had the Western example. The potted Victorian biography was a fixture, a way of learning about admired individuals. And it is interesting that the first work to be translated into Japanese was Samuel Smiles' *Self Help*, a selection of short, didactic biographies extolling the Victorian virtues of ambition and hard work. In Japan it was explicitly titled *Saikoku Risshihen (Accounts of Western Self-Made Men.)*

Ogai stood against the morality-mongering of such works. As his son later remembered, his father said that for him working with biographical sources constituted a form of scientific research. He was interested in the mundane, the quotidian, because it has once been. It had truly existed, which is perhaps more than can be said for unspoiled civic virtues.

These *shiden* thus brought something new to biography, and both Chinese and Victorian models were superceded. As Marcus indicates, this new approach was that of "the first-person quest technique."

Ogai included himself and his own efforts in reconstructing these lives. This sober self-inclusion "stands as the most elaborate expression of Ogai's aversion toward the tawdry confessionalism and literary self-indulgence that followed in the wake of the Naturalist movement."

An enemy of the newly-emerged *shishosetsu* (the first-person "I novel") with its sometimes overweening and occasionally vulgar confessional style, Ogai also rigorously excluded any psychological portrayal—indeed, this is so absent that "one is inclined to regard the project as a deliberate critique of the sort of psychological novelization mastered by Natsume Soseki."

As Marcus has noted: "Biography is by its nature a literary

tango and its great choreographers—Johnson, Boswell—have emerged as equal partners in the dance." Ogai makes a minor presence on this dance floor, but he (unlike any Japanese before him) is palpably there.

He is present both in that his *shiden* is also an account of the making of the *shiden*, and because, like any editor, he picks and chooses what to put in and thus creates an image of his own values and tastes.

Here we find Ogai creating, whether he so intended or not, another kind of idealization: his examples tend to illustrate Confucian virtues: self-sacrifice, forbearance, magnanimity. If the *shiden* are truly unreadable, this might be the reason. In backing away from Chinese-style hagiography, Ogai backed into a new Japanese kind.

That he consistently chose from his sources to create an idealized version is demonstrated by Marcus who brings originals and finished material together and finds that Ogai "has produced an abstract, detached and refined version of lively, if occasionally rough-hewn narrative."

When Edwin McClellan set out to make the first (and only) translation of any of the nine (that devoted to Shibue Chusai), he discovered that "it is so full of esoteric detail—which even the educated Japanese reader finds daunting—that I could hardly expect the lay Western reader to tolerate it in its entirety."

This *shiden* emerged in translation as the admirable *Woman in the Crested Kimono*, McClellan having had to do with his original text just what Ogai did with his. Ogai's relation to his material became clear when he was writing the last of the nine. He confessed that he had become increasingly disappointed in the man and that this made it difficult for him to continue.

For a biographer to be disappointed in his subject argues for certain prior assumptions which have little to do with the subject himself but everything to do with the biographer.

Perhaps it is this attitude, then, which makes the *shiden* difficult. On the other hand, Marcus's accounting for them is not difficult at all. It is thorough, reasoned, generous, and extremely lively.

Paragons of the Ordinary: The Biographical Literature of Mori Ogai, by Marvin Marcus. Honolulu: University of Hawaii Press, 1993.

Ito Sachio

Ito Sachio's literary reputation is that of a poet. During his short life (1864–1913), he wrote over 3,000 poems and some of these are found in most major collections. His popular reputation, however, is that of a novelist. He wrote 26 of them, and several are still widely read. One in particular, his first, greatly impressed Natsume Soseki, who wrote to and about the author, thus insuring his novelistic reputation from the start. The book was *Nogiku no Haka*, which appeared in 1905 and soon achieved the status of a popular classic. It has only now, however, been translated, along with a shorter work, the 1908 *Hamagiku*.

A Grave amid Wild Chrysanthemums, to give the translated title of the first (the other is rendered as *Beach Chrysanthemums*) was written when the author was already forty-one and is considered to be autobiographical. The young hero, son of a well-to-do farming family, becomes attracted to a cousin, two years his senior, who has come to help with the farm work. The family and the neighbors begin to gossip about this, detecting an improper romance when, in fact there is yet none.

The narrator is sent away to school, and the girl is married off. It is only then that he realizes that his affection is love. She, already knowing her own emotions, has had a miscarriage and dies. When he returns his mother tells him this and implores his forgiveness. He visits the dead girl's grave, finds it banked with the wild chrysanthemums she loved. "No matter how far it may be from this world to the next," runs the translation of the last sentence, "not a day passes without my thinking of her."

Soseki's high opinion of this work might be due to his soft spot for the sentimental (and certainly this quality must account for its continued popularity with the ordinary Japanese reader), but a part of it might be that it appeared at a time when "naturalistic" tendencies were being fought, by Soseki among others.

Though Ito was, himself, to write a number of "naturalistic" novels—*Akigiri (Autumn Fog)* is the best known—the 1904 work is introspective, impressionistic, and evocative—non-naturalistic qualities all. In addition, it was said, this work embodied the spirit of the *tanka*, a spirit I do not myself detect in it and one which the translation does not assist me in recognizing.

The translator has defined, I think, the reasons for the popularity of the work when he writes: "We are moved not so much by the finesse of the writing, or the adroit plot but by its simplicity and sincerity." This quality of the *makoto* always seems to lie in the intention rather than the accomplishment, and all too often indicates a facile appeal to sentiment. I find it pervading the work. So, of course, does the Japanese reader—thc difference is that he approves and I do not.

A book is popular precisely because it has, intentionally or not, reached and reaffirmed a number of (usually ethical) unspoken assumptions. I find Ito's getting rid of his rather attractive heroine (he does so in the most open possible manner) distasteful because she is sacrificed to a need for easy sentiment. My assumption is that even imaginary people must be allowed to live their own lives, that they are independent and responsible.

The assumption of Ito and his readers is quite different. Much more important than any belief in the reality of little Tamiko is the idea that love is always star-crossed, that death is our common end, and that enduring memory is much more important than transient living. To my mind, this comes perilously close to the vulgar *shikataganai* syndrome. For them as well, with the difference that the syndrome is readily and happily accepted.

It is interesting to compare this work with a foreign novel on precisely (minus miscarriage) the same theme: Colette's splendidly sincere (my version) *Le blé en herbe* of 1923. Her book is about the awakening of love between two rural adolescents, the various oppositions to this attachment and its denouement.

Her work (never among her more popular) upsets a number of French assumptions, one of which might be that the two would be happy together. Instead, she allows them to live on and then part because of what they are—adolescents. As in the Ito book, it is the boy who is scarred, but the reasons are quite different. It is easy enough for Ito's hero (the beloved antagonist safely dead) to give himself over to comforting thoughts on evanescence; Colette's boy-hero must live on with the knowledge of his own failure.

I realize that a comparison such as I have just made is invidious. We are not to compare the works of one country with those of another—particularly if they are Japanese. Nonetheless, my concern, as I suppose has become apparent, is ethical—and I wonder about Ito's ethics—full knowing, of course, that it is just these which contribute to, or entirely create his popularity.

I might mention that other Japanese share this doubt. When this short novel was made into a film in 1955 (*Nogiku no gotoki kimi nariki* from the best-known line in the book: "You are like a wild chrysanthemum"), the director, Kinoshita Keisuke, and his writers realized that the structure of the book was not strong enough to bear the weight of the emotion called for. Therefore, they took the first paragraph and the last and made separate sequences of them. The now aged hero is making a pilgrimage to the grave, and he remembers the past events (all very faithful to Ito) and then, in the ultimate sequence, he silently (important point) reflects.

As Henry James is forever telling us, endistancing always accomplishes intended effects. In the film version, we no longer have the hot breath of the narrator in our ear, we are not involved in all the *makoto*-esque goings-on and consequently are free to offer our emotion. We do this because the emotion has not been called for—or, at any rate, been called for in a much less direct manner.

I have happily wept through many a showing of this picture. The difference between Ito, on one hand, and Colette and Kinoshita on the other, is I think basically ethical. The latter two show a respect for their material; the former, to my way of thinking, does not.

Perhaps in reaching these conclusions I have been aided by the translation. Perhaps the original contains felicities I have missed. If so it may be my inattention or it may be that translations are—naturally—inadequate. Naturally, because one cannot translate out of one's own language and into another; one can translate only out of another and into one's own. It is not a question so much of accuracy but of nuance. I can never know the nuances of Japanese, and for the same reason Yamamura Saburo (and all other Japanese translating from their language) can never know the nuances of English.

"As might be expected of the gentler sex," cannot be used, even in translating a 1905 novel; "my ill-natured brother's wife" seems to refer to the brother's ill-nature, while actually it refers to the wife's; "I felt … I would be unable to turn her down," cannot be used in a book which nowhere else ("I suppose she must have felt chagrined at my rebuke ...") uses the colloquial; "It is craven for one so young as you to retire from active life" is something I think even a hero as priggish as this would not have said. Yamamura's translation is no worse than any of its kind—it is just this kind is not adequate.

Nogiku no Haka and *Hamagiku*, by Ito Sachio, translated by Yamamura Saburo. Tokyo: Hokuseido Press, 1979.

Kunikida Doppo

Kunikida Doppo, born in 1871, dead at thirty-seven, is one of the least celebrated of Meiji writers. Japanese readers seem to prefer easier authors, Koda Rohan, for example; Japanese critics, more classifiable ones. Foreign criticism often follows: *The Reader's Guide to Japanese Literature* does not mention Doppo.

There are a number of reasons for the neglect, one being that the author did not live long enough to fulfill his full potential—to the extent that any author ever does. Another is that Doppo, an original and even experimental writer, was continually changing his stylistic approaches, and this always confuses opinion-makers. As a result, he is nearly unclassifiable, which in local literary circles means undiscussable.

Nominally, Doppo is listed as a "naturalist," mainly because Shimazaki Toson in 1906 called him one. He shares little with others of this genre, however, and the influences of Turgenev and Maupassant (neither a naturalist in any European sense of the term) are much stronger than those of the "great naturalist" Zola.

Actually, the largest influences on his writing were

Wordsworth and various Victorian Christians, none of whom could be accused of naturalism. As Donald Keene (the only Western critic to treat this author at deserved length) writes: "It is hard to fit Doppo into any school. He was basically a romantic and … expressed in lyrical prose a sense of wonder before nature and man with burning sincerity."

It is the lyrical insight that Doppo brings to his work that keeps reminding one of poetry, though (except for the several volumes of poetry he also wrote) Doppo is usually considered a prose writer. Nevertheless, infused into stories and novellas is an attention, a rigor of observation, a celebration we associate with lyric verse. As Akutagawa Ryunosuke, a strong admirer of Doppo, wrote, "the poet within him was eternally the poet."

This is particularly apparent in his earlier work of 1897– 1901. Included would be "Old Gen," Doppo's best-known work, "Musashino," "River Mist" and the wonderful "Unforgettable People."

A story set within a story, this last is, I think, completely representative of his strength and originality. A writer shares his sketches with a casual stranger whom he meets at an inn. These are all brief pictures of people he met and could not forget. He describes one, then concludes with "for almost ten years now I have thought of this man in the shadow of the lonely island and whose face I never saw." As the sketches continue it becomes apparent (without Doppo's ever having to tell us so) that the young writer's sensitivity is almost as great as his need for friendship.

He tells the stranger, a young man in his early twenties named Akiyama, that once near Mt. Aso at sunset a young packhorse man passed him. "He was a sturdy young man in his early twenties, but as his back was to the light of the early evening moon, I could not make out his profile clearly. Even so, the dark outline of his brawny figure remains before my eyes to this very day. I followed him for a while with my gaze and then turned my attention back to the volcano's smoke." Two years later, we find the writer back at the same inn writing away on his manuscript, "Unforgettable People." We learn about others he met, but "of Akiyama there was no mention."

This is the last line of the piece. Nowhere does Doppo say that here was perhaps the friendship the writer sought; yet the fact that he chose to end the piece in this manner implies just that. With subtlety and tact, with the assurance of a poet, Doppo allows the reader to complete the true meaning of the work.

Subtlety and tact are not qualities one associates with Meiji Japan, and perhaps it is Doppo's complete lack of didactic intent that has resulted in his relative neglect. It has certainly resulted in his being more than occasionally misunderstood.

For example, of the beautifully balanced "Deer Hunt," one critic has said that its effect is somewhat marred by the inclusion of tragedy (a suicide) into an apparently realistic description. Properly read, however, this man shooting himself balances perfectly the shooting of the deer and establishes an equilibrium so delicate that to state it is to destroy it. As in all poetry, unspoken apprehension is the goal, and Doppo certainly overestimated his readers.

One of the results is that, though there have been a number of translations of the works and some quite distinguished—Jay Rubin's translation of "The Suburbs" that appeared in *Monumenta Nipponica*, for example—none of them have been collected. In 1973, however, the late David Chibbett made this collection of fifteen of Doppo's works, including all those mentioned above, and wrote a full introduction to the life of the man and his writings.

Chibbett's death in 1977 occasioned considerable delay in the publication of this manuscript. It was copyrighted by

UNESCO in 1982 and published a year later and is now generally available. My enthusiasm for the author and for Chibbett's edition of his work, should be apparent. It is precisely Doppo's unclassifiable originality that I esteem, particularly his unwillingness to subscribe to Meiji literary vogues. His voice speaks directly and personally over this near-century which separates us from him. It is a small voice, but it is utterly authentic.

River Mist and Other Stories, by Kunikida Doppo, translated by David Chibbett. Kent: Paul Norbury Publications, 1983.

Koda Rohan

Koda Rohan (1867–1947) is often thought of as one of the great writers of the Meiji Period. Several years ago, an academic journal found that his popularity put him in the top three (the other two being Natsume Soseki and Mori Ogai) well ahead of the nearest competition (Shimazaki Toson).

Nonetheless, among all these writers, he is the one with the least translations into other languages. There have been several of *Goju no To* (two in English—1909 and 1959—and one in German) and a few stories and essays have appeared in English. And now there appears a new collection with translations of the former work: *The Five-Storied Pagoda* and two others, *Tai Dokuro* ("Encounter with a Skull"), and *Higeotoko* ("The Bearded Samurai").

There are reasons for this Japanese acclaim and this foreign neglect. As Kato Shuichi has observed: "The eighty years of Rohan's life coincided with the years of Japan's 'modernization,' but he was unconcerned with the question of how this should best proceed. Rather his work testifies to the continuity of traditional culture despite this process."

Some critics find his commentaries on Basho's seven volumes of haiku to be his finest work and traditional writers have long found much virtue in him. Tanizaki, writing of Rohan's *Ummei* (a 1919 work as yet untranslated) said (in Donald Keene's translation): "In this day and age when things resembling pages from a mundane diary pass for fiction, this historical treatise is a novel in its genuine sense."

In its genuine Japanese sense, one would imagine, for though Rohan himself listed Shakespeare, Milton and Goethe as influences on his work, these (in Keene's words) "were more apparent to Rohan than to any subsequent critic." And translations reveal works which do not sit well with Western sensibilities.

Rohan's works are, somewhat like others of the late Tokugawa, Bakin's for example. The characters are not "developed" in any Western sense, nor did the writer intend that they should be. Rather, they are two-dimensional in the accepted Sino-Japanese manner. "A born Edoite polished and sharpened to the core, Genta was no more sparing in his benevolence than he was in his rage." They are also presented in the self-consciously "poetic" Tokugawa fashion. "Baba swung his eyes up, sprinkling a few icy teardrops over the flaming face of Dairoku."

All of this, while quite acceptable to the Japanese reader, Tokugawa and later, goes against Western prejudices which (during this century at any rate) have demanded something more realistic. Yet it was "realism" as understood by Meiji writers that Rohan stood so valiantly against and is for this reason prized.

Another difficulty encountered by the prejudiced Westerner is the Rohan narrative itself. It is very much in the didactic Sino-Japanese tradition and the point is always ethical. In "The Five-Storied Pagoda," two carpenters (master and apprentice) both wish the honor of constructing the pagoda, and the problem is solved by a wise old priest.

Though several other narrative layers are suggested, (for example, the major characters are given names which indicate their symbolic functions), the Western reader is unlikely to consider this just compensation.

In "Encounter with a Skull," there are again long speeches and a didactic intent. A brash young man encounters a mysterious woman who tells him her story and is revealed as a ghost. He, having been enlightened, picks up the skull at his feet and lectures us about suffering and compassion. In *Higeotoko*, the pure love between two samurai is interrupted when one of them is killed in a fight. The killer is apprehended, and in the speeches which follow, he indicates just why he did what he did, how a higher loyalty was involved, etc., etc., etc.

This antipathy, which the prejudiced Western reader might feel need not limit enjoyment of Rohan's work. It merely indicates that it is to be enjoyed in a different manner—one perhaps more sociological or even anthropological than literary. Perhaps it is best to read Rohan as one reads that other Meiji favorite, Bulwer-Lytton—that is, if one reads him at all. Or perhaps as one reads Washington Irving. His "serious" works (*The Life of George Washington*) are unreadable. He lives only in his sketches and his adaptations ("Rip Van Winkle") and because he is still taught in school, or at least was when I was still going to school.

The reason for making youngsters read *The Sketch Book* was that American literature had to begin somewhere if it were to be taught. It wasn't that Irving was any good but that he was first. American Lit. needed an early master. In the same way, I suggest, Japanese Lit., Meiji Period, needed a traditional example. Rohan's present popularity is indicated by a poll taken by and of academics, people who teach Japanese Lit. When I asked my non-literary Japanese friends about Rohan it turns out they have all read him—once—in school.

Be that as it may, the Western reader must face one more problem with reading Rohan. How does one translate him? The current translation is by Chieko Irie Mulhern, the leading foreign expert on the author, her 1977 biography being the standard work, and even she has her problems.

If one translates with straightforward accuracy, one finds people "gnashing the invisible fangs of bitter regret," explaining that "such a move would be nothing short of suicidal, like eggs throwing themselves against a boulder," and crying "how I regret that I was born a samurai, to squander a whole lifetime fretting and gloating over vain glory!"

Then if one tries to lighten all of this and assume a more colloquial stance ("You're giving me a hard time," and "I'll take a rain check on your dinner invitation,") the convention of language level is breached, and the results become even less persuasive. And searching for the arresting word will not help much. "Her silent hospitality was more winning than a mouthful of piddling lecture." Since this hospitality consists of cups of tea, one finds the adjective problematical.

Indeed, as the translator herself writes: "... no translator can ever hope to approximate, let alone re-create, Rohan's resonant, surging poetic prose, which has its own force and rhythm so inimitably Japanese." Probably not and perhaps, after all, just as well.

Pagoda, Skull and Samurai; Three Stories, by Koda Rohan, translated by Chieko Irie Mulhern. Rutland: Charles E. Tuttle Company, 1985.

Tokuda Shusei

Rough Living is, I think, the first translation into English of a novel by a writer whom Japanese themselves find one of their finest. Tokuda Shusei (1871–1943) was thought by Kawabata Yasunari to be the most Japanese of all modern novelists, and Nakamura Murao stated that, after Saikaku, only Shusei portrayed the true characteristics of the Japanese people.

One of the reasons for this adulation may have been that Shusei was among the earliest modern writers to concern himself with "lower-class" characters, to abandon upper-class Meiji aspirations and to reflect the actual life, the "true characteristics" of Taisho/Showa people.

At the same time, this was the audience for whom he was writing—a popular audience for whom he adhered to generic conventions. As the translator, Richard Torrance, has explained, he "punished the rich and powerful and sympathetically portrayed the weak and oppressed."

Shusei is thus usually classed as a "naturalist," though he was sometimes denied the literary standing of his almost exact contemporary Shimazaki Toson. Perhaps it was this "lower-class" identification that disputed his literary status. Natsume Soseki complained that *Rough Living* contained (in Donald Keene's paraphrase) "nothing that was ennobling, nothing that could bring comfort or relief, nothing to suggest the joy of life."

Perhaps such descriptions have discouraged would-be translators. Though there have been several in French, until now there has been only one English translation of Shusei's work, the story "*Kunsho*," rendered as "The Order of the White Paulownia" by Ivan Morris. Thus the appearance of *Rough Living* (a translation of the 1915 novel *Arakure*) offers the opportunity to make the acquaintance of this naturalist author.

In *Rough Living*, probably his most famous novel, Shusei was explicit in his intensions: "I was trying to write about a modern person who is constantly in action, never revealing a flicker of interest in such concepts as *giri* and *ninjo*, extremely coarse-grained and unable to understand the feelings of others."

Oshima is thus a person who refuses the role that society has allotted her. Determined to get ahead in the world, she fights and struggles, attaching herself to one man after another, successfully clawing her way to success. During her various trials, she displays no insight at all into herself, and though she may weep at her plight, she then pulls herself together and does something about it. She is, indeed, the opposite of that social fiction, the demure and helpless maiden who becomes the good wife and wise mother.

We may now see her as a variation of the "modern woman," one who will no longer put up with the discrimination hitherto forced upon her. Oshima's determination, like that of the class from which she springs, is that of a healthy human demanding its rights.

Of such organized society does not often approve. Indeed, a literary descendent of Oshima went on to become the heroine of *Shukuzu* (*Miniature*, 1941) and landed her author in trouble. Though this rebellious geisha was, as Robert Rolf has written "treated in depth and with sympathy" the publication was halted by wartime authorities, and the work consequently never completed, and two years later the disappointed Shusei was dead.

Rough Living (a title which Donald Keene translated as *The Wild One* and which I rendered as *Untamed* when the novel was filmed), was written for serial publication. It is consequently highly episodic and, as is common with some Japanese popular literature, tells much more often than it shows.

Also, we are, to an extent, dealing with known types. No matter how often they appear, the characters wear their tags. Oshima's father, for example, is on most appearances called her "stern, old-fashioned father" There is also an amount of melodrama, people slashing about with straight razors, leaping into wells.

One is not then surprised to encounter the problems the translator writes of. Indeed, what to do with "she felt anger constricting her chest" or "her subdued heart sprang to life." These are, I am sure, perfectly adequate translations. The problem is that in English the thought itself seems inadequate—or at least adequate only in careless, popular publications.

Maybe that is the reason that I feel the novel was more adequately presented in its 1957 film version, written by Mizuki Yoko, directed by Naruse Mikio and with Takamine Hideko radiant as the untamed heroine. The melodramatics were toned down and stereotypical tags were not possible. Also nothing could be told to us because we had to be (this being the nature of film) shown.

Reading the novel itself, I was in the fortunate position of being able to visualize Takamine as Oshio and could understand her partners through such actors as Mori Masayuki, Kato Daisuke and Uehara Ken. For those who do not know the film and are consequently not so fortunate, this novel, though of major historical important, is perhaps of more sociological than literary interest.

Rough Living, by Tokuda Shusei, translated by Richard Torrance. Honolulu: University of Hawaii Press, 2001.

Tayama Katai

At the beginning of this century, the Japanese were still openly and avidly learning from abroad. Government missions were studying foreign methods, engineers were learning their trades in other lands, and artists were looking to other countries for both inspiration and technique.

In the arts, the current international style was

naturalism—an influence which took various forms upon reaching Japanese shores. A well known painter returned from abroad with Japan's first full-front nude, consequent police investigation and a narrowly averted prosecution. To public indignation, Japanese dramatists were beginning to explore low life in full detail. And novelists, following the reigning example of Zola, were displaying the often unattractive personal emotions upon which most social life is based.

Among these latter was Tayama Katai (1872–1930), a writer who was thirty-five years old when his *Futon* appeared in 1907, a work which raised him to instant fame and exposed him to immediate abuse.

A great reader of Zola, Hauptmann, Sudermann and Maupassant (references to whom stud his pages), Katai wanted to write about emotions as they actually were and not as society preferred to view them. He aimed for a new verisimilitude and thought, like most naturalists, that their mere recounting was enough. What acclaim he received was because this was an extremely new idea for Japan, and he is even now given credit for having instigated the idea of the *shishosetsu* novel form. The criticism was because official Japanese society then and now prefers the assumption of some ideal (specifically Confucian) basis and resents the wanton protrusion of reality.

Katai's self-appointed task was large, larger I feel than his talents warranted. *Futon*, for example, is naturalistically detailed but completely misses (does not even aim at) the assumption of detachment upon which any kind of realism, including naturalistic realism, must rest. "He was in torment, his thoughts in confusion. Feelings of jealousy, regret and vexation merged together and spun round his mind like a whirlwind." This kind of generalized description tells us nothing. Later on the same page, however, he does tell us something: "He just lounged in his wisteria chair—cold to the back now that it was coming into autumn—and gazed at the streaming rain ..." There is a realistic detachment in this latter example; there is only woolly description in the former.

Such overstated vagueness is much more typical of the very kind of Japanese writing which Katai was presumably fighting against. It is the opposite of the truly realistic new writing of the period, that mainly of Natsume Soseki, which was deliberately anti-heroic, purposely analytical, and depended upon a very real assumption of detachment.

Katai, then, is a minor writer who has come to stand for much of the intellectual ferment of his time and is accordingly locally admired. Since he has been so far little translated (into English, only the Sargent translation of "One Soldier"—though *Futon* has been translated into German), it is good to have the present collection which contains *Futon* and seven stories including "One Soldier." At the same time, however, I would also want to add that Katai is not to be compared with the great Meiji innovators, Mori Ogai and Natsume Soseki—though this opinion does not agree with those of Japanese scholars nor with that of the present translator.

I am in no position to attest to the fidelity of the translation. I do, however, have a few quibbles about presentation. Why are anachronisms permitted?—we have a policeman plunging into a crowd "to tell someone off" in a 1912 story, and in a 1908 tale, we are told that "when it gets to that state even a train's had it." And why such infelicities?—the hero is called "the young sir of a wealthy country family." Sadler (the example is from "One Soldier") translates it as "the eldest son of a prosperous country household." Even if "sir" is a misprint for "sire," the use of that antique word is still an infelicity, particularly when surrounded with such contemporary jargon as telling someone off and saying that something has had it.

Also, while I am at it, I think that the translator's introduction, too, inflates the importance of this particular author. If one is going to devote time and skill to the rendering of an author, one need not, and should not, be defensive. One ought, rather, to place him fairly. In the case of Katai we have a minor author of decided historical interest. Since that is what we have, such an introduction ought to have been enough.

The Quilt and Other Stories, by Tayama Katai, translated with an introduction by Kenneth G. Henshall. Tokyo: University of Tokyo Press, 1981.

Natsume Soseki

Now Japan's most celebrated novelist, Natsume Soseki (1876–1916) was delighted to leave the country in 1900. His marriage was not a happy one, and he disliked teaching in Kumamoto. Perhaps he thought he could find happiness in England. Whatever, he failed to do so. "The two years I spent in London," he later wrote, "were the most unpleasant years of my life. Among English gentlemen, I lived in misery, like a poor dog that had strayed among a pack of wolves."

He selected the place himself. Originally, he had thought to go to Cambridge but feared that his stipend from the Ministry of Education would not be enough. Then he fancied Edinburgh but was afraid of picking up a Scot's accent. And so he settled for London and moved from one awful lodging house to another. He had no letters of introduction, no good friends, no one to show him around. "Nor did I trust myself to a train or cab ... their cobweb system was so complicated."

Amid all this distrust, the English he met seemed

friendly. One of the guards at the Tower of London went out of his way to show him a suit of Japanese armor; when he wanted to witness Queen Victoria's funeral cortege and was too short to see what was happening, his landlord let him sit on his shoulders.

Nonetheless, Soseki elected to remain unhappy and based his later opinion of the English character upon those of the landladies and tradespeople with whom he unsuccessfully attempted to deal. Letters home urged wariness of uncritically accepting Western civilization. This unattractive helplessness is emphasized in a small essay he wrote while in dreadful London (though only published in 1905, back home) about his unhappy visit to the Tower of London.

Since he refused public transportation, he naturally had some difficulty locating the place, and once there he did not always know what he was looking at. He reports that the armor of Henry VI was "gorgeous" but that its owner must have been unusually tall. This was because he was really looking at the armor of Henry VIII having, it turns out, mistaken the label.

Still, looking around and observing things, he timidly began to enjoy himself. Though he was not equally polite to the guard who was polite to him ("I merely nodded without a word"), he did note that the pattern of his uniform, "a combination of straight lines … reminds me of an Ainu coat."

And at several historical spots, Soseki allowed himself reveries. One such was a vision of the two little princes in the Tower, and the resulting conversation of their assassins. He takes it all down: "When I strangled the boy, there was a quivering of his lily lips. The purple veins stood out on his clear forehead. Still I can hear his groans."

The influence is perhaps Shakespeare, one Englishman whom Soseki did like. However, he did not like him well enough to visit Stratford-upon-Avon when he had the opportunity, preferring to stay with his books in his awful room. And, in any event, he liked him mainly through what Carlyle had written about him. Carlyle Soseki really liked. He went to visit his famous house four times.

In later reveries, the Carlyle influence is noticeable. For example, an unknown lady is seeing the Tower in company of the Japanese author. He notices her always near; then he comes to realize that she is nothing other than the spirit of Lady Jane Grey, an innocent girl who "was like a rose pistil trampled to pieces, only to leave her fragrance up till today." He touches the wall. "My fingertips were all red. The blood shed in the 16th-century seemed to reappear and wet the floor or the 20th-century, I felt I could hear groans coming from behind the wall."

Peter Milward feels that rather than the Shakespearian influence Soseki claims, the spirit behind such fancies is more like Dickens or even Ainsworth. This is probably so. And behind them stands Ueda Akinori and other writers of the fantastic reverie based upon ancient history. This the author candidly admits, when in his postscript, he states that "the reader may think I have written the above as a statement of fact. But, in fact, it is mostly fictitious."

It is also negligible, but the author is not, and thus all kind of information is welcome. There is a Soseki Museum in London now, chronicling his misery, all five of the horrid boarding houses are identified (addresses given hopeful pilgrims in this edition), and here we have this damp *jeu d'esprit* through which the unhappy author kept his courage up, went back home, and wrote his finest work.

The Tower of London, by Natsume Soseki, translated and edited with an introduction, commentary and notes by Peter Milward and Nakano Kii. Brighton: In Print Publishing, Ltd., 1992.

In 1908, already an established popular writer, Natsume Soseki turned to more experimental forms of expression. Among these was his accounting of ten dreams he purportedly experienced. All are fairly dark. One finds a man killing pigs on the edge of a cliff over which he himself eventually tumbles; another is about a man being ridden by a blind child who turns out to be the son he once killed—simultaneously, he is his own descendant and his own ancestor.

Though all ten are as arbitrary as real dreams are, one is inclined to read further meaning into the collection. One of the reasons is that there is nothing more boring than listening to other people's dreams. Some sort of meaning seems to be required. Hence, the reader turns psychiatrist, and the critic begins to look for structure. Another reason, however, is that it is possible to see the pig dream as a kind of allegory on the problems of the individual in society, and the blind boy as having something to do with questions of identity in the Meiji era.

Both of these were major concerns of Soseki. Indeed, they constitute two of his major themes. He later incorporated them in *Sanshiro*, that classic study of a search for identity which he began just after he had transcribed his ten dreams; and in his masterpiece, that study of a solitary individual, *Kokoro*.

Ten Nights' Dreams, though not perhaps the most popular of Soseki's works, has long appealed to translators. One of the earliest versions in English (by Miyamori Asataro) first appeared in 1917, followed by an anonymous translation in 1922 and one by Hara Sankichi and Shirai Dofu in 1934. Postwar translations include that by Earl Miner and Oura Yukio, 1961, another by Ito Aiko and Graeme Wilson, 1969, and the present translation. There was also from the 1950s one by George Saito, though it is not included in either the Kodansha nor the P.E.N. listings of Japanese literature in foreign languages.

The present translation is the work of five translators—though only one is mentioned on the title page. Consequently, the reader will not find a single style, the unified tone which might be otherwise expected. Each of the five does two dreams each, and there are consequent stylistic differences. In addition, since they are all translating out of their own language and into a language not their own, there are anomalies.

One of the most persistent is the use of indirect discourse when Soseki specified direct discourse. This smoothes the text, to be sure, but it also adds an anodyne quality not often encountered in so specific a writer as Soseki. At the same time, however, there is a tendency toward another kind of specificity which the foreign translator avoids.

For example, when the man carrying the blind child reaches the grave marker, he finds, in this translation, that the characters on the stone were "scarlet like the stomach of a newt." In the Oura/Miner translation this is given as "bright as the marking of a lizard," a description which fits the ascribed literary tone but is, in fact, not precisely what Soseki wrote.

In the eighth dream, the dreamer finds himself on a large ship. It is filled with foreigners and is proceeding West. He asks a crew member who replies with a song. Oura/Miner have the final lines as: "So we float along on the waves, the rudder our pillow, drifting, drifting along." The present translators, having decided that the song was a "sea shanty," have rendered this as "My ship is my home and ever I roam. Sail on, sail on, sail on. Ho!"

Vagaries of translation aside, one may, I think, find this dream frankly allegorical. Japan is sailing West and is filled with foreigners, and the solitary Soseki wants off. In the dream he jumps overboard. In real life, a like situation made him just as miserable but had a less permanent result.

This was the trip to London in 1900 where the West

was finally met face to face. How surprised he would have been to see that this modest translation has been published to celebrate his arrival in London a hundred years ago. And how astonished he would be to learn that it is the work of a Soseki Museum in London, located right across the street from where he lived in Clapham.

Ten Nights' Dreams, by Natsume Soseki, translated by Kashima Takumi, Nonaka Kyoko, Oiwa Hideki, Kawashima Horikatsu, Fujioka Katsunori. London: Soseki Museum in London, 2000.

In the autumn of 1909, Natsume Soseki, by then a well known author in Japan, was invited to tour Manchuria and Korea. The invitation was from the South Manchurian Railway Company, the president of which was an old school friend. The company picked up all the expenses, and the *Asahi Shimbun*, the newspaper which published Soseki, encouraged the project. The young railway would profit by association with the author's name, the newspaper would sell more copies when the results were published, and government policy would be gratified.

Soon, however, things went wrong with this publicity scheme. For one thing, Soseki was not well. He suffered much from stomach ulcers (a complaint which would eventually kill him), and every page is as devoted to the trials of gastritis as it is to the glories of the far-flung Japanese empire.

Too, the author seems to have been at least somewhat aware that he was being used for political purposes. A particularly sincere author, he coped with this by fully revealing his former schoolboy association with the railway president and picturing himself as awkward, a jocular ploy which had proved popular in such works as *Botchan* and *I Am a Cat*.

In the very first sentence of the journal, the author

ingenuously wonders aloud just what exactly this Southern Manchurian Railway Company is, to which his school pal, now the president, can say: "Old boy, you really are a fool!" This exchange sets the tone for what is to follow. Soseki is the blundering but well-meaning intellectual amid all the power people who run the railway, the occupation of Manchuria, and the Japanese government itself.

That this is a distancing device comes ever more clear as the account progresses. Though Soseki was truly a bad traveler (as his disastrous sojourn in England indicates), he now had more reasons to be (ulcers, being used for advertising), and he outdid himself on this Manchurian jaunt. In fact, he never reaches his destination. Though the account's title speaks of both Manchuria and Korea, he stops writing while still in the former occupied area and never gets to the peninsula so soon itself to be occupied.

A number of reasons for this have been given. One is that he much admired Laurence Stern who in his *A Sentimental Journey through France and Italy* never gets to Italy. Another is that this Manchurian travel journal was published up the end of the year (1909), and the paper thought it fitting to begin the new year with something else.

A perhaps more likely reason for the dropping of both the journal and its publication, however, was that during this season Ito Hirobumi was assassinated by a Korean secessionist. This prompted the *Asahi* to run a vitriolic series entitled "Dreadful Korea." It ran side by side with Soseki's Manchurian pieces and must have caused the author many a gastric attack. But the new series on dreadful Korea served the government's purposes. During the next year Japan would annex that unhappy peninsula and (for a time) enlarge its overseas empire.

Soseki's unhappiness with the project upon which he is engaged shines forth from every page. He, who once criticized *Gulliver's Travels* for being too political, now found himself in a political adventure which he did his best to poeticized. He talks about the color of the sky, the sea, about various natural sights such as the flights of northern birds. He carries this to such an extreme, jumping from one safely poetic subject to the next, that dissatisfied readers gave the journal the name of *Soseki Here and There* (*Soseki Tokoro Dokoro*), a play on the original title, *Here and There in Manchuria and Korea.* (*Mankan Tokoro Dokoro*).

The author has also been criticized for finding the Chinese dirty and for using pejorative terminology ("*chang*," somewhat like the now ostracized English "chink"), but political correctness had not yet been invented in 1909, and Soseki was merely echoing public opinion, no matter how deplorable we may now find that opinion to have been.

One might more fairly criticize the author for getting himself into such a compromised venture in the first place and then to have continued even when he knew what it was. His old school pal states his own intentions clearly: "You know, it is interesting to go and have a look at what the Japanese are doing abroad. Guys like you who know nothing at all take patronizing attitudes and create misunderstandings."

But Soseki swallowed no bait. He was not about to endorse his country's expansionist ambitions. Instead, he talks about the local soybean soap, the beauty of the northern sky, the curious situation at Mukden where the ground "had for countless centuries been saturated with urine and excrement," with "the disastrous results still noticeable in the drinking water." And, on one page, he exposes the whole set-up. His companion asks just how far they will travel and Soseki says: "Well, if I didn't reach Harbin, it would look bad."

The translators in the preface plainly state that this has long been Soseki's least popular book, and it has certainly had to wait longest for an English translation. One may say that it is a project which the author himself aborted, and he himself rarely referred to it—nor does anyone else: Donald Keene does not mention it in his monumental survey.

At the same time, however, it is an interesting glimpse into the mind of the author and a lesson on how to comport oneself in a difficult situation. Also, in case of an author this good as well as this famous (his face is on that thousand-yen bill in your pocket), one must read just everything.

Rediscovering Natsume Soseki: Travels in Manchuria and Korea, introduction and translation by Inger Sigrun Brodey and Sammy I. Tsunematsu. Folkestone, Kent: Global Books, 2000.

Natsume Soseki's 1914 novel *Kokoro* is one of the finest works of Japanese fiction. As Donald Keene has written of it, the book "succeeds in a manner that marks Soseki as a writer of the first magnitude: The story is simple, but the characterization is not."

Neither is the structure—it is a complex system of parallels which illuminate the story without ever commenting upon it. The young student, drawn to his teacher, finds in him a father while denying his own. He loses both and, in so doing, is himself guilty of an act which resembles that committed long ago by his teacher and which may account for the latter's suicide.

This tight shape is beautifully fleshed out and articulated in a spare narrative which supports the largely unstated moral of the work. To identify this is to cheapen Soseki's intentions, but most critics agree that it has to do with egotism and the lack of human understanding that ensues.

It is fitting then that this new edition of *Kokoro* includes a translation of the famous 1914 essay, "My Individualism," which has many connections with the novel. (Also included is the 1911 essay, "The Civilization of Modern Day Japan.")

In the essay on individualism, candid and disarming, Soseki says that he discovered that "my only hope for salvation lay in fashioning for myself a conception of what literature is." What he discovered was an ability for introspection. "Self-centeredness became for me a new beginning ... I found a belief that I could get my hands on, the conviction that I was the single most important person in my life."

This was probably said smiling, and the author was quick to add that "one must grant others the freedom to develop their individuality for the sake of their personal happiness, even as one secures it for oneself ... I can turn left, while you turn right, each of us equally unhindered so long as what we do has no effect on others. This is what I mean when I speak of individualism."

The "best of Soseki" is thus packaged but the editorial presentation is inadequate since little scholarly care is evidenced. The translators are not identified, nor is the publishing history of the translations. For the otherwise uninformed reader, then, this translation of *Kokoro* originally appeared in 1957 from Henry Regnery, Chicago. Edwin McClellan is the distinguished translator of several other Soseki works, among them *Grass on the Wayside*. Jay Rubin is a major authority on Soseki and his times. He is the translator of *Sanshiro*, and the author of that major work, the 1984 *Injurious to Public Morals: Writers and the Meiji State*. His translation of "My Individualism" originally appeared in *Monumentica Nipponica* (34:1) 1979.

Kokoro: A Novel and Selected Essays, by Natsume Soseki, translated by Edwin McClellan and Jay Rubin. Lanham: Madison Books, 1992.

With the republication of *And Then* (*Sorekara*, 1909), Natsume Soseki's "first trilogy" becomes locally available in paper. As the quotation marks indicate, these "trilogies" are not unified by their chronologies, nor do the same characters appear in the various volumes. Nonetheless, the themes particularly in the first "trilogy" are intimately connected. Soseki himself explained that *And Then* would be about the same kind of main character "in a more advanced state" and that the final volume would lead a similar kind of character to yet further "advancement."

If "advancement" is at all the proper term, because in these three books we see a young and inexperienced student, Sanshiro (a serious Botchan) turn into the definitely alienated Daisuke (the main character of *And Then*), who, in turn, becomes the punished, if accepting, Sosuke of *The Gate*, now definitely outside society—a most uncomfortable place for anyone but particularly so for a Japanese.

In her illuminating "afterword," Norma Field speaks of this "black sheep" theme in all of Soseki's mature work—and some of his immature as well, *Botchan*, for example. It is really the delineation of this decline which concerns this "trilogy" and which binds its parts together.

While the middle years of the Meiji Period are still officially seen as decades of progress and glory, Soseki saw them as they also were—years during which the Japanese were subjected to the most intense dislocation. "Modern society was nothing more than an aggregate of isolated individuals. The earth stretched boundlessly, but the instant [that] houses were built upon it, it became fragmented. The people inside the houses became fragmented, too. Civilization took the collective we and transformed it into isolated individuals." All Japanese, in this sense, became black sheep.

Daisuke, like all the characters in the "trilogy" is filled with unknowing, packed full of unawareness. The hope of Sanshiro is gone and the tranquility of Sosuke is yet to come. Though quite capable of cynicism (speaking of his parent's noble "service to society and country," he says: "If serving society and country earns you as much money as it has Father, I wouldn't mind doing it either ..."), he is quite incapable of that kind of objectivity which would allow him to become what he is.

This leads directly to an existential crisis and the (possible) madness which ends the book. "Daisuke, who had been quietly soaking in the water, mechanically lifted his right hand to his left breast; no sooner had he heard the throbbing of life" than he, terrified, quit the tub. "There, sitting cross-legged on the floor, he stared absently at his legs. They began to look strange. They no longer seemed to grow from his trunk at all, but rather, completely unconnected, they sprawled rudely before him ..."

Passages like this are amazing for 1909 and completely unique in pre-World War II Japanese literature. Not until Sartre's *La Nausée* would such dislocating observations become common. What is being described is, precisely, existential shock, that awareness of self as "other."

It is Soseki's superb delineation of these passages (based, it is said, in part upon his own "breakdown") which makes the middle volume, *And Then*, the finest and the darkest of the three books. Daisuke almost discovers the truth—discovers enough to know that he cannot live with it as he is. In describing it, Soseki indicates that he himself could and did.

The trilogy as a whole (and the quotation marks may now be dropped since the three volumes are seen as unified by this painfully aware accounting of a lack of awareness) gives a very lively picture of middle-Meiji, but this middle volume presents a reflection of all of us.

And Then, by Natsume Soseki, translated by Norma Field. Baton Rouge: Louisiana State University, 1978.

Nagai Kafu

In 1903 a young man who was to become one of Japan's finest writers left for the United States. He did not particularly want to go—he would much have preferred France—but his father insisted.

Kafu, the pen name the young man was later to take, had proved a disappointment to his bureaucrat parent. The trip was to give him enough prestige to return as a *kichosha* (a person who had been abroad) and settle down as a respectable businessman.

This he was determined not to do and though he moved around the country (Tacoma, Seattle, Kalamazoo, Washington, D.C., New York) he wasted no time learning trading expertise or American know-how. Instead, he profitably spend his years (five, including one in France) by observing what he saw and jotting it down.

On the West Coast, he saw (and experienced) prejudice. "The way Japanese people are ostracized in this place is almost unbelievable ... no decent house or apartment will rent to Japanese or Chinese." At the same time he chronicled the awful way that these stigmatized people turned against each other—as stigmatized minorities will.

He talked with many of the people there and recorded the degrees of their unhappiness, but he also knew that "the United States is a country where you can see both the best and worst in society, so that it is possible for a person to go in either direction, following his inclination."

Kafu's own inclinations had been formed first by being upper- middle-class Japanese and second by becoming early besotted with French literature. He was thus gifted with a kind of double vision.

He saw America through Japanese eyes. The Saint Louis Exposition was a "nightless city," after the example of Tokyo's Yoshiwara. The train trip from Kalamazoo to Chicago was "like passing by the vicinities of Shimbashi and Shinagawa." Mount Rainier became the "Tacoma Fuji," and New York turned into something in a late Japanese print.

"From the tall Times building and the Astor Hotel up north to the opera house and the faraway Herald Square with department stores like Macy's and Saks Fifth Avenue in the other direction, the rows of buildings loom like clouds ... only from the windows, higher up and lower down, lights are shining like stars, or fireflies."

The twenty-three-year-old's other lens was French literature. The *American Stories* are studded with quotes from Verlaine and, Kafu's favorite, Baudelaire. New York's Chinatown is, for example, described in terms of Victor Hugo and its pleasures are referred back to Baudelaire's *paradis artificiels* (sic). The major French contribution, however, was the stance offered the young Japanese traveler. He could assume the role of *flâneur*—one cultivated by Baudelaire himself—the stroller on the pavement, the uninvolved observer, he who sees the heights and depths but remains himself unmoved.

The stance served him well. How unlike Kafu was to Natsume Soseki, miserable in London. Both may have been lonely, but Kafu had an excuse for it—the *flâneur* is always lonely. It is part of the definition. "Alone," he says, sitting in Central Park, "looking at each occupant of the passing cars, I comment endlessly on the person's choice of fashion and degree of tastefulness." His apartness became not only a protection but also a way to communicate.

From this comes the authentic Kafu tone—apart but empathetic. Though it occurs little enough in an early work such as this collection, there are pregnant passages: "As the piano and violin played on, the sight of sailors and laborers embracing these women ... in a dim electric light that was yellow from the dust on the floor, the smoke from cigarettes, and the smell of alcohol, gave me an indescribable sensation of pathos, going beyond disgust or detestation."

This sense of pathos in ordinary things—identified as Japanese, though this country certainly has no monopoly on it—is in the work of Kafu particularly linked to the lives of prostitutes, and here the double lenses of old Japan and literary France fuse.

The best of these American stories, "Ladies of the Night," is a description of goings on in a high-class New York whore-house in the spring of 1907. Its great anthropological interest is surpassed by the artistry with which the scene is conveyed. Kafu sees and feels everything, but he is never mentioned. He is not there at all except as a compassionate observer, alive to the pathos of these lives around him.

In "Midnight at a Bar," he is downtown, just off Chatham Square, watching the misbehavior of the lower-classes. But it is not a matter of class. It is the matter of being human, a classless state. And it is the pathos of this condition which Kafu so clearly sees and which, after he had returned to Japan, he would so successfully communicate in such masterpieces as the 1921 *Quiet Rain* and the 1937 *A Strange Tale from East of the River*.

That his theories about prostitutes were backed up by healthy practice is something well known. While he was sitting in a bar in Washington, the woman next to him struck up a conversation. Later, he confided to his diary (not included in the *American Stories*) that "at her invitation, I went to her house." This began a fairly long affair with Edyth (for such was her name), one which provided the template, as it were, for those lovely, lonely relationships (such as that with O-Yuki in *A Strange Tale from East of the River*), which so distinguish the Kafu page.

(Edyth, incidentally, goes strangely unmentioned in

Iriye Mitsuko's otherwise informative introduction. The full story is wonderfully told in Edward Seidensticker magisterial *Kafu the Scribbler* and further details are to be found in the Kafu sections of Donald Keene's *Modern Japanese Diaries*.)

It is perhaps telling that once out of America and into longed-for France, Kafu did not like it. He made, indeed, something of a specialty of not liking where he was. He loathed Meiji Japan until it became Taisho Japan, then he longed for Meiji. Ditto for Showa. But this too is part of *flâneur*-ship. It is essentially antiquarian since it looks for timeless values in the transient present.

And even in a work as uneven and, at times, as callow as the *Amerika Monogatari* (and continuing in the *Furansu Monogatari* which followed) there are passages which clearly foreshadow the hard-boiled compassion of this vulnerable observer.

The work was an instant success in Japan when it was published in 1908 because it gave such first-hand news of what had not hitherto been reported. We now read it because of the angle from which Kafu viewed America—one which both preserved and illuminated what he saw happening, one which insisted upon the pathos of all existence.

American Stories, by Nagai Kafu, translated with an introduction by Iriye Mitsuko. New York: Columbia University Press, 2000.

Young Kimie, straight from the provinces and into prewar Tokyo, had already slept with so many men that she'd lost count. A waitress working in the newly popular cafes, she had "never sought the kind of love that is described in novels." And "that is why she had never experienced the emotion called jealousy."

"Rather than have one man deeply fall for her, and because of that enduring his angers and grudges ... Kimie thought it best to frolic on the spot, as the spirit moved her and to her heart's content with anyone who presented himself, be he young or old, handsome or ugly. That way there was no bad aftertaste."

With the creation of Kimie, heroine of the 1931 *During the Rains* (*Tsuyu no Atosaki*), Kafu sprang back into literary prominence. Tanizaki Jun'ichiro was among the first to recognize that here was a major work, one which continued a major theme. Major in a double sense. The vital scramblings of the Tokyo demi-monde had been a major concern of the author just as it had been of much Edo literature. This Tanizaki recognized when he said that "the oldness of the form stands in subtle contrast to the modern colors of the material."

In quoting this, Edward Seidensticker in his *Kafu the Scribbler* says that, in this work, the view unveiled is that "of a muddy expanse, dotted here and there by an unmade bed and an unwashed chemisette." True, but such a prospect —and I am sure that Seidensticker would be the first to agree—is not without its charm.

The charm of the proletariat at play, the appeal of the open watonness of the poor, has its darker side—indeed such a display of *la nostalgie de la boue* tells much about the wealthier person indulging in it. Yet it just this which animates an entire strain of Japanese literature—from Saikaku and the *gesaku* writers, through Nagai Kafu, the late Yoshiyuki Junnosuke and beyond into even such further fields as the films of Imamura Shohei.

The raffish author, who is a connoisseur of such good times, runs, however, the risk of moral disapproval. Donald Keene writes of this work: "Kafu may have been impelled to write [it] in his capacity as the chronicler of disappearing Tokyo because he feared that cafes and waitresses might not survive the rigors of … the war with China, but readers of a later generation are likely to decide that this would have been no great loss: Kimie and her friends arouse little nostalgia."

Kimie is neither lovable nor pitiful. Keene feels but "the reader does not despise her either, and her last gesture, giving herself to an old man out of compassion, recalls the courtesan's generosity, as described in a work of Edo fiction."

This gesture is also, just as importantly, completely in character. A pragmatic young person, she is free from social cant. She is thus capable of disinterested actions such as—a marvelous passage—her giving herself to the old man. Kafu's demi-mondiennes deserve more approbation than blame.

They deserve something like admiration, as is seen in this beautiful passage in which the author further describes Kimie. "Everything about her, not just particular parts of her body, breathed out a lovely, alluring charm not to be seen in a respectable woman. Such charm, no doubt, was the same in kind as the difference in the everyday demeanor of a tea-ceremony master from that of an ordinary person, or the physical alertness of a swordsman even at his most relaxed."

Equally worthy of regard is the kept-man hero of *Flowers in the Shade* (*Hikage no Hana*, 1934). Jukichi has lived off women ever since his school days and has rightly come to regard this as a kind of profession. It has its demands, like any other line of work, and he, a good *shokunin* satisfies them to the best of his abilities.

Kafu reveals in this working-man's relations with his older lover-employer a tenderness, a dedication and moral acuity which is both amusing and touching. Theirs is almost a parody of a proper marriage and yet, at the same time, there exists true feeling.

This is based upon a pragmatic regard of things as they are and an acceptance which dignifies necessity. O-Chiyo, the older woman, does not want to prostitute herself to get money for life with Jukichi, but when an earlier customer returns and says he must have the same woman as before, she cannot refuse. "And so, night by night, O-Chiyo descended further into the depths. However, she was able not only to pay off the interest at the pawnshop but to pay in full that month's back rent."

This nod in the direction of convention ("the depths") followed by a precise account which amounts to a vindication is typical of Kafu and is indeed what makes him one of the most honest of authors. This candor is difficult to catch (Seidensticker's translations are a master class on how to get tone exactly right) and, as will have been seen in the quotes above, Lane Dunlop well duplicates the nods and the deflations which make Kafu such a moving author.

Though little enough is translated, (the Seidensticker volume, parts of *Udekurabe* [*Geisha in Rivalry*], some uncollected shorter pieces), it is apparent to the Western reader that here is one of the finest of modern Japanese novelists.

During the Rains and Flowers in the Shade, by Nagai Kafu, translated by Lane Dunlop. Stanford: Stanford University Press, 1994.

Saito Mokichi

A well known, even popular poet famous for his devotion to the *tanka*, Saito Mokichi (1882–1953) wrote 17 full collections and had a "*tanka*-life" which extended nearly 50 years. The authors of this new translation speak of his "enormous, almost monumental devotion to the form."

They have also accepted what might have been

Mokichi's definition of the form itself when they write that "the *tanka*, as poetry, is so connected to a poet's life that, like the I-novel of Japanese literature, one must examine that life and those elements that shaped it."

While this is certainly true of Mokichi's version of the *tanka*, it is not true for that of others. The 31-syllable, poem, consisting of five lines in the pattern 5-7-5-7-7, is a poetic form of many uses, only one of which might be the autobiographical.

At the same time, the uses of the *tanka* certainly shifted between the 8th and the 20th-century, as did the needs of the poets. The fortunes of the *tanka* were at low ebb before it was once again taken up by Yosano Akiko, Ishikawa Takuboku, Masaoka Shiki (Tsunenori) and Mokichi at the end of the 19th and beginning of the 20th-century. The translators call their subject "one of *tanka*'s saviors." Certainly, he found new uses for the form, among them the strictly biographical.

One of the ways in which poems could be made to serve as chronicle was to compose sequences devoted to the same subjects. Thus, the famous *Sad Tidings* sequence which begins the *Red Lights* collection is a series of 10 poems reflecting the state of mind of the poet upon hearing of the death of Ito Sachio, the poet who had done so much to encourage Mokichi.

The focus is not only autobiographical, it is deeply interior. What is important is not the death of Ito but the disturbed feelings of Mokichi. The translators maintain that "read in sequence, these *tanka* vividly describe the movement of the poet's mind in the same way that successive frames of a cinema film reproduce a man's motion."

This is the technique of *rensaku*, a chain of compositions on the same subject for a total effect amalgamating what is seen and what is felt. It was also, perhaps, the first time that what was felt took such extraordinary precedence.

A frankly interior view, it may well have accounted for the great popularity of *Red Lights* when it was first published in 1913. Everyone likes psychology, the baring of strong emotions, even—or particularly—psychodrama. This Mokichi offers in such abundance that the translators' claim that his *rensaku* form a kind of "I-novel" seems justified.

This being so, one would have thought that every piece of this vast psychodrama would be necessary for the complete presentation of the poet's life since, when everything is as arbitrary as this, everything counts.

The publishers, however, did not think so. To include all 834 *tanka* in the collection, along with the *romaji* renderings, the notes and the long introduction would have required too many pages. So, "we had to decrease the number of *tanka*," with the result that 298, more than a third, have been left out.

Consequently, the subtitle must speak of "selected" *tanka* sequences, though we are assured that only the better were selected. However, when all bear the same biographical burden, what does better mean? And in any event, when one publishes a work, one publishes it.

But often, particularly in academic presses, books fall prey to formats. I remember Keiko McDonald's full-length study of the film director Mizoguchi Kenji, which lost many of its most valuable pages because the publisher insisted upon cramming her book into format size.

Purdue's is then an editorial decision with which one may disagree, particularly in that the translators had done their work well and translated the entire cycle. Certainly better to have cut the *romaji*, particularly since the poems are already printed in a bilingual format.

Even better, perhaps, to have shortened the long and somewhat hagiographical introduction which seems to insist upon every last detail, including some curious ones, such as Mokichi (also a practicing psychiatrist) being the doctor who prescribed the sleeping pills with which the author Akutagawa Ryunosuke ended his life.

Having said this, one must, at the same time, welcome this partial translation as the first substantial rendering of Mokichi into English. There had been good translations of several lyrics by both Howard Hibbett and Edith Shiffert, but this is the first extended translation.

Red Lights: Selected Tanka Sequences from Shakko, by Saito Mokichi, translated with an introduction and notes by Shinoda Seishi and Sanford Goldstein. West Lafayette, IN: Purdue University Press, 1989.

Santoka

The poet Santoka (born Taneda Shoichi in 1882) led an early life of particular unhappiness. His mother killed herself, his own marriage failed, any business to which he turned his hand foundered, and he could find respite only in alcohol. Finally, in 1924, in middle-age, he decided to end it all.

Just in time, the train screeched to a halt, and the unharmed Santoka was taken to a nearby Zen temple. There he was not questioned nor reprimanded, not even his name was asked. Instead, he was fed and told to stay at the temple as long as he wished.

Two years later, with his only possessions—his priest's robe, his straw hat, and his begging bowl—he set off, and for the rest of his life (he died in 1940) he became a mendicant Zen monk, following the tradition of the earliest Chinese sages and also such later wanderers as the poet-monks Ikkyu and Ryokan.

It has been estimated that, during these years, he walked more than 28,000 miles. It has never been estimated how much he begged, but it could not have been very much. Usually, he had to visit no more than 20 homes before he had received, enough for the day. As soon as enough rice and money had been received, he stopped begging, never providing for the next day. "How," he once asked, "can you be a beggar if you have extra money?"

During all of this walking and begging, Santoka also meditated. His was not the Zen of sitting nor the Zen of the *koan*; his was the older Chinese form of Zen which consisted of putting one foot in front of the other, gaining (says Santoka's translator and editor) "realization through contact with nature on long pilgrimages from one mountain temple to another."

This Santoka celebrated in one of his haiku: "Without anger, without speaking/Without covetousness/Walk slowly, walk steadily!" For Santoka was a haiku-making Zen priest (ordained finally at 44), like Ryokan and like Basho—whose narrow road to the deep north he had once retraced.

Indeed haiku (along with sake) had been his solace in the earlier part of his life. Now haiku (again, along with sake) sustained him on his rigorous marches all over Kyushu, Shikoku and southern Honshu. How many haiku he wrote (and what his apparently voluminous journals contained) will never be known because he used to destroy his manuscripts if he found himself becoming too attached to them.

Into the thousands certainly, these haiku—and most of them imbued with the spirit of Zen which he was recreating in himself—as in the most famous of his poems: "If there are mountains, I look at the mountains; On rainy days I listen to the rain/Spring, summer, autumn, winter/Tomorrow too will be good./Tonight too is good."

The years passed. Santoka's walking figure became well known. Often the figure also lurched. On occasion, he was even arrested for public drunkenness. He himself said he could do only three things: walk, drink sake, and make haiku. But he could also do a fourth—he could bring them all together, as in one of his finest poems: "Sake for the body, haiku for the heart/Sake is the haiku of the body/Haiku is the sake of the heart."

Then one day, after a poetry meeting during which Santoka had been quite intoxicated, the wife of one of the poets went to see if the poet was still sleeping. He was dead—having lived two lives: first, the tragedy-filled existence common to us all; second, that extraordinary and illuminated experience, a record of which he has left us in his poetry.

Santoka, both as a poet and a person, has only recently become widely known. At present, however, says his translator, "more books on Santoka are available than perhaps on any other Japanese poet, ancient or modern." In addition, he has come to be rightfully regarded as a great Zen-poet in the tradition of Ikkyu, Haikuin and Ryokan. It is perhaps telling that his deserved elevation occurs only now in a materialistic, commercialized Japan—the kind of Japan that badly needs someone like Santoka.

And it is now also that the first collection of his verse in English appears. (Heretofore, there have been only translations of a few by James Abrams and, notably, R.H. Blyth.) Over 370 of Santoka's poems (mostly "modern" haiku in form) have been gathered and uniformly well translated. The poems are given both in *romaji* and in their English versions and capture well the spirit, the patience, the dedication, and the honesty of the man who could write: "My heart is weary—/The mountains, the sea/Are too beautiful."

Mountain Tasting: Zen Haiku, by Taneda Santoka, translated and introduced by John Stevens. New York: Weatherhill, Inc., 1980.

Nagatsuka Takashi

The Soil—usually translated *The Earth* (*Tsuchi*)—is the best known of the novels by the poet Nagatsuka Takashi. Originally printed in 1910, it is a detailed and partially autobiographical description of the hardships of the traditional farmer's life. The dirt-poor hero loses his wife when she attempts to abort a baby she knows she cannot feed. He tries to get along with only his daughter to help, but since he must steal to feed his family, he creates bad relations with the other farmers. Yet, finally, after a disastrous fire, he comes to accept the closeness of the community.

Written with no apparent political purpose, the novel—as Donald Keene has noted "differs from later 'proletarian' writings on the peasantry in that Nagatsuka put forth no thesis, but seems to have had no other object than to present an accurate description of his subject."

Nonetheless, political uses were shortly discovered for the book. Marxist critics, to be sure, could find no good in a book on peasants written by a landlord's son, and leftist readers during the 1920s could find little about an oppressed proletariat in a novel which had nothing to say about the causes of rural poverty or its coming cure.

Still, other uses were found. It was discovered, as Japan mobilized for war in the 1930s, that the book could be perceived as a celebration of community. A drama was made of the book and, in 1939, a movie by Uchida Tomu. Here the message was that, everyone working together, a New Order was possible.

Such interpretations were far from the intentions of the author. Following his teacher—Shiki (Masaoka) and his objective descriptions of nature in what became known as the *shasei* style—Nagatsuka refused to judge his people, politically or otherwise.

This admirable stand was not observed by subjective critics. From the very first, the book excited passions. Originally serialized in the *Tokyo Asahi*, the author was midway requested to wrap up the story as soon as possible because "the common reader" did not appear to like it.

Natsume Soseki, who had originally encouraged Nagatsuka, found that the results were most distasteful. The author, he wrote, "portrays every detail of [these peasants] almost beastly, impoverished lives. He describes their vulgarity, shallowness, superstitiousness, simple-mindedness, cunning ..."

Other vaunting men of Meiji agreed that those who read the book would "feel themselves dragged into the mud," and Nagatsuka received no credit at all for having written what was, in fact, Japan's first unaligned naturalistic novel.

Gratuitous interpretation of the work continued. After World War II, the novel became a quaint reminder of what Japan had once been like and as Ann Waswo writes in her interesting introduction, *Tsuchi* took its place among other gentrifications (real *irori* in fake *inaka ryoriya*) attracting urban tourists.

Now cleansed of all the mud originally thrown at it, the novel has achieved the sterile eminence of becoming a part of the Japanese language section of the university entrance examinations. The opening passage is quoted, followed by eight multiple-choice questions. And so the novel is now read because the Education Ministry likes its collective flavor and because students want to pass exams.

This opening passage affords the reader some indication of the style: "The powerful west wind had tormented the forest all day, striking the trees with invisible blows until the leafless branches moaned in pain.... Abruptly the wind ceased [and] as if remembering their suffering, the branches trembled from time to time, their rustling breaking the eerie silence."

Whether one wishes to endure such a heavy dose of the pathetic fallacy must be up to individual judgment, but it should be remembered that nature anthropomorphized is very much a part of the Japanese poetic tradition and that Shiki himself would have found nothing pathetic in the above passage.

The present translation is suitably plain, and, as Waswo has indicated in her introduction, her major interest is in an ethnographic reading of the novel: "It has been as a historian and not as a specialist in literature that I have approached the task," she writes. Consequently, her style is factual, laconic—one which suits the author's intention. Her's, however, is not the only English translation available. Kawamura Yasuhiro (thanked in this edition for helpful comments) himself published in Tokyo a 1986 translation (unmentioned in this edition) which suggests a different perspective.

The Soil: A Portrait of Rural Life in Meiji Japan, by Nagatsuka Takashi, translated with an introduction by Ann Waswo. Berkeley: University of California Press, 1989.

Ogawa Mimei

An anomalous figure, Ogawa Mimei (1882–1961) was a fantasist who later became a socialist, a fairy-tale author who almost became an anarchist. He fits few literary categories and, consequently, plays a small part in literary histories. Ogawa is remembered, however, for his children's stories—short works penned between those he thought more important, such as the socially concerned *To the Lowest Rung of the Ladder* (*Soko no Shakai e*, 1914) and *Death of a Tenant Farmer* (*Kosakunin no Shi*, 1918).

The children's tales live on and have given the would-be

anarchist the unavoidable sobriquet of "the Hans Christian Andersen of Japan." A number have been translated. A first collection, *The Rose and the Witch*, appeared in 1925, the work of Myrtle McKenney. It was followed by another collection, *Tipsy Star* (1957), translated by Akiyama Yoshiko. Other translators of single stories include Kanayama Atsumu (1962) and John Bester (1964).

Of the 25 stories collected in this volume, only three have been previously translated (the title story, "The Cow Woman" and "A Big Crab"), and the interested English-language reader will find much that is new. All, however, as one would expect, have similarities.

Many are laid in the far north (Ogawa, like the much more famous Miyazawa Kenji, whom he sometimes resembles, was born in Tohoku) and are concerned with cold, snow and ice. Most are about children of what the author would have called "the proletariat." Like Andersen's little match girl, they are mainly undeserving victims of what the author would also have described as the class struggle.

Sometimes they are not, however. It depends upon which phase of Ogawa's political career they came from. By 1920, he was a member of the Japanese Socialist League and the Japan Fabian Society, but when the socialist movement came under the control of Marxists in the mid-20s, he joined an anarchist writers' group that formed in reaction, before deciding to free himself entirely from this involvement.

What the stories have in common is that, like Miyazawa's, they rise above political concerns and describe a child's world in terms a child would understand. They are all, for example, animistic. Everything thinks, and most things react: "The coals in the trolley laughed, showing their pretty, glittering teeth." Here, mountains talk, trees proclaim, and stars murmur—there is a consciousness in everything.

Despite this, the stories rarely descend to sentimentality (which those of the Danish Ogawa Mimei almost always do). Further, they do not reveal themselves as symbolic or allegorical, or contain beneath their often sweet surface the sour core of a moral precept intended to help turn the child into an adult.

For a man who apparently believed in the constraints of socialism (and the even heavier burden of anarchy in which you have to make your own organizational rules), these stories are surprisingly free.

A seal has lost her pup and laments. The moon takes pity and looks for it. He does not find it, but he does find a drum. This he gives to the bereaved mother: "The seal seemed pleased. Several days later, when the moon lit up the sea, the ice was beginning to thaw, and the moon heard the sound of the drum among the waves." The end.

Story after story ends in no way the reader could have expected. This I take to be a strength. When "nothing happens," one may be sure that something is happening in an unexpected way. A result is that even adults (me) start somehow "believing" in these mythic non-fables. That a socialist could encourage such individuality argues that the author knew the world to be a more complicated and personal place than his politics allowed.

The same is true of his work for adults. In "Aerial Stunt" (*Kuchu no Geito*, 1920), a man accepts a wager to stand on his head atop an 85-meter smokestack while other workers gape below. Ogawa wrote the story when he was 28 and just coming under the influence of socialism, so he may have thought he was writing a political parable. It is nothing of the sort. *The Introduction to Contemporary Japanese Literature*, the first English publication to translate—though in paraphrased form—this story said that it failed.

In actuality, this splendid story transcends political limitations to become a strong delineation of the paradoxes of psychology. When I first heard about it back in 1947 (courtesy of the Introduction), I wanted to make a movie of it. (Someone still ought to.) I also met the author (a mild man with glasses), and a kind of translation resulted. But that is all that came of it except that later Ivan Morris splendidly translated the story as "Handstand" (1962). It appears in his *Modern Japanese Stories*.

Red Candles and the Mermaid and Other Tales, by Ogawa Mimei, translated by Watanabe Masao, Sato Hiroshi and Sanford Goldstein. Tokyo: Nihon Tosho Kankokai, 1997.

Shiga Naoya

Shiga Naoya (1883–1971) remains for the Japanese the most important and influential of writers. As Donald Keene has written: "No modern writer was more idolized ... a half-dozen authors were so greatly influenced by his writings as to recall Shiga on almost every page." Indeed, "his works were accorded such reverence that he was referred to by some critics as 'the god of literature.' "

It has hitherto been difficult for the Western reader to understand the reasons for this adulation. His single long novel, *A Dark Night's Passing*, was only translated a decade ago (by Edwin McClellan) and has yet to be given the critical attention it deserves. A couple of famous works have been translated a number of times (four translations for "Razor," sixteen for "Han's Crime") but these are not Shiga's finest nor his most typical work.

Really, only one work was available in English translation which indicated what a remarkable writer Shiga was. This was "At Kinosaki" in Edward Seidensticker's translation. The 1917 story is perhaps typical of the best of Shiga in that, with the slenderest of means, it suggests a fullness of experience.

The first-person narrator, ill, goes to recover at Kinosaki—there he leads a quiet life (tuberculosis of the spine threatens), and in the course of the story, there are three incidents: first, he notices a dead wasp; second, he witnesses the torture and probable death of a rat; and third, he in an idle moment, tosses a stone and kills a small lizard.

That is all the "story" there is (and some critics have consequently refused to call the work a "story"), and its précis can give you no idea at all of the enormous effect of the work. By such a severe restriction of means, by such careful choosing of such mundane material, Shiga endistances his reader—you lean forward, as it were, to see better, to learn more.

In so doing, you are open to Shiga's real subject: the will to live, the inevitability of death. Such quotidian matters are illuminated by the author, and their original delight and terror are returned. You learn the worst but, like the narrator, are spared.

These small miracles occur again and again in this new edition of the short pieces of Shiga, a collection for which we must thank the translator Lane Dunlop and his enterprising publisher. Of the seventeen short works included, a number have been translated already (including the three so far mentioned), but none have been collected and, in any event, many of the earlier translations were not serviceable.

Completely new to English are the 1911 "The Paper Door," the 1923 "Rain Frogs," the 1925 "A Memory of Yamashina," the 1926 "Infatuations" and the 1927 "Kuniko." Also translated for the first time is a 1913 piece, "An Incident," which is, I think, the best work of Shiga I know.

Before describing it, I might mention that many of Shiga's best pieces consist of a simple incident upon which is brought to bear an enormous weight. Disliking plot with its editorial falsifications, Shiga (like his admirer, the film director Ozu Yasujiro) returns to the simple happening all of its original meaning.

Shiga was a conscious stylist and one who worked hard. As he has himself written, "just as there is only one word to express each particular thing, the author must discover the one method, the one feeling, the one attitude appropriate to a given piece of material." And this he did by sheer intensification.

In the admirable 1923 "Rain Frogs," a wife's unfaithfulness is equated to the natural mating of these little creatures which the author views and of which he approves. In the splendid 1919 "The Shopboy's God," the incident turns slowly into anecdote and just before it can develop into plot, the author deliberately exposes his hand—and his astonishing and absolutely right reason for doing so is that he felt that such a (plot-like) ending would be cruel to the shopboy the story is about.

In the 1908 "As Far as Abashiri" absolutely nothing "happens," as we observe a young impoverished mother and her fretful children. Yet, through the art of Shiga (showing "the one attitude appropriate") we will never forget her. In the same way, "An Incident" is made (apparently) of very little. The first-person is in a trolley on a hot July afternoon. The passengers sit, dozing, indifferent. There is also, it is noted in passing, a butterfly fluttering about inside.

Then there is the incident. A little boy almost gets run over by the trolley. Taken inside the stopped car until his parents arrive, he is examined for scratches. The child struggles and pees on the man holding him. When the family comes, the young man has taken off his shirt and is mopping himself off, the passengers are all revived by the incident, and the butterfly has flown away.

What is this all about? It sounds like some kind of comic sketch, but it is not; it is told in a completely serious manner, and no one is made fun of. The butterfly is not a symbol nor is the little boy nor is the trolley life itself.

On paper it reads as factually as a newspaper clipping, and yet the enormous incongruity (the way the boy is described, the way the young man is described), the sense of something absolute occurring before the reading eye, the apparent emphasis made of simple juxtapositions when such enjambments of events are not simple at all—all of this imbues the "incident" with the clarity of something seen as a child and never forgotten.

Like several others among the great writers (Anton Chekhov, Henry Green, Nagai Kafu, few of whom Shiga knew), the author of "An Incident" feels such curiosity and interest in people and has so high an opinion of human intelligence (ours, theirs, his own) that he denies himself the undoubted convenience of a plot, conventional dialogue, and stereotyped language.

Instead, all is new, all is strange, and all is quivering with a naturalness which brings tears to the eyes—and delight to the intellect as one observes with what skill all the parts in this strange and beautifully detailed story are made to play their parts.

One is indeed grateful to Lane Dunlop for making this selection of the shorter works of Shiga Naoya available. It is now possible for the English reader to begin to appreciate just how fine a writer Shiga Naoya was, and to understand the extraordinary honors given him by his countrymen.

The Paper Door and Other Stories, by Shiga Naoya, translated by Lane Dunlop. San Francisco: North Point Press, 1987.

Western criticism of Shiga Naoya's work often focuses on whether it is autobiography or fiction and judges it accordingly. Japanese criticism need not concern itself with this question since the *shishosetsu* (the form Mori Ogai adapted from the German *Ich-roman*) does not admit such a division.

As a result, Western critics, for whom fiction is a higher category than autobiography, spend much of their time wondering what it is that the Japanese rate so highly in Shiga. One thing would be that the Japanese critic considers the *shishosetsu* to be a major ingredient in *jun bungaku* (serious literature); another would be Shiga's celebrated style: terse, laconic, concerned as much with what is left out as what is included.

That this writer should be considered by his compatriots to be the quintessential Japanese writer of his age baffles Western critics. One of them, driven to desperation, writes: "Like tofu, a dish which most Westerners find insipid, Shiga's fiction is an acquired taste." Another speaks of "a form of autobiographical jotting that may scarcely seem to deserve the name fiction at all." Yet another complains of the "triviality."

The fault, if that is what it is, lies in the assumptions of these critics. They expect Western literature in Japanese, a plotted narrative with a beginning, a middle and an end, all tightly constructed with causal connections. If this is the criterion, then Shiga is indeed guilty of penning "unformed reminiscence."

But this is not the criterion. There are many other ways of shaping narrative, and Shiga's is among them. This is the theme of the book under review, and the author is rightly concerned that Shiga has been much misrepresented in Western criticism.

He points out that in "At Kinosaki" (1917) the relationship among the three incidents described is not causal, as in conventional narrative, but associative, as in poetry. "Bonfire" may indeed be a "plotless story," but this is because the lyrical mood rather than a highly structured plot line is the unifying principle of the work.

Indeed, says the author, Shiga's stories "have an integral

structure, an almost rigorous internal logic of their own … a connecting principle is very much there if the critic takes the trouble to look for it." As for triviality, "once Shiga has turned a 'trivial' incident into a short story, it no longer seems trivial."

Starrs compares Shiga to a near contemporary, Ernest Hemingway, and finds many similarities between the traditionalism of the Japanese and the modernism of the American. The eventless, closely patterned Nick Adams stories are as "naturally plotted" as Shiga's *shishosetsu*. Ezra Pound was quite right to find something "haiku-like" in early Hemingway.

"The Big Two-Hearted River" is compared with Shiga's "Bonfire," and their similarities, gratuitous but real, are noted. Among these is that both authors knew precisely what to leave out. Of his story, Hemingway said that "it was about coming back from the war, but there was no mention of the war in it."

In accounting for the Shiga style, the author does not credit modernism itself (though this "foreign" style was certainly forming contemporary writers such as Kawabata Yasunari) but something more traditional, something that creates "this central vision, redolent of the mainstream spiritual culture of the Orient, especially of Zen Buddhism."

Here the critical ground grows less firm. The author, aware of soggy footing, seeks to forestall argument. Naturally, Shiga was not a "Zen artist," and the critic is not trying to show that his author embodies "Japanese tradition" with his "Zen aesthetic." Nonetheless … etc.

Actually Shiga does, in his way, discuss Zen in one of his works, the single novel *A Dark Night's Passing*, and if one may argue that haiku is somehow Zen-like, then one can argue the same for Shiga. Both arguments, however, risk essentializing "Japanese culture" in a way all too common, and Starrs is aware of this danger.

A result is that the Zen trappings of this important and full exegesis of Shiga and his work are worn a bit uncomfortably. This is perhaps because they are unnecessary. One does not need to account for Shiga's style through reference to his cultural entity—one need only account for it through his personal entity.

The "Japaneseness" of Shiga, however, is too good a weapon with which to assail those many Western critics (a majority) who have failed to appreciate the writer for what he is. It is consequently often brandished, and Starrs, endlessly repeating his evidence, belabors the dead horses among his colleagues. He, in a way, becomes guilty of just what Shiga avoids—overkill.

The second half of the book is given over to translations of six Shiga works, two of which—the 1917 "Reconciliation" and "The Diary of Claudius"—are here translated for the first time. "Bonfire" has been previously translated by S. F. Richards and Dennis Keene; "Manazuru" by William Sibley and Stephen Kohl; "Akanishi Kakiṭa" by Haneda Saburo, Elizabeth Schultz and Sakamoto Tadanobu; and "At Kinosaki" by Lane Dunlop, Haneda Saburo, William Sibley and Edward Seidensticker. This information is not included in this edition, but the reader may desire alternative translations.

An Artless Art: The Zen Aesthetic of Shiga Naoya: A Critical Study with Selected Translations, by Roy Starrs. Richmond, Surrey: The Japan Library, 1998.

Izumi Kyoka

When Akutagawa Ryunosuke committed suicide in 1927, he had a book open on his desk, a volume of Izumi Kyoka (1873–1938). Whatever else this might indicate, it suggests a similar concern with death. Indeed, most of Kyoka's works deal with it, usually romantically, often involving a beautiful and mysterious woman whose role before she dies is to educate the hero.

All of the three stories in this newly translated collection share this theme. In the 1895 "Surgery Room" (*Gekashitsu*), the lovely countess refuses anesthesia because she fears she will reveal her love for the surgeon. Midway through, she grabs the scalpel and completes his work. The next day, comprehending all, he dies by his own hand.

Though the work is, in the words of Donald Keene, "impossibly melodramatic," it belongs to a genre of fiction which is supposed to be. This, Charles Inouye, the translator of these tales, identifies as "Japanese Gothic."

Influenced by the romantic excesses of the French, by such Symbolist works as Oscar Wilde's *Salome*, and Stephen Mallarmé's *Herodiade*, the genre saw the heroine as a melodramatic feature, part whore and part saint, or—like Anatole France's *Thaïs*—simultaneously both.

In Kyoka, this bifurcated creature takes on the aspects of scarlet temptress or virgin-white mother. And since he also wanted both in the same person, the women in his tales move rapidly between tossed underclothing and motherly caresses.

In the second of them, the 1906 "One Day in Spring" (*Shunchu*), the heroine is a Melisande in far Zushi. She has "locks like clouds, her hairpin like a star, her lips a red blossom, the corner of her eyes like hollyhocks; leaning back like a willow upon the grass, she was like a dandelion with its skirts floating in the air."

Luxuriating in this symbolist excess, she is, besides being a loose woman, something of a mother to the hero. If she is also tiresome, this is because, in such fantasies, the femme fatale is never a real person and always a reflection of the author's emotions.

But then she is not supposed to be real. One of the rules of Gothic fiction is that it must be all effect, everything visible upon its florid surface. This is acknowledged when one of Kyoka's characters turns to a carved figure of that ambivalent goddess, Kannon.

"You could say a carved figure is nothing but wood or metal or earth, decorated with gold, silver and gems ... but what about people? Skin, blood, muscles, the five senses, the six organs, join them together, put some clothes on, and there you have it. Never forget, sir, that even the most beautiful woman is nothing more than this."

Men, too, are then nothing more than this, but such a thought would be unwelcome to the Gothic artist who needs his *princesse lointain* precisely in order to define himself. Such would certainly seem to have been the case with Kyoka. Indeed, his translator has here isolated a basic myth common to most of Kyoka's work:

"A young or otherwise sexually hesitant man encounters a dangerously alluring yet nurturing woman in a watery and therefore threatening environment. The hero trespasses the world of the sacred and the dead, experiences both horror and fascination, and returns from the encounter having learned something important about his own nature and about the deeper meaning of love."

This pattern is quite visible in the third of the tales, the 1920 "Osen and Sokichi" (*Baishoku Kamonamban*). Glimpsing an apparent whore, the hero remembers the prostitute who was more than a mother to him. Moving between now and then, the author weaves a fantasy which may owe something to the admired French fin de siècle, but owes equally to the Edo literature he read as a child.

It is this fusion of the two worlds of high fantasy that is most admired by critics. This and the fact that Kyoka is famed as a stylist. Mishima Yukio said that no modern author has more explored and developed the possibilities of the Japanese language than did Kyoka, and Tanizaki Jun'ichiro has stated that "we should read Kyoka in the way we read Chikamatsu or Saikaku."

This celebrated style poses its problems for the translator. Perhaps this is the reason that Kyoka has, despite his fame, not been much translated. Edward Seidensticker has published (in *Modern Japanese Literature*) a translation of "A Tale of Three Who Were Blind," and the Izumi Kyoka Translation Committee (which published the present volume) has put out prior translations of "The Saint of Mount Koya," "The Song of the Troubadour" and "Of a Dragon in the Deep."

Charles Inouye, the present translator, understands well the Kyoka style and renders an English equivalent which has its own logic and its own compulsion. He would believe, with Arthur Waley (whose translation of the *Genji* is a triumph of the Symbolist style), that the translation of a work of art should be a work of art itself and that if it is philology it is not literature.

Inouye is also aware of some of the more troubling implications of Kyoka's work, particularly the assumption that women must die so that men may live. That the author is locally known as a feminist is to be understood only if the term is used in its Japanese sense.

Japanese call "feminist" any author who takes an interest in women for whatever reason. Thus, the film director Mizoguchi Kenji is locally known as a feminist, though his own attitude toward women in both life and films was concerned only with the negative aspects of women's attempting to achieve a better position in a man's world.

(It is perhaps fitting that Mizoguchi very much admired Kyoka's work and filmed several, including "Osen and Sokichi" in the 1934 *Oizuru Osen*. Suzuki Seijun is another admirer, and he put parts of "One Day in Spring" in his 1981 film version of the play *Kageroza*. More recently, the celebrated *onnagata* Bando Tamasaburo turned film director in his adaptation of "Surgery Room.")

This edition (part of continued publishing efforts by Kyoka's hometown) brings together, in the most polished form, three of the author's most typical works.

Three Tales of Mystery and Imagination, by Izumi Kyoka, translation, critical essays, notes and preface by Charles S. Inouye. Kanazawa: Izumi Translation Committee, 1993. (Reprinted as *Japanese Gothic Tales*. Honolulu: University of Hawaii Press, 1996.)

Izumi Kyoka was much admired by Tanizaki, with whom he shared an esteem for Edo culture; by Mishima, who cherished his elaborate style; and by Akutagawa, who much admired his handling of supernatural themes.

Ghosts, goblins and the life beyond are the stuff of Kyoka's drama, all presented in high Edo style and laced with lavish language. These plays were, however, not at all well known during most of the playwright's life. The only one of them staged during his lifetime was *Demon Pond*, and though the author so wanted to see *The Castle Tower* on the stage that he offered to pay the actors and waive his royalties, it was not performed until fifteen years after his death. One of his best plays, *Yamabuki* was only put on in 1977, and some of his other plays have never been staged at all.

There are a number of reasons for this late approval—the rise of a less realistic theatre, the interest of such avant-garde playwrights as Terayama Shuji and Kara Juro, the devotion of such actors as Bando Tamasaburo, and (as Cody Poulton, author of this interesting study of Kyoka's plays, suggests) changes in the Japanese language.

"Never an easy writer, Kyoka now is practically impenetrable for the modern reader. His images are far more accessible to modern audiences through stage or film than through the thick weave of his language." This, coupled with what is taken for his "new age" interests (astral beings and the like), has made the drama fairly popular.

Also, the eccentricities of the author himself contributed to his late popularity. Superstitious, he entertained a number of taboos and fetishes concerning the use of language. Rough drafts were offered before a photograph of Kyoka's mentor, Ozaki Koyo, and then burned. The ashes were later eaten as a talisman against cholera, a disease of which Kyoka was in mortal fear. Such entertaining anecdotes can only appeal in age of pragmatic standardization, and a result is that Kyoka is an established, if marginal, playwright.

This is ironic because, while the plays were being ignored, stages were brimming with Kyoka's language, the reason being that his fiction proved so popular that adaptations were being made for the Shimpa theatre.

Intended as something of an antidote to kabuki, the marginally more realistic Shimpa had a need of new vehicles, and popular literature was continually being raided to provide these. Since this fiction thought itself realist and was usually sensational, it consisted often of melodrama.

In exploring this irony ("that the Shimpa adaptations which have been performed continuously for close to a century now, have faired much better than his original plays"), Poulton finds himself in an interesting scholarly position.

This he acknowledges when he writes in his concluding chapter that "this study has been in part of a defense of the Shimpa and an apology for the melodramatic element in Kyoka's literature." Though quite aware of the sentimentality and stereotyping of melodrama, he argues that this is as much a part of "theatre" as is anything else. And if this leads to cant, cliché and kitsch, then this, too, is part of stage presentation.

In his argument, Poulton shows not only the influence of noh and kabuki but also such Symbolist playwrights as

Haupmann and Maeterlinck. He notes the effect of Wilde's *Salome*, seen in Japan as early as 1907, and reaches a number of conclusions. Among these is that in his fiction (and I think his plays as well), Kyoka was "reworking the same kind of moral schematization seen in Edo drama, one predicated either on the vindication of good over evil or the encouragement of virtue and the castigation of vice." Kyoka's contribution was to problemize the notion.

How this was done is indicated by the study of the work, a complete translation of three plays (*Demon Pond*, *The Sea God's Villa*, and *The Castle Tower*) and a full essay on each. These in hand, the reader is prepared for an encounter with one of Japan's most romantic moderns, a man it is said who created a dramaturgy of the sacred from the dregs of the past.

Spirits of Another Sort: The Plays of Izumi Kyoka, by M. Cody Poulton. Ann Arbor: Center for Japanese Studies, University of Michigan, 2001.

Tanizaki Jun'ichiro

Chijin no Ai (often translated as *A Fool's Love*; here given simply as *Naomi*) was written in 1924 when Tanizaki (1886–1965) was in his mid-thirties. It begins around 1918 and ends (Tanizaki projecting into the future) around 1926—just the period when, World War I ended, Japan was once more looking to the West with typical and acquisitive adulation.

Naomi is a *modan garu*, a "modern girl," a type which proliferated in Japan after World War I. Independent, outspoken, she takes her models from American films—"Mary Pickford's smile, Gloria Swanson's eyes, Pola Negri's wrath, Bebe Daniels' suave affection."

Having seen *Neptune's Daughter*, she delights in imitating

the noted swimmer Annette Kellerman, whose diving pose shows off Naomi's good legs—long, like a Westerner's. During this, she continues her imitations: "Pickford laughs like this; Pina Menicheli moves her eyes like this; Geraldine Farrar does her hair up this way."

She takes up with the *mobo* as well—"modern boys" with short haircuts, pencil moustaches, and modern ideas. One such is invited someplace but "it's so stiff and formal, we're planning to run away without eating." Asked if it is really that bad, he replies: "Unbearable. The maid gets down and does that ceremonial, three-fingered bow. It's depressing."

Naomi also takes up with Joji, a perfectly ordinary-seeming middle-aged man short of any post-World War I affectations, even a bit given to traditional Confucian virtues. Nonetheless, Joji (whom Naomi is shortly calling George) falls deeply and permanently in love with the Westernized youngster.

He sees through her—knows, for example, that she is limited. When he first meets her, she is fifteen and "tended to hide in a corner as she did her work silently and nervously. This may also be why she looked intelligent." But, as he soon discovers, intelligible thought is not one of her qualities. At the movies, for example, "she watched in silence, her intelligent eyes wide open like those of an alert dog listening to a distant sound." Yet, though "she'd betrayed my expectations for my mind … her body now surpassed my ideal."

And "here I have to acknowledge how base males are. Whatever transpired in the daytime, I always gave in to her at night." Later, voicing the theme of the story of life with Naomi: "It's fine to give confidence to the woman you love, but as a result you lose confidence in yourself. And when that happens, there's no way to overcome her sense of superiority. This leads to undreamed of misfortunes."

Joji speaks of an ideal. He is that kind of man: he has

ideals. Nothing *mobo* about him. He enshrines Naomi and like all women-worshipping idealists from *Pygmalion* on (including Shaw's Professor Higgins and Nabakov's Humbert Humbert) he is sacrificed to this ideal.

The limited Naomi indeed becomes something of a goddess as George, besotted, looks at her face from below, up close: "Seen in this way, her beauty had the grandeur of a giant. It forced itself upon me with volume and substance. The fearfully long slits of her eyes; the nose, as prominent as a splendid building; and beneath the lines, the richly, deeply chiseled, red lips."

This view of Naomi becomes a metaphor for large alien attractions, and it is this which is one of the themes of Tanizaki Jun'ichiro's splendid realization of Joji's passion for his Naomi. Through it, and many another, one realizes that the author is writing about something else as he recounts the plight of his ludicrous lovers.

It would be too much to say that this fine Tanizaki novel is an allegory and that Naomi stands for the West and Joji stands for Japan. Yet, just as one must not make too much of this, one must also not overlook it, for it is this quality which gives the book—here in an exemplary translation—its extraordinary resonance.

Naomi, by Tanizaki Jun'ichiro, translated by Anthony Chambers. New York: Alfred A. Knopf, 1985.

Quicksand is the long-awaited translation of the Tanizaki's seminal 1930 novel *Manji*. Though early rendered into Italian (1982) and French (1985), this is the last major Tanizaki novel to be translated into English because, says the jacket, of "the extreme difficulty in capturing the narrator's precise tone."

It is a novel written in the Kansai dialect—more specifically, that patois spoken by women in the Hanshin district during the late 1920s. In addition, the narrator is, by no means, reliable and behind her self-serving language, the translator must somehow suggest what (perhaps) actually occurred. At the same time, the structure is such that the narrator (speaking to a transcribing *sensei* who has to be Tanizaki himself) often states something as true only later to reveal that she had been narrating only that truth she knew at the time, not the "real" truth.

She—Sonoko by name—has fallen in love with a beautiful younger woman named Mitsuko, and the novel is an account of this thoroughly destructive infatuation. In his 1991 study of Tanizaki, *Visions of Desire*, Ito Ken calls the novel "a catalogue of dissimulation," and finds Mitsuko "a resourceful and pathological liar, full of stratagems for making others submit to her sexual wiles."

In this, she joins many another Tanizaki heroine—Naomi, Shunkin, Ikuko: all of them demanding women who practice varying degrees of deception and exercise various disciplines. The "masochistic overtones" of Tanizaki's sexier novels are commonly acknowledged but to use such a clinical term for what is, after all, a human passion is to misrepresent the works themselves.

Tanizaki is writing about desire, and this occurs in many forms. In a novel like *Manji*, desire is naked. It can be confused with pornography (and has been there is an Italian soft-core film of this very novel) because, as in porn, these people are their passions—there is nothing else.

Pornography, however, ends there; Tanizaki does not. The lesbian relationship, for example. Many men find the idea of women making love exciting, and most porn spectacles, whether on stage, screen, or the printed page insist upon some kind of lesbian simulation. Tanizaki may have been excited himself, for all I know, but in his novels love between women is not used for titillation.

It is used, as in *Manji*, as illustration, since it is a powerful source of desire. Also, since it remains socially proscribed, it also lends itself to necessary dissembling. Of this Tanizaki—unlike the porn peddler—is continually aware.

Sonoko is "confessing" to *sensei*. Her husband is standing helplessly by, and she says "head down on the table, I sobbed like a spoiled child, and I kept repeating: 'I want to die! Just let me die!' By that point, saying I wanted to die was the best tactic. What else could I do? All I thought of was how I could go on seeing Mitsuko the same as before—really, what I feared most was being divorced. Anyway, now that he knew all this, surely our married life would be harmonious. I'd be very considerate of him, if only he would understand my attachment to her and accept it."

The catalogue of deception, including self-deception is long and detailed—Tanizaki's *liassons dangereuses* are just as convoluted as those of Laclos, and like those of the French author, they are used not to titillate but to point a moral—a thoroughly conventional one.

Unbridled desire creates, just as the Buddhist church maintains, a true hell on earth. "Day by day our torment deepened.... Neither my husband nor I could go off with [Mitsuko] and leave the other person alone. So we had to stay home, where one of us was always in the way, unless the other was tactful enough to withdraw. And yet Mitsuko ... knew just what she was doing ..."

As these extracts indicate, the problem of tone has been solved. Howard Hibbett, translator of *The Key*, *The Diary of a Mad Old Man*, and various shorter works of Tanizaki, has been working on this translation for years, and the result is a beautifully realized rethinking of the work in English.

Ito has said that the "narrative effects achieved through the use of dialect ... would be difficult to reproduce in English," and so I am sure they were. He adds that Sonoko's vernacular has a more fluid sound than the clipped syllables of standard Japanese and that this gives her voice a heavy, cloying sensuality. At the same time, this accent seems to imbue her with an intense femininity.

If Tanizaki's "transcription" of these confessions in patois Japanese is masterly, so is Hibbett's parallel rendering into English. One's only complaint—something for which the publisher, not the translator, is to blame—is the rendering of the title. One cannot (though the French translation did) call it swastika, precise translation though it is. The Italian title managed a kind of faithfulness with *La croce buddista*. Ito refers to it as *The Whirlpool*, but Tanizaki—who knew English—apparently did not like this title. Would he, I wonder, have preferred the even more melodramatic *Quicksand*? Whatever—the rest of the translation is a masterful rendering of a very particular kind of masterpiece.

Quicksand, by Tanizaki Jun'ichiro, translated by Howard Hibbett. New York: Alfred A. Knopf, 1994.

Around 1930, Tanizaki Jun'ichiro changed his style. Before, he wrote in a manner he himself described as "orthodox ... propelled by strictly objective description and dialogue." After and periodically, during his long writing career, he experimented with what he called "essay-fiction," attempting to "find the form that would convey the greatest feeling of reality."

At the same time, as had indeed been evident since 1927, he experienced a new interest in Japanese history and aesthetics. From this conjunction of tradition and experiment came a number of extraordinary works: *A Blind Man's Tale* (1931) and *A Portrait of Shunkin* (1933)—both available in Howard Hibbett's translation—and the two works here translated by Anthony Chambers: *The Secret History of the Lord of Musashi* (1931–32) and *Arrowroot* (1931).

As Chambers has noted in his introduction, both of these latter works seem to have been initially inspired by Stendhal, by one of the *Chroniques Italiennes* which Tanizaki had translated into Japanese in 1928. At least the narrative technique of these two works—old manuscripts, antiquarian interests, the present peering into the past—seem derived from the French author. (With the difference that Stendhal used real manuscripts in *The Abbess of Castro*, and Tanizaki made his up—though the sources mentioned in *Arrowroot* are all authentic.) With the difference, too, that Tanizaki is, in these works, aiming at "the greatest feeling of reality." His historical novellas are completely consistent imaginary worlds, and one much regrets the unachieved "long historical novel ... with courtiers, shogun, priests, and beautiful women involved in deep, complex relationships and undergoing vast changes," of which Chambers tells us.

At the same time, Tanizaki's method in these historical works, complete imaginative reconstruction, perhaps could not have been successfully sustained over a vast number of pages. Perhaps his greatest "long historical novel" is his translation into modern Japanese of *The Tale of Genji*. Certainly, for the longest and arguably the finest of his novels, *The Makioka Sisters*, he returned to his "orthodox ... strictly objective" style.

Musashi purports to be the examination of two ancient manuscripts from which the story of Lord Hoshimaru emerges. Still very young, he witnesses the ladies of a besieged castle dressing the decapitated heads of the enemies (a celebrated passage), and his emotional direction is set for all time. He will always yearn for the imperious woman, and he will himself become, as it were, the severed head.

The attractions of that form of emotional communication known colloquially as s/m have been quite fully described in many Tanizaki works, from the early *Naomi* to the last work, the superlative *Diary of a Mad Old Man*. In the Musashi diaries, however, it receives, perhaps, its most colorful treatment.

One of the reasons is that Tanizaki is also, in part, writing a parody of traditional Japanese histories, inserting everything which they, for reasons of propriety, would have left out. "The ... aspects of life that the Confucian historians piously omitted from their accounts, Tanizaki presents in outrageous exaggeration," Chambers writes.

Thus we have not only the eroticism of severed heads and sliced-off noses, we also have secret passages which lead to directly under the palace lady's toilet and all sorts of quite brutal s/m frolics. (Chambers says that, in addition to parodying official Japanese histories, Tanizaki is also parodying his own emotional inclinations. This I do not quite believe. Love, in whatever form, is not an emotion amenable to humor, in whatever fashion. Actually, s/m is treated quite seriously here—this attitude indeed giving the work much of its power.) The effect is, however, purposely grotesque, as though Yoshitoshi had illustrated the *Genji*, and yet, at the same time, there is an abundance of emotion. The result is certainly a "feeling of reality."

Arrowroot is a different matter. Again, it is an historical investigation but one based on actual records. Two friends go into the mountains of Yoshino to look for remains of the pre-Muromachi exiled court. Nothing is really found but atmosphere, but what atmosphere, and with what skill past and present are seamlessly woven to evoke an almost invisible past. Later in life, Tanizaki always said that this was one of his favorites among his works. One can see why. In just a bit over fifty pages, he has created a magnificent evocation.

It, too, is not without its domineering lady, but here the effect is not intended to be grotesque, nor is it. The figure becomes metaphor in which love for mother, love for an ideal woman are mixed as magnificently as they are in, say, that later masterpiece "The Bridge of Dreams," and the feeling for the past is as achingly present as it is in that astonishingly beautiful essay *In Praise of Shadows*.

The Secret History of the Lord of Musashi and Arrowroot, by Tanizaki Jun'ichiro, translated by Anthony H. Chambers. New York: Alfred A. Knopf, 1982.

In Praise of Shadows is the first complete English translation of Tanizaki's splendid 1933 essay *Inei Raisan*. Over half of it was translated in 1954 by Edward Seidensticker, appeared originally in the *Japan Quarterly*, and was later reprinted in the *Atlantic Monthly*. Some time later, the remainder was completed by Thomas J. Harper (who also wrote the postscript for this edition). It has now finally, several years after the manuscript was completed, been published.

Its concern is with aesthetics, but its ramifications are much broader since it is also an explication (and a defense) of an attitude which permeates (and, Tanizaki would say, delineates) traditional Japanese culture. The attitude has no name—which is perhaps the reason for the author's evocative title—but it certainly exists (or existed) and runs precisely counter to Western aesthetic regards.

The opening sets both the tone and the direction with a spirited defense: "Every time I am shown an old, dimly lit ... toilet ... I am impressed with the singular virtues of Japanese architecture. The parlor may have its charms, but the Japanese toilet truly is a place of spiritual repose ... the perfect place to listen to the chirping of insects or the song of the birds, to view the moon, or to enjoy any of those poignant moments that mark the change of the seasons. Here I suspect, is where haiku poets over the ages have come by a great many of their ideas. Indeed, one could with some justice claim that of all elements of Japanese architecture, the toilet is the most aesthetic."

It is most aesthetic because it combines silence with darkness, and it is the latter quality which Tanizaki finds not only typical but also illustrative of traditional Japanese aesthetics. To this he adds the quality (already present in the toilet itself) of an aesthetic appreciation of the mundanely human.

Of the prized quality of patina, he continues, "this 'sheen of antiquity' … is in fact the glow of grime … a sheen produced by the oils that naturally permeate an object over long years of handling [and] can well be described as filthy … For better or worse, we love things that bear the marks of grime, soot, and weather, and we love the colors and the sheen that call to mind the past that made them."

This calls to mind the conditions under which these objects of the past were originally to be appreciated: "Artisans of old, when they finished their works in lacquer and decorated them in sparkling patterns, must surely have had in mind dark rooms and sought to turn to good effect what feeble light there was. Their extravagant use of gold, too, I would imagine came of understanding how it gleams forth from out of the darkness and reflects the lamplight."

The appreciation of a natural dark and signs of a purely human use permeates much of the earlier traditional art. The noh, for example (and certainly not, the author makes clear, the bright and gaudy kabuki): "The darkness in which [it] is shrouded and the beauty that emerges from it make a distinct world of shadow which today can be seen only on the stage; but in the past, it could not have been far removed from daily life. The darkness of the noh stage is, after all, the darkness of the domestic architecture of the day …."

Toward the end of the essay Tanizaki gives some reason why all this should be—or have been. "[We] Orientals tend to seek our satisfactions in whatever surroundings we happen to find ourselves, to content ourselves with things as they are; and so darkness causes us no discontent, we resign ourselves to it as inevitable. If light is scarce, then light is scarce; we will immerse ourselves in the darkness and there discover its particular beauty."

This was as true as it is beautiful, but, even as Tanizaki was writing, this aesthetic had almost vanished. He has many hard things to say about the bright lights of Ginza and the general electricity-mad atmosphere of prewar Japan. It had managed to spoil everything: "In conversation ... we prefer the soft voice, the understatement. Most important of all are the pauses. Yet the phonograph and the radio render these moments of silence utterly lifeless." What, one wonders, would he have made of our loudspeakers, hi-fi, and ubiquitous TV tubes? Well, one knows. Sitting with half an eye and half a mind in front of television is the precise opposite of sitting alert and appreciative in the Japanese toilet.

Tanizaki had already seen the neon on the wall, but he hoped for at least one area of respite: "I would call back at least for literature this world of shadows we are losing. In the mansion called literature I would have the eaves deep and the walls dark. I would push back into the shadows the things that come forward too clearly ... perhaps we may be allowed at least one mansion where we can turn off the electric lights and see what it is like without them."

Or, perhaps not. Contemporary Japanese literature is now all lit up too, and shadows of any kind (as distinguished from vagaries and obscurations) are very difficult to find anywhere in the land. The notion that to be well lit is to be well displayed has taken hold and only the likely national energy crisis can save us now.

Even in his lifetime, Tanizaki was accused of being reactionary and (as though it followed) romantic. To critics who find nostalgia a fault, this may, indeed, have seemed so, but a close reading of this essay will disabuse any of such ideas. Quite to the contrary, Tanizaki is here concerned with the precise definition of an important and a very human quality, one typically but not only Japanese.

Always realistic and always pragmatic, Tanizaki saw just what was being lost and just how hollow an ideal progress always is. The appeal in this essay is for an acceptance of mere self—but of that this vaunting century has little appreciation. So little, indeed, that this essay of Tanizaki is one of the few reminders that such a natural acceptance was once an unremarked part of everyone's lives.

In Praise of Shadows, by Tanizaki Jun'ichiro, translated by Thomas J. Harper and Edward G. Seidensticker. New Haven: Leete's Island Books, Inc., 1977.

A Cat, a Man and Two Women is a translation of the 1936 *Neko to Shozo to Futari no Onna*. It is one of Tanizaki Jun'ichiro's most interesting and most curious works, and the foreign reader will long have been intrigued by its reputation—and perhaps by seeing the 1956 film version by Toyoda Shiro. Now it has appeared in a fine translation by Paul McCarthy.

The structure of this short novel is as simple as the title. Indeed the title contains the story but under the anecdote lies the vast import of the theme—the ramifications of love.

Shozo, a feckless Osaka-type, has just gotten rid of one wife, Shinako, and taken another, Fukuko. This is the work of his mother, determined that her idle son bring in some money, if only in the shape of a dowry, which the new wife has. She is also a bit wild but "once she had a husband, she wasn't likely to be unfaithful to him—and even if she was, it wouldn't matter much."

The weak-willed son, however, is already in love. He has a cat—named Lily. This affection is divined by his mother who says: "Now, Shozo, it doesn't matter whether it's a cat or a human being: if you pay too much attention ... and forget your brand-new wife, why, it's only natural she's upset." Lily upsets both wives. The first even warns the second, "and he always paid much more attention to her than he did to me at the dinner table and in bed." Shinako, the first, believes that once she has Lily she will get Shozo once more, and so the women begin to concern themselves with the unfortunate animal.

Shozo regards the beloved beast and sees her sad eyes. "When Shinako got that sad look in her eyes, it didn't bother Shozo very much; but for some reason, when it was Lily, he was strangely overcome with pity." And Lily was getting old fast, being only a cat. She was getting scrawny flanks, her head drooped. She wobbled when she walked and Shozo felt "an indescribable sadness ... as if he were being given a personal demonstration of the Buddhist truth that 'all things pass away'."

This is the true Tanizaki tone: humor and irony all marbled with compassion and wisdom. The statement is literally true and yet when confined to an old cat and the suspicious affection of a wastrel its dignity turns softly human—and we smile.

The author chose not to end his tug-of-war. Like much Japanese fiction, this novella stops rather than ends. (That lovely coda of Shozo in the rain looking for the elusive Lily is a contribution of the film version.) But not before it has made its classic point about evanescence, about the suchness of things, about—indeed—*mono no aware*.

I wonder if Tanizaki knew Colette's *La Chatte*, which was completed three years before *Shozo*. The parallels are startling. Saha the cat belongs to Alain, just married to a really terrible young lady, and he continues to love the animal more than the human. Like Lily, Saha sleeps with him, thrusting careful claws through his pajamas, giving him kisses with her chilly nose. These are love scenes between a childish man and a womanly cat. The true marriage is theirs—the wife is the troublemaker. Not that a resemblance between the two novels makes any difference. One great work is often piled on top of another, and many artists are most inspired by other art. Still, it would be interesting to know.

Tanizaki had in his earlier years, something of a magpie reputation. Indeed, when he was writing *Manji*, it was rumored that this was really a translation or adaptation from the French—a rumor occasioned by his having hired two young women to render the dialogue of that novel into proper Osaka dialect.

Though not true in fact, the rumor was true enough in spirit. During the writing of *Manji*, Tanizaki was reading Radclyffe Hall's *The Well of Loneliness*—in the original. Many of its more technical passages may have found echoes in the Tanizaki manuscript.

Certainly, however, the foreign writer to whom one might most profitably compare Tanizaki is Colette. Both were supreme stylists, both had the most intimate knowledge of and interest in the senses: the taste, the smell, the feel. And both had a very personal interest in the anomalies of love.

Would that Colette had also had as fine a series of translators as Tanizaki has had, Seidensticker, Hibbett, Chambers, McCarthy—all are themselves stylists, all are concerned not only with accuracy but also with voice, with tone, with the specific gravity of prose.

Filling out the length of this collection are two minor works. "Professor Rado" is slight self-parody about the great writer being interviewed and being found out. It was originally written in two parts, 1925 and 1928. They are here united but to small effect. The other piece "The Little Kingdom" (*Chiisana Okoku*, 1918), an early story but a very fine one. In it the anatomy of power is laid bare in its frightening parable of a grade-school student who takes over his class, his classmates, and finally his teacher.

A Cat, a Man and Two Women, by Tanizaki Jun'ichiro, translated by Paul McCarthy. Tokyo: Kodansha International, 1990.

Nearly forty years ago I read, in Donald Keene's *Anthology of Japanese Literature*, Edward Seidensticker's translation of a portion of Tanizaki's *The Mother of Captain Shigemoto*. It was the section where the young Shigemoto follows his father out into the night and then watches as his bereaved parent goes to the graveyard and contemplates the spectacle of dissolution.

I, like many other readers, never forgot it, and over the decades I often wondered what the rest of this haunting novella might be like. Now I know, and memorable it is. The pages I had remembered slip into their context, and the whole is as beautifully disturbing as ever the portion was.

As in many of his historical novels, Tanizaki erects a frame of antiquarian scholarship upon which to hang a story of contemporary relevance. Himself a scholar, he had between 1935 and 1941 been working on his first translation into modern Japanese of the *Genji Monogatari*. From 1951 to 1954, he produced another, and between these two (1949–50) he wrote *Shosho Shigemoto no Haha*.

The work opens with a quote from the *Genji* about some of the personages appearing in that novel. Other authorities are quoted, selected passages are given, a scholarly apparatus is erected, and all the while Tanizaki is securing (from behind as it were) a tale of completely contemporary interest.

The main document is a manuscript, one "not so widely read," in the collection of the Shukokaku Library which is called "Shigemoto's Diary." A provenance is given along with the information that the "full text has not survived anywhere," and that "only fragments remain, apparently written sporadically ... beginning with the spring of 942."

A reason that the text has not survived is that the entire manuscript, like so many quoted in Tanizaki, is a literary invention. Ito Ken quotes the author on this: "No matter how attractive a certain subject seems, I can muster neither desire nor ability to write about it unless it is a fantasy born of my own mind. I have written a work or two that resembles historical fiction, but by and large, these are things I made up."

Sometimes these inventions are used for sheer delectation. Matching the very sober incident of the hero's father mediating on the dissolution of a corpse is an earlier scene where the amorous but disappointed suitor decides to contemplate the excrement of the beloved, for "when he realized that he, too, grimaced and produced the same dirty stuff, he would feel an aversion for her at once."

At this point, Tanizaki interrupts with "by the way, the author does not know what chamber pots were like at the time," and off he goes into lists of possible antiquarian and literary sources, all of them amusing, all of them irrelevant.

More often, however, such historical badinage has a serious purpose. Tanizaki finds that in the fake fragments "Shigemoto's yearning for his mother fills their pages." And we find that, in the pages of this spirited historical reconstruction, that we can recognize a like theme. Much of Tanizaki's fiction is about the missing mother.

This is also the theme of the 1932 *Ashikari*, here translated as *The Reed Cutter*. Again, there is an historical scaffolding, this time the 13th-century, the court of the

Emperor Gotoba, again an amount of looking on, of spying, and indeed of what one must properly term voyeurism. And again it is the story of a yearning for mother so vast that it consumes the entire work.

That the historical setting is needed for this contemporary story, is indicated by the curious film *Oyu-sama* that Mizoguchi Kenji made of the novel in 1951. He dispensed with all historical references and treated the story as a modern anecdote. The result is curiously pointless and eventually tiresome. The film director and his writer, Yoda Yoshikata, in eliminating the history, took away the resonance, the sounding board which allowed the tale to reverberate within the reader's mind.

The power of the past is the power of the dead, and yet it is equally true that the dead are brought alive through an evocation of the past. This is the aesthetic of Tanizaki's historical fiction. My forty-year gap, years of idly wondering about the Shigemoto novella, was seamlessly sealed and, at the same time, made whole by the author's showing me that the whole of the past lives on in the present detail.

The coupling of these two novellas is also particularly apt in that, separated by nearly two decades though they are, both share so much with each other. They share also Anthony Chamber's fine translation.

The Reed Cutter and Captain Shigemoto's Mother: Two Novellas, by Tanizaki Jun'ichiro, translated by Anthony Chambers. New York: Alfred A Knopf, 1994.

Here is a collection of six of Tanizaki's shorter works, given to us by two of the most eminent of Tanizaki's translators. Including work as early as 1911 and as late as 1955, this volume encompasses some forty-five years in the career of one of Japan's greatest modern writers.

Tanizaki's novels are well known, but some of his

finest works are his stories, few of which have ever before been translated. The earliest here included is the 1911 *Shonen* (translated by Chambers as "The Children"), a famous text about how children really play with each other, here serving as a curtain raiser to some of the other stories displaying the author's full blown interest in what doctors call sadomasochistic sex.

The 1911 *Himitsu* appears in Chambers revised translation (the first appeared in the University of Michigan's 1993 tribute to Edward Seidensticker, *New Leaves*) as "The Secret." The secret is that the protagonist hides his gender under the kimono of a traditional Japanese woman, doing so in part so that he can continue his affair with a real Japanese woman.

Both of these early stories are delightfully illustrative of the erotically grotesque world of the young author, full of aestheticized sex, a quality suggested by the term *tambishugi*, one by which Japanese university professors still designate the author.

Tanizaki had, however, numerous styles. One of them is illustrated in the 1918 *Futari no Chigo* which McCarthy has translated as "The Two Acolytes." Spare, elegant, restrained, this is the story of two young student priests and the separate ways they chose. Any temptation to return to the hot-house world of "The Children" is resisted, and the placid style of classical Japanese narration is sought—and beautifully found.

The final three stories in the sextet finds Tanizaki back in mature, outrageous form. That he is one of the great comic writers of the century is not known abroad since the great comic stories have not been hitherto translated. Here, however, is proof.

The 1919 *Boshoku Kurabu*, which Paul McCarthy translates as "The Gourmet Club," is filled with a typical and glorious excess. The overflowing sensuousity of Tanizaki turned on full is palpable in this story of a strange Chinese-style eatery where "Phlegm-and-Spittle Liquid Jade" is among the least repulsive items on the menu.

Aozuka-shi no Hanashi, the 1926 story which McCarthy translates as "Mr. Bluemound," reflects both Tanizaki's early interest in the cinema (he once worked for a film company and wrote a number of scripts) and his lifelong obsession with appearances and the possible realities behind them. This particular excursion goes so far that it was originally censored by the government. Its logical but outrageous conclusions about virtual reality are a shock even now.

The final story is *Kasankamangansui no Yume*, written in 1955, just ten years before the author's death. Translated by Chambers as "Manganese Dioxide Dreams," it was written more or less at the same time as that final masterpiece *The Diary of a Mad Old Man*.

Again, the work is in journal form and seems merely the digressive jotting of some elderly party until we realize the dangerous direction in which it is flowing. As the jacket blurb succinctly puts it, we are offered "a tantalizing insight into the author's mind as he blends Chinese and Japanese cuisine, a French murder movie, and the contents of a toilet bowl."

One of the joys of reading Tanizaki is while the most basic of the human passions are fully explored, this is done with an honesty and a delicacy not often associated with such subject matter. As one's own worse nature threatens to be revulsed, one's better is melted by the beauty of the observation.

The Gourmet Club: A Sextet, by Tanizaki Jun'ichiro, translated by Paul McCarthy and Anthony Chambers. Tokyo: Kodansha International, 2001.

For a long time the young Tanizaki Jun'ichiro used to lie awake at night. He was waiting for his mother: "You can get under the covers now, Jun'ichi; but be sure not to fall asleep 'till Mama comes back to say good night." And, after lying sleepless for what always seemed the longest time, finally "there came a sound, at first faint and distant, then gradually growing clearer and clearer—the familiar, longed-for sound of mother's *geta*."

Like the young Proust, Tanizaki—also to grow into his country's finest novelist—allowed his mother the greatest influence. Not only could he not sleep unless she was there, but after he was grown, she became, in various forms, visible once again in many of his works.

She was a part of all of the women, real or imagined, in his later life—she, of whom he remembered that "the flesh of her thighs was so marvelously white and delicate that, many times when we were taking a bath together, I would find myself looking at her body in amazement."

And with her remembered presence came—as with the young Marcel—the entire, detailed procession of the past. It was always a part of the mature Tanizaki, and in 1955, when he was in his late 60s, he wrote his remembrance of things past, *Yosho Jidai*, now translated by Paul McCarthy as *Childhood Years*.

In these magical pages, the whole world of mid-Meiji, the last decade of the 19th-century comes again to life. The sights and sounds, the very smells of downtown *shitamachi* Tokyo become real once more. Tanizaki remembers the taste of the first mackerel, the first flickerings of the first movies, that when he first heard Kansai dialect he thought it sounded far too much like "rough male Tokyo speech" and was concerned that it was his mother's lady friend who was using it.

He remembers old-fashioned toothbrushes made with tufts of shaved wood, so that "every morning after you cleaned your teeth, you found your mouth full of little bits and pieces of the brush," and that chicken used to be called *kashiwa* (and not *niwatori* or, more likely nowadays, *chikin*), and that the bathhouse was called *yuya* and not *sento*.

It was from the *yuya* that Tanizaki's mother nightly pattered back in her *geta* to the waiting Jun'ichiro. The family was poor but genteel—the Tanizakis had seen better days. Perhaps consequently, the young Tanizaki spent a good deal of time outside the house, playing in the labyrinth of old *shitamachi*—now so changed.

And so changed in Tanizaki's lifetime. When writing these remembrances he consulted a 1953 map of Chuo Ward, looking for the world of 1891. Vanished. "Even the positions of the bridges in the area have shifted, so it is difficult to fix any landmarks at all."

Changed though old Tokyo was it continued to live in Tanizaki's memory, and it continues to live on these pages for us. Here the young Jun'ichiro, open-mouthed, watched the *kagura*, then one of the few amusements of the young or observed with interest the Asakusa archery booths and their pretty and painted attendants. He did not realize what these concessions were a front for and "did find it odd that the customers spent all their time laughing and talking with the women and never seemed to get around to drawing their bows."

Later he falls in love with the kabuki, then so different from now. So much more detailed, realistic—as in the murder of Yoichibei in *Chushingura*: "Sadakura mounts on his chest like a horseman; the knife slowly, carefully carving away at Toichibei's entrails; his last, agonized breath."

And he remembers, son of a merchant family, the prices. In 1893 a good box in the orchestra at the Kabukiza cost ¥3.50. In 1897 it cost ¥20, causing his uncle to explain with exasperation: "I can't afford to go to the theater just when I feel like it any more!"

(Besides inflation, there is precious little left of this old Tokyo to be recaptured. I was therefore surprised and pleased to find that one day, "after viewing the morning glories at Iriya," they went to have tofu at the Sasanoyuki. The place is still near Iriya and it still serves tofu. Though now also housed in a concrete box, the taste lingers.)

Among all that Tanizaki remembers, recalling before our eyes a vanished civilization, are many of those small and telling details which are usually the first things to get lost in history. He remembers that in primary school "when you knelt in formal posture with your lower legs folded under you, without a cushion, the pattern would impress itself on the insteps of your bare feet."

And he remembers his father telling him that, when he was young and working as a delivery boy, Tokyo used to get so cold that "he could continue to walk only by letting his warm urine stream down onto his half-frozen feet." Of such accepting, human—and hence Tanizaki-like—details is this marvelous memoir made.

And it speaks to us directly. The translation becomes transparent—as though Tanizaki were writing his own pellucid English. One of the reasons is certainly the empathy of translator for writer. Paul McCarthy has long been a student of Tanizaki. It is this feeling for the author that drew McCarthy to him, and it is this continued bond which accounts for the rightness of this translation.

Childhood Years: A Memoir, by Tanizaki Jun'ichiro, translated by Paul McCarthy. Tokyo: Kodansha International, 1988.

Muro Saisei

Now considered one of Japan's finest poets, Muro Saisei (1889–1962) himself thought most highly of his prose works. While some critics would agree, this prose has not been widely translated, though the poems are included in most foreign-language anthologies. Until now, the major Saisei prose translation has been Edward Seidensticker's of *Ani Imoto* (*Brother and Sister*), an atypical work which does not reflect Saisei's major prose concern: his own life.

He once made the famous claim that a writer could never exhaust the meaning of his own life no matter how repeatedly he wrote about it. A writer, he said, was under an imperative to show how he had lived. This he did in his lyrics as well as his early prose. James O'Brien here translates two of the three extant biographical pieces in which the poet first began showing how he had lived.

"Childhood" (*Yonen Jidai*), "Adolescence" (*Sei no Mezameru koro*), and "The Death of a Certain Girl" (*Aru Shojo no Shi Made*), all published in 1919, remained the most fully formed of his biographical writings. They reflect an unsettled childhood. Son of an ex-samurai and a household maid, the illegitimate Saisei was sent to foster-parents and eventually ended up as the adopted son of a priest.

He seems always to have yearned for the settled home he never had—even constructing one in his memory. Poet Ooka Makoto has said that Saisei's most typical poems are those in which a man now living in the city remembers the countryside of his childhood. As recounted in O'Brien's translations, this childhood was filled with longings. In the latter work, the title of which is literally translated as "An Awakening to Sex," these unsatisfied inclinations take a more definite form.

As a youth, he wanders about the temple yards and finds one of the omen slips tied to a branch, left there by one of the local geisha. "I could detect on the paper the heavy fragrance of lipstick, the unbearable sweetness of which gave rise to agonizing dreams and the wish to hug something, if only a tree."

Later he spies on a girl while pretending to pray stealing

from the donation box. Though excited by this, he does nothing, though he imagines a lot: "How tantalizing to admonish her then, and to observe her heartfelt tears of remorse. If the penitent were grateful and eventually fell in love, my days of loneliness would be over. If she remained unmoved, I would subject her to all kinds of perversities."

In fact, however, he becomes her accomplice. He replentishes the offerings from his own funds, and when these prove not enough, he steals from the priest.

Obsessed with the fair thief, he even follows her home, creeps into the entry, steals one of her sandals and takes it home. "The sandal had a palpable heaviness about it and gave off the strange, oily fragrance of a woman's heel."

One might compare this heated awakening to sex with that of Mori Ogai, as chronicled in the famous *Vita Sexualis*, published just ten years before. The older author was interested merely in vindication and, in Donald Keene's phrase, "demonstrated his conviction that not all men are governed by lust ..."

Saisei, a poet, was interested in authenticity and has captured well those days of adolescent fever when the body is maturing but the mind remains a child's, when one is constantly thirsty and no drink slakes. That much of his recounting may be fiction is of no matter. Saisei is constructing an inner reality.

The concerns of these far off days of adolescence are concluded with "The Death of a Certain Girl," and I very much wish that O'Brien had chosen to translate this work rather than the novelettish "Stolen Incense Burner," a much inferior piece which is the third of those in this collection. We should, however, be grateful for what we have—part of a moving and convincing evocation to memory and the past.

Three Works by Muro Saisei, translated by James O'Brien. Ithaca: Cornell University, 1985.

Uno Koji

This is the first translation of Uno Koji (1891–1961), an author who originally perhaps excited more attention by how he acted than by what he wrote.

He used to go the Paolista Cafe on the Ginza wearing a blue fez and a red cravat tied in a big bow; at one literary banquet, he appeared in his idea of a kabuki costume with his face painted white, and on a lecture tour organized by Kikuchi Kan, he stood at the podium, eyes closed, and refused to open his mouth when his turn to lecture came.

Such eccentricity (not all that rare—Sato Haruo used to turn up at that same Paolista Cafe in a crushed velvet suit and a bright red fez) did not excite much interest in the author's work, and, indeed, he did not write anything until well into his twenties, very late for an author.

His first effort, and the one most critics still think his best, was obviously inspired, however, by something he loved—clothes. This is "In the Storehouse," the first of the two stories, written in 1919, here appearing in a beautifully colloquial translation by Elaine Gerbert.

The first-person narrator ("As I go on talking, you'll realize that I'm not the most trustworthy person,") is so in love with clothes that he pawns what he has in order to buy new ones. Then, stricken, he goes to the pawnshop (the storehouse of the title) to visit the neglected garments and to curl up in a particularly beloved but equally forsaken futon.

If Uno had a model it was Nikolai Gogol, whose stories had already appeared in Japanese translation, and whom he loved all of his life. But he also had a number of antimodels as well. These were the solemn confessional authors of the so-called naturalist school, the kind we now associate with the dullest of the first-person "I-novel" authors.

It was one of these, Chikamatsu Shuko, a man equally attached to his wardrobe, who unwittingly offered the anecdote upon which this story is based: "When I actually saw my dear kimonos so well cared for, I felt like a parent must feel when he learns that the son he gave up for adoption or the daughter he gave away in marriage are really well off."

Though Uno gave this literary form its popular name of *shishosetsu*, he was no friend to its self-serving aims. He parodied its authors and attacked the establishment. In another story, he has his young hero state: "I haven't the slightest intention of saving the human race or contributing to the improvement of society."

Though his close friend Akutagawa Ryunosuke called him "a spiritual chameleon," Uno remained true to his own ideals throughout his long life. They were often quixotic and usually counterproductive, but they were real and were based upon his ideas of literary excellence.

Late in life, he, alone among established authors, took a stand against Ishihara Shintaro's *Taiyo no Kisetsu's* being awarded the Akutagawa Prize. It won anyway (and was translated as *Season of the Sun*), but Uno was right. He also involved himself in the Matsukawa Incident, a controversial criminal affair of the Occupation period, because he believed so strongly in the innocence of the accused—and again he was, by his lights, right.

In all, Uno is a most attractive figure and one rare in Japanese literature. He has consequently been accounted for in various ways. Donald Keene classifies him with the "mental-attitude novelists" and finds that "it is questionable whether or not the critics have been right in classifying him as an 'I novelist.' " Dennis Spackman finds him "representative of a certain middlebrow element in modern Japanese literature," and discovers in him "a popular and prolific practitioner of the magazine story of his period." He also finds waggish humor and jocularity.

Elaine Gerbert, on the other hand, finds a much more interesting author, one given to parody, to satire and to a self-referential style which was avant-garde for its time (Uno was one of the earliest writers to complain that readers always confused the first-person narrator with the author). Though his tone was purposely unbuttoned (Sato Haruo guessed, correctly, that like Ivan Goncharov's Oblomov, the author wrote lying down), it is also sharp and sarcastic.

In explaining the acquisition of his *futon*, for example, his narrator says: "I was trying to be as carefully choosy as a soldier is when he gets his horse, or a geisha her kimonos, or as the literati of old were when they chose their inkstones."

Certainly, no one else in militant 1919 was writing anything as delightfully mordant. Nor did he continue to write in this manner very long. There were a few more stories, including the 1922 "Love of Mountains" (here translated), and then a long silence.

This was occasioned, it is commonly believed, by the suicide of Akutagawa (about whom Uno later wrote a book) and by the state of Uno's own health. What he wrote after this crisis was much more conventional and was, for a time, more highly regarded. Yet his early, strident, convoluted, playful voice is certainly worth listening to — particularly when it has been so aptly, adroitly and even lovingly transcribed by Elaine Gerbert.

Love of Mountains: Two Stories by Uno Koji, translated by Elaine Gerbert. Honolulu: University of Hawaii Press, 1997.

Akutagawa Ryunosuke

Though he is one of Japan's best known and most

widely read authors, the literary reputation of Akutagawa Ryunosuke (1892–1927) remains anomalous both in Japan and abroad.

There are various reasons. One is, perhaps, his very accessibility. He remains a popular author and one of the easiest of all Japanese modern writers to read. There is, consequently, less for literary scholars to do. This being so, he is not given critical attention—not to the degree given Soseki, Kawabata, Shiga, etc. Another reason is that he does not favor the confessional mode which has long been a major concern of Japanese critics. Yet another is that Akutagawa is an extraordinarily imaginative writer, even a fanciful one, and literary opinion in Japan has long been controlled by the various schools of realism.

The result is that his work is codified as minor, and Akutagawa is himself regarded as a literary symbolist (the Japanese place him among the *shinrichi-ha*, whatever that may mean—it translates as the Neo-Intellectual School). His true worth, as one of Japan's most personal writers, one of its most accomplished stylists, remains largely unacknowledged; and he is downgraded to the position of a children's author, or one, at any rate, whom young people may profitably read. That he was also an anti-social maverick has not endeared him to the Japanese literary establishment and even the fact that he committed suicide (in itself often enough to ensure canonization—as in the case of Dazai Osamu) was not considered sufficient to award him a proper place in the literary pantheon.

This being so, one might expect, as had often been the case, that the foreign scholarly community would come to the rescue. But, here again, there are problems. One of these is Akutagawa's sheer availability in English. He is the most translated of all Japanese authors. More than one hundred thirty stories, the form he favored, are translated: fifteen whole pages are devoted to these in the International House bibliography; *Rashomon* alone has been translated forty-two times. With so much already available, foreign scholars are not much interested—they prefer to make reputations by staking out their own territories, preferably virgin.

Another problem militating against a general foreign acceptance of Akutagawa's worth is that he was translated early. One of the results is that the translations range from unscholarly to appalling; another is that these early translations insist upon the exotic—this being one of the few ways to sell Japanese literature in the early days—with the result that the unfortunate author is made to seem quaint and curious. Thus, Akutagawa has come to have a bad literary reputation in the West: he is perceived as a purveyor of exotica—which he is not.

To be sure, Akutagawa has also had excellent translators (Arthur Waley, Howard Hibbett, Ivan Morris, Paul McCarthy, Richard McKinnon), but these have contented themselves with a story apiece, published in collections or journals, and such efforts have not been enough to raise Akutagawa's reputation to its deserved level.

None of this would make much difference to the general reader except for the important fact that Japanese indifference and foreign misunderstanding have prevented our receiving what Akutagawa deserves: a completely new and first-rate translation of the complete works.

These thoughts on the vagaries of Akutagawa's literary reputation are prompted by a new reprint of one of the early translated collections. This book originally appeared in 1964, though the various stories had also appeared in earlier publications. (The same translator has another volume as well, *Rashomon and Other Stories*, which appeared in 1952.)

These translations are, to put it charitably, not distinguished. Since English is not the translator's mother tongue, he cannot be expected to understand the nuances of that language, and no number of American/English eyes overlooking his labors (and there seem to have been quite a few) can supply this lack. Further, there have been a number of simplistic additions (the cast of characters added to *Genkaku-Sanbo*, the introduction to *Nezumi Kozo*), no indication being given that these are not the work of the author. I am in no position to check the accuracy of the translation itself, but, comparing it with other translations of the same material, I believe it to be what was once called (innocent word) "free."

Something, to be sure, remains of Akutagawa—he is a strong, highly pictorial writer—but not enough. *Jigokuhen* is much more powerful in the W.H.H. Norman translation (included in Keene's *Modern Japanese Literature*), and *Hana* (Natsume Soseki's favorite Akutagawa) is much better served in the Morris translation (uncollected: *Japan Quarterly* (2:4) 1955). *Kumo no Ito* is more moving in the Daniels translation (out of print: *Japanese Prose*, 1944), and "A Clod of Earth" is much more persuasive in the McKinnon translation (out of print: *The Heart Is Alone*, 1957.)

At least no matter how difficult to obtain, we thus have some alternate translations. More serious difficulties are occasioned by works of which there are no others. One of the pleasures of *Heichu*, I am told, is that the style is a parody of that of the *Uji Monogatari* from which work the story is taken. And one of the charms of *Yonosuke no Hanashi* is the pastiche of the style of Saikaku, the author of *Koshoku Ichidai Otoko*, that book of which Yonosuke is the hero. You could never guess this from the present translations, however. There is no lightness, no wit, no playfulness (and Akutagawa can be a very playful author); rather the slow, quasi-accurate, pedantic pace of English as an acquired language.

With diligence and imagination, the English reader may garner some slight inkling as to why Akutagawa is such an important and rewarding author, but few will be willing to exercise themselves to this degree. Rather, he or she will lay down the volume believing that the author is quaint, grotesque, a little dull. And this, I claim, is a misrepresentation as well as being a shame. Until there is an adequate body of informed translation, poor Akutagawa will continue to languish in his literary netherworld.

Japanese Short Stories, by Akutagawa Ryunosuke, translated by Kojima Takashi. Tokyo: Charles E. Tuttle Company, 1981. (Reprint of the 1964 Liveright edition.)

In the essay used as introduction to this new collection from the works of Akutagawa Ryunosuke, Jorg Luis Borges found these "enchanting and sometimes terrifying" works typical of the troubled interchange between East and West.

Indeed, "one might say that the meeting of the two cultures is necessarily tragic," that it results in "a heart-rending and sorrowful spiritual crisis." It follows then that Akutagawa is "one of the artists and martyrs of that metamorphosis."

The unhappy childhood (mad mother) and early life of the writer is well known, as is his troubled career and eventual suicide. Well known also are a handful of works, the novel *Kappa* (a favorite of Borges) and the stories *Rashomon*, *In a Grove* (the combination of which made the famous Kurosawa film), and the 1918 "Hell Screen."

It is this famous story which opens the present collection. In it, the artist who wants to paint hell is presented as model his own daughter; he accepts (so great his devotion to his art), and she is burned alive.

Of this work Sakai Kazuya (translator of Akutagawa into Spanish and probably the editor of this collection) has said that this story is "a descent into the hell that the author felt was beginning to close in on him."

The other works in the collection ascertain that this destination was indeed reached. "Cogwheels," found among

Akutagawa's papers and probably written in 1927 is, as Donald Keene has said, "perhaps his masterpiece." A series of six short interrelated pieces, it is "about" mental disintegration (or reintegration) and ends with the cry: "Isn't there anyone to come and strangle me quietly in my sleep?" As Keene has said of this work: "After reading [it] we can only marvel that Akutagawa did not kill himself sooner."

This is followed by "A Fool's Life," written a month before the suicide. It is a collection of fifty-one short sections; a tiny, fragmented *shishosetsu* in which the suffering author remembers life. Experience and literature (the mad Strindberg appears) mesh, and the 1923 earthquake is distilled into 13 lines, beginning with that famous reference to the corpses: "The odor was not unlike that of rotten apricots."

Concluding the selection is his suicide note, or one of them: "A Note to a Certain Old Friend," addressed to Kume Masao and including that well known phrase "*bonyari shita fuan*" (which Keene translates as "a vague uneasiness"), one of the apparent reasons for the suicide.

The Akutagawa who appears in this collection is the tortured, tormented intellectual who found death preferable. A reason for the exclusivity of this presentation might be that all the works refer to each other—that is, in "Cogwheels" the author makes reference to "Hell Screen" and to "A Fool's Life," where occurs the phrase: "Life is more hellish than hell itself." Another might be that many readers and writers (including Borges it would seem) prefer this version of Akutagawa (an accurate one so far as it goes) to any other.

Another presentation, however, is quite possible, and other Akutagawas are waiting to be introduced. The one I would like to meet would be the mature and compassionate man who wrote the fine "middle-period" stories and revered Shiga Naoya and paid homage in such splendid narratives as "Hand Car" and—for me the most moving of all Japanese short stories—"Tangerines." There are several new translations of Akutagawa collections being made at present. Perhaps one of them will not so insist upon the demonic and the death-prone.

And perhaps it will have translations all of a piece. The present collection does not, though some of them are excellent. Particularly fine is that for "Cogwheels" by Cid Corman and Kamaike Susumu, originally published by New Directions in 1974. "A Note to a Certain Old Friend," is translated by Beongcheon Yu (who has also made a distinguished translation of "Cogwheels" which remains uncollected).

"A Fool's Life" is translated by Will Petersen—it is a translation which originally appeared in 1968 and was later printed in book form by the Mushinsha Ltd. publishing house. It is poetic, laconic, and reads extremely well. It does, however, abridge. The last section, "Defeat," for example takes over eighty words in Keene's translation (an excerpt in his *Dawn to the West*), and in Petersen's version it takes less than fifty. The information is the same, but the styles are various.

"Hell Screen" is given in the old Kojima translation. Since the editor could have availed himself of W. H. H. Norman's much better work, I do not know why the Kojima was used. This is not said to denigrate the work of this early translator (who has translated more Akutagawa stories than anyone else), merely to indicate its limitations.

This new collection, certainly a product of these interlaced times—edited in (apparently) Argentina, printed in Italy, and published from Colorado—may be seen, I hope, of a renewed interest in this popular but critically neglected author.

Hell Screen/Cog Wheels/A Fool's Life, by Akutagawa Ryunosuke. Colorado: Eridanos Press, 1987.

Sato Haruo

As Thomas Rimer remarks in his introduction to this translation, the particular kind of lyric melancholy which Sato's prose (and much of the poetry) exhibits might indicate a Buddhist pessimism over the state of the mundane world, but it is perhaps also an attempt "to recast certain attributions of that melancholy in terms of modern alienation."

Like Baudelaire, whose poetry he knew and had translated, Sato defined for Japan that sense of apathy and world-weariness which the French author had written about in "Le Spleen de Paris." The term which Sato used, *yuutsu*, occurs often in the work and figures in the titles of two of the works here translated. *Denen no Yuutsu* (*Rural Melancholy*) appeared in 1918, and *Tokai no Yuutsu* (*Melancholy in the City*) in 1922. In both, ennui is the theme. The former finds the narrator unhappy in the country; the latter, disconsolate in the metropolis. In this he is indeed much like Baudelaire to whom spleen was a way of life.

The resemblance extended, in the early years at any rate, to an eccentric dandyism which saw the youthful author as a Keio student wearing a velvet suit and a red fez and on the Ginza sporting a bowler hat and flowing cravat. He also carried around D'Annunzio and Oscar Wilde, particularly *The Picture of Dorian Grey*, a work he revered, as well as volumes of Nietzsche and Blake.

It was the latter who contributed a major theme to *Rural Melancholy*, a rose with canker in the bud. Indeed, echoing a beloved line from Blake, the first version of this work was called *Yameru Sobi*, which is the "sick rose" of the title of this volume.

Like many another dandy, Sato turned in later years as conservative as he had been bohemian. He supported the Japanese invasion of China, became actively involved during the Greater East Asia War, and both his prose and poetry voiced patriotic sentiments much different indeed from the poses of alienation in the early work.

It is, however, perhaps just this need for active guidance that the dandy is originally exhibiting in his sartorial experiments. He is searching for a style. And often the dandy (D'Annunzio, Pound; Sato, Mishima) finds it in the socially repressive.

Before settling for conformity, however, Sato was interestingly unconventional. It was he who, notoriously, fell in love with the first Mrs. Tanizaki and then had to convince the famous author (who did not love her but apparently had strong feelings about property) to give her up.

Sato also unconventionally attacked his literary elders. The leading Japanese authority on Wilde, as Donald Keene has told us, was savaged by the young Sato, who found this *sensei*'s translations of *The Picture of Dorian Grey* much lacking. "Somehow I cannot quite believe that lilac is the plural of lily," wrote the icy young author, adding: "My edition does not contain that passage."

Rural Melancholy (Keene's translation of the title and better, I think, than *Gloom in the Country* which is used here), was the product of a young and precocious intellect. Sato had read the fin-de-siècle writers and found himself responding. The result is something like Huysmans in Hachioji.

Francis B. Tenny, who has so admirably has translated these two works (and added the interesting character sketch, "Okinu and Her Brother"—Okinu to Sono Kyodai, 1918) knows quite well that small works, important to contemporary literature history, are also "period pieces."

And so, "beyond the attempt to be faithful to the meaning and style of Sato's prose, I have sought to find English equivalents natural to the readers of literate English of the 1920s. This has guided me in the choice of English words and idioms and in the romanization of Chinese names and places and some Japanese words and names." In this context it may also be seen that, as a title, *Gloom in the Country* indeed has a 1920s like ring to it—early Lawrence.

In any event, the translation is consistent and illuminating. It is not, oddly, often that a translator from the Japanese knows about the historical levels of English and realizes how important they are in approximating the original effect of the work being translated. This, however, Francis Tenny certainly does and has, as a result, given us in this volume the fresh and rose-like smell of these lyrical effusions written over seventy-five years ago.

The Sick Rose: A Pastoral Elegy, by Sato Haruo, translated by Francis B. Tenny, introduction by J. Thomas Rimer. Honolulu: University of Hawaii Press, 1993.

Yosano Akiko

Yosano Akiko (1878–1942) is one of modern Japan's most celebrated woman poets. Her *tanka*—the form she favored—were several times collected, and she has been much translated over the years.

The single work for which she is most famous is the *Midaregami*, a 1901 collection of 399 *tanka* (115 of them translated here for the first time) which was so frankly sensual that it caused a sensation, the reverberations of which are still felt. For example: "Spring is short!/Nothing endures!/I cried,/Letting him touch/These supple breasts!"

One may imagine the stir caused by poems like this in prim Meiji Japan. The poem flew in the face of a number of received opinions, among them that women were to curb their sensuality and that nice women did not even experience such emotions. More importantly (Nothing endures!)

the poem even attacks the official optimism of the period.

Yet, as Yosano often suggested in these hundreds of diary-like *tanka*, she early knew what the world was really like: "Even at nineteen I knew/The violet would fade,/The brook would dry up and life would pass away."

To read such Heian-like thoughts in 1901 must have been disconcerting for the reader, but Yosano was in many ways both before and after her time. While frankly sensuous, well aware of her human nature and society's double standard, she was at the same time filled with that tragic sense of life without which real poetry is impossible. And she knew what such poetry costs: "After my bath/At the hot spring,/These clothes/As rough to my skin as the world!"

Though she wrote modern (even by contemporary standards ultramodern) *tanka*, their content was often concerned with a timeless past. "In the dark/palace corridor/suppressing her cry/With the sleeve of her dancing robe—it was he!"

Here she is, a Heian Period dancing girl (albeit one who has obviously seen 19th-century melodrama), glimpsing the beloved. And in many of her poems she lingers in the classical ages. (And more than lingers: her 1912 rendering of the *Genji Monogatari* into modern Japanese remained the authoritative edition until Tanizaki's in 1941.)

"Complain not,/but hurry on your way—tonight, other soft hands/will be waiting,/ready to undo your clothes!" Now she is one of the serving girls at a wayside inn. And here she is as both herself and whole generations of women before her: "Whispering goodnight/this spring evening/and leaving the room,/I take from the rack/his kimono and try it on."

The honest feelings shown in *Midaregami* have kept it alive during the decades and contributed much to the image of the brave poet. One who, as the years passed, grew even braver. When her soldier brother was at Port Arthur, she wrote poems urging him not to die for his country. When reprimanded for her lack of patriotism she replied that women everywhere have always hated war.

Yosano also went on to become a better poet than she had been in 1901 and eventually came to dislike even hearing of the early *Midaregami*, invariably—then as now—the single work everyone knew.

As Donald Keene has observed, like the aged Theophile Gautier who was "always remembered in terms of the red vest he wore to the opening of *Hernani*, Yosano captured so vividly the headstrong emotions of a sensual girl that readers never permitted her to grow up."

Tangled Hair: Selected Tanka from Midaregami, by Yosano Akiko, translated with an introduction by Sanford Goldstein and Shinoda Seishi. Tokyo: Charles E. Tuttle Company, 1987. (Reprint of Purdue University Press edition, 1971).

In 1928 the now famous poet Yosano Akiko was invited to travel through northeast Asia by the South Manchurian Railway Company. This quasi-governmental organization often invited famous folk. No only did it publicize the railway itself, but it also served to validate Japanese Manchurian military adventures.

The largest coup was Japan's most famous author, Natsume Soseki, who had been, in 1909, induced to take to the rails and publish the results. Aware that he was being used for political purposes, the author of *Botchan* turned jocular, a ploy he had often used to endistance himself, and in the end, exposed the whole set-up.

Yosano, though writing at a time when Japan's expansionist ambitions were even more evident, sometimes seems carefully unaware. As the translator of her journal writes: "[She] never mentions that all the extraordinary courtesies she and her husband received during their weeks in Manchuria and Mongolia might in any way influence what she was writing about Japanese activities there."

At times, her comments seem purposely naive. Delighted to find an acquaintance now in a position of some power, she marvels at the "good relations" he has contrived between Japan and Manchuria. And, in a gracious reference to her hosts: "I was happy to see the sagacious manner in which the South Manchurian Railway Company assigned the right man to the right place."

At other times, she is more astute. "When I consider the Sino-Japanese issue ... I imagine that Japan will end up isolated from the world, and it saddens me." When soldiers (Koreans recruited by the Japanese military) are billeted in their hotel, she writes that "imperialism and the smell of liquor [were] incompatible with our desire to write poems about ... willow catkins."

This what she and her husband often did—view something local and then pen a verse. Both were, after all, poets—she now much more famous than he was—and her poetry, as well as her presence, was what the railroad was paying for. In addition to being conventionally poetic, her journal also sometimes becomes commonly genteel. "We appreciated that the maids all preserved the humility of respectable young women and had nothing of the air of waitresses about them."

Though given the subtitle "A Feminist Poet from Japan Encounters Prewar China" there is little in this journal to indicate what we now know as feminism. Little too of what Yosano herself once demonstrated years before when her brother was at Port Arthur and she wrote poems urging him not to die for his country.

Now, traveling first-class, her feminist concerns seem fewer. She finds herself "delighted to the point of tears to find that women of such elegance [as a certain Mrs. Wu] in war-torn China still existed." Listening to a railway director she notes that "one point he made, about the difficulty faced by Japanese women born and raised in Manchuria in finding husbands, struck me as particularly melancholy."

Not only is there little forthright feminism, there is also a certain tone which signals acceptance of received ideas about the sexes. One of the reasons for the society-column sound of the journal is, to be sure, that she was not alone and so wrote in the third-person plural, a form which always lends a suggestion of the spurious. "We much enjoyed the landscape" seems not only less personal but also less honest than "I liked the view." Another reason was that, as a professional writer, she knew what her audience would expect—well-bred reactions to the new territories. Yet another reason for the shallowness of many of the observations was that, while writing, she knew that the Japanese military was looking over her shoulder.

Joshua Fogel, who translates this edition, is an authority on the subject, having written *The Literature of Travel in the Japanese Rediscovery of China, 1862–1945*. Many Japanese authors went—Tayama Katai, Akutagawa Ryunosuke, Tanizaki Jun'ichiro, Sato Haruo and others. Many had met with other Chinese writers. By 1928, however, with Sino-Japanese tensions high, such meetings were impossible and cultured Japanese travelers had to content themselves with a genteel tone, a safe antiquarianism and writing poems about willow catkins.

Perhaps for this very reason, this translation of the *Man-Mo Yuki* is important. It was written by a major poet, and it gives an insight into the dilemma of a sensitive and individual writer in circumstances where she could not write freely.

Travels in Manchuria and Mongolia: A Feminist Poet from Japan Encounters Prewar China, by Yosano Akiko, translated by Joshua A. Fogel. New York: Columbia University Press, 2001.

Tsubota Joji

Kaze no Naka no Kodomo by Tsubota Joji (1890–1982) was originally serialized in the *Asahi Shimbun* in the fall of 1936—thirty-eight short chapters printed over three months. It proved quite popular and was shortly made into a much-praised film by Shimizu Hiroshi.

It also made the forty-six-year-old author's reputation and established him as one of Japan's foremost writers about children. Some translations of other works into German appeared, and *Children in the Wind* itself was rendered into Italian in 1966. Aside from a single story translated by the late William L. Clark in 1958, however, this is the first appearance of Tsubota in English.

The story of this novella is soon told. The father of the children, two little boys, is accused of embezzlement and imprisoned; mother finds the original document, however, and, his name cleared, father returns home. Interest in this anecdote is sustained in that, as the translator writes in his afterword, "the adults in the story do not seem to understand what is happening in the boys' world any better than the boys understand what is happening in the adults' world."

This is a most fruitful confusion, and it has resulted in several masterpieces—both *Huckleberry Finn* and Henry James' *What Maisie Knew* are built around this recipe. This, however, is the only similarity between these works and Tsubota's much more modest effort.

A major difference is that there is no irony in the Japanese work because the children are denied any serious status. We are invited to regard them with a common if affectionate amusement. Irony, however, can operate only if both we and the children remain seriously unaware. Huck's resolve to be "wicked" and not turn in the runaway

Jim is ironic because he turns to the true good by being socially "bad"—something of which he is unaware (as were a majority of Twain's adult readers until they had it pointed out to them).

Tsubota is altogether easier on the reader. We are told what is happening and are then invited to share an indulgent smile as we observe what the children make of it. To this end, we must continually switch points-of-view, an operation which always ruins believability.

Mother and children are on a bridge. Mother looks at the rushing torrent. Given her troubles, we can guess what she is thinking. Nonetheless she turns to her youngest and says: "What if Mother died?" The little boy does not take this in, and his mother, touched by such innocence, "then and there ... made up her mind. No matter what happened, she would go on living. She would bring up Sampei."

This sudden change of viewpoint, this dull iteration in the final sentence, may make a rousing ending for a newspaper installment, but it defeats any possible irony. If children and adults do not understand each other's worlds, this is merely stated, rather than expressively shown.

Thus, at times, the text reads like a children's book rather than a book about children. Indeed, the publisher seems to think that this popular novel *is* a children's book. The afterword asks: "Do these Japanese boys have feelings that differ from yours? Do you imagine that the things which made them feel happy or sad, angry or afraid, might also make you feel happy or sad, angry or afraid?" These are questions to be asked a child, not an adult. Yet Tsubota intended his tale for grown-ups, and in any event, the *Asahi Shimbun* is not read by small children.

The translator, Robert Epp is known as a translator of popular literature. He has hitherto given us works by Kinoshita Yuji, Shiina Rinzo, and Sono Ayako, not to mention Ikeda Daisaku. His rendering of Tsubota is sturdy and straightforward in a way which compliments the author.

I might have wished for a bit more awareness of historical levels of language. "Knock it off" and "really neat" are examples of post-World War II juvenile American slang and are not appropriate for 1936. Also, there is the problem of the cliché. When mother is kept "busy as a bee with her sewing," and "hadn't slept a wink all night," the reader is forced to wonder whether the author intended the cliché or not. In this case, however, clichés fit well into Tsubota's style and, in any event, the question of a sophisticated author's knowingly using a cliché for ironic effect is not applicable to this novel.

Children in the Wind is an example of what the average Japanese reader liked and felt at home with. Since such examples of popular literature are rarely translated, one must compliment Epp and his publisher for making one such available to us.

Children of the Wind, by Tsubota Joji, translated by Robert Epp. London: Kegan Paul, 1991.

Yoshikawa Eiji

Musashi, Charles Terry's English translation of Yoshikawa Eiji's *Miyamoto Musashi*, has now reached the American bestseller charts. It is time to examine this phenomenon.

Since the phenomenon is not, I think, literary, it would be best, perhaps, to first dispose of *Musashi*'s pretensions in that direction since these tend to obscure the true accomplishments of the publishers.

Yoshikawa Eiji (1892–1962) was a Japanese popular novelist, popular in the *taishu-sakka* sense (for which term

Kenkyusha gives the translation of "dime novelist") who, between 1936 and 1938, serialized his long saga of *Musashi* in the *Asahi Shimbun*. It was published in book form and eventually appeared in four separate editions, selling—say the publishers—a total of one hundred twenty million copies, a figure which (if accurate) would indicate that every man, woman and child in Japan owned one.

The work has been, in other words, a popular success. It has also been filmed a total of seven times, and there have been three TV series based on it. It is conceivable that there is not a single Japanese who has not heard of Musashi himself. Yoshikawa's Musashi, that is.

As for the real swordsman upon whom the saga is based, he has been completely obscured by the novel—just as has been Will Adams by *Shogun*. The real Musashi, for example, as Charles Terry has elsewhere noted, probably never had a duel with Sasaki Kojiro, but since this event is the climax of the legend, it has now gone into "history," and the Japanese layman is convinced that it occurred.

The book which the real Musashi actually wrote, the *Gorin-no-sho* (A Book of Five Rings), shows the man to have been as austere and devoted as his fictional counterpart and as rambunctious and feckless, but history often pales before irresponsible dramatization and, consequently, Yoshikawa's has become the real Musashi.

And popular this popularization is. So popular indeed that Edwin O. Reischauer in his introduction to the translation speaks confidently of its being the "*Gone with the Wind* of Japan." Such comparison, however, is surely as inaccurate as it is well-intentioned. Margaret Mitchell was a highly competent writer, and her book is a well-researched historical novel with a beginning, a middle, and an end. Her characters are believable and can think as well as act.

A closer comparison to Yoshikawa, if one is necessary, would be, I think, Hervey Allan and his now long forgotten

Anthony Adverse. This novel had, like Yoshikawa's—and at about the same time—an enormous popularity. Anthony swept America in the same years that Musashi was sweeping Japan for the first time, and the reasons for the popularity had, in both cases, nothing to do with literature.

Both countries needed affirmative national heroes at the time. America was coming out of the Depression and was getting ready for its new role as world leader. Like many states during the 1930s—Germany, Italy and Japan among them—it needed a glorified national past. A like zeitgeist was operating in Japan. Social forces, both "natural" and manipulated, resulted in instant bestsellers which satisfied the need and filled the vacuum.

Anthony Adverse is, like *Musashi*, really a children's book disguised as adult reading. Precisely, both are boys' books—Frank Merriwell in, respectively, 18th-century America and 16th-century Japan. Both are about wild action for its own sake, both keep the psychology (and the believability) down to a minimum, and yet both pay a kind of lip service to aspiration. Musashi is presumably looking for "enlightenment," and Anthony is looking for "fulfillment." Both were ideal fodder for countries and populations looking for historical respectability, an affirmation of "ancient" virtues, and a new place in the sun.

In his introduction, Reischauer goes on to be kind to *Musashi* at the expense of *Shogun*. He finds that the latter "flagrantly flouts history," and is often "without a shred of plausibility." But, if this is true of *Shogun*, then it is equally true of *Musashi*. Though there is indeed a *Shogun/Musashi* connection, of which more later, such comparison is perhaps not to the point—one might as well compare the Big Mac with the Dairy Queen Hamburger Special.

Let us look more closely into the ingredients of *Musashi*. Charles Terry has described these as well as anyone could. "There is something in it for everybody: history, romance, a guided tour of the countryside, a fairly simple philosophy of life, a melodramatic love affair (by this I mean one in which the lovers travel all over everywhere, missing each other by minutes …), local color, a modicum of religion, a great deal of patriotism, poetry … talk about art, glorification of traditional culture, and sword battles galore."

"There is also a gallant hero, yet with human flaws; a despicable villain, yet with redeeming features; a beautiful Japanese heroine, all meekness and inner strength; a learned priest who condemns but always forgives … a determined old woman bent on revenge … a great and elegant geisha; not one but two impish but adorable little boys; a shogun, several daimyos … a cast of thousands."

These two-dimensional people swarm through their two-dimensional settings at the pace required by daily newspaper installments, each section a cliff-hanger. (One of them literally so. The lovely Otsu falls off a cliff in one section, and we never do learn how she gets back up.) Only rarely, outside children's literature, does one encounter such bustle.

To very small end. Something for everyone means nothing for anyone, and, consequently, action unsupported by thought remains merely itself. As an example: the real Musashi, and supposedly his fictional counterpart, was looking for enlightenment. Indeed, Yoshikawa makes much of this supposed ambition. Yet at the first encounter (and all those further), we are told nothing. The Musashi in this book is locked up for three years by the priest Takuan in order to study and prepare himself and learn something of the ways of the spirit. The hero tied up in the tree, which occurs just before the incarceration, takes pages: the swordfight which occurs after it takes a whole section; yet this potentially fascinating period of three whole years is disposed of in just a paragraph. One sees where the true interest of the novelist lies.

Further, though there is a cast of thousands, each turns out to be not a character but an exemplar we have often met before. Musashi, for example, is the strong man who grows weak at the sight of the opposite sex, full as he is of that reassuring horror of women which is even now an attribute of Japanese machismo.

Otsu is rebuffed at every turn but displays through her near masochistic devotion the long-suffering loyalty insisted upon as an attribute of the truly feminine Japanese female. Musashi's sidekick, Matahachi, is bumblingly there so that the virtues of our hero can seem the more sterling. Takuan, comic relief, yet knows, behind the smiles and simpers, the "true way." The entire gallery consists of personifications of received ideas.

The book itself is also a collection of *idées reçus*. Let us deconstruct a single sentence: "Even children have a sense of feminine beauty or at least they understand instinctively whether a woman is pure or not." Jotaro (one of the "impish but adorable little boys") is making friends with the long-suffering Otsu, and the sentence is the author's comment.

One first notices that "feminine beauty" is being identified with "purity" which here means virginity. In other words, a woman with some experience cannot be truly feminine. The obvious "truth" of this observation is emphasized by the further suggestion that, if "even" children can make this association, how much more "true" it is for adults. In practice, if little boys sense this, then grown-up men know it. Thus one of the hoariest of received ideas is pushed forward to take the place of psychological investigation and consequent character revaluation. And now imagine almost a thousand pages of this kind of stuff.

Here, of course, we also have an added reason for the popularity of *Musashi* in both countries. Received ideas are always popular. They reassure they maintain an agreed-upon status quo; they do not upset nor surprise—rather, they lull. Hence the good Japanese *yomi mono* (which is what *Musashi* is) and the "rousing good read" (which is what the *Washington Post* called *Musashi*) consists of little else. Indeed, the true difference between pop lit (or *taishu bungaku*) and literature (*jun bungaku*) is simply that the former is always a construct of reassuring truisms based upon moral conventions, and the latter is an often accurate reporting of disturbing amoral life as it is. The fanciful one of the pair is the pop novel, not the literary one, and it always sells better.

In the case of *Musashi*, much better. Better, despite or perhaps because of the nonsense. The *New York Times* found that "finishing *Musashi* is a small act of heroism in itself...." and said that the book was "a ludicrous series of accidents and coincidences." I would certainly not deny these statements but would suggest that these might, in some manner, account for the very popularity of the book. One may not know what one likes, but one usually likes what one knows, and *Musashi* is familiar ground indeed.

Let us attempt to account for the popularity of *Musashi* in America, other than in terms of its easy assurance that people are limited everywhere. First, Musashi is a swordsman and the American martial arts boomlet has been large enough to render the judo/karate phenomenon visible. Not only are American readers fairly familiar with *budo* (in whatever form), the idea of strenuous exercise coincides with that nation's belated passion for "physical fitness"—solitary sport (jogging, judo *kata*) is currently a good thing.

Too, swordsmanship (whatever the Americans think that means) is connected with the aspirations of Zen. Thus a sport which makes you more fit, not only physically but spiritually as well, is an even better thing. Though Musashi appears to know as much about Zen as the average Jersey City jogger, that is not the point. The point is that both are attempting.

Also, *Musashi* is not an historical reconstruction, it is a *chambara*, a sword-play romance, and Americans have seen many filmed *chambara*. Indeed, they have often enough seen *Musashi* itself, all three parts of the Inagaki version (*Samurai*) with Mifune sweating and straining as the hero. Prints of these films have been in the United States for years now and have been very widely shown. In addition, many another *chambara* (*Sword of Doom*, *Kill*, etc.) have long been house-fillers. Thus Yoshikawa's audience finds a somewhat prepared audience since his action-filled book is the original *chambara*.

In continuing to search for reasons for *Musashi*'s current American popularity, I would mention its rendering into English. I have nothing but praise for Charles Terry's translation. Though he himself possesses a distinguished English style, both clear and lucid, (apparent to any who have read his other work), he seems to have realized from the beginning that such would not benefit *Musashi*. So he took, I think, a calculated risk and translated into an exquisite pastiche of pop-book style.

Sample: "Saved again ... somebody's on our side, that's for sure." Another sample: "Aw, Oko ... don't be that way.... Is that any way to treat an old friend?" And just as Edward Seidensticker in his monumental *Genji* translation brings something of himself, his love for Jane Austen, into his language, so Terry brings something of his own as well, the language of his own Southern childhood: "Run as fast as your legs can carry you. Fetch your daddy right away. Then go down to the river bank and get Uncle Gon! And hurry!"

These examples I would argue are right for *Musashi*, even (or particularly) the rustic confusion of Mississippi and Iga. Terry's triumph (and I am not, at least not here, speaking ironically) is that he has recreated the thought of Yoshikawa in a language suited to it.

He has also energetically pruned. Indeed, this translation is only (if you count pages, a somewhat suspicious undertaking when one set is in Japanese and the other in English) two-thirds of the original book. I think this, and his other simplifications, a good thing, and cannot imagine that the missing third could add anything to our pleasure.

Yoshikawa's Japanese is convoluted and elaborate. He also often uses very difficult *kanji*, and it is indeed this use of such that has perhaps so long fooled Japanese readers into thinking he has anything to say. Obviously, such a style does not suit the content of his book. Terry's rendering magnificently does.

There are doubtless other reasons for *Musashi*'s U.S. popularity. Curiosity about a country which can so disrupt America's economy, nostalgia for a land where the work ethic persists, etc. Also, perhaps, an interest in finding something usable. The translation of Musashi's *Book of Five Rings* has sold, I have been told, 30,000 copies in the United States, apparently to those who are attempting to use it as a guide to better selling and distribution techniques.

But among all these reasons, the great one is, of course, the popularity of *Shogun*, the book which started the whole thing. The publishers of *Musashi* are quite aware of this. The copy for their *New York Times* ad is indeed quite explicit: "If you loved *Shogun*, you're ready for the authentic samurai classic from Japan." Despite the implication that *Musashi* is authentic, one can see upon whose coattails this translation comes riding, those of the Shogun's *haori*. Indeed, without Clavell, we would have in English no Yoshikawa.

(No one has mentioned that this is Yoshikawa's second appearance in America. In 1956 Knopf issued his *Shin Heike Monogatari* as *The Heike Story*. Though a better book than *Musashi*, since the author had to stick to very well known history in that one, it was roundly reviewed as dull, episodic, shallow, and disappeared without a trace. Now we have a book which is just as dull, episodic, shallow and it ends up at the top of the bestseller lists.)

So, popular this translation of *Musashi* is, and detractors from this achievement will be told that the publishers will cry all the way to the bank. This admonition, however, is one whose sting is felt only if one believes that bank balances represent the greatest good. Others may rejoice that at least something seems to have penetrated the *kanji* curtain.

Terry has elsewhere written that "my own belief is that if a Japanese bestseller … becomes a bestseller in the United States and other countries, one small step will have been taken toward the creation of a better Japanese image abroad." Reischauer has also, without having indicated that *Musashi* is any less than a rousing read, suggested that its importance in English might be elsewhere. "*Musashi* … gives both a glimpse into Japanese history and a view into the idealized self-image of the contemporary Japanese" and is hence, presumably, all the more worth reading.

I wonder. I notice that both use the word "image." I trust that both are using it in the sense in which my *Concise Oxford Dictionary* gives it: "artificial imitation of the external form of an object …"

Musashi: An Epic Novel of the Samurai Era, by Yoshikawa Eiji, translated by Charles S. Terry. Tokyo: Kodansha International, New York: Harper & Row, 1981.

Uno Chiyo

Uno Chiyo (1897–1996), writer, ex-housewife and later what the press called a "femme-fatale," was in 1930 finishing a short novel and had decided to include a double suicide, man and woman done in by love.

Uno had thought of gas but since she did not know the mechanics involved, she called up the artist Togo Seiji, a celebrated survivor of just such a pact but one involving the much more dramatic means of knives.

Realizing that such a matter could not be satisfactorily discussed on the telephone, they arranged to meet at a bar. The result was instant attraction. She was a brave, intelligent and extraordinary self-possessed woman. He was perhaps not a very good artist, but he was dashing, particularly with that white bandage around his throat.

One result of this meeting was that Uno went home with Togo, where they spent the night together on the very same blood-stained futon where the failed suicides had taken place. Another result was the beginning of an entirely new novel, *Iro Zange* (*Confessions of Love*), which was published to scandal and acclaim in 1935.

The confessions involved were those of Togo himself—Uno stated that she did not change a word. Perhaps so, Togo was known to have been something of a raconteur. At the same time, it is difficult to imagine one of the most spirited women of her times simply sitting and taking dictation. Too, if it were really his recounting, one might expect that self-regard alone would have painted a more flattering picture.

As it is, the hero emerges as a real *nimaime*, the kind of weak-chinned, weak-willed character often found in Japanese fiction, drama and—particularly—film. His indecisiveness is equalled only by his vanity; he regularly has dizzy fits or faints dead away, and he completely botches the celebrated suicide.

This bedraggled little man is involved with three splendid and willful women who lead him about, yet at the same time seem oddly dependent upon his invisible charms. In rebellion against the constraints of social opinion, these women are forever running off to foreign climes, but they always return and again set up housekeeping with our weak-willed hero.

Which is, of course, just what Uno herself did—upon numerous occasions. She lived with Togo for a number of years, and her time was spent successfully peddling his indifferent paintings. During this period Uno wrote not at all—she was too busy helping pay for their Le Corbusier-style house, their fancy bedroom, their new borzois.

Though she could leave husbands dramatically (she left one in Hokkaido with a sink full of dirty dishes, saying she was just going to Tokyo for a day and never went back). she usually returned—even if it was to a different husband.

Perhaps like their author, Uno's three women in this novel are very much themselves yet, at the same time, strangely dependent. Uno is not like, say, Jean Rhys, whose career hers much resembles. Rhys, the author of *After Leaving Mr. Mackenzie*, is quite cynical about the possibilities of love (or even friendship). Uno, however, is a true believer.

She is not, like Tanizaki, capable (or even interested in) the delineation of a pathologically weak-willed man as in *Naomi*. Rather, perhaps, it is precisely this oscillation between freedom and dependence that Uno (however unwittingly) celebrates in much of her work, particularly in *Confessions of Love*.

Now in her nineties, Uno has kept the integrity, even bravery, which has always marked her work and her career. Winner of many literary awards, much admired for the limpidity of her style, she has gone from being something of an embarrassment in the literary establishment to becoming one of its stars.

This quality is recognized and well served by her translator, Phyllis Birnbaum, who in addition contributes a very interesting introduction to this translation. Birnbaum is also the author of a splendid profile on Uno which ran in The *New Yorker* and which I very much wish the University of Hawaii Press had found room for in this edition.

In a way, Uno is more interesting than her work, but in any event, it is the conjunction which will captivate the reader. A unique Japanese author (and for once the adjective is warranted), Uno exemplifies the bravery and common sense so much a part of Japanese women and so little celebrated.

Confessions of Love, by Uno Chiyo, translated by Phyllis Birnbaum. Honolulu: University of Hawaii Press, 1989.

Ibuse Masuji

Japanese novelists have a feeling for history. The best have an ability to recreate past sights, sounds, smells—and to do so with naturalness, with none of the paraphernalia with which the "historical novelist" is otherwise apt to surround himself.

I do not mean such historical novels as *Musashi* or *The Heike Story* by Yoshikawa Eiji. He is a "historical novelist," writing the Japanese equivalent of *Forever Amber* or *Shogun*. What I mean are those serious novelists who occasionally write historical fiction.

For example, Tanizaki Jun'ichiro in his historical recreations, the historical stories of Mori Ogai, or those of Inoue Yasushi. Writers this scrupulous about the past have few counterparts in the West: perhaps Janet Lewis, certainly Marguerite Yourcenar.

Now, into this company comes a new translation of two short works by Ibuse Masuji (1898–1993), both of which present past events with an honesty and an immediacy which both respects history and which recreates it for us.

Ibuse is, of course, well known to English readers for his contemporary fiction. Most interested foreigners have read *Black Rain* and the excellent short story collection *Lieutenant Lookeast*. Ibuse's historical fiction, however, is not nearly so well known.

Not among foreign readers at any rate. Japanese readers, however, have long known *Sazanami-gunki* (1938) as one of the masterpieces of modern Japanese fiction. It (now translated under the title of *Waves*) purports to be the sections of a diary kept by one Tomoakira, a very young Heike commander, from the summer of 1183 to the winter of 1184.

This was near the end of the Heike campaign. It was during this period that the Battle of Ichinotani occurred, which they lost, and the rout to Yashima, and the beginning of the Kyushu journey which led to the debacle at Dannoura. And it was during this period that Ibuse's Tomoakira was forced by the extraordinary demands of his time to become adult.

By deciding to write in the form of a diary (and the inspiration for this work came from the author's hearing of just such a Heike journal, one which the owner would not show to him), Ibuse has at once simplified and complicated the problems facing any novelist writing in the historical-present.

In creating a diary or journal, the novelist becomes one with someone who actually lived back there. He has at his command the eyes, ears, nose of the dead. He can record sensation as he never could using a third-person singular character. And he also can avail himself of that apparently built-in belief which most of us have in any work written in the first-person.

On the other hand, the author runs great risks. The most formidable of these is the danger of intruding himself and what he knows into the consciousness of his character. He always runs the danger of making him (or her) modern. (One remembers that ur-JAL-stewardess Mariko in *Shogun*.) If the first-person is used, then that person must belong to his century and not to ours. (The perfect example of the problem overcome is seen in the title character in Yourcenar's *Hadrian's Memoirs*. The dying emperor is completely of his time, not ours, and it is, consequently, that we can put our trust in him and his observations, that we can, in short, believe in him.)

For Ibuse, as for many Japanese novelists, the past is still alive and he can, perhaps consequently, cast himself back into the person of this 12th-century youth. He does not need to make that awful effort that Western writers of historical fiction seem to find necessary.

At the same time, he has so well researched the period that he knows just what to leave out—a question just as pressing as what to put in. His Tomoakira can take much for granted and so therefore must we. (We don't even see Yoshitsune's celebrated descent down the cliff at Ichinotani.)

But what he does notice (wonderful scenes: loyal horses following the fleeing barges and one by one drowning in the wake; an old retainer cropping the grass but refusing to remove the arrow which has stuck into the turf near his lord; the brutal details of battle—an arm lopped off here, a number of heads there) is made for us memorable.

The chronology, the ordering of events, is wonderfully done: vital, exciting and yet frugal. And equally splendid is Ibuse's delineation of that other dimension: the interior chronology of the youth, his coming of age. Here the evidence is all indirect, since he himself is not aware of his growing maturity. We see it, though, in the way he expresses himself, in his reactions to what he experiences—for example, his early sentimentality about the young girl he finds and parts from, then his later "adult" unconcern when her house is burned.

(The second work translated, the 1946 *Wabisuke*, here given as *Isle-on-the-Billows*, is both slighter and more conventional, though equally well done. It is about an island prison-colony during the time of the "Dog Shogun," Tsunayoshi, when arrests were daily, the offense always being the mistreating of dogs or even the inconveniencing of them. There are many unstated parallels—the work was written during World War II, a time of even stronger repression—but the whole is comic as well as satiric.)

Both have been well translated—particularly *Waves*. (I judge from the English style, a proper way to judge in an English translation). David Aylward and Anthony Liman, the two translators, went directly to Ibuse with any problems they had and some of the successful compromises are apparently his. Certainly, it was a sound idea to use words which are archaic and/or from special vocabularies: "affrays," "abatis," "cheval-de-frise." And the tone seems quite right: "The men sleep quietly all around us on makeshift pillows of helm and quiver."; "She rattled on as if her tongue had wheels...."

I am not certain, however, that the translation of place names is ever a good idea. The "Clear Spring Palace" the "Miscanthus Pavilion," "The Hall of Balconies" sound too self-consciously picturesque. And in any event when Tomoakira thought of Kiyomizu he did not think of clear springs. Also questionable is the use of modern names in historical fiction. Back then, for example, Kyoto was still known as Heian-kyo.

Finally, even nominal place-name translation has its dangers. To speak of the ancient capital's Third Avenue does not make us think of Kyoto but of the Bowery. However, in large, the translations are superior and Ibuse's splendid recreation of living history is well served.

Waves: Two Short Novels, by Ibuse Masuji, translated by David Aylward and Anthony Liman. Tokyo: Kodansha International, 1986.

Last year Kodansha published two of Ibuse's short historical novels; now it has published two more: the 1952 *Oshima no Zonnengaki* (*A Geisha Remembers*) and the well known 1937 *Jan Manjiro Hyoryuki (John Manjiro: A Castaway's Chronicle).*

Ibuse began writing historical fiction in 1930 perhaps as a comment, even a criticism of his times. *Waves*, though short, took eight years to complete; this powerful story of a sensitive young man in a brutal war-filled world appearing at the very time when Japan was fast turning fascist and a new war was coming.

John Manjiro (hitherto known abroad through Kaneko Hisakazu's 1940 translation and several original English works based on the story—all now superseded), itself a story of Japanese-American cooperation, appeared in 1937, at the very moment when all notion of such cooperation was fast disappearing.

All during the ensuing war, Ibuse wrote historical fiction. It was one way to keep on writing and not bring down the military authorities. It was also one way to keep on writing about what he wanted to write about.

This theme—a major one in the historical fiction—is the testing of the solitary individual. Whether he is a young Taira warrior or the peasant Manjiro, a castaway picked up by an American ship, we witness what happens to his individuality. The shaping force need not be war, nor the vagaries of wind and waves—it can also be a repressive government as it is in *A Geisha Remembers*.

Here we have the story of the samurai scholar Takashima Shuhan, an early advocate of Western learning at the end of the Tokugawa Period, the very time when an increasingly insecure government was hounding such advocates. Mizuno Tadakuni (notorious for the 1841 Tempo Reforms) and such of his toadies as Torii Yozo, were responsible for the arrest of Takashima, whose individuality was much tested during these trials.

(And vindicated. He went on to a high position in the Meiji government—as did John Manjiro—and both Mizuno and Torii died in despair: one under house-arrest, the other banished.)

To tell this story, Ibuse (famous for knowing just how to do this) chooses the perfect point-of-view. Just as the enormities of Heian-Kamakura war are best shown through the purported diary of *Waves*, so the inquisitions of the late Tokugawa Period are seen through the supposed memoir of a geisha, quick to notice things but not too smart, who has a sentimental crush on the imprisoned hero. Thus, though she gets everything right, its import keeps escaping her, and the result is history seen from an angle informingly oblique.

Big, fat, official "history" is kept at bay, and what is presented is something more like life experienced. And it helps enormously that none of them—Heian youngster, geisha, John Manjiro—know how to write.

Ibuse's style here is one which was influenced or perhaps even formed by Mori Ogai's historical fiction. It is notably a spare style, one in which every word counts, in which description is kept at a minimum, one where any grand effect is not even attempted.

(In Ibuse's most recent historical work, *New Records of the Tea Gathering at Tomonotsu (Tomonotsu Chakai-ki)*, the style is even more severe—it consists only of those laconic notes (*chakai-ki*) kept at tea ceremonies, but through them a whole turbulent era is suggested.)

This style admirably suits the author's purpose. The Taira warrior's writing is sparse; that of the geisha is simple, and John Manjiro is an unlettered peasant whose story is being told by someone (not named) who is no "writer" either.

(All of this is respected by these able translators. In particular, the story of the castaway John Manjiro, with its Robinson Crusoe-like overtones, is grateful for the simplicity and Defoe-esque brevity of the English here used.)

The Western reader, used to large purple patches—whole savannas—in historical fiction, used to lots of unlikely dialogue and arbitrary violence, may find the effect of Ibuse's historical novels bracing indeed. A cold, clean wind blows through them, and the effect is invigorating. Only a few Western writers present history so plainly and so imaginatively and with such scrupulous adherence to the fact that history was once alive. Ibuse's historical fiction truly makes us one with the past.

Castaways: Two Short Novels, by Ibuse Masuji, translated by Anthony Liman and David Aylward. Tokyo: Kodansha International, 1987.

Miyazawa Kenji

Miyazawa, who died in 1933 at the age of 37, remains a legend and is still remembered, at least in Iwate where he was born and lived, as "Kenji *bosatsu*."

Though the author has been made a *bodhisattva* because of his mystical visions and his efforts to help the local poor, his popular elevation in the rest of the country is almost as extreme.

In both his poetry and his prose, it is the man himself who occasions the admiration. Poet Takamura Kotaro, one of his earlier enthusiasts, made the distinction that he was not so much a poet as a man who wrote poetry. It is the moral strength of the person that is admired equally with the work.

This is true of the prose as well as the poetry. Though many of the pieces are unfinished and a number seem pointless as well, they have been given almost classic rank by the agreed upon status of the man. Most of these pieces are in the form of folk stories, and many are indeed distinguished by an endearing homeliness of invention.

In one tale, stars "were winking and blinking and switching themselves on and off all over the firmament." When a baby mouse is popped into a cello, his mother cries: "I'll go with him. All the hospitals allow it." The Pleiades and Orion's Belt "glimmered now green, now orange, as if they were breathing."

Much of the logic in the stories is of that circular variety beloved by the fairy tale. "In those days there was an order to things: it was a matter of course that Kojuro should get the better of the bears, that the shopkeeper should get the better of Kojuro and the bears ... but since the shopkeeper lived in the town, the bears couldn't get the better of him, for the moment at least."

There is also that delight in recounting consecutive events over and over again, in great numbers of things (5,000 of this, 10,000 of that), and in constant repetition, all found in children's stories. There is evidence that Miyazawa (whose stories often take place in other lands) read Western children's tales. "A carriage made of a great white mushroom appeared, drawn by a horse of a most peculiar shape and gray in color—just like a rat, in fact."

Given the nature of these stories, it is curious that we find the publisher observing that to call the collection children's tales "would have been misleading from the outset: mere children's tales could not have commanded, for some 70 years in a violently changing world, an increasingly wide following among adults."

But Japan is a country where otherwise mature adults continue to read comic-strip *manga* and indeed childishness is an ingredient necessary to complete popular approval. Many of these stories have been made into children's dramas and animated cartoons. And in addition, it is unlikely that Miyazawa would have called children's stories "mere."

In any event, Miyazawa actually did intend these stories for children and indicated as much when the first collection appeared in 1924. No less an authority than Kenneth Yasuda has written that these "children's stories ... were intended as an aid in moral education." And it is this combination of the childlike with the moral earnestness that many Japanese admire that makes them attractive to adults to this day.

This body of work has found an ideal translator in John Bester, winner of the first Noma Translation Award. He has already translated both longer Miyazawa works and an earlier collection of short tales, the 1972 *Winds from Afar*. These 16 stories are here recast and reprinted, and eight more are added to form the present collection.

Bester brings to the original a practical seriousness which matches the Japanese author's careful naiveté, and both thus prevent the stories from becoming sentimental. The pragmatic logic of the child is observed, and this combination of wide-eyed belief and nascent sophistication renders the story and its translation that approximation of the child's-eye view which has kept these stories so popular.

Once and Forever: The Tales of Kenji Miyazawa, translated by John Bester. Tokyo: Kodansha International, 1993.

This year [1996] is the centennial of Miyazawa Kenji's birth; it also marks his canonization. There are already translations of the major works including this one, *Ginga Tetsudo no Yoru* (1927) which already has a good translation by John Bester, as well as a popular animated cartoon version, a TV drama version and a radio version; in addition there is a TV account of his life, several new biographies and two hagiographic movies, both showing at present: Shochiku's *Miyazawa Kenji: Sono Ai* and Toei's *Waga Kokoro no Ginga Tetsudo: Miyazawa Kenji Monogatari.*

The title of the last indicates the placement of *Ginga Tetsudo no Yoru* (here newly translated as *Milky Way Railroad*) in the pantheon. It is considered emblematic of the author and is, indeed, probably the most beloved modern children's story in Japan.

Part of its popularity is the fact that it was written by a man whose legend shows him helping the farmers, lecturing on rice cultivation, loving children and writing all sorts of stories for them. That all of this is true only makes his popular appeal the stronger.

Another reason for Miyazawa's popularity has to do with the work itself. Though some of it is sentimental and much of it is quaint, part of it has great power—the *Milky Way Railroad* included.

Two boys, friends, are, during the Tanabata festival, suddenly transported on a magical train to the Milky Way. They meet various people, and it only slowly becomes apparent that these are the dead and they are on their way into the beyond. In fact, one of the boys is dead as well—having drowned in the Tanabata festivities below. The other one, not yet dead, returns shaken but safe.

The power of this short saga is to be accounted for in a number of ways. Miyazawa was an autodidact. He taught himself everything and as a result became a true eclectic. A strong believer in Nichiren Buddhism (a faith which early separated him from his Jodo Shin father), he also took a passing fancy to Christianity and at the same time, steeped himself in the folk religions and legends of his native Iwate. He read foreign philosophy and made somewhat cursory studies of other languages.

Consequently his own style is a compound of foreign words, scientific terms, Chinese compounds, Sanskrit phrases, even some Esperanto. At the same time he believed in various types of synesthesia—music becomes color, and this he couples with spoken rather than literary language, with rice planting and manure-gathering imagery. His poetry—he wrote some 400 free verse poems and many *tanka*—is distinguished by what Kenneth Yasuda has called "bold rhythm patterns and cadences, repetitive vowel sounds, [and] a great freedom of diction."

This extraordinary eclecticism resulted in heavily layered work—poems and stories capable of multiple interpretations. In *Milky Way Railroad*, we have not only the bridge of dreams from the *Genji*, but also a personification of the Tanabata legend (Weaver meets Cowherd in the persons of the two boys on their journey). We even have the flocks of magpies forming the bridge to bring the two together. In addition (and this is the result of Miyazawa's random and eclectic learning), there occurs a quite successful syncretism: the imageries of science and religions, of West and East, all brought together.

In the original story, the two Japanese boys are even given Western names, after two of the Renaissance Italian proto-scientists whom Miyazawa admired. Since this particular syncretism was not successful, I think that the translators are quite correct in giving the two properly Japanese names. There are other felicities in this adaptation (the original Sigrist translation is from 1971, one year earlier than John Bester's, though not originally published until 1984), as well as an introduction which gives the book its literary due.

Stroud speaks of "transcendental realism," and this rare quality Miyazawa truly has. To speak of something which transcends what is spoken or written about is difficult, but—as an indication—when I was reading this

Miyazawa, I was constantly reminded of something in Lewis Carroll (another synesthesist) but could not remember what.

Then, as these things will, it surfaced: the third chapter of *Through the Looking Glass*, where Alice suddenly finds herself in a railway carriage going where she knows not, where horses look in through the window, a goat turns to converse with her, and a gentleman in a white paper hat leans gently forward to observe that "so young a child ought to know which way she's going, even if she doesn't know her own name," and later advises her to "take a return ticket every time the train stops."

The realism of the passage points to something quite beyond reality, to some world where connections are made in a different way, where logic has relinquished the upper hand, where connections are governed by something other than mere common sense and where coherence grows so large as to be the whole meaning. *The Milky Way Railroad* is like this.

It is, in Miyazawa's words: "as if all the world's diamonds, that the diamond companies hide in order to keep prices up, had been abruptly dumped out and scattered recklessly all over."

Milky Way Railroad, by Miyazawa Kenji, translated and adapted from the Japanese by Joseph Sigrist and D. M. Stroud. Berkeley: Stone Bridge Press, 1996.

Yokomitsu Riichi

Yokomitsu Riichi (1898–1947) is now considered one of the marginal figures in modern Japanese literature. At least this would seem the opinion of the local literary establishment. No adequate edition of his collected works has appeared, and his importance is restricted to the merely historical. If mentioned at all, he is seen as indicative of the failure of "Japanese modernism."

Just what "Japanese modernism" might be need not concern us since, like so many labels, it obscures rather than reveals the workings of the Japanese literary stock market: Shiga Naoya rising, Tanizaki maintaining, Mishima declining. That strange critical game of rank and worth is played by Japanese critics with such a plethora of rules and lack of criteria that both foreign critic and foreign reader are well out of it.

One of the results, however, is that, while the Japanese reader is not encouraged to hunt out and read one of their country's most interesting writers, the foreign reader—immune to the reputation game—is now in a position to make the fairer judgment, if judgment is necessary.

This new collection presents eleven of the stories, including some of the longer ones. "Time," not included in the collection, and perhaps the author's best work, is currently available in two different translations: Donald Keene's in *Modern Japanese Literature*, and Richard Foster's in *Time and Others*, published by Hara Shobo. "Silent Ranks" is also published by Hara Shobo; "Young Forever," by Hokuseido. In addition, back numbers of the *Japan Quarterly* and the *P.E.N. News* offer other stories.

As Dennis Keene has pointed out in his introduction, the contribution of Yokomitsu lay in his new interpretation of the uses of the *shishosetsu*, the first-person, so-called "I" novel. He makes a useful comparison between the work of this author and one more conservative: "... he wished to transform ... life into a fictional work of art, unlike Shiga Naoya, who seemed to feel that life as it had been lived was a work of art already."

Though all writers begin with biography, it is only, I think, the Japanese who have also stopped there. Yokomitsu found this position so limiting that it amounted to a special kind of falsehood. He wished, he said, to create "fictions" and not record "the enormous lies" that appeared as *shishosetsu*. Consequently, willy-nilly, he was one of the first Japanese writers to concern himself with what the West calls psychological realism. This means the construction of likely thought processes in characters other than the first person. Since this has long been the mode of most Western literature, it is hard for the foreign reader to realize the innovation and the difficulty of effecting it.

It means, for one thing, letting go of the apparent stability of self, and for another, the assumption of responsibility for the thoughts and actions of someone else—and all without the safety net of "I thought" or "it seemed," or "I observed." These are two things which many Japanese and most Japanese writers have found difficult. It assumes a kind of omniscience, something which no self-respecting *shishosetsu* writer would claim.

This is, more or less, just what Yokomitsu attempted, however. If the results are various, the attempt is real. And it is more important than such labels as "Japanese modernism" would indicate. Though, indeed, many of the stories are written in the first person, they are, as the author intended, "fictions."

Yokomitsu energetically forged his style early and then, to an extent, coasted. Properly, therefore, Dennis Keene has drawn his collection in large from the early work. Further, he has translated works which throw light upon each other. "After Picking Up a Blue Stone" is relevant to both "The Pale Captain" and "The Depths of the Town." "The Defeated Husband," a work much rewritten, shows the author's processes more clearly than the more polished works. "Love," "The Child Who Was Laughed At," "The Machine," "Spring Riding in a Carriage," "Ideas of a Flower Garden," "The Carriage" are all early works—

some of them famous—of which the author remained fond. The single exception collected here is a late work (the author died in 1947) published after the war called "Smile."

Here one sees clearly the author's accomplishment. There is a third-person narrator who now, after the war remembers a wartime occurrence. Yokomitsu and the reader observe only his thoughts. There is evidence (a book title mentioned) that the narrator is, indeed, Yokomitsu, but his thoughts are not the focus of the story. Rather, it is about a young lieutenant who, though boyish and in other ways unformed, invents a secret weapon. Whether this pure and brilliant lad is, in reality, insane is the subject of the story.

By writing his story in the mode that he does, Yokomitsu is able to suggest (and his means are subtle) that the wartime Japanese as a whole were equally brilliant, and equally crazy. To state this baldly, as I have done, is plainly outrageous—but real literature is often composed of outrageous statements skillfully suggested and meticulously presented.

In a story such as "Smile" (and one quite agrees with Dennis Keene's calling it perhaps the finest postwar Japanese story), Yokomitsu achievement is plainly visible. Though patently a fiction, the story is all the truer because a created pattern always shows more than an accidental (*shishosetsu*) one does. A controlled and largely fictitious third-person viewpoint avoids completely the myopia of the literal first person.

Some Japanese critics have enthusiastically pointed out that Yokomitsu is therefore not in the true Japanese tradition. One would agree that he is not. But at the same time, one would want to indicate—as the translator has done in this excellent volume—that because he is not, he had widened and deepened that tradition.

Love and Other Stories of Yokomitsu Riichi, translated with an introduction by Dennis Keene. Tokyo: Tokyo University Press, 1974.

Yokomitsu's first novel, *Shanghai* was published in magazine installments between 1928 and 1931. Based an a short visit there in 1928, it concerns a 1925 incident (the so-called May 30th Movement) when Chinese workers at a Japanese spinning mill staged a strike to the consternation of the resident foreigners.

Though this was the kind of "proletarian" material that was animating Japanese literary circles at the time, Yokomitsu's novel contained no message calling for workers to unite, nor any apology for Japanese capitalists aboard. Indeed, in a later essay the novelist said ("rather ominously" writes Washburn) that "only Japanese militarism possesses enough power to rescue the subjugated East."

Rather, the novelist's interest lay in this international city as vehicle for his modernist ideas. In it he could find a paradigm for no less than "the state of contemporary man." Explicitly stating that his aim was to create a new realism in order to combat the Marxist proletarian school, Yokomitsu told his story of a group of Japanese expatriates in the "festering" city through many of the techniques of international modernism.

Washburn, in his postscript, indicates some of them. "He uses catalogs of images as well as broken phrases and clauses to create ... the sense of a camera eye. Dashes visually break up almost every page, setting off the internal thoughts of characters to allow the narrative to shift between [them] and the third-person narrator."

Also, the use of a city as a formal unifying device was one of the most useful techniques of modernism. Joyce's *Ulysses* which uses Dublin as paradigm had been mostly published by 1922 (and partly published in Japanese translation by 1930); Proust and Gide on Paris were translated in part by 1929, though Andrei Bely's *Petersburg* was known only by reputation.

Just how familiar Yokomitsu was with any of these works is unknown since he rarely talked about foreign literature. Kawabata Yasunari, his fellow theorist (the Shinkankaku-ha, "New Sensationalist" school) apparently at least knew about *Ulysses* when he wrote his big-city modernist novel, *Asakusa Kurenaidan*. In any event, the only resemblance between Yokomitsu's modernist work and those of the Europeans is a reliance on lists of otherwise unconnected visual impressions ("gutted domesticated duck, pork kidneys, baby mice soaked in honey") and a purposefully laconic diction.

Such had long been part of his New Sensationalist style but had not always been successful. Donald Keene has written of Yokomitsu's 1923 *The Sun*, an historical novella inspired by the Japanese translation of *Salammbo*, that "the uncouth short sentences are reminiscent less of Flaubert than of Tarzan ... at best they suggest a primitive people who had yet to discover subordinate clauses."

More serious was a perhaps consequent lack of characterization. One critic wrote that "the author is absolutely determined to describe only the surface ... not a single real human being exists within this atmosphere." Indeed most of the characters in this novel are implausible from the start, which is the reason that I here include nothing about the extended plot.

This lack of believable characters is perhaps intentional. Kawabata stated that *Shanghai* was the summation of the methods of New Sensationalism and indeed this school's style had never been strong on character. The reason that Kawabata's *The Scarlet Gang of Asakusa* is so much more readable than *Shanghai* is that the author chose to use a picaresque modernism (closer to Paul Morand than to Joyce), which did not take the characters seriously and accepted their purposely *manga*-like dimensions.

If *Shanghai* exhausted its author, as he later said it did, I can imagine what it did to its translator. The book is long, prolix and at the same time fantastically detailed. Washburn in his postword writes that "I have tried in this translation to recapture the effects created by these stylistic elements and thus preserve the quirkiness of the original, by starting with as literal a version as I could manage." At the same time, he knows that translation is merely an analogue and that he could only aim at replicating the "strangeness of Yokomitsu's novel—a rather elusive quality that for me made the novel worth translating." And for us, worth reading.

Shanghai, by Yokomitsu Riichi, translated with a postscript by Dennis Washburn. Ann Arbor: University of Michigan Press, 2001.

Kawabata Yasunari

Kawabata Yasunari (1899–1972) sometimes intimated that he believed that the finest of his work was to be found in the series of extremely short stories which he wrote intermittently between 1921 and 1972.

There are 146 in all, written over this half-century, and most are so short that the author called them *tanagokoro no shosetsu*—stories that fit into the palm of one's hand. They took various forms—a haiku-like composition, a truncated novel, a long work compressed, a short work expanded to a page—but all indicated Kawabata's attitude toward his art and his life.

For him writing was a process, and the works themselves were segments of a continuum. He might formally end a larger work only to continue it some years later. Or he might rework or even reuse. The 1949 "Boys" contains material which might have been taken from the 1926 *Izu*

Dancer. Kawabata's last work *Yukigunisho* ("Gleanings from Snow Country") (1972) is a palm-sized reduction of the 1936 *Snow Country*.

Kawabata's attitude toward writing was a radical one—something which we are apt to forget since the later and more popular works are all in the realist mode. He was, however, certainly no less a modernist than, say Yokomitsu Riichi, a writer with whom he is seldom compared; he had read or read about *Ulysses*; and he wrote the script for Japan's first experimental film.

This was Kinugasa Teinosuke's 1927 *Kurutta Ippeiji* (*A Page Out of Order*, aka *A Crazy Page*), a highly experimental picture, modernist in structure. The 1929 fit-in-the-palm novel "Man Who Did Not Smile" is about the filming of the picture and how Kawabata felt about the mask-filled finale he had written. Though the style is realist in mode, the narrative is not. It is often this combination of a realistic style and "unrealistic" occurrences (or vice versa) which lends these short stories their peculiar flavor.

In "The Rainy Station" (1928), for example, the narrative is straightforward but the prose is not:

> But was the happiness of makeup like the fruit high up in a tree? The neighbor's wife was no female acrobat, used to scrambling up the tree of makeup like her enemy. Although, riding on her enemy's back, she'd pecked at the fruit of being a writer's wife, the enemy had flown away out of the treetop on loudly flapping wings of adultery. Unless someone gave her a hand, she could not get back down to the ground to join the crusade of honest women. Although she waited and waited, her husband did not come to rescue her. The wives, wives, wives, collecting their husbands, husbands, husbands, dispersed into the rainy dusk.

Metaphor run wild is one of the stylistic extremes typical of these stories. Another is an extraordinary compression of events. The 1963 "Earth," for example, is a very long novel pared down just four pages. "The Silverberry Thief" (1925) fits between two lines of a folk song.

These are often written in the expressionist style, popular in Japan during the late 1920s. There are dream scenes, descriptions of "morbid" moods, lots about sex. As for example in the 1929 "Samurai Descendants" where the hero "like the baby who ate newspapers ... wanted to sink his teeth into her flesh and devour her ..."

Others are somewhat collage-like in the sense that the 1930 novel *The Scarlet Gang of Asakusa* is constructivist-collage. Still others are in that extended form of metaphor we call surreal. "The Bound Husband" (1930) is literally that—a man with a rope tied to his leg.

All, however, are distinguished by that Kawabata's characteristic sensibility: watchful, waiting, uninvolved—and then the sudden telling detail which seems to affirm what went before and yet casts any single meaning into grave doubt. In the 1946 "Silver Fifty-Sen Pieces," the girl remembers receiving her allowance as a child, then remembers buying a glass paperweight with a dog carved in it. Other shopping days are remembered.

Then, from a scene where she is shopping with her mother, we are swung to postwar Japan ... and the paperweight, which has somehow survived the war. There in the rain, standing in the bombed and burned area that was once home, she looks at it. "Suddenly, she realized that there was not a single dog left in the whole burned-out neighborhood."

This sudden shift from carved dog to real dog is a carefully contrived shock—and we realize that all the other parallels in the story (and there are many in these five pages) have pointed the way and narrowed the passage. We are suddenly confronted, as we often are in Kawabata, with mutability, the past, loss, and at the same time its beauty.

Over the years, these small hand-palm stories have been occasionally translated into English. (I have counted some 10 and there are more if other languages are included.) Here, however, is a real handful—70 of the 146, about half of them. These translations are the work of Lane Dunlop and J. Martin Holman, both of whom have long been interested in this collection and have a feeling for the form.

Palm-of-the-Hand Stories, by Kawabata Yasunari, translated by Lane Dunlop and J. Martin Holman. San Francisco: North Point Press, 1988.

Kawabata's *Izu Dancer* (*Izu no Odoriko*), a short, early novel about an adolescent student on a walking tour of Izu who becomes infatuated with a very young girl, a dancer from an itinerant traveling troupe, is among the most famous of his works. Autobiographical, as are most of Kawabata's writings, it has captured whole generations of readers. One of the reasons is the autobiographical basis of the writing.

Donald Keene has indicated the extent by comparing an unpublished 1924 memoir with this 1926 novel. And, indeed, seemingly artless, this first-person narrative folds the past into something like an idyll, an evocation of first-love itself. Martin Holman's collection (1997), which begins with a 1914 diary, indicates just how close fact and fiction were for the writer and how Kawabata carved and fashioned narratives from what had been life.

The work has been several times translated—by Hayashi Eichi, by Martin Holman, and by Edward Seidensticker. This latter's translation has appeared in two versions. First, that which was originally published by *The Atlantic Monthly* in 1955. It was reprinted in the Asia Society's

"Perspective of Japan," was later printed by Hara Shobo, and still later was republished by Tuttle and is the translation used in this new edition.

It was the first Kawabata to be published in English, but it was also cut by the then-editor of *Atlantic* who forced Seidensticker to remove whole passages. Though the reason was nothing more sinister than lack of space, the translator had long regretted having been made to do this, and when the opportunity presented itself, he reinstated all the missing passages. This full version was published in *The Oxford Book of Japanese Short Stories* (1997) where it is at present to be found.

The Izu Dancer, by Kawabata Yasunari, translated by Edward Seidensticker. With *The Counterfeiter*, *Obasute*, *The Full Moon* by Inoue Yasushi, translated by Leon Picon. Singapore/Boston: Tuttle Publishing, 2000/1974.

Written in 1954 and only now translated into English, *The Lake* belongs to Kawabata's most productive decade—one during which he also wrote *The Master of Go* and *The Sound of the Mountain*. Unlike either of those works, however, it is inward, searching and deeply romantic.

Gimpei, a schoolteacher fired from his job for an affair with a student, has made his life into a search: he follows women on the street. In his way, he is, like all romantics, searching for perfection. And, like all romantics, he never finds it. He may discover the perfect voice, the perfect nose, but never his ideal—the perfect woman.

Not that Gimpei knows that this is what he is searching for. All he understands is his compulsion; with it, he keeps fresh the self-loathing with which he protects himself. Reality can never satisfy him, but memories of his past women and fantasies of his future women make the dreadful present livable.

But if Gimpei does not understand himself, Kawabata does. With knowledge and compassion, he shows that a compulsion is always much more than just a compulsion. It is a spiritual quest, a journey leading toward a perhaps unattainable ideal. The very structure of a compulsion, the same act repeated over and over again, need not be seen only as a private hell, some infernal hall of mirrors. It may also be seen as a way of hoping, striving, living. Like all roads, however, it also leads to the grave. Any man driven toward perfection is driven toward death because the absolutely perfect is also the absolutely dead.

Usually regarded as unfinished, *The Lake* is a fine example of that blending of wry detachment and the most involved compassion which defined Kawabata and all of his best writing. Toward death the romantic road may lead, but Kawabata shows us how to accept life along the way; the destination is darkness but hope and bravery and the will to continue still illumine the way.

The Lake, by Kawabata Yasunari, translated by Tsukimura Reiko. Tokyo: Kodansha International, 1974.

Beauty and Sadness is a translation of Kawabata's last novel, *Utsukushisa to Kanashimi to*, first published in 1961, some ten years before the novelist's death. The story, as so often in Kawabata's work the pretext for the novel, is soon told. A novelist, now getting on in years, goes to Kyoto and sees the woman who was his mistress a quarter of a century earlier, when she was just a girl herself.

He finds her with a woman only a bit older than she was at the time of their liaison. Returning to Kamakura, he is eventually seduced by the girl who then turns her attentions to his son. In the end, there is a motorboat accident on Lake Biwa. She is saved, the boy is drowned.

As with many Japanese plots, a précis makes the work sound like melodrama. The girl is so apparently motivated by a desire to revenge her lover, the older woman is so much a mover of the plot that the structure sounds simplistic. The effect of the novel, however, is entirely different. This is because the plot is only ostensibly the subject of the book. The real subject is far less easy to describe. Its quality, however, is indicated by the way in which Kawabata constructs the work. This is, roughly through a series of parallels leading, as it were, into the distance.

Among them are the parallel of the novelist seducing a young girl and, much later, being seduced by another; his ruining the life of one girl and having his own life ruined by another; the older woman bearing and losing his child and his "bearing" and then losing his son; the older woman having lost this child, a girl, and then finding another daughter-like child in the young girl; and many, many more, the novel being a most elegantly fashioned bundle of parallels.

One of the effects of such a structure is a growing, and intended, feeling of claustrophobia. Wherever one moves one strikes a parallel—a bar in the cage. Another effect is the growing feeling that life, after all, is not merely the inchoate mess upon which we daily open our eyes but a structured and, as it were, intelligent pattern we both create and exist within. If Kawabata were Hardy, this would be Fate; if he were James, it would be the beautifully incidental (but all-important) "figure in the carpet." But Kawabata is Kawabata and the quality has no given name.

It does, however, in this effect, resemble something else—this is the ordered view which religion gives. In this, *Beauty and Sadness*, like other novels of Kawabata's, lends evidence for a kind of karma. Actions are repeated endlessly, the identical reverberations echoing through the corridors of the novel. The theological point is that punishment consists of repetition. Kawabata, however, does not call it punishment. He calls it life.

The parallel construction and its consequent effects are set, in this book, against a massive and beautifully contrived contradiction. The fatalistic progression of the parallels is hence questioned every page of the way.

The contradiction is, likewise, not to be found in the plot but its treatment. Kawabata has, to begin with, set a very long (quarter-century) story into very few pages. Though he avails himself of flashbacks, literature's tendency to always seem in the present tense is skillfully exploited. This book, as with all good novels, appears to happen right now. With so much material to be fit into a slender volume, Kawabata restricts description to an extraordinary extent.

"Keiko reached behind Otoko's obi and gently straightened the back seam of her kimono." In that sentence is packed the concern, the habits, the regard, the affection of those two women who live together. Nothing else need be said about the domestic aspect of their lives, and Kawabata says nothing more.

An example of the contradiction within the book is, for once, well described in the blurb: "At once lyrical and terrifying, it is a tale of passion told with the most unsettling dispassion." The happenings are of an erotic nature, but the style of their being told is carefully mundane. They are emotionally explosive, but the surface of the page is "as placid as a still pool in a temple courtyard."

One of the effects of this contradiction is that the reader is troubled and does not know why. One of the results of this is that the dramatic goings-on seize the imagination in a way perhaps otherwise impossible.

Certainly this is the kind of experience that only a novel (and a very fine novelist) can create. This book was made into a film in 1965. Directed by Shinoda Masahiro, it was called (in a translation which perhaps better suits the tone of the original) *With Beauty and Sorrow*. This was the only improvement, however. Film cannot handle the kind of complexity that a novel can. It emerged as mere story, mere melodrama—all of the allusions and reverberations of the original were missing. This marvelously nuanced work became a parody of itself.

The book, to be sure, is "about" all of its happenings, but it is also and more purely about the patterns that shape us, the dichotomies that divide us, the identical happenings that unite us, and the great nameless and unsettling void in which we all live.

Beauty and Sadness, by Kawabata Yasunari, translated by Howard Hibbett. Tokyo: Charles E. Tuttle Company, 1975.

First Snow on Fuji, a collection of stories, plus an essay and a dance-drama, was originally published in 1958 as *Fuji no Hatsuyuki*. It is late Kawabata—most of the major works had already appeared; the author wrote much less during these years, and he died in 1972.

That these works form a meditation on death is not surprising. Many of Kawabata's works—early and late are just that. He called himself a master of ceremonies at funerals, and though he was referring to duties at the demise of friends, his writing was from the earliest informed by thoughts of death.

Indeed, this awareness of transience creates the Kawabata tone. In a way it makes him "Japanese" because these people are traditionally less inclined to deny the facts of life (and death) than are those of at least several other countries. It also makes him universal because these are facts that, like it or not, we must all face.

This lends Kawabata's work a certain cohesion—this and the facts that he often finished works long after they were originally published and that all of his writing shares a relatively narrow repertoire of themes.

Readers of a work as early as "The Diary of My Sixteenth Year" will find that one of the stories here, "Nature," might be considered a continuation. The story "Yumiura" could be seen as a late metamorphosis of *The Izu Dancer*. Indeed, one Japanese critic saw it as that, stating that the aged woman turning up at the novelist's door is really the child dancer now grown old. In any event, Kawabata included both works in a collection of his favorites published shortly before he received the Nobel Prize.

A theme that is often found in Kawabata's works (as well as in the writings of many other authors) is the nature of self-awareness. The woman in "This County, That County" is surprised to discover that two entities can express themselves through her; the man in "Nature" has lived a life as a woman, and Kawabata is very interested in what Thomas Rimer has called "the interplay between character, gender and self-knowledge."

In "Silence," the author visits another writer, victim of a stroke, who can no longer speak and seems "a living ghost." Interwoven into this is a "real" ghost story, one side of the theme lending body to the other. The essay "Chrysanthemum in the Rock" contains its own ghost, since the rock is eventually a grave stone and the various themes of awareness, ghosts and death are all gracefully gathered together.

Kawabata's means are famously economical. Indeed, perhaps the only way to treat the great truths he deals with is through a style this laconic. Through ellipses, thrown-away observations and intimations, Kawabata is able to suggest his meaning without explicitly stating it. One must infer when reading Kawabata, and this modest exercise means that one brings to him what is necessary for his intentions to flower.

The sense of death that hovers just over the Kawabata page would, indeed, be impossible were it directly delineated. Rather, author and reader together weave the pattern. Translating this into another language is a problem. This work has been translated into German and Russian, and I can have no opinion as to their success. In English, Kawabata is fortunate in having had good translators—Edward Seidensticker, Howard Hibbett and now Michael Emmerich.

This sense of evanescence that is so palpable in Kawabata is what, I believe, links him so strongly to his country and its culture, and what makes him at the same time so universal. He wrote about the most important subject and his words directly reach us. After his suicide, no note was found, but one obituary remembered something he had said: "A silent death is an endless word."

First Snow on Fuji, by Kawabata Yasunari, translated by Michael Emmerich. Washington, D.C.: Counterpoint, 1999.

Ozaki Kazuo

Though Ozaki Kazuo (1899–1983) is very popular in Japan, he is barely known at all abroad. Of the same generation as Kawabata and Yokomitsu Riichi, he has not achieved their foreign reputations. One of the reasons might be that he wrote almost exclusively in that local literary form called *shishosetsu*—a term which the translator of this new collection of Ozaki stories parses as "*watakushi wa shosetsu de aru.*" In this "I-am-a-story" genre, the author believes that "daily life itself provides literature with an adequate context." For him "'plot' is what he naturally pens … not what he makes his characters do."

This, the translator finds, accords with the Japanese traditional aesthetic which "assumes that art should deal with what lies closest to actual experience, with what the artist feels most intensely."

The results are various. Stories can be as illuminating as those of Shiga Naoya or as deadening as those authors who seem (in the words of Donald Keene) "to have derived a masochistic pleasure from disclosing not only their most contemptible actions but also [their most] shameful thoughts," all the while concentrating "on probing the inner significance of their most trivial gestures. . . ."

Not only does Ozaki write in this troubled genre, he specializes in a further sub-genre. This is known as *shinkyo shosetsu* or "a story of the state of the *kokoro*" which term the translator renders as "the heart of mind—what makes the human being human."

Indeed, the unity of life and art is stressed in the most direct fashion by Ozaki. Right in the middle of "Rosy Glasses" (*Nonki Megane*, 1933) the story that established his reputation, the author suddenly writes: "I had little trouble getting started on 'Rosy Glasses' once I got the idea to write it." Fiction has turned into autobiography, and literature has become self-referential.

In this new selection of stories, prefaced by a long and informative introduction to Ozaki and his work, Robert Epp presents the author in full detail. The ten stories (only two of which have been previously translated) are selected from those written during the Period 1933–1964 and hence offer a whole slice of Ozaki's life.

They are "Rosy Glasses," "Yoshibe—On Conventions," "Guile," "Land of My Fathers," "Entrance Bath," "Crickets," "This and That about Bugs," "The Skinny Rooster," "Day of the Nuptials," and "Putting in for Retirement." All are taken from the 1968 revised Shincho Bunko edition of *Megane Nonki*. "This and That about Bugs" (1948) has been translated twice before; once by Kumai Hiro in 1951 and again by the late William Clark in 1958. "The Skinny Rooster" (1949) has been translated in its entirety by Edward Seidensticker (1955) and in part by Donald Keene (1984).

It is perhaps indicative of Robert Epp's approach to his author that he calls *Yaseta Ondori* "The Skinny Rooster" while both Seidensticker and Keene call it "The Thin Rooster." Epp prefers to translate in boldly colloquial English and consequently, given a choice among words chooses the most colorful, the most idiosyncratic. This becomes evident if one compares his translation with Donald Keene's. The passage is from *Yaseta Ondori*. (I am, making this comparison, while in no position to check the original Japanese. It is the English styles that I am comparing, and their effect upon the reader. Every translator, because of the very nature of translation, must create his own "version" of the text he is translating.)

Keene's version runs: "Ogata had been bed-ridden for years.... The pain seemed to be brought on by cold and dampness. Overwork, too, was dangerous, but for Ogata, reminded by the slightest exertion that he was a sick man, there was neither work nor overwork. He did no more than the little writing he had to. For the most part he moved only his hands and mouth, which he could manage satisfactorily lying down."

Epp translates the same passage as: "Ogata has already spent four years flat on his back.... Generally speaking, chill and dampness appeared to spark off the neuralgic pains between his ribs. Over-exerting himself had the same effect. Even the slightest movement let Ogata know in no uncertain terms that he was a sick man, so aside from the unavoidable task of writing manuscripts every once in a while, there was little or no work in his daily life. The only parts of his body he put to work, in fact, were hands and mouth, which he could use even in bed."

Epp's version of Ozaki is very engaging, very down-to-earth, very colloquial, as will have been seen in many of the terms used in his translation above: "flat on his back," "generally speaking," "no uncertain terms," etc. His Ozaki, though sick, poor and put-upon is nonetheless resilient, quick to notice the quirks of human behavior, and full of his own kind of common sense.

Indeed, as the translator insists in his introduction, this attitude "also saved him from the de rigeur pose of being angry at the world or 'alienated.'" So much does the translator insist upon the colloquial in this version that he is quite ready to sacrifice considerations of historical levels of usage. For example, in a 1946 story ("Crickets,") he has people using 1970s colloquialisms: "'Hey you guys,' I said, 'don't go cramming all those bugs in here like this.'" In another story, he renders a line as "'Wow!' he rasped," for which I should dearly love to learn the Japanese.

Saved from poses, Ozaki has a wholesome sense of perspective and retains his humor and an ability to smile at his own foibles. In the words of the translator, Ozaki strives "to find life's meaning, not to vent his anger over its meaninglessness."

Which—if one were to agree that life has a meaning—makes perfect sense. In this translation of his stories, Ozaki appears as a real survivor, something even of a humorist, a very down-to-earth person with a bit of the rural about him. In all, a most attractive personage. One which Ozaki himself would have liked one feels, and perhaps was even partially responsible for. The cover blurb for this collection says that the translator "worked closely with the author over several years in preparing this English version."

Ozaki idolized Shiga Naoya (some of the stories are about this attachment), and his bug story is often compared by Japanese critics to Shiga's 1917 "At Kinosaki," which perhaps inspired it. There is a great difference between the two. The Shiga is informed with a sense of transience, of futility, which makes it one of the most intensely moving short works of Japanese literature.

This kind of pessimism (if that is what it is) is beyond Ozaki and, in any event, not to the taste of his presented persona. While searching for the meaning of life, he also permits himself a little smile and a little tear and this perhaps accounts for his permanent Japanese popularity.

Rosy Glasses, by Ozaki Kazuo, translated with an introduction by Robert Epp. Woodchurch, Ashford, Kent, England: P. Norbury Publications, 1988.

Ishikawa Jun

Despite his eminence in Japanese letters, Ishikawa Jun (1899–1987) is barely known abroad. There is Donald Keene's translation of the *Shion Monogatari* ("Asters") in his *Three Modern Japanese Short Novels*, and William Tyler's translation of *Meigetsuju* ("Moon Gems") in *The Showa Anthology*, and that's about it. But here is Tyler's translation of *Fugen* (*The Bodhisattva*), the 1936 novel which won its author the Akutagawa Prize and which is still regarded as one of his finest works.

One of the reasons for Ishikawa's neglect is his difficulty—both for translator and for reader. Often called *saigo no bunjin*, the last belletrist, the least of Ishikawa's concerns was making what is now called a good-read. As he himself said, "the breezes that stir the pages of [my novels] are a far different wind from the gusts of the mundane world."

The narrative of *The Bodhisattva* involves an impoverished novelist living in downtown Tokyo and writing about Joan of Arc. Paralleling this devotion is his love for a young woman involved in the political underground.

Several friends are also around, and there is a lot of circular dialogue. At the end, there is a kind of tragedy but art (the Joan of Arc book) goes on.

If the interest in this novel were merely on this anecdotal level, it would have been difficult to find a publisher, let alone a translator or a reader. But it is not. As the author says during its course: "Were I to take these details, fit them into a peaceful setting replete with birdcages, and give them a clever twist or two, no doubt I would have the makings of a novel of manners." But simple narrative is not the intent.

Rather, as the translator observes: "The brilliance of Ishikawa's writing ... lies in his special ability to order multiple levels of prosody, allegory, and satire into an intricate whole."

This novel then best demonstrates "the blend of Ishikawa's modernist and literati tastes." This is a confluence that brings together a first-person narration which is like that of the novel within the narrative in *Les Faux-monnayeurs*, the prolix mannerisms of Santo Kyoden in his sharebon writings, and something like the *mitate* techniques of analog images in Buddhist texts.

The influence of Gide, particularly *The Counterfeiters*, is paramount. Ishikawa was reading this novel during the writing of *The Bodhisattva* and was translating Gide's *L'Immoraliste* and *Les caves du Vatican* as well. In addition, he had the highest admiration for Gide's early (1895) *Paludes*, a study of intellectual impotence much like that he himself had observed.

The influence of Gide was strong in Japan—and in a way it still is. Many writers were influenced, and one, Nagai Kafu, said that a day spend without reading Andre Gide was a day wasted. The French author certainly influenced Ishikawa, and the dialogue in this novel contains many Gide-like passages. For example:

> "Is there any human habit more nasty than eating?"
> "You think there's something despicable about food?"
> "No, on the contrary, I feel insulted when I realize how much I enjoy it."

At the same time, as a vehicle, Ishikawa adapts a *jozetsu* (garrulous) style, one with Edo roots but which was, in his time, typically used only for jocular purposes. Here it is rendered sardonic, as though the Soseki fun-figures (as in *Botchan* and *I Am a Cat*) had suddenly started to think.

One of the reasons for the marked sardonic in this novel was so that (another layer in this patterned fiction) the author could more precisely target the object of his parody: the solemn I-novel which then had a stranglehold on serious literature. Ishikawa speaks of the awful search for "sincerity" which these self-consumed works represented. "One proceeds to read a novel but ends up seeing instead the big, fat face of the author." This is something the reader of Ishikawa will never have to put up with. The I-novel style is so severely put down that its demands are deflated even before they arrive.

Donald Keene, in writing of this novel, has called attention to a passage where the author's high-flown style is interrupted by his landlady wanting to introduce the neighborhood junkman. "The incongruousness of a Japanese writing on [Joan of Arc] in a dirty lodging presided over by a woman wanting to make some money out of scrap iron is one of the effects at which Ichikawa aimed."

A book like this, self-referential, playful, and unconcerned with any of the reader's expectations, would even now be called modernist. And like much modernist writings it is, beneath its dappled surface, healthily subversive.

Gide wished to subsume bourgeois prejudices, and Ishikawa uses his sardonic humor to serve as antidote to the ultra-nationalist thinking of his time. For this his hero has a very bracing scorn: "I asked myself what was to become of this land, an imperial realm no less, in which such mindless breeds prevailed and proliferated."

But having strong moral concerns is not truly important to the structure which the author is creating. He himself offers a paradigm when he mentions a "time-honored form of child's play in which one draws different parts of a pictures on six small squares of paper. By rearranging the pieces, it is possible to assemble the images in six different combinations." The intent is as formal as it is playful, and the result is both self-effacing and moving.

All of this is beautifully explicated by the translator in the terminal essay on the book we have just finished reading. He describes, quotes, and illuminates the text in a fashion rare in Asian studies. It is certainly not often that we find a scholar of Japanese literature as sophisticated as Tyler.

Revealing Ishikawa's modernist precedents, the translator has constructed a text which manages in an alien tongue (English) to amply mirror the author's stylistic concerns. It is a thoughtful, subtle, informed translation, a full presentation through which we are allowed to read Ishikawa's novel on its own terms.

The Bodhisattva, or *Samantabhadra: A Novel*, by Ishikawa Jun, translated with an introduction and critical essay by William Jefferson Tyler. New York: Columbia University Press, 1990.

Ishikawa Jun still remains less known in the West than other Japanese writers of equal stature. With the publication of this volume, however, several more of his works become available in English. This is due to the devotion of William Tyler, whose translations of the 1936 *Fugen* (*The Bodhisattva*, 1990) and the 1946 *Meigetsuju* ("Moon Gems," 1985) introduced Ishikawa to English readers.

A reason for the relative neglect in the West is perhaps

the difficulty of cataloging him, that is, placing him within the framework of received opinion about Japanese literature. Japanese critics have the same problem—he does not seem to fit anywhere. Though he is commonly given a place in the *burai-ha* (decadent school), the designation means even less than usual when applied to a writer of such subtle variety.

One of the reasons for dropping Ishikawa in the *burai* bin is that he is not "politically committed," since he often consciously availed himself of earlier styles, such as the garrulous manner typical of the *gesaku* writers of the Tokugawa Period. Of his literary life he once said, "I did my study abroad in Edo."

At the same time, though not politically committed, Ishikawa was capable of political action. His 1938 *Marusu no Uta* ("Mars Song." translated in the present volume) is an example. It is about a writer who cannot write because of the constant dinning of military songs. Though no actual "Mars Song" existed, similar patriotic songs were everywhere in 1938 and shortly became ubiquitous.

To speak out against such jingoism, even in symbolic terms, was a brave political act—and one for which Ishikawa was punished. The magazine that had printed the piece was banned by the censors, and Ishikawa wrote nothing of any political import until the end of the Pacific War in 1945. Of course, this abstinence, this refusal, was also a political action.

Many other Japanese writers were incapable of it. Some, like Takamura Kotaro, jumped right on the military bandwagon. Others, like Tanizaki Jun'ichiro after *The Makioka Sisters* was criticized, simply stopped publishing but went on writing. Only Kafu stopped writing at all—except for his journals.

Takami Jun has noted that not one literary man in Japan died for the sake of freedom of speech. But several refused to be literary any longer (Donald Keene has an excellent essay on this subject), among them Kafu and Ishikawa.

The war over, Ishikawa began to write again. *Moon Gems* (here republished in an amended translation) *Ogon Densetsu* (1946) ("The Legend of Gold"), *Yakeato no Iesu* ("Jesus of the Ruins") and *Taka* (1953) ("The Raptor"), all included in this collection, show the author picking up where he left off.

In several respects, the wartime and the postwar Ishikawa share a political bravery: When "The Legend of Gold" was to be anthologized in 1947, the Occupation authorities suddenly took exception to it (an American soldier purveys black-market items to his Japanese girlfriend) and refused to allow it to be published.

Thus the resolute Ishikawa, true only to himself, had the honorable distinction of being banned by both the Japanese and the American censors. If his personal, layered, sometimes involuted style demands careful reading, it is that utterly intimate loyalty to self that makes reading him worth all the effort.

The Legend of Gold and Other Stories, by Ishikawa Jun, translated by William J. Tyler. Honolulu: University of Hawaii, Press, 1998.

Sumii Sue

This is a translation of the first volume of a very long and very brave novel which Sumii Sue, born in 1902, published over the years 1961–73. It made its author famous all over Japan and sold over four million copies.

The book is brave because it is a passionate and unsparing account of the lives of Japan's proscribed class, the *burakumin*. Their history is one of enduring the intolerance and bigotry of the citizenry at large—a history which continues to this day.

Though the so-called Edict of Emancipation was promulgated in 1871, it has never been widely observed. Only several years ago a number of major local companies were revealed as having subscribed to a directory which listed the "outcast" settlements and gave new and old names. In this way the companies could avoid accidentally hiring *burakumin* descendants.

Indeed, as one of the characters in this novel says, upon remembering the days of the edict: "You needn't think you can start rejoicing yet: it won't make a scrap of difference for at least a hundred years." And, it turns out, not even then, not even then.

All of this prejudice is directed against a group which is in no way different from the majority except for the degree of bigotry it must endure. There are various theories as to the origins of this class. One of them says it was because this group originally engaged in despised trades, working as butchers, tanners, undertakers. Another says that it was because this group was forced (then as now) into such despised trades. Yet another suggests that the group was originally priestly, designed to protect against the evils with which they later in the public mind became confused.

There are, however, no historically valid reasons for the continuation of the ban, though there may be some psychiatric causes—such as the compulsion of the nation to discover a "pure," unique and homogeneous quality in itself, and the consequent need of some "other" against which to define this.

It is the "invisible" quality of being *burakumin* that so bewilders and eventually infuriates young Koji, the main character in this first volume of the novel. We follow his growing consciousness from 1908, when he was six, through the beginnings of adolescence. Though the full novel carries his story to 1924, in this volume all of the major themes are stated.

One of the strongest of these is the sense of injustice. The proscribed children cannot even use the same water bucket at school, are constantly assailed by cries of "dirty, dirty," are targets of the many bullies, and are continually discriminated against by their teachers.

In fact, the entire social system seems to be designed against them. Perhaps it was. The anthropologist Emiko Ohnuki-Tierney says that the group was further degraded because of the uses to which a growing government could put it. The central government deliberately tried to create fruitful antagonisms by placing these people in the midst of farming communities, or by insisting that they take the hated role of executioner/torturer, or even by deliberately elevating some of their number in order to create rivalries. If popular dislike could be directed against such a proscribed folk, a totalitarian government would receive less of it.

Koji understands that it is as "natural" for the other children to despise the lowest as it is to worship the highest, the Emperor, but he refuses to himself believe (as many of his relatives do) that since he was born "defiled" he must resign himself to his state. He sees the proscription and sees how cynically it is manipulated. As his mother, a young widow, innocently says: "When it comes to war, we end up the wives and mothers of dead soldiers like everyone else."

During maneuvers the Emperor himself attends and the excited village folk, rummaging about afterward discover his cigarette butts, each with its imperial seal. Even more excitement is occasioned when one townsman discovers what he takes to be the Emperor's excrement.

"Funny what a difference there is between people

when we're all the same human beings," says a relative of Koji's. "There they are, treating the Emperor's crap like treasure, but in our case they think even the rice we grow is dirty and stinks." For Koji the main interest, however, is just in this homely proof that the Emperor is not a god, that the Emperor is himself human. It marks the beginning of a new awareness.

It also makes a splendid symbol—a concrete embodiment of purity/pollution and displays (rather than merely recounts) one of the major concerns of this work. Such occur, however, rather rarely.

Often the most liberal of sentiments is voiced through the most conservative of styles, and this is certainly true here. The book is realist, intensely discursive, and naturalistically detailed. It is also didactic, usually after the fact. We are shown the plight, the cause, and hence do not need the assurance that they "knew in their bones how much evil could come of a society that placed the authority of an emperor above all else."

But perhaps literary standards are of less importance here because the message is the most important thing about this multipart novel, and it is one which can scarcely be stated strongly enough.

That four million Japanese have over the years read it is heartening. But, as always, the problems of a country are not with its people but with its government. Perhaps now that this translation informs foreign opinion, the "invisible minority" can be more openly acknowledged and the 1871 edict can be put into full effect.

The River with no Bridge, by Sumii Sue, translated by Susan Wilkinson. Tokyo: Charles E. Tuttle Company, 1990.

Yamamoto Shugoro

Ichi is a woman married to a ranking official in 18th-century Japan. She leads a secure, easy and unquestioning life until tragedy strikes. Her husband is involved in some questionable political business. She and her baby must flee. Having entrusted her with some valuable papers he is, apparently, killed.

In hiding, she takes up mat weaving, and one of her products is of such beauty that the local lord allows her an audience. Though ill and failing, she presses him to read the papers. She now knows what the political business was and is determined to vindicate her late husband's name.

The vindication comes in the person of the husband himself. Now reinstated, he thanks her for her devotion and approves of her protecting her mother-in-law (his own mother) even though their child was lost in the process. Then, in a moment of tremulous emotion, she actually hears him begging her pardon.

If this sounds like one of the more popular television serials, it is only fitting that it should. *Hanamushiro*, the 1948 novel of which this is a translation, did indeed become just such a TV serial. It obviously abounds in "the common touch" of which the blurb so enthusiastically speaks.

Just what this consists of, however, is not easy to discover. Yamamoto (1903–1967) is perhaps the best-loved of all contemporary novelists and his position is probably unique in that it is not only the occasional reader but also the intellectual who speaks well of him. Critics who castigate the modern masters of *jun bungaku* will rush to the appreciation of this exponent of *taishu bungaku*. Speak bad of Kawabata, but not a word against Yamamoto.

Pressed, the informed reader will refer to the "common touch," and then go on to praise the author's "lyricism."

Further questioned he will reveal that Yamamoto is especially highly regarded as adept at a sub-literary genre, the *shomin* novel, tales about the Edo Period merchant class. Of this, the common or, at least, the popular touch is apparently made.

None of this, however, clears up the mystery of what is so good about Yamamoto. By Western literary standards, this book is quite thin: the characters are shallow; there is lots of pathetic fallacy (including a flood timed to coincide with the heroine's emotions); a tiresome tendency to resort to indirect discourse when any action threatens, and a general lack of purport.

But, of course, it is precisely Western literary standards which should not be brought to bear on works such as this. Such standards can reveal nothing when the passage in question is one such as: "The eager expression in her eyes, which were dimmed with fever, had a desperate power which would not allow him to refuse her." By such standards, this would not even make the pop category. It would have to be relegated to the pulp.

Nor do I believe this lack of excellence to be in any way the fault of the translation which is occasionally so stiff as to seem literal. (I would, however, complain about its ignorance of proper historical level: I cannot believe there were 18th-century equivalents for "It looks as if he's checking into something," or "I bet you'd like to wipe the perspiration off.") No, I think the problem is more serious. I do not believe it is possible to translate popular fiction of this sort. Literature (*jun bungaku*) by its precision, its explicitness transcends boundaries; pop fiction through its very reliance upon popular unspoken assumptions trips over them.

The West knows nothing of Yamamoto as yet (saving Kurosawa's *Red Beard* and *Dodes'ka-den*, based on his work, and John Bester's translation of a single story) and indeed *taishu bungaku* has not been widely rendered—the one exception being Yoshikawa Eiji. Given his limitations and those of his genre it will be interesting to see if Yamamoto finds a home abroad.

The jacket-blurb speaks of his limitations as though they were virtues: "This translation puts Western readers in touch with the tastes and emotions of the average Japanese reader and enables them to share, for a little while, a very Japanese view of life." To which the only answer is: Yes, but....

The Flower Mat, by Yamamoto Shugoro, translated by Inoue Mihoko and Eileen B. Hennessy. Tokyo: Charles E. Tuttle Company, 1977.

Koda Aya

The subtitle "A Japanese Literary Daughter" indicates the choice of the biographer. Koda Aya (1904–1990) is to be the literary daughter of the famous Koda Rohan, noted Meiji critic and novelist, best known as the author of *The Five-Storied Pagoda*. She is to be defined by him during his life and after his death.

This thesis would prove limiting in a discussion of, say, Tsushima Yuko, the daughter of novelist Dazai Osamu, to say nothing of Yoshimoto Takaaki's daughter Banana—so different are these literary offspring. Koda Aya was, however, truly formed by her father. She did not begin writing until after he had died, and she herself described her writings as "the grumblings of a woman blinded by the light of death."

When she was young, her father apparently once told her that it was best to communicate with him without words. This advice at the time she may have heeded but, as her biographer writes, she later "spent her career attempting to communicate with him—and in some way rejoin him."

This dialogue with the dead resulted in a literature very different from that of the author's father. His prose was seen by critics as like "an old samurai wearing armor—heavy on stylistic flourishes and requiring slow, careful treatment." Hers, on the other hand, was fluid, immediate, personal. Critics were initially divided on the literary daughter's style. One found it "unbearably" perfect, and another said that it represented "the crumbs of genius left to her by her father."

Now the former opinion holds and the celebrated Koda Aya style is discovered to be a late manifestation of that which has long animated the finest in Japanese literature—the voice of a woman writing from personal experience, one which echoes from Heian verandas to Tokyo apartment complexes.

Alan Tansman writes that Koda consciously confined herself to "the language of restrictive and confining domesticity" and that her concerns were all for the concrete everyday. It is this which would distinguish this main stylistic line from any other. It is resolutely concerned with the real, the actual, the indubitable—as distinguished from the ideal and the theoretical, which would be male concerns.

If the author makes much of these presumably different provinces, it is because he wishes to define Koda more precisely than is critically common and also to find her and her works germane to what he believes to be "the most public and explosive of issues … the problem of gender in the modern world."

While it is true that she writes of a restrictive and confining domesticity, her passivity is merely ostensible—it is a stratagem long known to women writing in and against a patriarchal culture. This apparent compliance was, however, with Koda extreme—so much so that this presumed valorization of "feminine aesthetic values" invited an adoption of "oppressive social norms." At least, this occurred in the minds of a number of critics, where she is perceived as confirming "what men think—and hope—women are."

This, however, writes Tansman, is more apparent than real. A true artist, Koda used the persona of the traditional Japanese woman to write honestly about that state. If the outlook was narrow, this could well be a literary virtue. As Edith Wharton observed: "The creative mind thrives on a reduced diet." Koda's world, so richly made of real sights and sounds and smell and tastes is all the more real for being narrow.

This is certainly true of her finest work, the 1955 novel *Nagareru* (Flowing), of which Tansman writes that "everything she wrote prior to it seems preparatory, and everything after it reads like a coda." This beautifully controlled novel about the decline of a geisha house on the Sumida River contains the whole postwar world in miniature.

The events which create this world are all mundane: bills pile up, customers don't come, the women argue. But all are observed by the new maid, who is herself not a part of this world. Her angle of interpretation is that of an outsider who can, consequently, see deeper since she is not blinded by self interest. She is thus also a critic and can understand what others cannot. In addition, she has her own life to think about and wants to get on with it.

Tansman finds Koda's continual theme to be that of "the transformation of identity" and in his book intends to show how one writer "picked up the pieces left by the Pacific War." In the novel, "the narrow parameters of her world allow [the maid] ever-expanding possibilities for action." Just as they did for Koda herself.

In his exegesis, Tansman translates many pages from the 1955 novel, and in this way, the reader can get at least some idea of its quality. In addition he offers in full translations of four stories: the *Kunsho* ("The Medal," 1949) *Kami* ("Hair," 1951), *Hina* ("Dolls," 1955) and *Kuroi Suso* ("The

Black Hems," 1955). Since Koda's work is not at all widely translated, it is good to have these stories—though the last of them already exists in a beautiful translation by Edward Seidensticker (*Japan Quarterly*, 3:2 (1956), later twice collected), a fact which is unrecorded here.

There would have been other ways to approach Koda and her work rather than through the grid of psychology and such heavy emphasis upon paternal relations. On the other hand, the shape of Koda's life seems to justify it. At the end of her career, she devoted herself—using both her royalties and those of her father—to rebuilding a five-storied pagoda in Nara.

The Writings of Koda Aya: A Japanese Literary Daughter, by Alan M. Tansman. New Haven: Yale University Press, 1993.

Koda Aya's life with father was not easy. Nonetheless it is commonly observed that she "spent her career attempting to communicate with him—and in some way rejoin him." These attempts have attracted the attention of a number of scholars. Tansman locates her "a Japanese literary daughter." Ann Sherif, on the other hand, in this new study, is critical of such a psychological approach. For her, Koda Aya is a voice in the feminist debate.

She finds that "the resilience, strength, and maturity of the [Koda Aya] persona differ sharply from the masochistic, self-sacrificial attitude prescribed for women—an attitude of persevering and not complaining about the oppression of patriarchy, the exploitation of the brutal capitalist, the barrenness of Japan's rural landscape, the bankruptcy of unexamined habits of heterosexual marriage."

Yet Koda Aya is not to be fitted into the ideal feminist mould and of this Sherif is quite aware. Indeed, the author's present popularity (and she is far more popular than her once more famous father) seems to rest upon her perceived ability to, in herself, suggest a kind of compromise. Though a dutiful daughter, she was also, at the same time, an independent person.

The independence is seen not in the essays about her father and herself but in the autobiographical fiction which she began writing later on in her life—in particular the 1955 novel *Nagareru* (*Flowing*). Here the father vanishes, and the daughter takes his place as an autonomous artist who imparts her darkly beautiful view of women's lives.

Though this seminal work remains untranslated, Tansman's book gives some passages, and Sherif's a few. Both authors, however, have chosen the same format: a biographical introduction supported by full translations from the works. Sherif offers two essays, "Fragments" (*Kakera*) and "A Friend for Life (*Mono Iwanu Issho no Tomo*) and two short stories—"Dolls" and "The Medal"—two of those already translated by Tansman.

Such duplication seems wasteful, and, in any event, we are in both books given a lot of opinion about Koda Aya but not much proof. While it is undoubtedly true that she is her father's spiritual daughter and, at the same time, some kind of proto-feminist, it is the work which is important, not the writer.

Mirror: The Fiction and Essays of Koda Aya, translated by Ann Sherif. Honolulu: University of Hawaii Press, 1999.

Enchi Fumiko

At the end of *The Waiting Years*, the best known novel of Enchi Fumiko (1905–1986), the heroine comes to realize that "everything that she had suffered for, worked for, and won within [her] restricted sphere of life ... lay within the confines of that unfeeling, hard, and unassailable fortress summed up by the one word 'family' ... she had suddenly seen the futility of that somehow artificial life on which she had lavished so much energy and wisdom."

Her disillusion and regret are understandable. She has been the perfect Japanese wife: she has managed the large house, raised the children, and put up with a tyrannical husband. More unusually, she has also had to choose for her spouse the fifteen-year-old girl who would be brought into the house as his mistress. When he tires of this one, she is forced to procure another. Later, she has to witness her husband's affair with her son's wife and, later still, must wonder about his intentions toward his granddaughter.

Though her time is one of change and growing freedom (the novel is set in the middle and late years of the Meiji Period), she can experience neither of these qualities. Her life is of the sort that could have been led equally well (or badly) in darkest Tokugawa. Her only respite is in her relations with other women—the two mistresses, with whom she is on excellent terms, her daughters, her grandchild. The men in her life—husband, son, various brothers-in-law—are all impossible. Only with other women can she experience affection and a kind of love.

At the very end of the book, dying, she makes her first independent decision—one which was regarded as sensational even as late as 1957 when this book was originally published. She lets her husband know that she does not want a funeral service. Rather, "tell him that all he need do is to take my body out to sea at Shinagawa and dump it in the water." This request finally upsets the husband's equanimity, and the book closes with a description of this welcome scene.

Just how efficacious it is or will be is not the novelist's point. Her concern is that it be seen that the heroine has finally had enough. A further concern might be that we understand this curious request as no real revolt at all: she merely affirms her husband's ultimate opinion of her.

I say "might" because this novel is purely descriptive, and one remains consequently somewhat unsure (and rightly so) about the opinions of the novelist. Though the work deals with the further reaches of male chauvinism, and though the prevalence of an unfeeling male world is patent, there is also the possibility that the heroine, by becoming so completely the proper wife, has brought it all on herself.

The book makes no judgments, it merely presents evidence. We are free to believe that a woman's lot is hard but that is the way that it is—that any woman who falls into the expected *musume-tsuma-haha* (daughter-wife-mother) pattern is going to regret it, that it is her own fault, that she did all this to herself—not as a woman but as a person.

This makes the novel pleasantly ambivalent and makes the original title more than a little ironic. *Onnazaka*, the original title, is better for the book than is *The Waiting Years*. It also, to this degree, makes for an amount of dissatisfaction in those readers who think that such a massive amount of simple injustice should somehow be righted.

Perhaps I am making this book sound more interesting that it is. It is not a distinguished work, and it meanders a good deal (I suspect it was written for magazine serialization originally); everything is told and very little is shown, and it is occasionally quite sentimental.

Nonetheless, the theme is an important one: a woman's lot is a difficult one; men are unfair, perhaps by nature, certainly by inclination; if a woman goes along with society's idea of what a woman is, she loses her life—all of this, moved to another plane, involves us all, men and women alike. Life itself is "unfair," and we had better get used to the idea. There is no solution to this "problem" but ways through it are possible.

Enchi Fumiko, perhaps not really believing that her heroine is culpable, suggests none of them, but I will. In Sartre's words: "It is not important what life has done to you. What is important is what you do with what life has done to you."

The Waiting Years, by Enchi Fumiko, translated by John Bester. Tokyo: Kodansha International, 1971, reprinted 1980.

Enchi Fumiko was, besides being a well known novelist, a scholar of Japanese literature. Like her father, Ueda Kazutoshi, she was a classicist. Her 1972–3 translation of *The Tale of Genji* into modern Japanese is popular, and her glossings of other classics are well read. The 1965 *Namamiko Monogatari* won her several major local prizes and represents still the best-known of her reinterpretations of classical texts. It is this work, translated by Roger Thomas, which is now given us.

A Tale of False Fortunes is consonant with *A Tale of Flowering Fortunes*, the title that William and Helen Craig McCullough gave their translation of the *Eiga Monogatari*. The English title was purposely chosen to echo the earlier work because the *Namamiko Monogatari* is a reinterpretation of the *Eiga Monogatari* itself.

That earlier work, an 11th-century historical tale, was presumably written—at least the first part—by Akazone Emaki, lady-in-waiting at the court. It is the first historical work written in the *kana* syllabary and is given over to the glorification of Fujiwara no Michinaga, whose principal wife was the lady on whom Emaki was waiting. It is a political panegyric devoted to a god-like Michinaga.

This means it also very pro-Fujiwara and champions that family which proved so adroit at handling reigning emperors and keeping the power in its own hands. There are, however, other takes on history and Enchi's is one of them.

She once said that she found all the Heian ladies, each one writing away, all rather alike, adding that she was, however, rather fond of Fujiwara Teishi, the consort of the Emperor Ichijo and found her appearance in the *Eiga Monogatari* both vivid and fresh.

So she set about making her even more so and wrote the *Namamiko Monogatari*, an innovative form of historical fiction, and a textual foil to the original—one where we may again view Michinaga but now find all of his god-like feats to be really political machinations.

Supporting Enchi's claim is *A Tale of False Fortunes*, a manuscript given her father by Basil Hall Chamberlain but now unaccountably missing. Nonetheless, she read it so thoroughly that she now remembers whole sections word for word, and it is these which are given us, along with commentaries on alternate readings, on probable motivations, and on her own suppositions.

So convincing and natural is the manner, so right-on is her pastiche of Heian Japanese, that some scholars are said to be searching for the missing document even yet. This the author encourages, often commenting upon her difficulties. "This kind of writing amounts to a sort of cut-and-paste work, rather irritating, but there is no other way to reconstruct."

The missing document, of course, never existed. The "source" is as fictitious as the result. Nonetheless, Enchi quotes from contemporary sources (Sei Shonagon is often there), and if she leaves out Murasaki Shikibu, it is perhaps because the original *Eiga Monogatari* quotes her. And at the end, she covers any error by asserting that her original tale "is a work of fiction and perhaps the order of historical events was inverted as a means for its author to suggest something."

Suggesting something is just what Enchi herself is doing in this spirited fake. In fact, faking in this manner is a known way of suggesting something. If is fascinating, effective and—right now—rather prevalent.

Yosano Akiko refurbished the *Genji* into a modern novel, and a publication by G.G. Rowley indicates just how she did it. Liza Dalby has Murasaki writing her memoirs in her *Tale of Murasaki*, and dedicating this work to her daughter, who in turn gives it to her own child, Murasaki's granddaughter. Thus excusing any chronological error, the author (Dalby) is able to piece together fragments from the real Murasaki diary, using the glue of her lively imagination.

Or, continuing the listing of contemporary attempts to fake history for a good purpose, I might modestly mention my own *Kumagai*, which purports to be the memoirs of the 12th-century warrior who famously took the head of the young and beautiful Atsumori. All of these books, including my own, are fakes, and all have ambitions to present something other than chronology.

Their common aim is to confirm the relevance of history by reinterpreting its motives and to validate the event by the interpretation. Being able to see further than did the various originals, these works attempt a contemporary interpretation which, far from endistancing the subject, brings it closer to us.

Thus, Enchi's *Teishi*, while never anachronistic, is our contemporary to the extent that the reader's is able to look deeper into motivation. At the same time, the conventional (classical) is revealed as naively partial or even (as in my *Kumagai*) an error. The result is that the reader is encouraged to revalue and (perhaps for the first time) take these characters seriously.

Enchi's book must have been a nightmare to translate. There are a number of levels of discourse, including Heian Japanese, all of them to be kept stylistically separate.

Thomas, who likes long, difficult, important books (it was he who devoted years of his life to translating Inoue Yasushi's *Confucius*) does so with skill and confidence—if they are still giving out prizes for translations, this effort certainly deserves one.

A Tale of False Fortunes, by Enchi Fumiko, translated by Roger K. Thomas. Honolulu: University of Hawaii Press, 1998.

Inoue Yasushi

One of Japan's finest novelists, Inoue Yasushi (1907–1991) has written a most impressive body of work, has achieved official honors, and has won true popularity, yet has still not been awarded, either in Japan or abroad, the critical attention he deserves.

One of the reasons would be that he is (a liability for critics both local and foreign) difficult to categorize. He seems to lack the strong (and categorizable) profile of, say, a Mishima; he does not write confessional fiction, a product Japanese critics find irresistible; he has no interest in "current events," and is the least political of writers. This being so, it's difficult to define him.

Also, his work is not all of a piece. It is, precisely, of two pieces. He writes contemporary-based fiction (the stories "The Opaline Cup," and "The Rhododendrons" in this newly published collection), and he also writes what we will, for the time being, call historical fiction—*Lou-lan*, "The Sage," "Princess Yung-t'ai's Necklace," and "Passage to Fudaraku," in this same collection. He does not specialize and consequently will not fit into critical pigeonholes.

Finally, even the "historical fiction" defies categorization. If both he and, say, Yoshikawa Eiji can fit under this rubric then the term plainly has small meaning. *Lou-lan*, for example, is historical fiction in that it is about time past, but it is also a meticulously observed piece of fictitious historical literature: there are no heroes, no characters—it is about a country and its two thousand years of history. But it is also fictional in that nothing really is actually known about this country.

The closest parallel that comes to mind is Borges, but the difference is that for Inoue the imaginary history veils no philosophical or existential assumptions. It reads as straight as a children's book (one of great sophistication, to be sure), and the fascination lies not in the presentation but in what is being presented.

"The Sage" and "Passage to Fudaraku" have characters but here, too, history and story are everything and characterization is kept carefully in its minimal place. There is some slight trace of plot in "Princess Yung-t'ai's Necklace," but this, too, serves the interests of history rather than fiction since it is a combination of then and now which provides the impetus of this short story.

What emerges most strongly from this beautifully composed fiction is the respect which Inoue shows for his imaginary history. He puts in no human interest; he refuses to tart up his chronicle, his suspense is the true suspense of life, which he renders with a scrupulous soberness which thrills and excites more than any *Shogun*.

Japan has no other writer like Inoue—though the historical reconstructions of Ibuse come close in tone. He is perhaps most like that other contemporary master (equally critically unappreciated and for many of the same reasons)—Margurite Yourcenar. She, with the appearance of *Hadrian's Memoirs*, proved herself one of the finest of all 20th-century writers—and she is still critically disregarded and (given the magnitude of her achievement) little appreciated.

Well, the only answer to critics is to bring out more evidence. I welcome and recommend this new collection of stories by Inoue. Two are not, to be sure, precisely new in English. Edward Seidensticker's translations of *Lou-lan* and "The Rhododendrons" also appeared in the bilingual Hara Shobo edition (where the latter was called "The Azaleas of Hira"), an edition now out of print. His translation of "Princess Yung t'ai's Necklace" is, however, appearing for the first time, as are James T. Arakai's equally fine translations of "The Sage," "The Opaline Cup" and "Passage to Fudaraku."

Lou-Lan and Other Stories, by Inoue Yasushi, translated by James T. Araki and Edward Seidensticker. Tokyo: Kodansha International, 1979.

The spare and beautiful novel *The Roof Tile of Tempyo* (*Tempyo no Iraka*), for which Inoue Yasushi received the 1958 Japanese Ministry of Education Prize, is about a group of Buddhist monks, four among hundreds, who left Japan during the Nara Period to voyage to Ch'ang-an, the capital of T'ang China. Their purpose was to bring back a Buddhist sage. This was finally accomplished, twenty years later when one of their number, Fusho, returned with the great monk Chien-chen, more commonly known in Japanese as Ganjin.

Based upon what few records remain, the novel is an exercise in controlled imagination. Lean, ostensibly factual, it recounts two decades of adventures with simplicity and directness. There are no purple passages, no indulgences. The wonders of Ch'ang-an are not even described. Everything is properly sacrificed to the quest itself, the often hopeless-seeming wanderings of the monks and their repeated attempts to fulfill their mission.

This Inoue novel, unlike some of his others, is not—

perhaps consequent to his scrupulous plainness—all that easy to read. It is definitely not a romance to be picked up and skimmed through. By forcing us to read slowly and to think about what we are reading, however, the author deepens our experience and enlarges our knowledge. At the end of the book, we realize that we will not forget it.

Its difficulties are not, certainly, the doing of the translator. He even simplifies our reading at one point by leaving out lists of sutra titles, and has substituted for the five-chapter structure of the original a twenty-one—section construction which approximates the serial form of the first publication. The translation seems smooth and simple yet the book must have been a translator's purgatory.

The thoughtful foreign reader, impressed by this book, will wonder why he had not heard more about Inoue Yasushi. Perhaps the reason is that, though he has been translated, the books themselves have been published mainly in Japan.

Perhaps this beautiful rendering of an important Inoue novel will finally call Western attention to the anomaly of knowing the novels, essays, and plays of Mishima Yukio, (even having available in English the early works of Ishihara Shintaro) yet knowing nothing, as yet, of Inoue Yasushi.

The Roof Tile of Tempyo, by Inoue Yasushi, translated by James T. Araki. Tokyo: University of Tokyo Press, 1975.

Tun-Huang is a translation of the Inoue Yasushi novel which was first published in 1959 and won the Mainichi Prize for the following year. In it Inoue continues his interest in medieval China, an interest which the West knows through the English translations of his *Flood* and *Lou-lan*, his later *Journey Beyond Samarkand* and the recent translation of *The Roof Tile of Tempyo*.

Inoue became interested in the territory of Tun-huang (Dunhuang) in middle Asia when he learned of many thousand Buddhist scrolls and manuscripts being found in the caves there. He set out in this book to account for them. Drawing upon his knowledge of the country and the period—the 12th-century—he has created a story about a young scholar who loses his chance to sit for the government examination. He becomes involved in the frontier wars and little by little is led to Buddhism. Eventually, it is he who hides the scrolls.

This is the anecdote, an imaginary one, upon which this novel, otherwise based in history, is built. An author handling this material has many choices of how to do so. He can turn it into blood-and-thunder and much dare-and-do—the choice of many historical novelists and hence the low critical estate of the genre. Or he can turn it into a psychological portrait of the man and times. Or he can make it a picaresque novel with many descriptive passages evoking the period.

Inoue does none of these things—and hence his worth as a novelist. He writes as though he were writing history—which in a very special sense he is. The chronicle is of major importance to him, and nothing intrudes into it. One remembers that in *The Roof Tile of Tempyo*, he did not even describe the fabled T'ang capital. *Lou-lan* is devoid, too, of any interpretive description. His description is limited to what we must accept as fact.

Take this passage from *Tun-huang*: "It was the middle of November, and the first hail of the season had fallen that day. The hail was the size of a man's thumb, and the noise it made as it hit the ground was deafening. No one could go outdoors for even a moment while it was hailing."

This is clear, factual, impersonal and concrete description—and nothing more. It could very well have been based on contemporary reports, and the resulting dispassion is precisely what Inoue wants. There is, likewise, no psychological description. Of one character (a major one), we read that "his characteristic sharp eyes glittered." This is as purple as Inoue ever gets and even there, words such as "characteristic" endistance the reader. The result is not a historical novel but a history novel.

Inoue's work never pulls the heart nor titillates the mind. Rather, through a sober recounting, a judicious chronicling, he succeeds in making the past authentic, and consequently gives his reader a real sense of the wonder of space and the awesomeness of time.

Tun-Huang, by Inoue Yasushi, translated by Jean Oda Moy. Tokyo: Kodansha International, 1978.

Though Inoue Yasushi is by now perhaps best known in the West for his meditative historical novels, in Japan he remains locally best liked for his fiction and his autobiographical writings. One of these has already been translated and published as *A Chronicle of My Mother*. Now the same translator has attempted the 1960–61 *Shirobamba*.

Or a part of it. When published after its original magazine appearance, this long work was issued in two volumes. What is offered here by Peter Owen is just the first of these, though there is no indication of this until the reader is well into the translator's introduction. Subtitled (by the publisher, not the author) "A Childhood in Old Japan," this initial volume covers the years 1915–16 when little Kosaku (the young Inoue) was about eight.

He grew up in Yugashima in Izu, having been sent by his parents to live in the house of a former mistress. Perhaps for this reason he was more solitary than most children and, perhaps consequently, more sensitive.

A young aunt, Sakiko, whom the boy loved, says as

much at the end of this first volume: "You study now. You're different from other children, and when you grow up, you must go to the university."

The other women in the child's life are Nanae, his real mother, a person who can find little good in him, and the old Onui, with whom he is raised. It is she who explains things: "The reason for [his] poor teeth is that his Mama didn't eat fish when she was carrying him." She also attempts to look after him: "Kosaku could not sleep. [She] noticed and offered to paste some pickled plum on his forehead."

The book is filled with the evocations of childhood one might expect from an author of the integrity of Inoue. Kosaku looked at Sakiko's illegitimate baby: "It was an exceedingly small creature and didn't look much like a human child. It couldn't talk to him; in fact he wasn't sure whether it was dead or alive."

Earlier, he and his friends climb trees to catch the first howl of the emerging infant, and, when that doesn't work, they crouch and put their ears to the earth. These and many other precise details render alive those days when "he could see hills, farmhouses, groves of trees, the white highway, and in the far distance, the beautifully shaped, tiny, toylike Mount Fuji."

All of this ought to be rendered in English as measured and objective as was Inoue's original prose. And some of it is. Also, some of it is not. He could never have written the equivalent of the translator's "the Numazu trip had an enormous impact on him" because he obviously did not use vulgarized Japanese. Nor, I think, would he have been guilty of a such pseudo-jocular usage as "after his umpteenth trip."

In addition, just as levels of usage are sometimes unobserved, there is a general heedlessness of gender differences: "Even Kosaku could see that her clothes were of exquisite quality." No boy in either culture would speak of "exquisite quality." To be sure, the book is supposed to be the recollections of an older man, but that is no reason for its being turned into what in this instance could only be the recollections of an older woman.

Also—while I'm at it—the notes (perhaps the work of the publisher rather than the translator) are maddening. They include the unnecessary. Both miso and samisen, for example, are in all big English dictionaries. At the same time, the notes vanish when we might want them. "She placed three kaoru antacid pills on the palm of his hand." Three what?

The original work is a subtle meditation on childhood, and the translator's inflated claims as to its equality with both *David Copperfield* and *Huckleberry Finn* are beside the author's point. Since Inoue's aim is, to this extent, unapprehended, the work reads in English more like a children's book than a book about childhood. One thinks of recent translations of such kid-lit as Tsubota Joji's *Kaze no Naka no Kodomo* and even the popular *Jiro Monogatari*.

These, however, were not, I think, what Inoue was thinking of when he wrote these memories of childhood.

Shirobamba: A Childhood in Old Japan, by Inoue Yasushi, translated with an introduction by Jean Oda Moy. London: Peter Owen, 1991.

The publication of a new translation of Inoue Yasushi is always of interest. When it is one of his finest novels, rendered by his most sensitive translator, it becomes an event.

Wind and Waves (*Futo*) was published in 1963 and won the Yomiuri Literary Prize for the following year. A historical novel of great originality, it recounts the tribulations of the people of Korea during the second half of the 13th-century when Mongol forces, under Kubilai Khan, occupied the country and were pressing for the invasion of Japan.

Korea was defenseless before the hordes, and Kubilai,

a military politician, alternately soothed and terrified. When he wished to be nice, he gave the departing ambassador ten camels. After considerable difficulty, the hapless man returned home "accompanied by those curious beasts which could not be put to any use in his country."

When Kubilai wished to threaten, he could be most forbidding. In 1262, the Korean government had sent every item stipulated except for baby sparrow hawks, which could not be found that time of year. Six months later, Kubilai accused the leaders of laggardness and stipulated a new levy—some 20,000 *kun* of fine copper. When he wished to further terrify, he knew just what to do. People were caned and "exposed to the elements for long hours, the naked flesh of the prisoners gradually darkened as if suffused with ink."

Hoping to retain something of their country and themselves, the Koreans were forced to give up the produce of their work, their property, and eventually all their men of military age. They agreed to put up with Tartar dress and coiffure—head partly shaved, the remaining hair plaited.

They put up with a Tartar princess as queen, a most capricious person: She had "the court musicians perform every night for her amusement ... a thousand lanterns lit the palace grounds ... once she had a tiger released in the garden and watched its capering from the upper floor of the pavilion."

Kubilai, however, was implacable. Also, he was wily. The Koreans never knew where they stood. He would smile and reassure and then order the Mongol army to march in. He was compared to one of the local animals in that "as a tiger approaches a rabbit, its eyes are said to be incredibly gentle."

The Mongol leader annexed Korea, but he was not interested in that unfortunate country for its own sake. Rather it was an avenue for him, created by his "unnatural fascination with Japan." Always intending invasion, he sent several ambassadors armed with letters. But then, as now, Japanese rarely answered letters from abroad.

Having failed through diplomatic means, Kubilai attempted through military force. There were a number of invasions each more ruinous to Korea, which was forced to join the attack. Finally there was the disaster of 1281 with the Mongol, Chinese and Korean ships and troops all lost in the lucky typhoon, the *kamikaze* that saved Japan. The sea was "a watery field of corpses," tens of thousands were killed, Kubilai himself eventually died, and conquest was forgotten. Not, however, before this rage had ruined Korea—and it is the ruin of this beautiful, brave and resourceful country which is the true subject of Inoue's powerful and memorable novel.

As in his other historical novels, Inoue goes directly to the remaining contemporary sources, in this case the 1240 *Secret History of the Mongols*, the 1370 *History of the Mongol Dynasty*, and the 1451 *History of Koryo*, as well as whatever else has survived. He also prepared himself by writing *The Blue Wolf* (1960), a novelistic biography of Genghis Khan (as yet untranslated), grandfather of the ruthless Kubilai.

And, as in his other historical work, Inoue creates a narrative of the greatest purity. Everything recounted exists in fact, and that which is reconstructed is stated soberly—as in "he could only hope the village elder had been mistaken" or "they exchanged sharp glances ... before involuntarily looking away."

This is Inoue's voice, heard against recounted history, but heard speaking the same dialect. It is, indeed, as the translator has stated, "like a 13th-century chronicle brought to life through spare narration, a minimum of dialogue, and slight yet lucid characterization."

And what an extraordinarily difficult book it must have been to translate. In it are layer upon layer of original documents, or commentaries upon these, all in different languages (Chinese, Korean), all with their own styles. And all of this to be translated into English that must also reflect Inoue's own style.

James Araki has already translated *Lou-lan* and other stories as well as *The Roof Tile of Tempyo* and knows Inoue well. Indeed, had not this most deceptively simple of styles been so perfectly understood, a translation as pure, as filled with integrity as this, would not have been possible. Its quality will have been perhaps evident from portions quoted above—it is faultless in that Inoue's powerful and elaborate construction has been rendered into an English structure which is equally complicated and equally congruent.

I also wish to compliment the publishers as well and to hope for the continuation of a program which permits the appearance of such works. This is not common. Japan's most prestigious English-language house recently turned down a translation of Inoue's splendid *The Emperor Goshirakawa* because it was felt that such a book could not sell in sufficient numbers.

Sufficient for what? Perhaps the historical novels of Inoue will never become bestsellers—indeed, they are too fine for that. At the same time, however, over the years they reach out and enrich a scattered audience which knows and cares. Now that *Shogun* is stone dead, *Tun-Huang* and *Lou-lan* are still in print, still enchanting and enriching readers.

Wind and Waves, by Inoue Yasushi, translated by James T. Araki. Honolulu: University of Hawaii Press, 1989.

Originally published in 1989 as *Koshi*, this novel about the last days of Confucius is the final work of the late Inoue Yasushi. It is also one over which he took unusual pains.

Though all of his historical novels are noted for their accuracy, their scholarship and their sense of reality, this one posed particular problems.

Among these was a major structural difficulty: how to reveal the man himself while at the same time maintaining the necessary mythic status of this teacher, this ethical paragon, this contemporary of the Buddha. The problem of distance is always crucial in historical fiction, but this was an exceptionally difficult instance.

Inoue's solution is brilliant in its simplicity. He casts his story as the reminiscences of a fictional disciple, one Yen-Chiang who at seventy-three is now approaching the age at which his master died, thirty-three years before. Removed from the reality of Confucius, we are carefully protected from the reality of the disciple by Inoue's casting the story in the form of a series of talks which are in turn answered by questions and observations from the invisible auditors.

This helps screen us from the awful arbitrariness of so much historical-fiction and, at the same time, allows full use of the only literary remains that Confucius left behind. He called himself a transmitter rather than a creator, and he wrote no original works, though he is supposed to have edited a few, including *The Book of Changes*. What is left of the man himself are the *Analects*, his collected sayings.

It is these which Inoue uses to provide the narrative of his novel. We, members of the congregation, watch the old follower remember the ancient days with the master as he for fourteen years wandered the Central Plain with his disciples and encountered those circumstances which resulted in the sayings now enshrined in the *Analects*.

These outline the ethics of the man (and Confucius must be seen as a social philosopher rather than the religious figure he later became) and define his ideas. He wished to restore a hierarchy which he believed that society had once attained. This being so, his tradition is generally quite conservative, and as a consequence, his teachings have appealed to rulers and been bent to reflect their interests. Like Plato, Confucius believed that the ideal social order was achieved by moral example.

Thus, in Inoue's version of the final years, we see these moral ideas in the making as observed by his follower: "In order for the master to bring a measure of stability to this confused world, it was necessary for him to begin by reforming the most fundamental things upon which society is founded. It must have been with these kinds of thoughts that he took up the problems of 'trust' and 'goodness'."

That the sayings would be edited by Mencius (playing St. Paul to Confucius' Jesus) and would later be turned and twisted by numerous political leaders, including Mao, cannot be known to this near contemporary who is telling his story. He can only report the original in all of its purity.

The famed and troubling "mandate of Heaven" is explained by simple observation: "To know what are the biddings of Heaven" is seen as "knowing what one should do as a human being." This is not reductive of either the disciple or of Inoue. It is, precisely, illustrative.

The illustrative principle which so animates this book is also, I think, responsible for its enormous local popularity. Inoue takes the familiar (those maxims descended from the *Analects*) and places them in a new context. Since a reigning Japanese interest is in just how cleverly the novel can be adapted to the familiar, his method fits (not I think intentionally) into a public concern. And it is the familiarity of Confucius which must account for some of his popularity in this land where even the most beautifully brushed of *kakejiku* still contains only the equivalent of "There's No Place Like Home."

For the foreign reader of this fine English translation,

of course, both maxims and circumstances are more or less novel. Further, some attempt has been made to make Inoue's spare, even austere narrative, more accessible. As the translator candidly states, his translation is abridged. An entire chapter, one dealing with philosophical discourse, has been left out. And there are doubtless other smoothings as well.

Intact is Inoue's particular concern, seen in all of his work. This is a constant theme which shows the struggle of a person not only to wrest some kind of order from chaos but to salvage the personal from the ravages of impersonal natural forces.

In this, Inoue's last novel, the humanity of Confucius is allowed to speak for itself. And this is to be apprehended through the words another person filled with a sense of his own common humanity. "This is nothing but a dilapidated hut in a mountain village where I live alone pretending to be a hermit. I can therefore offer you no amenities at all . . . ."

This result is a layered narrative of great strength and flexibility. Like all of his finest historical work, this final novel devotes itself entirely not to what might have been but to what truly was. Inoue's most acclaimed work, this is marvelously recounted history—sober, spare, alive.

Confucius, by Inoue Yasushi, translated with an introduction by Roger K. Thomas. Tokyo: Charles E. Tuttle Company, 1992.

Matsumoto Seicho

A listing of the foreign-language translations of works of Matsumoto Seicho (1909–1992) Japan's prolific mystery writer, reveals that the vast majority are in Chinese and Korean and that few are in Western languages. This may be because these stories and novels share much with the Confucian tale of detection. While there are no all-wise magistrates in Matsumoto's stories, his various sleuths exhibit the same kind of confidence. Says one, at the successful conclusion, "My reasoning turns out to have been flawless."

The wise, logical, problem-solver is a figure known and welcomed in Confucian Asia. And he has never, so far as I know, been regarded as insufferable. To be sure, he behaves with much more dignity and tact than does this condescending Western counterpart—Sherlock ("Elementary, my dear Watson") Holmes. Nonetheless, his assumption of superiority is something with which the Western reader has occasional difficulty.

Not that the Confucian influence is stressed in the work of Matsumoto, but it is there in that the characters are concerned with mundane ethics, with the letter rather than the spirit of the law, and with social relationships. The West prefers its authority figures to come garbed as commoners: the rueful inadequacies of Sam Spade, for example. The Japanese do not. Open authority rather than authority disguised as egalitarianism is accepted.

Matsumoto can so assume this that he may begin one of his stories with the prescriptive: "A wide range of crimes can be committed by one person working alone. The more accomplices there are, the higher the chances of failure." This is the accent of the Ming sage, speaking directly from a secure eminence.

And it is perhaps his continuation of this welcome tone that has made him what the jacket of this new collection of stories in translation calls "Japan's leading mystery writer." Certainly, he would seem to be drawing a self-portrait when he has one of his amateur sleuths, this one a newspaper novelist, flatter himself "that he had mastered the art of giving the public what it wanted."

One had not known that this talent was an art but the Matsumoto protagonist thinks it is. If so, then, as seen in the construction of these six stories, the art is very Japanese in that it describes ethics and does so in an economical, even minimal, manner. In fact these six stories, all written between 1959 and 1965, are made of very little and their structure openly displays Matsumoto's concerns.

The matter of murder, for example. Two of them, "The Serial" and "Beyond All Suspicion," favor cyanide, and several of the others, strangling. This is surely a slender repertoire compared with those of other mystery writers.

And the means of detection. In the above stories as well as in "The Face," "The Voice," "The Women Who Wrote Haiku," and "The Accomplice," the method is a long watch, over distance and time. Someone watches, waiting. The fear of just this, justified or not, is paranoia, and it is interesting that its exhibition should have helped create, as it apparently has, Matsumoto's extreme popularity.

Certainly, Matsumoto's choice of sleuths would support this thought. In all of the stories but one of the protagonists, though they may hire private detectives with abandon, are not themselves of this profession. They are just ordinary people who happen upon a clue. They push and pull and probe and get obsessed and end up uncovering a crime.

It is as though society encourages the informer. While this is no longer true, I believe, in Japanese society, it certainly once was, from the 17th to the mid-19th-century. And even now, the tattletale and the busybody (as well as other stock totalitarian figures, such as the bully, for example) are tolerated to a marked degree.

Certainly, Matsumoto's amateur sleuths are busybodies, often motivated by a quite abstract ethical concern. They have more than a taste for malicious gossip—they live for it, are consumed by it, And they—unlike a majority of contemporary Japanese, including most law-enforcing bodies—are all for the letter of the law. No case-by-case for them, and no sympathy, no understanding for the culprit. No matter what good reasons the desperate Yoshiko in "The Serial" has, she must pay society's price once she has done in the horrid victim.

This is the Confucian/Tokugawa side of Matsumoto. But he has another, though I do not know what to call it. It seems more "Yamato-esque," however, in that it indicates the natural frailty of man.

In story after story, it is the criminal's concern that leads to his or her capture. If they had only kept quiet about it, they would have been safe. But, no, they had to go and take elaborate precautions. "You were afraid of arousing suspicion, but you went a little too far," says one triumphant sleuth and that just about describes it.

The result is a pale irony, which readers of O. Henry might enjoy, and a simple affirmation of common vulnerability. And yet I would imagine that these two add to the author's popularity. Readers over the world like ironic twists, and the Japanese seem particularly fond of the ending with a fillip, a surprise conclusion which is not too surprising. Also, the assurance that the criminal really brought it all on him or herself appeals to the conservative, right-thinking reader.

These six stories are quite adequately translated by Adam Kabat. He is known as a translator of serious Japanese literature, including Yoshiyuki Junnosuke, a writer who deserves much further translation, a task to which I wish Kabat had rather applied himself.

It is not, I think, necessary to go into the stories themselves. If you like this sort of thing, you may already have acquired the book and, in any event, a disclosure of their plots would destroy the only reason for reading it.

The Voice and Other Stories, by Matsumoto Seicho, translated by Adam Kabat. Tokyo: Kodansha International, 1989.

Ooka Shohei

Ooka Shohei (1909–1988) is most famous for his autobiographical accounts of his Pacific War experiences: the 1948 *Furyo Ki* (translated as *Prisoner of War*), *Nobi*, 1951, (translated as *Fires on the Plain*) and the as yet untranslated *Reite Senki*, 1969.

Fine as these books are, they have tended to obscure other aspects of this remarkable writer. He was, for example, a specialist in European literature and published several critical studies of Stendhal. In addition, as a protégé of Kobayashi Hideo, he belonged to an influential literary coterie. He was also a modernist author who studied the styles of writers as various as Andre Gide and Raymond Radiguet.

In Japan, his literary reputation rests upon his modernist extensions of the Stendhalian psychological novel, two of the best of which are the 1950 *Musashino Fujin* (untranslated but Mizoguchi Kenji made a 1951 film of it) and the work under review, the 1961 *Kaei* (translated as *The Shade of Blossoms*).

Though both works take mundane subjects (in itself a modernist ploy), they delve much more deeply than is common in books about discontented wives and ageing bar women. The focus of the work becomes the thought processes of the woman herself, and the narrowness of this subject makes possible the depth of the analysis.

Yoko has been in the bar business for some time and has now reached an age when she is beginning to wonder if she can continue. Not only is her health compromised (by nicotine and alcohol), but she has reached the point where life has no further meaning.

Looking in the mirror, making herself up for the evening, she sees that the reflection speaks of "the melancholy of once again preparing to sell her love." She accepts the fact that "men knew nothing about her. They could care less about such things. It was enough if her body and the mood satisfied their desires." Later, she realizes that it was always "the same kind of man, saying the same old things ... Yoko was not especially aroused. It was all too depressing."

The couplings are always the same. "He embraced her from behind. What follows was what always followed." Eventually, she wonders, "floating for twenty years in the troughs between the waves of consumer life in Tokyo ... had she ever really been alive all those years? Was she alive now?"

Yoko has reached the reality of her dilemma. Like many other modernist protagonists (Stendhal's Julien Sorel, James Joyce's Leopold Bloom, Jean-Paul Sartre's Roquentin, Kurosawa Akira's Watanabe Kanji), she has been brought to the existential edge. She must somehow redefine herself, all the while knowing that she is merely the sum of her own actions.

Some of these characters are successful. Sartre's hero-affirming action is to stand and see that the veneer of life has melted, giving way, in one of the writer's most famous passages "to moist solidity, monstrous and chaotic—nude, fearfully and obscenely nude." Roquentin has the strength to stand there and affirm himself. So does Watanabe. His wasted years as a civil servant, half dead (the office force calls him the mummy) are redeemed by a single action: he denies the system (what Sartre calls the veneer) and affirms a single mundane reality—a park for children.

Some are not successful. Yoko, mindful but unheeding, watches her problems multiply and then decides to kill herself. She takes a bath ("I won't die naked," she says) and "back in her room, she spent time drying her hair until she could part it and braid it up like a girl." As she was doing this, "her breast welled up, and she thought that she was going to cry at last. But she let only a low moan escape her lips."

This low, inarticulate moan is nonetheless an authentic response to life and, that we accept it as such, tells much about Ooka's skill in making us understand the psychological processes of his protagonist and Washburn's dexterity in conveying her density and complexity.

This fine book is not in itself the slightest bit depressing. To face the truth as confidently and as acceptingly as Ooka does in this novel is to create confirmation and to succeed in the prime modernist aim: to find a pattern in the chaos of how we live.

The Shade of Blossoms, by Ooka Shohei, translated with an introduction by Dennis Washburn. Ann Arbor: Center for Japanese Studies, University of Michigan, 1998.

Dazai Osamu

Dazai Osamu (1909–1948) was a much more varied writer than he is usually thought to be. Thanks to the success and early translation of his two famous postwar novels, *The Setting Sun* and *No Longer Human*, thanks too (if that is the term) to his suicide, he has the reputation of being powerful if gloomy, honest if unpleasant.

There is another Dazai, however, one who is assured, satirical, showing more self-parody than self-loathing. It is this aspect of the author that has recently drawn translators' and publishers' attention. Dazai scholar James O'Brien has pointed out that the prewar Dazai is just as important as the postwar, perhaps even more so.

In his new publication, a revised edition of an earlier collection plus three new translations, O'Brien has taken care to choose works little known outside Japan. From the postwar period only one additional work has been chosen, the 1946 "Sound of Hammering" (which has had one other English translation, Frank Motofuji's in 1969.) Of the "autobiographical" Dazai there are two examples, the fairly well known "Memories," previously translated several times and the 1941 "On a Question of Apparel," here, I believe, translated for the first time.

Those who know only the serious Dazai will be surprised to find a comic author, mordant, filled with playful self-parody. In the drunken finale of the 1941 piece, the Yoshitsune-Benkei incident at the Ataka Barrier serves as inspiration for a bit of business that gets out of hand with amusing results.

That Dazai's tippling first-person narrator would know all about Yoshitsune and Benkei to the point of attempting to emulate them is surprising to those who know only the postwar author, but it is quite typical of Dazai's prewar writings.

He knew Japanese history well and loved Japanese folklore. Indeed, the Japanese reader knows him now mainly as a master storyteller, and his various collections are widely read, used as school texts, constantly in print.

Particularly admired is the wartime collection *Otogizoshi* (*Fairy Tales*), retellings of well known Japanese folktales—from which O'Brien gives us first translations of two of them: "Taking the Wen Away" and "Crackling Mountain."

Dazai was equally adroit at retelling classical literature. *Gyofukuki*, which O'Brien translates as "Undine" and which Thomas Harper called "Metamorphosis" in his 1970 translation, is a new version of a well known Ueda Akinari tale. Both "A Poor Man's Got His Pride," and "The Monkey's Mound" are rewritings from Saikaku's 1685 *Tales from the Provinces*.

Dazai also made up his own "classic" literature, as in the well known sketch "Monkey Island" (also translated in 1971 by Aileen Gatten) in which viewpoints (reader's and monkey's) are radically shifted in a way Saikaku himself might have admired.

In addition to Japanese literature, Dazai was also an avid reader of books from the West. He even wrote a "New Hamlet" (not yet translated) which has the hero remark upon learning that Claudius wishes to marry Gertrude: "Fallen for my mother? Why, every tooth in her head is false!" (The translation is Donald Keene's from his Dazai chapter in *Dawn to the West*.)

The popular "Melos, Run!" is partly based on the classic Greek story and partially on a later version of the same story by Schiller. Here O'Brien restores the original ending, often cut in textbooks, which finds Melos stark-naked at the end. *Kakekomi utae*, translated by O'Brien as "Heed My Plea" and by Katayama Takao as "I Accuse" in his 1958 translation, is based on Judas' betrayal of Jesus in the New Testament.

Like many Japanese intellectuals, Dazai was interested in the Bible and has here drawn a first-person character study of the celebrated traitor ascribing various reasons for his action. Judas, naturally, comes out as rather Japanese—indeed, as does Jesus, who tells Judas: "You may be lonely, but you can wash your face, smooth your hair with pomade, and smile as if nothing is wrong." The pomade is Japanese and so is the sentiment.

There is also a certain lightness in the writing which we ordinarily do not associate with Dazai. For example: "A flock of small birds rose silently from the treetops and flew off like sesame seeds cast into the sky." Or, the narrator down in the dumps thinks of his two favorite authors, but now "Pushkin and Gogol seemed as uninspiring as the names of several foreign-made toothbrushes."

Perhaps this lightness is the result of O'Brien's careful and, I would think, well-judged translations. While I cannot know what Dazai's Japanese style is like, I have been told about it and read about it. This translation, with its sudden unexpected word, its purposeful cliché, its abrupt slang, its ironical banality, may be the closest approach in English yet to just what Dazai's celebrated self-parody is like.

Crackling Mountain and Other Stories, by Dazai Osamu, translated by James O'Brien. Tokyo: Charles E. Tuttle Company, 1989.

Dazai has a deserved reputation for writings of great power and great unpleasantness. Kawabata wrote of the dark and sinister cloud shadowing his pages; Sato Haruo wrote that he had conceived a peculiar loathing for Dazai, though he admired his talent.

What is this then?—a new collection of Dazai's writings decorated with a bright, even cute cover and on the back, a *kawaii* sketch of Fuji and some flowers and the legend: "Fuji goes well with evening primroses." What's more, this new publication finds itself in a series which includes Kuroyanagi Tetsuko's adorable *Totto-chan*, lots of Akagawa Jiro's pop detective stories, and "the best scenes" from Yoshikawa Eiji's massive pot-boiler *Miyamoto Musashi*.

A look at the title page of this edition further suggests that some kind of popular rehabilitation of Dazai is afoot. Included are the author's brightest, sunniest sketches. "A Promise Fulfilled" is about a faithful wife; "One Snowy Night" is about a family squabble quelled; "Cherry Leaves and the Whistler" is about sisters consoling each other; "Run, Melos!" is about a man who keeps his promise at all costs and is fittingly rewarded; "Schoolgirl" is about (among other things) the satisfying pangs of adolescence.

"Eight Scenes from Tokyo" is a bit gloomy, to be sure, but it is all about things which are past, and in "One Hundred Views of Mount Fuji," we find that (in Donald Keene's words) "Dazai for the first time portrayed himself not as a self-destroying monster, but as a recognizable human being."

This, then, is a very "up" edition of one of Japan's most famous "downers." Dazai in this guise seems right at home with Miyazawa Kenji (some of whose titles swell this series) and such pop favorites as Murakami Haruki and Atoda Takashi. Here is the author with an uncharacteristic smile.

He does not at all seem the man who snarled at Kawabata and riposted back: "Does keeping small birds and watching dancers perform constitute such an admirable life?" On the contrary, in this collection he seems just the kind of person who would like watching dancers and keeping small birds. And after all he did write: "Fuji goes well with evening primroses."

Not that some of these stories are not excellent—it is just that they are unexpected. One has never before been treated to such a display of Dazai's brightness and light. Some of them have been translated before: "A Promise Fulfilled" by David Brudney and Shimizu Kazuko, "One Snowy Night" by T. E. Swann. Never, however, have they appeared in such charming packaging.

The reason is clear. It is hoped that this will appeal to the readers of the series. They have been treated before to a few chunks of *jun bungaku*, floating in the bath-warm spate of *taishu bungaku*, but these have been of a similar sunny variety: Soseki's *Botchan*, for example. And the Akutagawa chosen has been relatively pleasant—"The Spider's Thread" and other stories.

But what kind of readers are these? Since the series is entirely English translation, one might imagine that it is targeted for the foreign reader. But no, this Eigo Bunko series is for the Japanese reader. This then accounts for the image—the overtly *kawaii* is still a major selling style here.

Upon inquiry, I discovered that over seventy percent of the buyers of this series are junior and senior high-school students and that other readers include the retired and housewives. Editions are issued in the not-inconsiderable number of 15,000 to 20,000 copies, and the bestselling titles go into as many as eight printings. The *kawaii* look sells, so—apparently—does English.

Here, then, is a smiling and affable Dazai to be carried about and enjoyed. One hopes that his *Otogi-zoshi* will be issued next, for these are truly fairy-tales for adults. At the same time the reader will remember that the other Dazai—grumpy, destructive, sinister, and thoroughly unhappy—despite this Eigo Bunko gentrification, still lives in his cave deep in the recesses of *jun bungaku*.

Run, Melos! and Other Stories, by Dazai Osamu, translated by Ralph F. McCarthy. Tokyo: Kodansha International, 1988.

As James O'Brien remarks in the introduction to this new translation of selected stories and sketches of Dazai Osamu, most of what has been translated (into English at any rate) has been the postwar literature, and there is a feeling abroad that Dazai is a spokesman for the defeat. Having spoken, having said it all, as it were, he need speak no more. And it is true that, though modern Japan has turned out a number of personalist writers (indeed, turned out little else), no one was as personal as Dazai.

His life became his work. From the 1934 *Omoide* (included in this collection), himself, his thoughts, his feelings, are the sole subject of his writings. A true *shishosetsu-ka*, his works are solely about me, me, me. This is true as well of his historical works (the characters turn into Dazai) and his various retellings of Ueda Akinari and Ihara Saikaku.

Those who do not like Dazai feel that this excessive concern for self limits. And there is also the question of the kind of self: in this case someone who is apparently frivolous, brilliant but a wastrel, someone callous, cynical, yet excessively concerned about his own feelings, who can write amusingly about a double-suicide from which he alone was saved. In short, a deplorable person.

Those who dislike Dazai do so profoundly. I remember how much Mishima Yukio hated him. Though Dazai was older, and dead by the time that the younger writer began publishing, one would have thought, to hear Mishima carry on, that they were contemporary rivals.

Indeed, in a way they were. Mishima also wanted to tell (or at least show) all and seemed to resent the fact that someone had gotten there before him. But he also felt that Dazai's takings from his life were too transparent, too confessional, too inartistic. Mishima, just as concerned about self, was more artistic, that is, hid his traces better.

A reading of a wider sample of Dazai's work such as that presented in the present collection, however, makes one realize that Dazai also had his persona—that the decadent wastrel was, in effect, a literary creation and need not correspond with the actual Dazai just because the narrative is in the first person.

Of course, the life provided the raw material, as it does for any writer. And Dazai was much more direct about revealing this. *Tokyo Hakkei*, for example, makes reference to *Omoide*. The writer and the person seem identical. Yet, as O'Brien points out, the fictional text and the factual life are by no means the same. Dazai is continually editing his life and, in so doing, creating the persona of Dazai the scapegoat novelist. This figure he used for its rhetorical value. It was the consciousness through which the author chose to reveal his life.

That the two—person/persona—have much in common is not the point. The point is that they were long thought to be identical (and by many others than Mishima), and it is now becoming apparent that they are not. Dazai was much more than commonly thought the conscious artist.

One of O'Brien's contributions in this new collection is to indicate just how this persona grew in his work. He has arranged his translations of sixteen stories and sketches in chronological order and been careful to include those which refer to each other. As we read, it becomes clear that Dazai the writer is watching Dazai the first-person character, that they are not identical, that the persona provides the rhetoric, the stance, the style.

Osamu Dazai: Selected Stories and Sketches, translated with an introduction by James O'Brien. Ithaca: Cornell University Press, 1983.

Interest in Dazai and his work continues. His graveside memorial services are attended by television crews, and students still list *No Longer Human* along with *War and Peace* and *L'Etranger*. Scholarly and popular editions sell well, and abroad he is certainly as well known as Tanizaki, if not Mishima.

The man and his works—perhaps in that order, because Dazai's life was (or has become) legendary. Left-wing activities, underground causes, morphine addiction (temporary), lots of women (was once asked by a perfect stranger to be the begetter of her child, complied), and not one but five separate suicide attempts, the last one successful. And, through it all, writing away.

He was writing mainly (some critics say entirely)

about this extraordinary life of his, and thus the greater part of his work is in the *shishosetsu* or "I-novel" form. (Or, as critic Goto Meisei has noted, a parody of it.) Life and work form a double intertwined continuum.

Seeing this, Phyllis Lyons has written a new study of Dazai in which the first part examines the life and a number of the psychological problems, and part two covers the same ground transmuted into the many autobiographical stories and novels. The book concludes with translations of five of these stories and the "nonfiction novel" *Tsugaru*. The whole is finished off with appendices, bibliographies, photographs and an index.

Lyons sees almost all the work from 1933 to 1948 as a part of what she calls "The Osamu Saga." Supporting this are translations of not only *Tsugaru* but also the five stories, "Recollections," "Eight Views of Tokyo," "Going Home," "Hometown," and "An Almanac of Pain."

Several, if not all, have been translated before (James O'Brien et al.) so it is not as though an entirely new aspect of the author's work was being revealed in English. Also, Lyons' translation of the complete *Tsugaru* happens to collide with another complete translation by James Westerhoven, published by Kodansha International and released in almost the same month.

I am not going to report on which translation is "best," Lyons' or Westerhoven's, because I do not know. Comparing them (and they are not all that different), I was about to give one the edge over the other as being perhaps more colloquial or more graceful in English, but then I would turn to another page and find that the other was perhaps the more so. Suffice that both exist, both have full biographical material, both have maps and that one is twice the price of the other since the Lyons volume contains so much more besides.

The problem for any translator is Dazai's style. As

Miyoshi Masao has, in another context, written: "What saves Dazai's work from the dreary monotony of trivia that fills so many seedy I-novels ... is his dexterous manipulation of tonality ... from pathos to humor, from melodrama to comedy, from the ponderous to the light ... it is such irony and humor sprinkling from this discipline of language that restores his works from life's misappropriation of them."

He continues with perhaps the best summation of Dazai's work: "It survives, not because of his insight into human failures, or his Christian-Marxist critique of society, or his decadent satanism ... or his portrayal of the wretched life of the postwar years, but because—despite rather dubious achievements on all such scores—he never abandoned his love of the Japanese language."

The problem is, how well can this style translate into another language—though this is a question which must be addressed by all translations of anything. For example, Dazai is admired for irony. Is the following an example? "My disgracefully vulgar wish to stretch out at the fireside and have a drink of hot sake was miraculously fulfilled" (From the Westerhoven translation of *Tsugaru*. The Lyons translation has it: "My mean, disreputable prayer, to be settled by a fire with a flask of sake, was miraculously brought to pass.")

I do not think we would call the passage ironic. We could, in English, at the most call it jocular. In Japanese, it might well be received differently. Lyons herself mentions that Miyoshi "speaks of ... an inability of Japanese to understand what the West means by the self ... there always remains, even in the most seemingly intense engagement of author and subject, a distance that leaves the reader asking, 'But what is this man like, really?'"

What Dazai the man "really" was in his life and work is well explored in both books, particularly in Lyons' because this was her primary task. What his style must mean to the Japanese who still regard him as one of their finest modern writers is perhaps not so clear and perhaps cannot be so.

One is reminded (in more ways than one) of Mishima Yukio with his famous lapidary style. It is not that such styles cannot be translated; rather, it is that they cannot always be similarly perceived by the two cultures. And, for both Mishima and Dazai, the achievement of the writing will always be colored by the notoriety of the life.

Perhaps Mishima so disliked Dazai because they were so alike: both stylists, both drawing from personal experiences, both involved in a kind of psycho-drama in which characters became facets of themselves, both given to shocking the respectable, and both much drawn—eventually permanently—to self-destruction. And both are now just as remembered for the example of their lives as for the quality of their work.

The Saga of Dazai Osamu: A Critical Study with Translations, by Phyllis I. Lyons. Stanford: Stanford University Press, 1985. *Return to Tsugaru: Travels of a Purple Tramp, by Osamu Dazai*, translated by James Westerhoven. Tokyo: Kodansha International, 1985.

The local paperback reprint of two of Dazai's most popular postwar novels brings with it an opportunity to assess the state of other translations of his work. His foreign reputation rests almost entirely upon these two novels while his Japanese reputation now rests on other, earlier work.

Dazai soon achieved the style which is recognizably his: a largely autobiographical content, a stylist's concern for language, and a highly romantic temperament which included doses larger than usual in a Japanese author of self-pity and self-hatred.

Suicide is usually a successful conclusion for such an

author in that this act turns him and his work into myth. His act indicts the world, and the world responds by pondering and wondering and eventually elevating the author to perhaps a higher place than his work alone deserves. Sometimes.

But sometimes not. Mishima's suicide was very successful myth-making, but Dazai's has had mixed results—at least in Japan. After his death there was a larger than usual amount of adverse criticism—perhaps partly as reaction against the enormous popularity of the two postwar novels.

Yet, even now, though Dazai remains popular in that most of his works are kept in print, Japanese opinion appears to find best earlier work which is not so self-revelatory and which is not so exclusively concerned with the emotional states of the hero/author.

In the West, on the other hand, Dazai's reputation rests on the two postwar novels *Shayo* (*The Setting Sun*) 1947, and *Ningen Shikkaku* (*No Longer Human*) 1948, both of them evocations of Japan after the war and both filled with the nihilism then so much an intellectual recourse (and fashion) and now so completely missing from contemporary Japanese life and literature.

Western critics favorably compared these works to those of Dostoevsky (a comparison which would not occur to a Japanese) and called them consummate works of art—another statement one does not hear in Japan. That these two works were indeed somewhat overrated has become apparent in that Western interest in Dazai did not sustain itself and that this interest turned to the works of other postwar "representative" novelists—mainly Mishima.

This very strong similarity struck me when I was rereading this paper edition of *No Longer Human*. How very like Mishima's *Confessions of a Mask* it is. Though one is in third person and the other is in first, both are about the inner feelings of the writer-hero, and these, though their objects are different, share many more similarities than differences. Both hide their feelings (Dazai through clowning, Mishima through aestheticism), both are predatory to an extreme, both are almost excessively concerned about the world, which they assume the air of dismissing, and both fairly revel in the distrust (even dislike) of self which is indeed the motivating source behind both books. Finally, both include a kind of apotheosis at the end: Dazai reveals that what others find the writer-hero a kind of saint, a really good person; Mishima reveals that (like Proust) self-justification can only come through becoming a writer, in itself a saint-like profession.

Both obviously speak for not only themselves but for their times as well. Dazai's book appeared in 1948, Mishima's in 1949. Though their literary fortunes have much varied, their different but very similar pictures of the artist in postwar Japan are telling. This being so, they speak for an atmosphere, an ambiance long vanished but still there in these two books.

Is their only interest then, as I seem to be suggesting, historical? In a way, yes—but at the same time a cry of pain, which is what these two Dazai novels embody, is always audible and always ought to be. Dazai articulated his discontent and shared his discomfort to an extent now uncommon. Though not a Dostoevsky (and with no ambitions to become one), his view of life was tragic, his expression, direct and honest, his revelation of self, merciless. And for all of these varying reasons, unpleasant or not, he should be read.

The Setting Sun, by Dazai Osamu, translated by Donald Keene. Tokyo: Charles E. Tuttle Company, 1981. *No Longer Human*, by Dazai Osamu, translated by Donald Keene. Tokyo: Charles E. Tuttle Company, 1981.

Oda Sakunosuke

Though he died at thirty-four, had a writing career of merely seven years, and produced only some fifty stories, essays and plays, Oda Sakunosuke (1913–1947) has a permanent place in Japanese literature. One of the reasons is his individuality. He suggested his own category when he called himself a *shin-gesaku* writer, referring to those Osaka authors of the Tokugawa Period whose "playful compositions" reflected, says his translator, "not the ideals of society but its deplorable realities."

Here his model might well have been Saikaku, an author of whom he was fond and whose works he translated into modern Japanese. He was certainly aware of this possibility. In the autobiographical *State of the Times* (*Seso*) (1946) he is casting about for a really *gesaku*-like way to tell the story of the infamous Abe Sada, and rejects the most likely by saying, "but that would just be a rewrite of Saikaku's *Life of an Amorous Woman.*"

Oda created his own individual voice, and remained loyal to it. Censored and banned during World War II, he consoled himself by thinking of "all the writers of *gesaku* fiction in the Edo Period who ended up in prison because of their writings, and I felt a kind of perverse delight in what I was doing."

He remained true to himself during postwar attacks as well. The establishment had it in for him, and Shiga Naoya, doyen of Japanese letters, loftily pronounced *The State of the Times* to be "filthy." Oda returned the attack by loudly loathing the sainted Shiga. At the same time, he was content that the doyen's description had, in the words of the translator, "helped greatly to draw attention to the work."

Oda's style was achieved early. It is there, complete, in his first and most popular work, the 1940 *Meoto Zenzai*—a typical punning title that can mean either *Hurray for Marriage* or *Sweet Beans for Two*. Choko the geisha falls in love with Ryukichi, an extreme example of the Osaka *bonchi*. They have their ups and downs, Choko doing all the pushing and pulling, and in the end achieve a kind of happiness. The interest in the story (and in the delight in the style) is the dispassionate and Saikaku-like plainness in telling a tale so very far from the official ideals of the social community, and in the irony, as when a neighboring housewife sees Choko in a completely uncharacteristic fit of weeping and thinks that "for the first time … she had seen Choko act like a real woman."

(Foreign readers may be familiar with this novella through its famous film version, Toyoda Shiro's excellent 1955 *Marital Relations* with Awashima Chikage as the determined geisha and Morishige Hisaya as the spoiled scion.)

It is a plain style, even homely, yet extremely expressive. At least this is the way it is rendered by Burton Watson. The fit is very fine, and I cannot imagine Oda sounding any other way. For example, when the writer returns to the scenes of his youth, it seems that "the eaves of the houses were much lower than I had remembered … it dawned on me that this was because I was now quite a different height from … ten years ago."

This individual plainness (well reflected in Watson's adroit use of "ago" rather than "before") serves to reveal the ironic literalness of this prose. Here Oda has been compared with Nagai Kafu, for being interested not so much in nostalgic old ways already vanishing as in the raffish and human ways of those unaffiliated still remaining in an age of growing conformity.

Certainly, a further parallel would be that between Watson and Kafu's translator, Edward Seidensticker. Both have lived where their authors wrote, both—though respected and honored scholars—have their attractive *flâneur* sides, and both write strong and supple English.

Oda is thus particularly fortunate in having Watson as his translator. Not only in the two works above mentioned but also in "City of Trees" (*Ki no Miyako*) (1944) and "Six White Venus" (*Roppaku Kinsei*) (1946), included here, it is Watson's style which allows the nuances which comprise this major voice: the light-handed surface, the irony, and, under the levity, the deep sympathy that Oda feels.

Though the establishment has now placed Oda at the bottom of the *burai-ha* (variously "hooligan" or "decadent") heap, though various spokesmen have found him "no more than an interesting minor writer" remembered "more for his chaotic life than for his works," the author Oda speaks nonetheless directly, powerfully and in the most individual of accents. His place in Japanese literature is indeed permanent.

Stories of Osaka Life, by Oda Sakunosuke, translated by Burton Watson. New York: Columbia University Press, 1990.

Kinoshita Yuji

Though a well known poet in Japan, Kinoshita Yuji (1914–1966) is not considered one of the major moderns. Rather, he is regarded as a traditionalist, as a haiku master.

Certainly, more than half of his small output are haiku, some six hundred in all, and this classical training informed all of his free verse as well. In his preface, poet Ooka Makoto speaks of these "techniques of crystallization and focus" as well as "the charm of ellipsis." Also haiku-like are the small number of themes encountered in Kinoshita's work, the moments of enshrined feeling, and the reoccurrence of nature as a major concern.

And a troubled one. Kinoshita loved the city and wanted

very much to live in Tokyo, where he had gone to school. He had inherited his father's pharmacy, however, in provincial Fukuyama, and that is where he was forced to return.

He apparently hated it, and he could not have made too reliable a pharmacist. Tales are told of the time when, lost in thoughts of poetry, he lost track of the ingredients he was including and was much worried "whether the patient might die and he himself lose his license."

Other writers have left stultifying professions. Sherwood Anderson is said to have turned to his secretary with "it's all yours, dear," as he walked out of an Ohio hardware store, forever. Kinoshita, however, had no such freedom.

So, as his translator Robert Epp writes, "he had to forge a sense of continuity between past and future, between his rural identity and his alienation. At his late-night desk, he explored passageways linking these two aspects of his being and addressed the incongruity of his life."

"Shriveled moth eggs that had never hatched stick to the huge clock face labeled 'Out of Order.'" That is one self-portrait; another is himself as a wounded mallard: "I watch night's crystal sky through gaps in the branches/Blood dripping from my wound makes faint sounds on crinkled leaves ... so very far away."

A favorite symbol of self was the tree. He compares himself, in various poems, to a felled tree, to a wounded tree, sap running, and to a tree standing tall despite everything, hence the title given this collection of his poetry from 1939 to 1965.

Other guises include the Chinese poet Tu Fu, also exiled, and a peasant bound to the land. In "To a Friend in the Capital," he writes "I grew the rice myself and pounded it into *mochi*" and says that he made the enclosed rope as well. "Have a nice New Year," he writes "but don't think about how I wince when the rope touches my chapped hands."

Self-pity is not everywhere considered an attractive quality, but in Japan it is so well thought of that an entire literary convention, the *shishosetsu*, is based upon its ramifications. Thus Kinoshita's feeling sorry for himself at such length is, I believe, thought to be a more endearing quality than not.

Perhaps more to Western tastes are those many poems where he forgets his sorrows and turns to describing nature and making connections, an activity I take to be the proper business of the poet.

Though a number of Western writers are mentioned by Kinoshita and though he was very well read in world poetry, a major resemblance seems to be with a poet he perhaps did not know. As critic James Raeside once wrote, "Like Hardy, Kinoshita's observations of the country are detailed and accurate but absolutely without idealization. Rather, closely observed nature becomes the source of despondency and melancholy … a powerful sense of what has been called the 'landscape of loss.'"

In these lyrics on nature Kinoshita transforms his concerns into something universal. Indeed, "a fountain is loveliest/without water/for then into that chill space/I can sketch/what doesn't meet the eye."

This "landscape of loss" is beautifully delineated in the poem "February": "My boy came home from playing in the fields/He said the sun went down and he felt chilled/He smelled like burnt-over fields/like burnt eulalia fronds and briars and dry grass./And now/I lean on my late-night desk/calmly lighting private fires/to my mind/to the dry grasses in my mind."

Treelike, by Kinoshita Yuji, translated by Robert Epp, with a preface by Ooka Makoto. Rochester, Oakland University: Katydid Books, 1982.

Oguma Hideo

Though he died young, in 1940 at the age of thirty-nine, Oguma left behind a significant number of works including some of the most powerful political poems written in modern Japan.

Political protest is not a quality commonly associated with this country, but Oguma was, in this as in many other ways, an exception. While most of his fellow poets preferred the shorter and more traditional forms, Oguma was writing long poems, often with epic-like overtones. While others were ignoring the political causes of their darkening lives, Oguma was writing about them; while others went silent, he continued writing to the very end.

Born in Sakhalin, in 1901, Oguma knew poverty and privation, and later in Hokkaido he saw that he was not the only victim of the new expansionism. Early, he was writing "cruel pain/visits each season/with more solicitude than a loving mother...." Later, he wrote the 24-section "epic" called *The Flying Sled* with the dedication "For the Ainu People," since it is about their efforts to retain their culture in the face of Japanese expansion.

He also wrote for the unfortunate people of Korea, victims of a devastating occupation, one which openly avowed the destruction of native Korean ways and values. In "Long, Long Autumn Nights," he speaks for this people, assuming their voice: "About the Korea of old/The dirty wax in these ancient ears/Is forever murmuring."

The focus of this poem is a group of Korean laundrywomen who wear the traditional white of their country and who are told "starting tomorrow,/No one wears white Korean dress/In according with the regulations/Governing modern clothing/Everyone wears black, got that?/So there's no need to wash them."

That a Japanese could in 1935 write a poem this openly critical of official policy is surprising, but Oguma went even further in "The Tumbleweed Company" which is about a group of Chinese soldiers slaughtered by Japanese troops. While other Japanese writers were legitimizing the war (and poets were among the most bellicose), Oguma was maintaining both his standards and his humanity.

As David Goodman writes in his perceptive introduction, "Far from 'sneering at defeated enemies,' [he] sympathized with their plight and dramatized their condition. In the Ainu 'aborigines,' Oguma found nobility; in the 'archaic' customs of Japan's Korean colonial subjects, he found beauty; and in the gory demise of Chinese soldiers, he found humor."

A very special kind of humor—complex and compassionate. When the dehumanized Chinese soldiers finally meet the Japanese soldiers, they find them just as dehumanized. Through humor—and the poem is funny—Oguma humanizes the Chinese and helps us understand their debasement. At the same time, the poet exposes the falseness of Japan's mythical "humanitarian mission" in Asia.

Like many of his contemporaries, Oguma had early become a "proletarian" poet. Seeing the injustice of government and its politicians, he was among those who turned his attention to the dispossessed and spoke for them.

He was, to this extent, a Marxist and it is perhaps telling that until now his poems have been translated only into Russian, at least those poems which could be construed as following the Soviet political line.

These are very few, however, for unlike many intellectuals he soon saw through Marxist pretensions and by the time of the Communist purge was no longer involved. Many others were, and there was a disorderly exodus from the Communist movement as writer after writer recanted all belief in Marxism and declared allegiance to the Emperor.

Those less showy opted for silence. Oguma, however, believed that a poet should speak out, and he did. "I know well enough/that silence is a form of cowardice." He believed that poets should "talk furiously!/Until our enemies fall silent."

The enemies did not fall silent, and Oguma became more and more outspoken. "Politics and literature/Are both dirty laundry/Occupying the same tub./And the washer-man has only been in business a year."

Reading these poems (in Goodman's committed, informed, fluent translations) now, in this time of cultural and governmental uniformity, it is surprising and reassuring that such a brave and able dissident was both alive and working during the dark prewar years.

He had the true vocation: "If they cut off my hands, I'll write with my feet./If they cut off my feet, I'll write with my mouth./If they gag my mouth,/I'll sing with the hole in my ass."

Long Long Autumn Nights: Selected Poems of Oguma Hideo, translated with an introduction by David G. Goodman. Ann Arbor: Center for Japanese Studies, University of Michigan, 1989.

Endo Shusaku

The novelist whom Graham Greene has called "one of the finest living," Endo Shusaku (1923–1999) is much concerned (like Graham Greene himself) with Christian, specifically Catholic, problems. He was born into a Japanese Catholic family, " ... in other words, my Catholicism was a kind of ready-made suit." His solution was "to take the Christian religion, which was so uncongenial to me as a Japanese, analyze why it was so uncongenial, and in some way to make it something more compatible—in other words, "with my own hand I would remodel the ill-fitting suit of European clothes that my mother had dressed me in, and I would make of it a kimono more becoming to me as a Japanese."

Endo's life and works can be seen as a series of such attempts— all of this often skillful stitching and basting resulting in one good fit, the 1966 *Chinmoku* (*Silence*). Now we have a translation of one of the earlier endeavors, the 1959 *Kazan* (*Volcano*).

It is a fairly straightforward allegory involving two older men dying in a hospital and their involvement with a volcano situated outside their windows. They represent two attitudes toward the ineffable as symbolized by the perhaps extinct, perhaps dormant, perhaps active volcano.

Suda, a retired volcano specialist, has lived the unexceptional life of the academic bureaucrat and paid small attention to the demands of any inner self. Now, however, he finds that his family loathes him and, further, that even the volcano might betray him, his life-long thesis having been that it is quite extinct.

Durand, an ex-priest, has also not paid sufficient attention to his inner self, and further, his Catholicism has been of a superficial variety. Now, he finds that his life (and his faith) have come to naught. For him, the volcano is active, evil, and will shortly erupt.

Both are projecting inner needs onto the mountain and in so doing are neglecting any feeling of warmth or love in themselves. The volcano is fittingly silent in its role of, I suppose, God. There is no resolution to this slight story, the purpose of the book having been its presentation.

There are some complications. Suda has assured a hotelier that it is perfectly safe to build a big hotel on the mountain; Durand is hoping that the coming eruption will completely eradicate a Christian retreat already built there. These, however, do not disturb the simplicity of the structure—a triangle with the volcano as the peak, the two men as either leg, and their similarities as the base.

Both Durand (a character who appeared in Endo's earlier *White Man, Yellow Man* and later appears, in another form, in *Silence*) and Suda are alike in that they have not attained a state of grace nor shown signs of achieving it. One has rejected the church outright, and the other has rejected faith as well in his own completely superficial piety.

The basic cut of Endo's kimono is French. He was the first postwar Japanese to go and study in that country and there he devoted himself entirely to French Catholic literature: Bernanos, Maritain, Claudel. Though he realized the differences of their positions and possibilities from his own, he quite accepted their notion of an all-loving and compassionate Deity, one whose ways are perhaps inscrutable but are, at least, well-intentioned. From this, he elaborated his own ideas of mystery and compassion, and his novels have been about little else.

In *Volcano*, we are presented with negative examples of this compassion—the novel is about this precise lack. Later, particularly in *Silence*, Endo went on to a more positive outline of the tenets of his belief. Love and mutual understanding are among the goals and the silence of God is specifically there to be transcended. Here Endo is quite close to Bernanos.

One might well ask what all of this has to do with Japan, a country whose truly dominant religion consists of the faith and dogma of being Japanese. Here Endo has already asked the question. It is, indeed, one of the themes of his work.

There are various answers. One (a theme in *Silence*) is that the opening of "soul" to the silence of God can be a particularly destructive operation to the Japanese. Another (one of the themes of *Volcano*) is that it is better to risk this upheaval if, through Catholicism, one is forced to account for the inner life. Another (voiced in a recent interview) has more to do with the advent of the Catholic church than it does with Japan: "Catholic writing in Japan, including my own work, is really not so important yet … [But] if we can succeed in plowing up the soil, things will be easier for the next generation."

Endo is not alone in his Catholic espousal. There are Inoue Hisashi, Sono Ayako, Takahashi Takako, and others. All are writers, all are intellectuals and all have found in Catholicism the antidote to the "optimistic nihilism" of the times. Endo comes right out and says it. "Since no literature or art can exist without form, you should be able to understand the reasons authors welcome the strong formalities and taboos of Catholicism."

Well, yes, you can. You can also understand why the formalities and taboos of organizations ranging from the Communist Party to the Boy Scouts are welcomed by those whose lack of inner resources make such outward buttressing attractive. The point certainly, however, is that literary and artistic form is the result of various inner convictions, often unknown to the writers and artists concerned. The danger of imposed forms is that a kind of propaganda often results.

Endo himself has avoided this danger, as have his French mentors. At the risk of seeming heterodox to the church itself, he has scrupulously attempted to adapt Catholicism to his own Japaneseness. This public spectacle is both touching and interesting, though whether it results in "one of the finest living novelists" is a matter of opinion. Certainly, however, it has resulted in the only Catholic in a kimono.

Volcano, by Endo Shusaku, translated with an introduction by Richard A. Schuchert. London: Peter Owen, 1978.

Tanaka, lecturer in the literature department of a

Japanese university, goes to Paris to research his topic—the life and works of the Marquis de Sade. Instantly, the unaccustomed weight of this experience falls upon him. He was aware that "the man who now stood ... in the pouring rain on a Paris street corner with heavy luggage in both hands, totally incapable of hailing a taxi, was not the university lecturer who had left Japan."

Indeed, he is something much less. He finds the fabled Montparnasse, but it now appears "darker and more deserted than the area in front of Ogikubo or Nakano stations...." He goes to Vincennes, where Sade was incarcerated, but finds that he himself is locked up as well, inside himself.

Nor does the company of compatriots help. Just the opposite. They are the sort of men "whose double chin and somewhat common features frequently adorned the advertisements for language tapes," and all are prey to "this strange tendency" among Japanese abroad to feel an intensification of professional rivalry and jealousy. "It's like ladies-in-waiting at the palace," thinks Tanaka. "That's what I hate most about the Japanese in Paris."

Indeed, "what was the point of coming halfway round the world just to keep up the same kind of intricate relationships one might expect in the sumo apprentice schools?" Yet, his failure to do so contributes to the decline which transplantation has begun.

His assistant (also treacherously in Paris) advises him to keep up with the other academics who nightly throng the Dome. But at the same time, Tanaka knows that his university is transferring him to another department, and the assistant is taking his place. The downfall began with his determination to study abroad.

But now in France, Tanaka cannot concentrate on his work. Only once, when he goes to see the ruins of the Marquis' chateau does he feel the ambition he knew in Japan. In the midst of a snow storm, he tries to reach it, and though he fails, he still feels he is doing right.

Later he comes to identify the two people in him. One is "the petit-bourgeois coward who was jealous ... the other was the one who tried to reach the castle." He continues to try to work, to attempt to ignore the awful other Japanese in Paris, but then he begins to spit blood—tuberculosis: the intellectual's answer.

And through it all he keeps repeating to himself: "Even if the worst comes to worst you must not settle abroad." And he keeps repeating the magical formula that caused all the trouble in the first place: "There's something uniquely Japanese about the Japanese." He writes of Sade that "he kept falling into the traps of the very society and laws he professed to hate," and does not realize how closely this also approximates himself.

It is quite apparent to Endo Shusaku, however, who in this 1965 novel, *Ryugaku* (*Foreign Studies*) gives a detailed and thoroughly repellent picture of bad faith and its consequences. Tanaka, however, unlike many of the other academics to whom we are introduced, has moments of insight, and it is this which makes his case interesting and his plight moving.

And in a way typical. One remembers Soseki miserable in London, even Kafu not having that much of a good time in New York. A kind of paralysis seems to attack the Japanese abroad. Not all certainly but a significant portion. And we are invited (in this Endo novel and elsewhere) to take the plight seriously.

Yet cultural differences are so various that, if this figure were foreign, an American say, who pined for apple pie yet resented the American Club, who had not the confidence to hail a taxi but was consumed with his sense of American uniqueness, then this figure could only be a figure of fun. Bad faith is never very smart, but here it would seem to approach stupidity.

Endo takes Tanaka seriously and consequently so do we, at least for so long as we are reading his novella. It is about life once removed. As are the two stories which support it in this collection. "A Summer in Rouen" is about the tortured inadequacies felt by a young Japanese student on home stay in France; "Araki Thomas" is about a Japanese abroad during the Momoyama Period who feels so inadequate that he apostates. Both are thus connected to Tanaka's story, which is called "And You, Too."

The customary fluency of Endo's style seems well captured in Mark Williams' translation; yet while it reads well in English, there are unavoidable difficulties. What should a translator do with a passage that defies translation? For example: "A Sunday in an unknown town in a foreign land. That was not a particularly good feeling. It felt as though a sprig of parsley had caught on his tongue." The above is Williams' solution—leave it as it is—and it is as good as any. The editor, however, might have avoided a few difficulties had he or she known a bit more French. It is not, for example "*Le carnet du balle*," but "*Un Carnet du bal.*"

Foreign Studies, by Endo Shusaku, translated by Mark Williams. London: Peter Owen, 1989.

Though Endo Shusaku has been called "one of the finest living novelists" in both the foreign and the Japanese press, though he has been widely translated and awarded various literary prizes, both abroad and in Japan, he has yet to produce a work which would seem to qualify him for this description. Even as a Catholic writer, a limited genre, his plays and novels lack the depths of other Catholic authors: Paul Claudel, Francois Mauriac, Georges Bernanos, to name but a few.

A reason for the relative shallowness of Endo's work

is, to be sure, that he is writing for the Japanese. This country may be, I think, safely described as non-Christian. Consequently, the writer must simplify, that is, become shallow, if his message is to get across. Another reason, perhaps consequent, is (a Christian virtue, perhaps; a novelistic virtue, never) the blindness of the faith he so often describes.

In Mauriac or Bernanos, faith is an articulate and dynamic quality; it is the dialectics of faith which concern these writers. In Endo, however, faith is an entity, a thing—there or not. So it was in *Silence*, his best known work abroad, and so it is in *The Samurai*, his latest novel, published in Japanese in 1980.

It is based upon an actual incident. A group of samurai were sent by their government to Mexico in 1613. While they were there, the government decided against trade and diplomatic intercourse, closed the country and began proscribing the Christian faith.

Upon its return, the group was met with suspicion, especially when it was learned that some of its number had, believing it would assist its mission, been baptized. The theme, a particular favorite with Endo, is the dilemma of the early Japanese Christian—here rendered piquant in that the faith had been improperly assumed.

This enables Endo, at the conclusion of the book, to demonstrate through the martyrdom of the samurai that, even improperly assumed, faith is still faith. Their death is not seen as tragedy—innocent men cajoled into professions of a faith meaningless to them. Rather, this death is, somehow, a triumph. Somehow, faith has redeemed and made important their short spans. Somehow, they have won rich reward in a better world—in which they do not believe.

It is difficult in this sense not to see the novel as propaganda. Endo is critical of the Catholic church, but he is not critical (in the sense of being dispassionate) of the quality of faith, as is, for example, Bernanos—that very quality being the burden of the *Journal d'un Curé de Campagne.*

Consequently, perhaps, Endo can tell us little about his subject; that is, little about what his characters are experiencing. To serve his purposes, he must give his main character thoughts unbelievable and, since the character is Japanese, inconceivable. "The samurai could not understand why he had become so obsessed with that emaciated man with both hands nailed to a cross. If this truly was a mere formality, there was no need to keep repeating the same words to himself over and over again. There was no reason why emotions as bitter as gall should swell up inside him. There was no reason he should feel remorse, as if he had betrayed his father...."

Precisely. No reason at all—except the overriding reason that Endo is making the moralistic message that faith is not a conscious state which one, precisely, earns. It is more like an obsession; it just happens to you, like influenza. Perhaps the reason that Endo so uncritically accepts such a shallow definition is that he is anxious to prove that there is at least one Japanese (the samurai) who can be so successfully attacked by faith—successful even to the point of martyrdom.

This is because the author has, in other works, and in this one as well, been so troubled by the apparent fact that the Japanese are immune to faith as he defines it. "Their so-called faiths exist solely for the purpose of providing as many worldly benefits as possible." And "the Japanese touch for acquiring worldly wealth is almost too sensitively attuned, but they have not the slightest feeling for things eternal." Or, as the priest in the book says: "When I look at the Japanese, I sometimes wonder whether a true religion—one that seeks after eternity and the salvation of the soul ... can develop in that country."

The answer is so plainly negative that Endo must seek

to prove its opposite if he is to have a case at all. Consequently, he is not interested in character. His are all two-dimensional, and his novel is consequently schematic. He shows this in several ways. His samurai, though he has a name, is always known as "the samurai," as if he were some allegorical personification, a lay figure in a pageant

Originally, Endo had wanted to call his book *A Man Who Met a King*. This is the title of a fable, or a parable; it is not, I think, the title of a novel. Also, the characters, not being based on life, are based on popular archetypes—like those in historical films. I discovered this when I found, reading the book, that I was also casting it: the worldly priest who nonetheless finds glorious martyrdom was Charlton Heston, the Pope was Alec Guiness, and "the samurai" was (who else?) Mifune Toshiro.

This is what I mean when I call the book shallow and consequently question Endo's right to be called "one of the finest living novelists." It is not the propagandistic element which troubles me so much as it is the quality, as it were, of the propaganda. Faith is a much more serious and far deeper thing than Endo makes it appear.

The Samurai, by Endo Shusaku, translated from the Japanese by Van C. Gessel. New York: Harper & Row, 1982.

This miscellany, the Japanese title of which is *Ikoku no Yujintachi*, is a collection of fifty short essays by the late Endo Shusaku that appeared in *The Daily Yomiuri* from 1989 to 1991 and were originally reprinted by the *Yomiuri Shimbun*. This new edition is bilingual, with English and Japanese on facing pages.

They touch upon a number of subjects—"Japan's Unique Family Unity," "Priest Saves Souls While Tending Bar," "Language Barriers Make Way for Friendship"—and all intend to instruct foreign readers. This is consistent with Endo's iterated desire to serve as a bridge between Japan and the rest of the world.

These essays indicate the author's hope "from the bottom of my heart ... that Japan becomes a place where it is comfortable and pleasant for foreigners to live." He is writing because, "while Japanese are not used to foreigners, foreign residents also need to acquire a better understanding of this country."

Such unexceptionable sentiments are touched upon again and again throughout these essays, which most earnestly attempt a reasoned balance. For example, Endo mentions the observation that Japanese seem to lack individuality and adds, "I think this is probably true. But then we all have both strengths and weaknesses, and we should bear in mind that a weakness has the potential to be turned into a person's strength."

It is difficult to prevent balance from turning to banality, and Endo is not always successful. On the other hand (here this reviewer is attempting to be balanced), when he feels strongly, he speaks strongly. For example, consider his outrage when he learns that some self-serving community in Tohoku wishes to construct an "Auschwitz Memorial Museum."

He is astonished and shocked that such a place of horror should serve as a pretext for a tourist attraction. He knows that visitors would see it as "just another stop on a sightseeing tour package." This he finds detestable, feeling it would be "a sacrilege toward those who died at Auschwitz."

Also, "if it is so important for young Japanese to learn about wartime tragedies ... informing them about Japanese atrocities ... (for example Japanese acts toward the Koreans) would have far greater impact than telling them what the Germans did." This is true bridge-building because facts take the place of generalities, and real feeling takes the place of anodyne agreement.

There is also an occasional lightness which does much to collapse the solemnity. In investigating a survey held to discover both favorite and least favorite foreigners on television, Endo discovers that, though the winner of the "least favorite" category was won by Agnes Chan, she was closely followed by Dave Spector (who also placed third in the "favorite" category) and Kent Gilbert.

This he cannot understand. "I have never met Dave Spector but … he is always sharp, direct and witty, and I am always impressed by his quick mind." As for Kent Gilbert, Endo actually met him. "He impressed me very much as a well-mannered person—a gentleman."

Why then was Anton Wicky (a foreigner once famous for an English-conversation morning slot) the most popular? This is because "Wicky comes across as gentle and kind—a safe person. Is this why, then, Japanese do not respond warmly to a foreigner with some individuality like Spector?"

Since he is writing for foreigners, Endo does not deliver himself of any of his more unpopular opinions ("Japan is a swamp"), nor does he much go into doctrinal differences between Roman and "Japanese" Catholicism. He is addressing people who are guests (albeit paying ones) in his country, and he addresses them in clear and simple language—though perhaps not so simple as the translation makes it and certainly more correct. "Language Barriers Make Way for Friendship," for example, is ambiguous English phrasing. There are other examples of imprecise usage and (on page 299) there is a reference to that famous Paris lodging, the "Gorge 5 Hotel."

To Friends from Other Lands, by Endo Shusaku, Tokyo: Koike Shoin, 1997.

Abe Kobo

Abe Kobo (1924–1993) seems singular in Japanese literature. Usually the Japanese writer avoids the abstract and favors the emotional; he prefers to examine life in small sections which may or may not have any connection with each other; there is usually little consideration for the structure of the work as a whole, but great attention is paid to the details. The aim is (with many a significant exception) a kind of synthesis.

Abe is analytical. Instead of combining to form a whole, he begins with a whole and at once starts to break it down—this analysis forming the substance and usually the story of the novel or the play.

The object analyzed is the subject itself, but this subject always takes physical form: it is a combination of the situation and the setting, and this becomes a metaphor. Thus the sand pit and those caught in it in *Woman in the Dunes*; thus the city in *The Face of Another* and *The Ruined Map*, the laboratory in *Inter Ice Age*, and the box in *The Box Man*. The metaphor is central to the work. Indeed, in a way, it *is* the work. Abe's disclosures, psychological and geographical, are abstracted from this central framework, and the results are often intellectually stimulating and usually emotionally stone cold.

Perhaps Abe's major singularity is that he is the only writer using the scientific method—by definition analytical. Trained as a doctor (he received a medical degree from Tokyo University but never practiced), Abe seems to see each work as an experiment which leads to philosophical conclusions. In *Woman in the Dunes*, the hero is himself saved through the scientific method. He learns how to extract water from sand, and thus (in philosophical terms—specifically existential) he learns how to cope with a life (and a self) which he himself has created.

The experiments continue—as in this English translation of the 1977 novel *Mikkai* (*Secret Rendezvous*). Here the central metaphor is, fittingly, a hospital. The ambulance comes and carries off the first-person narrator's wife and the resulting book is his search for her within the labyrinthine mazes of the hospital. This monstrous building becomes as central a metaphor to this book as does the castle in Kafka's novel or the palace in the Ghormengast trilogy of Mervyn Peake.

Wandering about on his quest, the "hero" comes to a number of conclusions, and in Abe's works, these conclusions are usually statements of the theme. Early on, he complains at the difficulty of finding his wife in such a place. Now, he is told: "Isn't that what reality is like? In a lottery, nothing says the first prize can't turn up until all the lots are drawn." Later, an aphorism is discovered: "A good doctor makes a good patient." And, at the end: "When will you ever accept the true ugliness of health? If animal history has been a history of evolution, then the history of mankind is one of retrogression. Hooray for monsters! Monsters are the great embodiments of the weak." And, finally, we reach a conclusion that to be truly civilized is to be truly diseased. The metaphor has been analyzed and now displays its own conclusions.

In writing allegory—which is what Abe writes—success often depends on an approach which is literally realistic. This hides the parable (we get to know every claw and feeler of Kafka's cockroach-man) and helps us accept what is also fantasy. As Cocteau has said, fantasy is only believable in the most mundane and detailed of surroundings.

In a work such as *Woman in the Dunes*, the surface realism is extraordinarily detailed. With its setting this vividly rendered, we accept the fantasy and swallow the allegory whole. The line between fantasy and whimsy is very thin, however. The danger is that the controlled fantasy slops over into the arbitrary and the freakish, that the whim has been inserted for its own sake.

Carried away in this 1977 novel by his unexceptional vision of the world as hospital, Abe turns surrealist (a high-tone word for whimsical) and eventually, I feel, forfeits not only the reader's belief but his attention as well. Allegory this undisguised and presented in such a wayward fashion is not palatable. The book may be, as the publishers call it, "a nightmare," but nightmares are only dreams, and it is just their arbitrary quality which makes the recounting of other people's dreams so notoriously dull.

Secret Rendezvous, by Abe Kobo, translated by Juliet W. Carpenter. New York: Alfred A. Knopf, 1979.

It is easy to become a box man. You take "any empty box, a yard long by a yard wide and about four feet deep will do," cut off the bottom and wear it over your head. An observation window should be cut, a plastic curtain over it ensuring privacy. ("For a box man the slit in the vinyl is comparable, as it were, to the expression of the eyes.") Then, arranging a few hooks inside upon which to hang necessities, ("radio, mug, flashlight, towel"), you are ready to venture forth.

Nor will you be any longer alone. "Though there can't be any statistics, there is evidence that a rather large number [of box men] are living in concealment throughout the country. But I've never heard that box men are being talked about anywhere. Evidently, the world intends to keep its mouth tightly shut about them." The reason one does not notice them is that sitting down they seem to be just a number of discarded cartons, a feature typical of the contemporary landscape. In actuality, however, they are inhabited, and they can be dangerous.

This is learned by the box man in *The Box Man*, E. Dale Saunders' excellent translation of Abe Kobo's 1973 novel, *Hako Otoko*. In it the author continues several of the themes common to his earlier work. Like the hero of *The Ruined Map*, the box man takes on the identity of someone else; like the leading character in *The Face of Another*, he does so because he is bereft of his own identity; and like the insect collector in *The Woman in the Dunes*, he finds a way, finally, to both exist and to affirm himself. "Instead of leaving the box," he says, "I shall enclose the world within it."

Unlike in the earlier novels, however, Abe here extends the search for identity into the form of the book itself. It is a collection of notes, journals, snatches of poetry, even pictures. The quest is for the reader as well as the box-man narrator. Both must make sense of this material.

It is not easy. One of the central problems is finally stated in the middle of the book: "Who is writing these notes and where are they writing them?" Investigating this new lead, the trail doubles back. The opening entries suddenly reappear, now in a new context. We realize that "this is a tale, of course," but that now "this story is in the act of taking place."

The tense changes from first-person past to second-person imperative. The present progressive descends like a smothering blanket. "Thus the world is always/A lap fast—" the box man tells us, "The world he thinks he sees/Has not yet begun."

Lost in the labyrinth, the reader is led along by his own curiosity and by the strange scenes he spies: two box men, one real, one false, seated watching a naked girl on all fours, rear in the air; two box men, both armed with air guns, spying on each other; a boy caught peeking punished by being forced to exhibit himself until he ejaculates.

It is the reader's own voyeurism that leads him to the conclusion of the book, a maze of mirrors where Abe's thesis discloses itself: upon reflection, the box man tells us, who we are depends entirely upon what people make of us.

Identity is to be equated with that self extracted by others. One is defined then, only when fully visible, and voyeurism becomes a timid and reserved confession of love, since "in seeing there is love, in being seen there is abhorrence." This is because "if the one who is looked at looks back, then the person who was looking becomes the one who is looked at." One must accept this identity when one is subject to "visual rape."

No one likes to be raped. Consequently, "by putting on clothes that are as much as possible identical and by having similar hairdos [people] manage to make it difficult to distinguish between one another." After all, "that the act of spying on someone else is generally looked upon with scorn is because, I suppose, one does not want to be on the side of being seen." Indeed, if you want to look, you usually have to pay compensation, as at the theater. "The fact that they keep on and on selling endless instruments for 'looking'—television—is excellent proof" of all of this. The box man's logic is impregnable as is his resolve that in the interests of "self" protection, "from here it is but a step, and a most natural one, to being a box man."

An amount of allegory is to be expected in the works of Abe. On one level, this book may be read as a parable of the ordinary, garden-variety alienated man, boxed in with wife, kids, and the eight-hour job. On another, however, the book reads as drop-out's pilgrim's progress. At the same time, the book may be seen as an affirmation of higher wisdom: find your limitations; these then become the limitations of your world.

One of the reasons for the various possible interpretations is that Abe is not involved with moral or ethical concerns. He is describing both the luck and the curse of being human, that is, being an animal who is conscious, who knows what he is doing as he does it, who consequently has been forced to invent both a self and an other.

The book itself is a philosophical essay confined inside a novel. And, as in those sets of boxes the next one of which always contains one more inside, there is no reason for the argument ever to end. Abe leaves his mirror maze by the simple expedient of writing the last page. The reader—fellow member of the search party—is not so lucky. There is really no way out of this labyrinth of reflections into which he has been most skillfully and seductively led.

The Box Man, by Abe Kobo, translated by E. Dale Saunders. New York: Alfred A. Knopf, New York, 1974.

Here is the third collection of Abe stories to be translated into English. The first was a group of four, translated by Andrew Horvat and published by Hara Shobo in 1973. The second, Donald Keene's translation of *The Man Who Turned Into a Stick*, and other stories appeared two years later, published by the Tokyo University Press.

Only one is duplicated in this new Kodansha collection, the minor 1949 story "Dendrocacalia"—man turns into a plant—which was earlier translated by Horvat. Most of the others in the book have, however, been translated into other languages: mainly Russian, Chinese, Czech, Hungarian.

That this should be so is perceived a tribute to the presumed Marxist orientation of the earlier work, an attribution I have never been able to understand, since the major European influence is obviously Kafka rather than Karl. Nonetheless, Japanese critics make much of a communist connection. They intend it as a compliment.

Perhaps they read Abe's various works on the emptiness of life in modern society, on the difficulty of communication, on the discrepancy between inner and outer realities, as some kind of indictment of the West with its democratic beliefs and searches for happiness.

It would be difficult to sustain such an interpretation. Abe is writing, rather, an indictment of life itself. Like Kafka, he sees the human state as interestingly hopeless, its essential idiocy only to be reached through such indirect devices as allegory.

In the 1961 "An Irrelevant Death," a man finds a corpse in his room. Like Ionesco's growing cadaver, this dangerous nuisance stands for all that is dead in society but still much with us. In the 1954 "Record of a Transformation," the dead soldiers don't die, they stay with us, observing—as indeed Japan's war dead have done.

"The Crime of S. Karma," the 1951 novella only a section of which is here translated, is that he lets his name card get away from him and the modest *meishi* takes over his personality—as indeed it does in ordinary Japanese life. In the 1951 "The Life of a Poet," a woman gets woven into the jacket she is making—a commentary on the nature of ordinary work.

Political intent can be read into the 1951 "Intruders." At least, it has been—the group of strangers who come into the hero's room, tell him to be more democratic and eventually hang him have been interpreted as the Allied Occupation authorities. Here too, though, the work has been widened. It serves as basis for the well known 1967 play *Friends*. What may have begun as political comment ends up an existential comment on life itself.

If there is an ideology behind Abe, it is certainly existential and hence metaphysical rather than political. His ultimate concern is with the snares of identity, and this theme has animated his finest work.

Here, too, the best story in the collection is the one which addresses itself directly to the theme of identity. In the 1966 "Beyond the Curve," a man loses himself. Suffering a sudden spiritual amnesia, he can remember nothing about himself, and yet he remains "himself" to the extent that he can think, can wonder, can suffer. This extreme state of spiritual malaise is consistently imagined, has no surrealist padding, refuses to opt out for a trick ending, and in the end becomes just as disturbing as the author doubtless intended it to be.

The closed and claustrophobic world of Abe, where one move brings you up against the next wall, has been in the past well served by Juliet Carpenter. Here again, she is equally adept at rendering the Abe style. Absurdly detailed descriptions come out "with the patient concentration of someone stripping shelled peanuts of their skins." The author's often lumpish lightness is rendered equally well. "She worked in order to stimulate the metabolism of her family of five, which tended to grow sluggish on her husband's meager salary."

Abe's existential thesis permits him to write only one way, and whether these twelve middle-period (1949–1966) stories are to be taken more often than once a day is for us readers to decide. Still, at least, we have the option.

Beyond the Curve, by Abe Kobo, translated by Juliet Winters Carpenter. Tokyo: Kodansha International, 1991.

Mole, 173 cm, 97 kg, lives under a mountain in a maze of shafts and tunnels left abandoned. There, he has set up his ark, a place of refuge from the coming catastrophe. It is coming shortly—indeed, it is almost upon us. And where Noah only had a flood to worry about, Mole must concern himself with terminal pollution and nuclear destruction. To this end, he has created an underground world of dead ends, false turns, booby-traps, and—as a centerpiece—a tremendous toilet that will flush anything away. Then, one day, he inadvertently gets his foot caught in it.

An allegory? Yes, indeed. Like other Abe works, this 1984 novel about Mole in the mountain, *Hakobune no Sakura* (*The Ark Sakura*) is intended to be read as comment on the current dilemma.

The major metaphor is waste—nuclear, industrial, human. The mountain is compared to a mass of intestines, the tunnels are bowel-like, and many of the similes are concerned with diarrhea, with irritable colon, spastic rectum.

The magnificent toilet is supposed to cleanse both the ark and the style, but it is Mole himself who makes this impossible and who becomes endangered, not by nuclear holocaust but by the very means through which it was to be rendered powerless. It is also he who finally fakes the atomic explosion that ejects him from the intestines of the ark that was to have saved him.

Paradoxical? Yes, indeed. In much of Abe's work, efforts result in effects opposite those originally desired. Mole, seeking to save himself, is ejected by his own concerns, but these, in turn, are what save him since there was, in fact, no atom-bomb attack, and he himself turned the ark into a tomb for those left behind. Afraid of the bomb, he himself simulates it; concerned with saving people, he condemns those who could not escape.

Or, more succinctly, would not: These folk, like the man in *Woman in the Dunes* who discovered a way to live in the sand, elect to remain behind. The characters in *The Ark Sakura* presumably have found a way to live in the dark. They so decide because it is paradoxical of them to do so—and paradox is the prime law of the Abe novel.

Not, however, before much discussion, and much mutual distrust. All the characters display a degree of paranoia—in Abe's novels you have to be crazy not to be. They always think the worst, and they invariably ascribe the most uncharitable of motives, and they do it at great length. Man caught in this great manhole that is life would be mad to trust, and this they demonstrate page after page.

It is this narrowness of Abe's world, his repetitive detail, and his relentless distrust that gives his books their power. They are fully imagined visions of a confined world, the projection of a powerful intelligence through whose hooded eyes we are forced to look.

This degree of expressionism can move, but it can also tire. The occurrences come to have the irrelevant logic of dreams—someone else's dreams. Unsustained fancy can soon seem fanciful, even (or particularly) if held up by the caparisons of allegory. If interest is successfully maintained through a novel such as *Woman in the Dunes*, it is because the surface realism of the story is enough to both contain and conceal the inner allegorical core. The later novels, however, stress their intent, and paradox displays only itself.

Like Kafka's mole in the story of the same name, Abe's is fraught with fear and suspicion, but Kafka's remains real, a small, distrustful animal, wonderfully anthropomorphized to fit our understanding. We feel its fears, but we also feel pity for its state. The story is parabolic of nothing, and this is what makes it immediate, memorable and moving.

Abe's Mole must carry such a heavy load of meaningful allegory that we can never much interest ourselves in him. He is not a person, he becomes a thing—merely a high-tech Mole for our times. And the Ark Sakura becomes an unalloyed symbol, forever in allegorical dry dock.

The Ark Sakura, by Abe Kobo, translated by Juliet Winters Carpenter. New York: Alfred A. Knopf, 1988.

Yamasaki Toyoko

It is commonly heard that Japan has now won through peaceful means what it failed to win through military methods. Not so commonly heard is any discussion of the nature of the means through which this was accomplished. For this reason the 1976 appearance of *Fumo Chitai* (*The Barren Zone*) by Yamasaki Toyoko (1924–) created something of a sensation.

Early on one of the characters says: "I'd say that an army command and a trading company are fundamentally the same." Later, he adds: "Economic strategy and the tactics of trading companies go hand-in-hand with the effort to revive Japan's economy. Instead of soldiers you have commodities, but the tactics are exactly the same."

Even wartime military language carries the message: "All I'm doing these days is stocking up on a commodity with a negative margin ... so my sword stays out of its scabbard." And "... the old military saying, 'Victory and defeat are constants in war,' applies to commercial wars as well."

The military/big-business connection is so elaborately spelled out in the Yamasaki novel that one would have thought that its translation would serve the foreign business person as some new Bible in further efforts to "learn from Japan." Yet, though this translation appeared in 1985, one does not hear of the American Chamber of Commerce's rushing to study it. They ought to—they'd learn something.

Not that Yamasaki had this aim. As in *Bonchi* and *Shibo Kiji*, she is writing a novel, a construct in which the wayward happenings of life are made to create a pattern. Her hero, Iki Tadashi, a Japanese army officer, is in Manchuria at the end of the war. Captured by the Russians, he is imprisoned, then returned to Japan as witness for the War

Crimes Trials, then returns to Siberia where he is sent to the worst of the camps. When finally released and repatriated, he returns a nearly broken man. Still, when approached by a trading firm anxious to make use of his expertise, he agrees. And even when he discovers that what they really wanted was his military connections with former higher-ups, now big men in the government, he still agrees.

Once a soldier, always a soldier—but this is not Yamasaki's theme nor does she treat her plot in the bald method this précis might have suggested. Rather, weaving through flashbacks, contrasting the past and the present, she suggests, through a series of parallels, the import of her story.

The Russians "planned to abrogate their neutrality pact with Japan and enter the war just as Japan was about to surrender to the Allies, thus allowing them an easy conquest of Manchuria. Iki burned with anger at this revelation of Russian deceit."

But that is only the beginning. He is imprisoned by the Russians for eleven years. During this time he learns of many further horrors. The treatment accorded Japanese prisoners of war is lucidly laidout—at the end of the novel is a listing of the twenty-two Siberian prison survivors interviewed by the author. The Japanese military was, of course, brutal (all militaries are), but one wonders if even here there was dehumanization so extreme as it is shown to have been in the Siberian camps.

Germane to Yamasaki's major theme is the further irritations of the "Democratic Committee" which is entirely composed of brain-washed prisoners. These Japanese soldiers torture other Japanese soldiers: they force a man to get on all floors and imitate a dog before giving him a message from his family in Japan; they force fellow Japanese to practice *fumi-e*, to step on the imperial chrysanthemum crest, before being given meal tickets.

Iki ponders this. "Japanese people are not endowed with a strong sense of individuality or of self-reliance, he told himself, and so they tend to fall in easily with the crowd ... [But] what, he wondered, has happened to our renowned Japanese fortitude? To our patience and honesty."

His own is rewarded. He survives though many do not. A comrade, unable to stand more, maims himself. He is sent even further north to an even worse camp. "No one ever escapes from Soviet justice." But Iki comes through. Only to end up in a new paramilitary big-business job in postwar Japan. But that is my way of putting it, not Yamasaki's. At the most, she has people say that "the only way Japan can rise again is by earning foreign currency. Lots of it. And we businessmen are the ones who can do that."

However, parallels within the book's structure reveal the author's real attitude. Toward the end, Iki notices that his trading company boss, being given red-carpet treatment, is offered chrysanthemums. "Iki ... stopped in shock. Once upon a time, and not that long ago, he thought, only the Emperor would have received such homage ... gold chrysanthemums." And the reader instantly remembers the *fumi-e* scene where these same chrysanthemum emblems were trod upon.

There are many such parallels shaping the moral import of this book. At the beginning Iki is in Manchuria. At the end, he is equally far away—in America. Also: "Iki, a survivor from a different war, rejoiced at the sight of a Japanese aviator sitting at the controls of an American plane as its test pilot, about to take off from an American air force base in California."

But the novel's final scene is Pearl Harbor, where Iki has gone because he is consumed with the need to see it. He has just learned that he was hired not for his military expertise but only for his military associations. He has also heard of the coming scandal. "These politicians are selecting the [fighter plane] on the basis of whether or not their choice will benefit the Prime Minister's party. They're putting the nation's system of defense in jeopardy, simply in order to maintain a majority in the Diet and to keep the position of prime minister within their party. This is no mere corruption. It is treason."

So reasons one of the characters, and it is sitting on a hill overlooking Pearl Harbor that Iki feels this stab in the back. It is here, associations reverberating, parallels clashing, that Iki decides.

And he decides on the last page of this extraordinary novel to go on, to continue—to be a successful postwar Japanese businessman. Some sort of cycle has completed itself. But what does the author think? What are we do think?

Perhaps these are questions a Japanese reader would not ask. Perhaps the statement of these similarities, these truths is enough. For the Western reader, it makes the reading not inconclusive but ambivalent. And, perhaps because of this, it makes the reading all the more moving, all the more powerful.

Why this book has not become widely read and widely known I do not understand. As one of the ways in which "successful modern Japan" can be understood, it is invaluable.

The Barren Zone, by Yamasaki Toyoko, translated by James T. Araki. Honolulu: University of Hawaii Press, 1985.

Yoshiyuki Junnosuke

Here is a translation of the 1970 novel, *Anshitsu*, a book

which won the author the prestigious Tanizaki Prize and became something of a bestseller. Already well known, both for his earlier novels and his translations of Henry Miller, Yoshiyuki Junnosuke (1924–1994) was now a celebrity.

It is an interesting and revealing work, beautifully translated, with all of his customary skill, by John Bester. The forty-four-year-old author-hero has in middle-age arranged his life the way he wants. This includes (or perhaps even consists of) having a number of complying women who, no more serious about their attachments than he is, are always ready to have him drop in for the night or accompany him to the nearest hotel.

Sex has become the major activity in his life. He does not find this exceptionable because, after all, one goes on living "just because there's nothing better to do." Nor does he seem to find it all that enjoyable, but, still, it is better than nothing—which seems to be the alternative.

He must make a number of small concessions, to be sure, but he is also careful to make no large ones. "… it's impossible to turn your back on society completely [but] … the marriage system … can be ignored indefinitely." Consequently, his days go by, and he lives mainly for his evenings.

Not that he likes women as such all that much, however. "If you said publicly that the ideal woman was a sex organ with arms and legs, a majority of women would get furious … among the men [however], there'd be a lot who'd agree," and "if you ask me, it's still true to say that where men have sex organs, women have reproductive organs."

He finds a kind of ideal in imagining the love-life of one of his friends who perhaps likes women more than she likes men: "No pregnancy, no domesticity, just the play of the senses," he muses, approvingly.

His relationship with his women, casual to an extreme, avoids all responsibility, all emotional investment, and if he misses emotional heights he also avoids emotional depths. He has, however, neglected to ponder upon one unavoidable fact.

This is that things change. Several of the girls get married, others disappear from his life. And he himself changes. Always subject to ill health and bad dreams, he drives himself further into this security he has created, then finds that it too changes. In order to continue to savor this content he has constructed, he is driven further. He can avoid commitment only through its parody, the sadomasochistic relationship, complete with submission, bondage, whips, etc.

Even this extreme fails to halt the natural and transient flow. Reduced to one woman (the least favorite), he finds himself hovering on the edge of that hateful involvement which we might also call love. The dark room is his metaphor for that condition. He has no idea what it may contain. The last line of the novel is "I was standing in front of Natsue's apartment. I grasped the knob of the door. The dark room lay beyond."

There are at least two ways this book may be interpreted, and one of its strengths is that the author gives no indication of which he favors. A conventional reading would see the hero deep in delusion, a user of people, a shallow, selfish, self-pitying man who gets his comeuppance.

A more rewarding reading would see him as a man of some strength who, knowing that life is not all that good (it's just all that there is), actively arranges it to suit himself. Unlike the majority of other men, he refuses to listen to the hollow blandishments of society and, following his own interests and observations, creates what is for him an ideal world.

His slow realization that this, too, is not enough can

then be seen as a natural tragedy—an everyday one, the kind we are all used to. Sex is not a cure. It is a palliative. We are still alone, and it was loneliness we sought to ease. Love also is no cure, but it works better and longer than casual sex does. So when the author puts his hand on the knob to that dark room, we know that he is entering another realm of illusion. There is no cure because life is the illness.

Such might be the ramifications of more extended reading of the book, but such the author himself merely indicates and never states. Indeed, one of the strengths of the book is that everything is implicit—one deduces one's conclusion.

It is fitting that this translator of Henry Miller won the Tanizaki Prize because his thoughts on sex, love, and being alone are between the sometimes empty but always affirming ideas of the former and the superlatively honest and unrepentant yet also affirming concepts of the latter.

In *Naomi*, Tanizaki shows that an s/m relationship (a term he would, rightly, never use) can be just as meaningful and just valuable and just as illuminating as, let us say, first love; in his last novel, *The Diary of a Mad Old Man*, he shows us that the erotic is by definition life-affirming and, no matter what crooked paths it is forced to take, its very presence assures continuation and, thus, fulfillment.

Yoshiyuki is perhaps not this wise, but his novel is definitely Tanizaki-like in that it implies that the erotic (sex, love, everything) is, indeed, just what the doctor (again, life itself) has ordered. As for the larger questions—being alone, dying, death—well, eroticism is one way to avoid them, for the time being.

The Dark Room, by Yoshiyuki Junnosuke, translated by John Bester. Tokyo: Kodansha International, 1975.

Mishima Yukio

The legend of Mishima Yukio (1925–1970) continues and grows. The suicide endowed him with a mythic status, and yet both our curiosity and our romantic imagination remain unsatisfied. He has become our Byron—with much of the same mystery, much of the same sense of hidden depths, and much of the occasional bad writing.

A book which exhibits all three qualities is this paperback printing of the original *Orian* (1978) publication of Kathryn Sparling's translation of the 1966 *Hagakure Nyumon*—here somewhat dressed up as *Yukio Mishima on Hagakure: The Samurai Ethic and Modern Japan.*

Here is the famous apologia for what was to occur several years later, one in which the most oft-repeated of the various maxims is the now well known "I Found That the Way of the Samurai Is Death."

The man who made this discovery was Yamamoto Jocho, who retired from the world and lived to a ripe old age, his words taken down by a disciple around 1710 and consequently published as *Recorded Words of the Hagakure Master.*

The young Mishima discovered this book very early in his life, and his devotion to it continued to the end. Hence, in 1966, he decided to publish a new edition of it in which he not only wrote the introduction but also provided full commentary on all of those texts he had selected for inclusion.

Jocho defined his way of the samurai in this fashion: "Depending upon circumstances, he may win or lose. But avoiding dishonor is quite a separate consideration from winning and losing. To avoid dishonor he must die." Mishima, with his much written about ideal of purity, was also considerably taken with ideas on honor and dishonor.

The idea of a pure and honorable death occurs in many

of his writings. It seems to have been, however, mainly a matter of appearance. Mishima says as much when he writes: "Cowardly words make the heart itself cowardly, and being regarded as a coward by others is the same as being a coward." In other words, if others think something about you, it is true. Here is Appearance with a capital A.

But before whom does one then thus appear? One's friends, one's countrymen, the world? No. Jocho is certain on this point. In talking about the need for a samurai always to look his best, he writes: "One may be run through at any moment in vigorous battle; to die having neglected one's personal grooming is to reveal a general sloppiness of habit, to be despised and mocked by the enemy."

Jocho in the early 18th-century may have known all about enemies, but Mishima in the late twentieth didn't have any enemies—merely, at best, those who mildly disliked him. Without constant contradiction, the way of the samurai is difficult indeed.

Consequently, Mishima (and it is he who makes this recounting of the *Hagakure* so personal, not me) had to cast about for other reasons for the necessary death. One is this: "To the man of action, life frequently appears as a circle to be completed by the addition of one last point ... The greatest calamity for the man of action is that he fail to die even after that last unmistakable point has been added." Another is this, quoted with apparent approval from Jocho himself: "If your name means nothing to the world whether you live or die, it is better to live." Therefore, if you are famous ....

That Mishima saw himself as a man of action is apparent, and his efforts to make this real—his toy soldiers, his sun-and-steel protestations, the hopefully political overtones of his final scene—are very touching. But the action-filled samurai must have his foe, and Mishima did not have one. Perhaps for that reason he had to construct one. He had few choices but seems to have settled for modern Japan.

Modern Japan was certainly the audience—it was to it that these annotations on the *Hagakure* were aimed, and it was those eyes before which Mishima was not to be "despised and mocked," was to prove that he was not "cowardly," and it was in front of these that he was to perform the act which was intended, at least partially, to indicate that he had avoided "dishonor."

This curious book, then, while it does not explain Mishima to any real extent, gives some insight into his manner of thinking. Certainly Jocho's *Hagakure* was seminal to his thought, and without it his life might well have been different. Or perhaps some other justification would have been found—there must have been many books like Jocho's, all aiming to explain and uphold a political status quo.

Certainly, Mishima's *Hagakure* is a major addition to the myth. Despite the fact that the tone, when not quixotic, is absurd, or perhaps even because of this quality, the legend has been enriched. Mishima represents, as he probably intended, a mystery, an enigma, and a rebuke. As long as we take seriously those things for which he stood, the mystery can only deepen and the legend grow.

Yukio Mishima on Hagakure: The Samurai Ethic and Modern Japan, translated by Kathryn Sparling. Tokyo: Charles E. Tuttle Company, 1978.

One of the last times I saw Mishima Yukio, he wanted, strangely, to talk about literature. Strangely, because when we were together literature was the one thing we never talked about. Even more oddly, this time, he wanted to talk about Ernest Hemingway. He was a writer whom Mishima had disliked to a marked degree, either because of, or in spite of, similarities.

Both were conscious stylists, both were romantics, both were given to macho posturings, and both were subscribers to obsolete codes. It turned out, however, that it was not the dead author's work that Mishima wanted to talk about. It was the American's suicide which interested the Japanese.

He might still dislike the man as a writer, I remember his saying, but he had come to admire the man himself. It was the suicide which had earned Mishima's new regard, and this I was to remember later in 1970.

I certainly did, as had perhaps been intended. And now, reading through this new paper edition of ten of Mishima's best stories, I find myself again remembering. And wondering—why is that, like Hemingway's, Mishima's best work is found in the stories and not in the novels?

Aside, perhaps, from the early *Sun Also Rises*, Hemingway's novels are as flaccid as the stories are terse, reaching an embarrassing bathos in works such as *The Old Man and the Sea*. In Mishima's work, the novels (except for his finest, the first, *Confessions of a Mask*, which is more autobiography than fiction) are as verbose as the stories are laconic, reaching true rhetorical windiness in the final books of *The Sea of Fertility*.

I had felt Mishima's resemblance to Hemingway in the work (a resemblance based, of course, not upon Mishima's actual prose, but rather the various English translations of it) but not known why. Now I think I do, though the reasons are not mine. They are those of Frederick Crews, and he outlines his thesis (confined entirely to Hemingway) in his review of several books on that author in a recent issue of the *New York Review of Books*, from which I quote.

"The short story and not the novel proved to be Hemingway's suited genre. The amplitude of a realistic novel calls for broad sympathies and a conscious, integrated understanding of characters and conflicts. A writer whose professed values serve as preventatives against self-insight will find it hard to sustain his characters' development over many chapters or to avoid recourse to stereotypes and posturing."

If one were to substitute the name of Mishima for that of Hemingway, I think that the argument would hold equally true. And certainly Mishima was as much as Hemingway "temperamentally inclined toward the economy of phrase and gesture required by a ten-page tale...."

Rereading these ten stories, I again admire what Mishima accomplished within this form. Some are anecdotal ("Thermos Bottles" is a single idea elegantly spun to its full length; both "The Pearl" and "The Seven Bridges" are small comedies of manners, or lack of them, encased in short-story form). Some are plotted ("Death in Midsummer"), and some are pushed into melodrama ("Swaddling Clothes"). Others are fables ("The Priest of Shiga Temple and His Love" and the powerful and prescient "Patriotism" of 1961), and others are in the form of observations ("Onnagata" and "Three Million Yen.")

(The tenth is not a story at all, and I do not know why New Directions included it in their original 1966 edition—it is *Dojoji* from the modern noh play collection and is an example of later Mishima psychodrama.)

Some of the stories verge on the sentimental. In "Three Million Yen," we are, I think, supposed to feel indignation that this beautiful young couple is "forced" to earn a future—they want a child, you see—by exhibiting the process in public. Others verge on the unlikely. In "Swaddling Clothes," for example. I know some ladies who might go about bothering rag-pickers but I do not know a single rag picker in this internalized society who would attack a lady.

Nonetheless, most are distinguished by the directness and economy which characterize the good short story. Indeed, much of the virtue of the Mishima short story comes precisely from his not having space enough to spell everything out. We run much less often into such phrases as "he thought that" or "she realized that"—phrases which must strike despair to every thinking reader's heart. Instead, we have precise description and crisp dialogue.

Mishima is in the short story (and again like Hemingway) under no compulsion to "make" character. Ten pages is too short a span in which to fully characterize. But it is just the right length for the telling observation. Both authors may sketch from life in their best impressionistic style. And both they and we are spared the hours of sheer toil with which "characters" are compulsively constructed.

Also, in the wise words of Frederick Crews, "we needn't know, any more than the author himself does, precisely what lurks within the gulf that every sentence barely skirts."

Death in Midsummer and Other Stories, by Mishima Yukio, translated by Edward Seidensticker and others. Tokyo: Charles E. Tuttle Company, 1987.

In his introduction to this collection of Mishima short stories, translator John Bester writes that it is now time, nearly twenty years after the writer's death, to put aside the accretions of "sensationalism, chic or special interest" and look at the work as literature.

Bester finds the best of Mishima, as do many critics, in the shorter works and has selected seven which illustrate Mishima's strengths as a writer and span his most productive years—1946 to 1965. The stories, "Cigarette," "Martyrdom," "Sea and Sunset," "Sword," "Fountains in the Rain," "Raisin Bread," and "Act of Worship," are not arranged in this chronological order; so without skipping they cannot be read to trace Mishima's stylistic growth.

Most of the stories have never been translated before. "Cigarette" appeared in English in 1972. "It was this 1946 work that the young Mishima showed to Kawabata and thus began his literary career. In it, he expressed concerns he would elaborate on in both "Martyrdom" and his first novel, *Confessions of a Mask*. The story also displayed what Donald Keene finds "the first, poignant expression of real feelings." Keene sees in this and the other early stories "an overly rich vocabulary and a penchant for obscure Chinese kanji"—a very self-conscious concern for writing itself. "Mishima," Keene continues, "never freed himself of these stylistic mannerisms, but he was eventually able to make them seen an integral part of his works."

It is this gradual stylistic growth which can be appreciated through a chronological reading of these stories. The following passage from "Sword" is indicative of the mannered prose of Mishima's earlier work.

"His own stamina had been like a country road beneath the midday sun, stretching smooth and uninterrupted as far as the eye could see. But now ..., the sun had suddenly set on the way, leaving him with an uneasy feeling that a little farther on the road would peter out without warning, perhaps plunge him into some waiting void."

This passage is taken from the most overwritten of the stories. Perhaps Mishima would have avoided the colloquial "peter out" and the cliché "uneasy feeling," but the translation captures the uneven mannerisms of the early style. "Up flew the purple of Jiro's helmet strings. Forth went his strength." Inverted runs the prose.

The style becomes both simpler and more compact in the later works, and in "Act of Worship," it is the resilient prose of the better novels, such as *After the Banquet*. Bester effectively demonstrates the growing security of the author and the forging of a personal, supple, precise style.

Throughout his career, Mishima was the kind of writer who preferred to tell rather than to show. The major points of any Mishima work are always related by the author, not by the characters. "Kagawa felt an immense irritation at seeing what should have been a simple, unclouded decision to leave Jiro prey in this way to a moment's clever calculations." Kagawa and Jiro show us nothing because Mishima tells us everything.

In Mishima's case, the origins of this common way of writing seem to have been French. He spoke of the influence of Raymond Radiguet, a stylist who had the advantage of dying before the age of twenty, something which the Japanese author sometimes spoke of with admiration.

Another influence, even a stronger one, might have been Jean Cocteau, a literary figure about whom Mishima was ambivalent but whom he in ways resembled. When Mishima writes that something "emitted the strange radioactivity known as beauty," it is pure Cocteau.

Acts of Worship: Seven Stories, by Mishima Yukio, translated by John Bester. Tokyo: Kodansha International, 1989.

Silk and Insight, published in 1964, six years before the author's suicide, is "late" Mishima. Late in several senses: not only was it written toward the end of the writer's life, it is also filled with his late concerns: authority, power, politics. Again, as in several of the earlier novels, he hangs these concerns upon an actual occurrence: the 1954 "human rights strike" at the Omi Kenshu silk plant, an event sometimes described as the most significant of its kind in the history of Japan's postwar labor movement.

In the novel, Komazawa Zenzo runs his business in the old Japanese way. He is the benevolent father to his workers, who " knew very well how much rain to confer, how much sun to confer." The rain included firing the ill, censorship of mail, and spy networks among the employees.

"You tried hard to pretend to be our father, did you not?" asks an adversary. "You always said women workers are my daughters, male workers are my sons, [yet] for all that did you ever once take a careful look at each of these daughters and sons of yours before the strike began?"

To which Zenzo answers: "My emphasis was on fairness, that's all. Fairness is different from equality." This belief in abstractions has him, at the end, making the deeply sentimental gesture of "forgiving" all the people who called him "an evil capitalist, a dated blockhead who made a personal possession out of a corporation."

The gesture is sentimental because it represents an excess of emotion as applied to an unworthy object—Zenzo's forgiving those he has wronged does not deserve our emotions. If this were simply reported, it would be a part of character analysis. Instead, however, it is presented as, somehow, a virtue. This observation is my own and not Mishima's. The writer himself found probity in the old paternalistic way and emotion in the old man's deathbed forbearance.

The depth of the writer's concern is indicated in his original intention to call the novel *The Father of Japan* (*Nihon no Chichi*) and in it, says the translator, he intended to describe the emperor in the person of Zenjiro. According to Mishima's biographer, Inose Naoki, the thematic origin of the novel was the author's witnessing the demonstrations against the renewal of the U.S.-Japan Mutual Security Treaty. From the first, his interest started shifting, says Inose, "from the demonstrators to those demonstrated against, from the anti-establishment to the establishment." And we all know in whose name Mishima later destroyed himself.

All this has given Mishima a definite place on the

political right and has attracted a number of followers who still, nearly thirty years after the event, hold meetings on the anniversary of the death. However, as Frank Gibney observes in his introduction, "I suspect that in a predominately rightist atmosphere, Mishima would have turned far left."

This, correctly I believe, suggests that Mishima's political interests were restricted to a dramatization of his own often conflicting emotions concerning power and paternalism. In this novel, as in so much of the late work, the action becomes a kind of psychodrama which illustrates the impulses of the writer. Each character becomes some aspect of Mishima himself.

A result is the omniscience of the late Mishima style. Everything is told, and little is shown: psychology is reported rather than presented, the reader is given small credit for any intelligence, and the tone becomes pedantic.

The result is a book which, as Donald Keene has said, "failed to enhance Mishima's reputation with either the critics or the public." At the same time, it remains relevant (particularly now) if read for its sub-text. As the translator has noted: the novel was Mishima's attempt "to explore what lies at the core of Japan—the 'power,' paternalistic, bureaucratic, what have you—that drives Japan."

Silk and Insight, by Mishima Yukio, translated by Sato Hiroaki. Armonk: M.E. Sharpe, 1988.

Mishima Yukio finished his play *My Friend Hitler* at the end of October, 1968—just two years before his death. It is thus a late work and, like all the later work, both moralistic and didactic.

The idea for the play came from events in Berlin during the summer of 1934. Hitler wanted to create a "legal" government and had carefully worked out a number of political ploys. Both Gregor Strasser, the socialist theoretician and national organization leader, and Ernest Roehm, chief of the SA, the Nazi military arm, were in the way—the latter, particularly, since he wanted to incorporate the regular army in the SA corps.

This indicated a political crisis Hitler was anxious to avoid and so he had them both killed. Later party propaganda accused them of conspiracy though there is no evidence whatever of any Strasser-Roehm connection.

These events and their various interpretations appealed to Mishima. He—whose later work is so filled with statements about purity and heartfelt fervor—was interested in the moment when idealism gives way to materialism, when revolutionary fervor turns to accommodating diplomacy. He found such a moment in these political events, and the last lines of the play gives the purport of the drama:

> *Krupp*: ... Adolf, you have done well. You cut down the left and, as you moved the sword, cut down the right.
> *Hitler*: Yes, government must take the middle road.

Such a moment, when belief gives way to practice, is indeed highly dramatic, and many fine plays (among them Mishima's "favorite" Shakespeare—*Julius Caesar*) have been based upon such. And there is no doubt that Mishima felt both personally and deeply the tragedy of pure idealism and a sincere and selfless devotion to a gleaming cause.

So deeply, indeed, that in this play he (unlike Shakespeare) is not content to show us these inevitable workings but has to tell us about them, at great length, and about how he feels about them. He hated accommodation, and anything that smacked of the pragmatic (indeed, the other character in this four-man melodrama is Krupp—portrayed as just the kind of opportunist Mishima most disliked); he exalted the loyal, the devoted, the single-minded, all of which, in his vocabulary, became the pure.

The result is that he interiorized all of the emotions in his drama. We are not shown four real men and asked to understand their problems; we are shown segments of the author's psyche and forced to choose sides. All the lines are loaded.

This is particularly evident on the level of metaphor (and the language is very self-consciously "poetic") and rhetoric. One of the principle metaphors is that of iron—one fittingly Hitlerian as well. If one examines its various metamorphoses throughout the play, one can see what Mishima is up to.

> *Roehm*: The only thing that can hurt me is a bullet. Or rather, when the steel of my body happens to betray me and attract into it the small iron lump of my comrade's—yes, when iron and iron, to be intimate, draw together and kiss, that's the only time I'll fall....
> *Strasser*: The pot that once swallowed a stray bullet put out blue flowers, but it puts out only insipid pansies now that the fertilizing bullet is gone....
> *Krupp*: For the guns ... they've shot the real human flesh to their fill for the first time in a long while, and should be able to sleep, satisfied ... like the soldiers who've been to brothels ... [And, later] iron ... by going through the storm of three thousand degree flames, iron ore turns into pig iron, etc.

The rhetoric plainly states not that iron must be put to a practical use (that ideals must give way to material considerations) and that this is the way of all things (one of the "messages" of the rhetoric of *Julius Caesar*) but that this unavoidable process is bad, bad, bad.

In this, Mishima was never more plainly a romantic—both works and life indicate a very real unwillingness to consider the world as it happens to be, and on this anecdotal level (the pure rebel, the idealistic example), his legend is going to live. Whether his work, particularly the later work, is going to live is more problematical.

On one level, it was dead the minute it was written. Unless we interest ourselves in Mishima's psyche, we cannot interest ourselves in this play. The characters are (by non-psychodrama standards) lifeless, their conversations are ploys, they are moved about like puppets, they spout rather than speak, and since they are all one-sided and obviously constructed for a purpose, they quite fail to gain our sympathy.

Which is perhaps what Mishima intended. He did not want them to gain our sympathy; he wanted his great idea to gain our sympathy. Didactic, he is laying down the law — we are given Mishima's opinion of the world. The play is propaganda.

As indeed, on some level, is most drama. The difference, however, is that the unavoidable "message" is usually not all of the play. Something timeless and hence true, and hence (and here is the leap into faith which art requires) good, is also visible and sometimes (as in Shakespeare) becomes the true theme of the play.

For a closer parallel to Mishima one must turn to an entirely different playwright—someone like Gabriele D'Annunzio (a writer Mishima admired enough to translate—that long psychodrama on St. Sebastian). The Italian symbolist loved the active life, adored "spiritual purity," got involved in the military, was quite quixotically implicated in politics. His *Il Fuoco* (*Flame of Life*) and *Francesca da Rimini* are now, I should guess, quite unreadable, and yet D'Annunzio remains unforgettable. The anecdote of his life has superseded all and as a flamboyant romantic hero—

Byron without the talent, Baudelaire without the doubts—he continues to live.

My Friend Hitler and Other Plays, by Mishima Yukio, translated by Sato Hiroaki. New York: Columbia University Press, 2002.

Spring Snow is the first volume of the four-novel cycle, *The Sea of Fertility*, Mishima Yukio's final work, completed on the morning of the day of his death in 1970. The title of the tetralogy, he told Donald Keene, "is intended to suggest the arid sea of the moon that belies its name. Or I might say that it superimposes the image of cosmic nihilism on that of the fertile sea." He also wrote that "I have put into it everything I have felt and thought about life and this world." His death indicates his feelings and thoughts during the last years of his life, and this final work somewhat explains them.

"The age of glorious wars ended with the Meiji era. Today all the stories of past wars have sunk to the level of those edifying accounts we hear from middle-aged non-coms in the military science department or the boasts of farmers around a hot stove. There isn't much chance now to die on the battlefield."

These are the words of Honda Shigekuni—friend to the main character in the first volume, Matsugae Kiyoaki, who is eighteen in 1912 and dead two years later—but they correspond to the young hero's own feelings. Later he himself is struck at "being alive as one age was ending and another beginning, like part of a great moment in history." At the end of the book, Kiyoaki's love affair has led him to go against imperial wishes, and he believes, in good upper-class prewar fashion, that there is nothing to do but die. "He held fast to that one thought as he stood there ... a thrill ran through him, but whether of joy or dread he could not tell."

Such thoughts were very much with Mishima during the six years he worked at this four-volume novel. The last time I saw him was about a week before he killed himself; though we spoke of many other things, Mishima returned again and again to Saigo Takamori, the Meiji Period military hero who had sought to reestablish ancient virtues by reinstating the Emperor, but who saw the new government delivered over to the bureaucrats and understood that the revolution had, for him, failed. Mishima spoke with admiration of Saigo, his final suicide by *seppuku*, and the faithful friend who dispatched him before committing suicide himself. He also spoke at length of the "beauty" of Saigo's act, that one superb gesture displayed when all had failed.

I remembered at the time a conversation we had had some weeks earlier, when Mishima had spoken of how he, like Saigo, hated the rationalizing, pragmatic, conciliatory ways that had become those of Japan in our time. I remembered his saying: "Japan is gone, vanished, disappeared." "But, surely," I said, "the real Japan must still exist someplace or other if you look around for it." He shook his head. "Is there no way to save it?" I wondered. "No," he said, "There is nothing more to save."

Now, speaking of Saigo and the beauty of his actions, Mishima added, "He was the last true samurai." I remember thinking at the time that Mishima knew what he was talking about, even if I didn't, because he had been born into a family that had been samurai, and he had in his own life practiced many of those samurai-like disciplines that still exist. It was only later, of course, that I realized he already knew that, within a week, it would be Mishima Yukio and not Saigo Takamori who would become the last true samurai.

When I found a passage early in the novel, "... a mere fifty years before, the Matsugaes had been a sturdy, upright samurai family, no more, eking out a frugal existence in the provinces" but that now "the first traces of refinement were threatening to take hold on a family that, unlike the court nobility, had enjoyed centuries of immunity to the virus of elegance. And Kiyoaki ... was experiencing the first intimations of his family's rapid collapse...."—when I read this, I knew who and what, in part at least, the novel would be about.

It is also about much more, because in these four volumes, extending from 1912 into the modern era, Mishima was writing of his times as well as of his life. As in *After the Banquet*, perhaps his favorite among his earlier works, Mishima in *Spring Snow* excels in creating the social and political life of an era as seen in the closed circles of the military, the court, and the aspiring nouveau riche.

One is reminded of Proust—not one of Mishima's favorite authors, though he much admired the many felicities of the Scott-Moncrieff English translation—and there are, indeed, similarities. An aspiring young man of a not particularly distinguished family finds that his father's money give him entree into society circles. Something of an aesthete (though Kiyoaki is an unlettered one), he keeps himself aloof from the issues of the day, remains emotionally drawn to the romance of history (Kiyoaki's interest in the neck of the Princess Kasuga is analogous to Marcel's infatuation with the profile of Oriane de Guermantes), and is very aware that he lives in a time of more than ordinary change: for Proust the First War was the end of France, for Mishima the Second War was the end of Japan.

Both authors are fond of the jeweled phrase ("... the Marquis' coarse, florid features could have served as a noh mask of the angry devil with fiercely contorted eyebrows"), the precious image ("'I can't tell you why,' she answered, deftly dropping ink into the clear waters of Kiyoaki's heart"); both loved and were influenced by Ruskin; both were involved in an explanation of, and an apology for, the perverse ways of love; and both are superb social reporters.

Spring Snow is filled with brilliant descriptions of meetings, gatherings, parties. Often an entire era is illuminated by a particularly apt reconstruction, as when Kiyoaki thinks of his Peers' School classmates and finds that "in their untried humanism ... their never faltering reverence for the talent of Rodin and the perfection of Cezanne—they were no more than the modern equivalent of the old traditional shouts of *kendo*. And so ... they went about wearing their arrogance much as the ancient courtiers wore their tall caps."

The comparison brings to mind one other book that shares something with this, the *Tale of Genji*. Like it, this *roman à fleuve* is a real *monogatari*, a (domestic) epic extending over a long period of time. The young and beautiful Kiyoaki is something like a latter-day Shining Prince, and one finds here the same objective descriptions of ritual and ceremony that distinguish the 12th-century novel. As in the earlier book, anything happening to those less than moneyed and/or aristocratic is dull and boring. One pitiful proletarian tale is dismissed in the Mishima book as "a common affair of the streets." The books also share assumptions, ironies, and—at times—even style: "[Kiyoaki's] tears soaked his pillow and he called her name again and again.

This said, I must add that the 19th-century is not the 12th, and that Kiyoaki is in no real way the new Genji. The latter was a handsome and complaisant young man; the former, on the other hand, is a beautiful young man who recognizes that "the symptoms of a man afflicted by true beauty are much like those of leprosy." Genji takes his conquests easily, Kiyoaki does not—pondering over Satako, "[he] thought that if the two of them were suddenly charred to ashes by a bolt of lightning, well and good. But what was he to do if no dreadful punishment fell from the skies and things remained as they were?" The Prince openly accepted his life, but the heir to the Matsugaes "drew comfort from the peace of mind that comes with loss. In his heart, he always preferred the actuality of loss to the fear of it."

Kiyoaki had doubts about a "virus of elegance" that Genji and his times had taken for granted. "His elegance was the thorn … he thought of himself as a … small, poisonous thorn jabbed into the workmanlike hand of his family." Later, "he had resolved that his beautiful white hands would never be soiled or calloused." And, later, "… the only thing that seemed valid to him was to live for the emotions—gratuitous and unstable, dying only to quicken again, dwindling and flaring without direction or purpose."

The hero is, in other words, a romantic. He is, at times, almost a kind of Roderick Usher in Japan; he so relishes the weight of decadence, is so determined to be the last of his line. Though he does not himself commit *seppuku* (this act is reserved for another hero in the second volume of the tetralogy), his death is a kind of suicide brought about by a completely romantic interpretation of life and the world.

Mishima himself was intensely romantic: his death was so romantic that its seriousness alone saved it from melodrama. But, as Mishima might have asked: what is the matter with melodrama?—it too is a form of drama, and drama is life. But when I say romantic, I do not mean a taste for its more conventional trappings (though Mishima certainly had these: his devotion to Beardsley, his lifelong admiration for Huysmans, his untranslated monograph on Saint Sebastian), and I certainly do not mean the kind of escapism the word romantic has now come to connote.

A romantic such as Mishima is a man who compares things as they are with things as they have been or could be and who, in the face of public indifference and private doubt, has the strength of character to live by those standards he himself finds suitable.

When he also has the strength to die by them, the act is astonishing because we have no word for this ultimate romantic gesture and because suddenly the man is all of a piece. When the fact was accomplished, it struck many of us as inevitable. Mishima's suicide was the final stone in the arch of his life.

Yet I do not want to suggest that *Spring Snow* is entirely autobiographical, for it is not. Kiyoaki is not Yukio. Not him as he became, though it is the portrait of the artist as a young man—a very particular kind of young man. Mishima usually had about him such a young man whom he would guide and look after much as Kawabata had looked after the young Mishima himself.

Such is common occurrence in literary circles in Japan, and the main difference was that the young men were all as much as possible the way Mishima himself had been at their age: they were often Peers' School (or some equivalent); they were always majoring in literature (Japanese or otherwise); they were literary, promising, and callow.

They were the mirror of Mishima at a certain age, and Kiyoaki is one of them to the life. Except that he cannot—no more than can any of these literary young—transcend this self as Mishima did. They cannot, as the death of the author revealed, contain in themselves that quality he most prized: a complete consistency of character, a more than ordinary sense of direction, and a more than human certainty of purpose.

Mishima was no more born with this than anyone is: he achieved it. All of his various activities (playwright, husband, actor, novelist, athlete, lover, singer, father) are now revealed as not only displays of the wholeness of a character then commonly criticized as too dispersed but also as the various ways through which such wholeness is achieved.

It is achieved by becoming the world in all of its parts. In his first novel, *Confessions of a Mask*, Mishima showed us the initial step, revealed the seeds from which his life sprang, when he spoke of the first of those who became an ideal. "I had a presentiment that there is in this world a kind of desire like a stinging pain. Looking up at that dirty youth, I was choked with desire, thinking, 'I want to change into him,' thinking, 'I want to be him.'" This is a common emotion, almost everyone must have felt it, but for Mishima the emotion was so strong that he truly became what he most admired.

This is the subjective (or the romantic) triumph. It is this that makes him an extraordinary writer as it made him an extraordinary man. As Mishima more and more became the man he wanted to become, he more and more saw himself (as every artist does) as, in his turn, an exemplar, a kind of model. His suicide, like his last novel, was a call to order. Both acts are consistent with this character that he (like all of us, but consciously) chose to create, and both (novel and death) are intended, in this sense, as creative.

We met often during the summer before his death (all of Mishima's friends saw more of him than usual that summer: he called more, wrote more letters, paid more attention to us), and one day we talked about writers and writing. I asked him what he was going to write after he had finished the very long novel (this one) that I knew he was working on.

"I don't know," he said. "I think I have said everything I can, for the time being, at any rate." I asked him why he didn't write a comedy—he never had. "I don't think I could write comedy," he said, "and, besides, this is no time for it." This was true, and though he himself could be very amusing, Mishima had never written anything amusing. He had a lively sense of the ridiculous and the incongruous, but his sense of humor was too barbed to be humorous, and though he loved aphorism, he was not witty. He liked Wagner better than Mozart.

"This novel I am finishing now is very hard, very hard work," he said, and then added, "And it's strange—I don't know how it is going to end. I have no idea, and I don't know how to do it. I am afraid to end this book." I was surprised because in all the twenty years I had known him I had never heard Mishima speak of fear. "What are you afraid of?" I asked. "It's just a big book, after all." "Yes, I know," he said, "I'm afraid, and I don't really know why."

Now, two years later, when I was reading this translation of that book, I found a passage that reminded me of that day. The count is looking at an old servant who had attempted suicide, and "he sensed the offensive aura that surrounds someone who has gone down the road of death only to turn back. He smelled the breath of defilement."

I think it was something like this that Mishima, the consciously self-created man, was afraid of. It would have been inconsistent with his ideal, with his choice of himself, not to have died and not to have finished the novel. He did both. Many puzzles remain—one does not so easily explain the mysteries of life and death and art—but among the certainties are this successful novel and that successful death.

Spring Snow, by Mishima Yukio, translated by Michael Gallagher. New York: Alfred A. Knopf, 1972.

The final volume of Mishima Yukio's tetralogy, *The Sea of Fertility*, has now appeared in English translation. As Donald Keene has observed, the four volumes of this last work, taken together, clearly constitute Mishima's testament to the world. In them, he plainly voices the motivating moral and ethical concerns that were presumed or implied in earlier works. Though not biographical in the ordinary sense of the word, these books do constitute a kind of autobiography in that they so fully display Mishima's personal beliefs and so strongly insist upon the vindication of those beliefs.

One of the moral assumptions central to this cycle of novels is clearly stated in its third volume: "There are only two roles for humans in this world: those who remember and those who are remembered." This had long been one of Mishima's maxims, and in both the method of his life and the manner of his death, the author was determined to assume the latter role. Indeed, this big book—it runs almost one thousand four hundred pages—which was finished in the early morning of the day in 1970 when Mishima killed himself, may be read as his final insistence on being remembered.

The entire *Sea of Fertility* cycle, in fact, is about remembrance—though not in any Proustian sense. Evanescence is the enemy, mutability the villain, and time consequently remains uncaptured. It is this theme which holds together a work which otherwise seems to be deliberately unstructured. The four main characters (one to each volume) are presented as a series of reincarnations.

Belief in the theory of reincarnation had apparently become necessary for Mishima. Always perturbed by change and disgusted by intimations of mortality, Mishima turned to the idea of a continued life. And reincarnation, of course, offers more than a promise of eternal youth: it is a way of being endlessly alive.

As Mishima saw it, the way to be both remembered and assured of being born again is through being "pure"—a word which occurs often in his works but never more than in this one. "Purity," he wrote, "[was] a concept that recalled … a child clinging to its mother's gentle breast, was something that joined … directly to the concept of blood, the concept of blades slashing down through the shoulder to spray the air with blood." In the context of this book, purity embraces steadfastness, determination, fidelity and all the other concepts opposite to the compromise and accommodation the author so hated.

The four main characters in *The Sea of Fertility* share Mishima's beliefs and all choose to die for a "purity," an attitude which can also be read as inflexibility. "If one wished to live, one must not cling to purity," Mishima wrote—and thereby suggested just how near death he conceived perfect purity to be.

Purity, of course, was also the theme of Mishima's last speech to the uncomprehending soldiers of Japan's Self-Defense Force just before he committed *seppuku*. And as he then admonished the soldiers, so he now exhorts us. As this book becomes more and more insistent upon the ethical and moral ideas that appear so naked on its pages, we realize that it too is a speech.

This, in short, is not a novel, that is a story recounted with expert observation and marked by ironic understanding. In *The Sea of Fertility*, Mishima's concerns are no longer those of the artist but those of the moralist. If this tetralogy is moving, it is as a cry is moving.

"People commit suicide to establish themselves," Mishima wrote in this final volume. Already established as a novelist, Mishima attempted, both in his death and in this book (and it is as impossible to separate them, as he doubtless intended), to establish himself as a true moralist, one who lived and died for his precepts. This display is as attractive as it is quixotic.

It has made these four volumes bestsellers in Japan, has inspired a stage version of the first and a proposed film version of the second. The attraction of such a firm and limiting statement as this book contains is that it makes the world a simpler place and a more exciting one. For this reason, this long testament will always have its admirers. It is also, however, clearly a formal declaration of a person's wishes as to the disposition of the opinion of the world.

One may read it as spiritual autobiography, as propaganda, as divine revelation or as empty self-vindication, but one can read it only as these.

The Decay of the Angel, by Mishima Yukio, translated by Edward G. Seidensticker. New York: Alfred A. Knopf, 1974.

Tachihara Masaaki

Tachihara Masaaki (1926–1980), one of Japan's most original contemporary writers, is not as yet well known abroad. His present translator has previously published three of his stories, and one of his pieces on the tea ceremony has locally appeared in English. The author's originality is in his fusing fiction with the aesthetics of traditional Japan, in discovering a correspondence between life and art.

Himself the son of a Zen priest, he has written widely on the noh and the traditional Japanese garden, insisting upon the identity between the sensual and the aesthetic impulses. His knowledge of traditional Japanese landscape gardening informs, in particular, his 1979 novel, *Yume wa Kareno o*, of which this present volume is a translation.

In it, a designer of traditional gardens seduces the wife of client through the design and effect of the garden itself. Even while it is being made, she is subject to moments of disquiet, and when it is finished she finds that "each perfectly placed stone seemed to be gazing ... with eyes that were alive."

When the gardener has his way with her, he lays her down and "realized how emblematic she was of both the path and the garden it penetrated." This fixing of both the lay of the land and the laying of the client is one pregnant with suggestion. "Viewed from one perspective, nature is really chaos, but this garden, while retaining that disorder, expressed a natural sort of beauty and contained nothing superfluous." On the other hand, it was not artificial.

The predatory gardener does not like artifice. He finds even "the Daiesen-in garden completely artificial ... the idea was immaturely expressed." Rather, his ideal—as expressed in both garden and client—is that "this garden was very naturalistic. The design seemed artless, yet it distilled nature."

All of this is expressed so indirectly by Tachihara that the story never joins the gothic romance standing right behind it. And the correspondence between lust and creation is so delicately suggested that such mighty polarities seem credible.

After all, the Genroku artist Moronobu also wrote about gardens and "the connection between the Moronobu who made erotic prints and the Moronobu who designed this garden was clear."

Tachihara thus shares with both Tanizaki and Kawabata a blending of sex with aesthetics. He does not have (nor apparently want) that objectivity which accounts for Tanizaki's humor and Kawabata's distance. Rather, he can say of his heroine: "And yet, she still had this thirst for love."

Her words recall the Mishima novel, *Ai no Kawaki*, (*Thirst for Love*) which also has an erotic gardener and a seducible housewife. And, like Mishima's people, Tachihara's are much concerned with vindicating their creative lust.

Both seducer and seduced think a lot about purity. He wonders if she "can purify such physical desire." Later, he wonders if she will "be able to purify [his] crude lust." Apparently she can, at least she says: "When I'm here with you ... I feel I've kept all my innocence intact."

A number of parallels are suggested. Landscape gardening tames nature. Such ideas as those about purity channel eroticism. Both nature and the sensual appetite are, in a way, vindicated. At the same time, gardening cannot respect the intrinsic entity of nature, and high-minded lovers cannot respect the full entity of physical desire.

The dilemma is not stressed in this book, but it is plainly there. At the end, the betrayed husband destroys the beloved garden, and the beloved herself, purity still intact, is left alone.

The originality of the author lies in the depth of his perception, his refusal to simplify (the book, for example, is not an allegory or a parable), and his vision of a natural, vital, and unacknowledged connection between what we think we feel and what we think we think.

Wind and Stone, by Tachihara Masaaki, translated by Stephan W. Kohl. Berkeley: Stone Bridge Press, 1992.

Kaiko Takeshi

"They have a repulsive, absolutely off-putting look. They are peculiarly timid and arrogant at the same time.... They have a frightened look about them and yet are filled with pride ... If they go to a restaurant, they sit in a corner as if glued to the wall, and they don't feel safe unless they're with other Japanese.... They say that they will become rootless if they don't continue to speak Japanese, and they must write in their own language; but that's a lie. The truth is that they can't function alone."

This is the view of one Japanese expatriate of other Japanese abroad: that of Kaiko Takeshi (1930–1989) in *Darkness in Summer*. His protagonist and her lover, separated for ten years, are both long out of Japan. They meet again and spend a summer together in Europe, eating, making love, thinking, talking, and demonstrating that the

Japanese cannot function alone. And, an achievement of this novel, they show that, indeed, no one can.

Harsh but never brutal, compassionate but never complaisant, the male member of the couple narrates the story of their renascent affair, which began in Tokyo and concludes in Berlin. Told with honesty and insight, the story becomes that of all rootless if needful love affairs everywhere. Metaphorically, all such couples end where this one does—riding the S-Bahn west to east and back again, these political polarities echoing all those personal ones the two protagonists have discovered in each other.

The first-person narrator, who, like his mistress, remains anonymous, is very Japanese. His only difference is that he knows it. He hates his country as only the disillusioned can and loves it as only the thoroughly dependent do. He does not sit as though glued to the restaurant wall, he does not pine for green tea over rice, he does not feel lost without a party of Japanese around—but he knows what all this feels like.

And he writes his book in a distinctively Japanese literary form, the *shishosetsu*—an intimate, formless first-person narrative, the main events of which are traditionally the seasons, the weather and the feelings of the narrator. Now, however, the ingredients are the distance of nature, the equal distance of self and the consequent pain of mere existence.

It is a measure of Kaiko's success that he not only makes us believe in these Japanese lost in the wide world, he also makes us see that we are all of us equally lost. His *shishosetsu* is so honest and so objective that he moves from the particular "them" to the general "us." By remaining absolutely Japanese, he has become completely international.

Darkness in Summer, by Kaiko Takeshi, translated by Cecilia Segawa Seigle. New York: Alfred A. Knopf. 1974.

Here are two excellent novellas, early works (1957 and 1959, respectively) by the writer known abroad mainly for *Darkness in Summer*. The first, *Panic*, is about a government employee who accurately forecasts a plague of rats, is disregarded by the bureaucracy, and must then suffer the consequences of having been correct.

The beauty of the story is in the balanced confusion between rat-pack and office-pack. The hero looks down at the head of the department "with [his] thin covering of hair and the scattered marks where he had scratched it and wondered how many rats lurked in the darkness of its interior." Most of the metaphors support this careful confusion: "This man, who had acquired a reputation for foxy astuteness … had finally fallen into a trap."—and the final suicidal migration of the rodents is balanced by a similar melee among the government officials. At no place is the parallel precise, but it is everywhere inescapable.

The second story, *The Runaway*, is about a common man in the Ch'in dynasty drafted to work on the Great Wall. Kafka-like ("The scale of the palace was so vast that it seemed likely that they would be kept working here till the day of their death."), it tells the story of a man who finally left "civilization" to go out and join the nomads—and here the parallel with Japan and its society is both precise and unspoken.

Panic and The Runaway: Two Stories, by Kaiko Takeshi, translated by Charles Dunn. Tokyo: University of Tokyo Press, 1977.

Komatsu Sakyo

This is a translation of *Nippon Chinbotsu*, the Japanese bestseller of 1973. It is about the volcanic destruction and eventual submersion of the archipelago in the very near future, and the efforts of the government and a few individuals to cope with the catastrophe. The book was extremely popular—two million copies in print—and there was much speculation in the dailies and weeklies concerning this bestseller phenomenon.

It does make one wonder. Fidelity to life as it is and people as they are, a general obedience to the laws of probability, and an observance of the complicated nature of human beings are not, to be sure, distinguishing features among the bestsellers of any country. Still, even among such, a book this heavily didactic, this transparently explanatory, this given to stereotypes must be something of a rarity.

One does not, naturally, expect too profound an analysis when characters are scampering out of the way of a shaking Tokyo and an erupting Fuji: One ought, however, to demand a certain appearance of probability and some indication that real emotions are being felt.

Probability is, from the earliest pages, sacrificed to the author's earnest need to dramatically inform. The cast of characters is collected time and again to witness some new terror so that we will have more eyewitness reports. No matter what they are doing, they always gather on the second to express their two or three emotions in the face of some further cataclysm. This involves some rather transparent manipulation on the part of the author who seems quite unaware that the laws of probability, and hence believability, are the first things to submerge in his novel.

As for the characters themselves, we have seen them all before—literally, in Japanese science-fiction films. For example, the self-sacrificing scientist, a brilliant maverick who does not enjoy the regard of the Japanese scientific establishment. Nonetheless, and against enormous odds, it is he who single-mindedly continues his studies and presents the unbelieving world with the truth. It is he who also elects to stay with the Japan he loves to the watery end.

I first saw him twenty years ago, grubbing around the bottom of Tokyo Bay trying to attach a bomb to the ankle of Godzilla. Later, I watched him combat Mothra and Baragon. Still later, he was successfully predicting an invasion from Mars. One came to feel a kind of affection. He was so reassuring.

Then there is the young hero. Stalwart, if not all that bright, he eventually "comes to understand" and then with might and main does whatever one can do against a submerging Shikoku and a Kyushu which is coming apart. He also undergoes a number of scenes which are called "obligatory" in bad movies.

There is the scene where he confronts the maverick but self-sacrificing scientist and fails to understand. Finally, after shuffling a bit, he does. Then there is the scene where he must quit his job in order to help the scientist in further studies. This his co-workers misunderstand, and he is accused of various things before it is all straightened out. Then there is the scene—obligatory sex scene—where horizontal love-making neatly coincides with a nearby volcanic eruption. Then there is the big scene where, having lost the heroine, he must rave for quite a while.

Since the heroine is put there for the hero to rave about, she is a somewhat dim figure. The author, however, cannily compensates by having two of them. The one the unmarried young man sleeps with is killed, as is the invariable rule in such books as this. The other, remains intact—at least so far as he is concerned. As for him, he ends up with in Siberia in a finale which eludes not only simple probability but even the major laws of raw chance.

Though the author's gift for prophecy occasionally falters, he doggedly scribbles his way through to the end, killing off his millions and regarding the eventual immersion with something approaching satisfaction.

Since there is no reality about the book we cannot, of

course, expect compassion. Nor, indeed, is any demanded. With its wooden characters and anonymous crowd, the book might well have been written with an eye to the Toho special-effects department. In any event, the book became a movie just as silly, and almost as popular, as the novel itself.

How does one then account for the popularity? Well, despite the fact that there is no proven connection between worth and popular acclaim, some kind of new horror seems to be necessary. In America, they burn tall buildings and are afraid of sharks; in Japan they feel the necessary frisson at what Berlitz calls total immersion. One of the conditions of such popularity is that you are never invited to really feel anything. The thrill comes in paperback and is, precisely, cheap.

Japan Sinks, by Komatsu Sakyo, translated by Michael Gallagher. New York: Harper and Row, 1976.

Tanikawa Shuntaro

One of Japan's most popular poets, Tanikawa Shuntaro has authored more than a dozen collections, several books of essays, has rendered Mother Goose into Japanese, and currently translates *Peanuts*. In addition, he appears as a reader of his own work and has given poetry recitals both here and on campuses and elsewhere across the United States.

His appearing across the U.S.A. is fitting because it was this country that most influenced his poetry. Though traditionally the foreign poetic influence in Japan has been French (Baudelaire, the later symbolists), Tanikawa and his generation took their influence from things American.

And in 1953, he and several others of his generation

(Ibaragi Noriko and Kawasaki Hiroshi) founded a magazine, *Kai*, which displayed their unconventional verse and their anti-traditional attitudes.

Tanikawa, for example, is publicly proud that he never went to university; he pretends never to have read the *Man'yoshu*, and has often said that he became a poet suddenly, that it was like learning to ride a bicycle.

When his first collected verse appeared, its freshness and newness made a considerable impression. It was not "deep" in the accepted and somewhat gloomy sense of neo-symbolist poetry in Japan, but neither was it shallow. It was light, sharp, sophisticated.

When I asked Kanaseki Hisao, the literary critic and translator, to suggest a parallel, he said that this would have to be someone less academic than Betjeman, yet more formal than Ferlinghetti, someone as knowledgeable as Francis Ponge.

Recently, a further comparison was offered. James Kirkup said that "Tanikawa is the poetic equivalent of Okamoto Taro's meaninglessly banal and hideous sculpture." While one must, of course, agree with this appraisal of the work of Okamoto, one cannot, at the same time, but wonder if the parallel is precise. To be sure, Kirkup ought to know. He was one of Tanikawa's translators and three of the poems appear in his versions in the Penguin *New Writing in Japan*. To say, however, that (apparently like Okamoto's) Tanikawa's "later work is ... childlike inconsequence masquerading as spontaneity" seems to me to do the poems less than justice. With Tanikawa the childlike quality is real; so is the spontaneity.

This has itself occasioned some criticism. Donald Keene has written that "Tanikawa was sometimes criticized for his readiness to compose poetry that amused, rather than moved, his readers." Also that, though Tanikawa "gained a wide following for his fresh, affirmative poetry," this actually "acquired its full impact only when read aloud."

Foreigners who have or have not heard Tanikawa reading on U.S. campuses now have three more volumes of Tanikawa's poetry (in addition to the early North Point Press *Selected Poems of Tanikawa*) to help them make up their minds.

Japanese critics and poetry enthusiasts go on about Tanikawa's extraordinary gift for word play, his beautiful way with the resonances of the language, his often surprising spontaneity. Just how well such qualities lend themselves to translation may be open to doubt—though something quite attractive does come through.

The three volumes (all translated by William I. Elliott and Kawamura Kazuo) are: *Tabi* (1968), given as *With Silence My Companion; Yonaka ni Daidokoro de Boku wa Kimi ni Hanashikaketakatta* (1975), translated as *At Midnight in the Kitchen I Just Wanted to Talk to You*; and the 1980 *Coca-Cola Lessons*.

It is the latter which contains the celebrated Tanikawa version ("for Jimi Hendrix and Yano Akiko") of "Kimigayo," the last stanza of which goes: "May our Great Knight the Emperor reign for one-thousand,/nay, eight-thousand nights,/and through all eternality/may pebbles grow into a great boulder/mucked with a mess of moss!"

The other two collections are a bit more formal, and the 1975 volume contains this very Tanikawa-like verse for his friend, the composer Takemitsu Toru: "As usual, you're out drinking tonight, aren't you?/I heard ice cubes smacking the glass./I suppose you drone on and on, and suddenly fall silent./Although there's only one reason for suffering,/people fool themselves in lots of ways./Do you beat your wife?"

With Silence My Companion, by Tanikawa Shuntaro, translated by William I. Elliott and Kawamura Kazuo. Portland: Prescott Street Press, 1975.
At Midnight in the Kitchen I Just Wanted to Talk to You, by Tanikawa

Shuntaro, translated by William I. Elliott and Kawamura Kazuo. Portland: Prescott Street Press, 1980.
Coca-Cola Lessons, by Tanikawa Shuntaro, translated by William I. Elliott and Kawamur Kazuoa. Portland: Prescott Street Press, 1986.

Yamazaki Tomoko

In 1968, Yamazaki Tomoko went to Amakusa to research the true story of the *karayuki-san*, those women who had formed the vanguard of colonial and commercial expansion as "military comfort women." Twenty years ago, little was known of this exploitation, and Yamazaki was in the vanguard in exposing what had happened to these trusting and unfortunate women.

In 1973, one year after the publication of her account, she was awarded the Oya Soichi Prize, and a year later the book was made into a film by Kumai Kei. *Sandakan Brothel No. 8* is now in its twenty-fourth printing, and last year this English translation was released. The "comfort women" issue has been much more fully exposed and work on an assessment and recompense continues.

This initial document remains important for a number of reasons. One of them is its directness. All by herself, Yamazaki went looking and found a woman, Osaki, who had had these experiences. Thc firsl part of her book is about how this was accomplished.

Though Osaki had returned to Amakusa, she was very poor (her Borneo earnings had built her brother's house for him, but she was given no room in it), and Yamazaki determined to share this poverty with her.

As she tells herself: "If you can't eat Osaki's barley rice day in and day out, sit on rotten tatami crawling with centipedes, and sleep on her futon of Borneo cotton on which she had to lie with thousands of men, and, finally, if you can't dig a hole and do your business below the cliff out back, how can you expect her to look at you as an equal? If you can't do that, surely she won't tell you about her life as a *karayuki-san*."

The second, and major, part of the account is Osaki's story: Where and when she was born—1907 or 1908, she was not certain—and how she was sold and shipped off to Borneo. "It was two or three years after our arrival that we were forced to take customers. I had just turned thirteen. I will never forget that day."

Initially, she refused, but the boss said: "I've invested ¥2,000 in your body. Pay it back, and you can forget the customers! If you can't, then you just better settle down and start taking in men from tonight."

Osaki and the other girls scheduled to begin with her had not really known what this meant. "It was so horrible, we could hardly believe it … sometimes I thought I was going to die. You'd think that at least when we had our periods we wouldn't have to take customers, but the boss wasn't one to let that get in the way. 'Just stuff some paper up inside you—it's no big deal,' he would say."

Later, talking with Yamazaki, she said that some women had different experiences and "even let out cries of ecstasy, but I never felt this way. Of course, I also uttered those cries. What did they call it? Service, that's it, extra service. But in my heart I just wished that the man would hurry and be done with it and leave."

Yet she was forced to continue and so she did. More fortunate than many, she did not succumb to any of the prevalent illnesses and very gradually was able to pay back her debt. Eventually, she returned to Amakusa, where she had been born, but she was now old, as well as poor, and (the community shunning her) had only other repatriated *karayuki-san* women as companions.

All of this Yamazaki discovered. "As I lay in bed at

night listening to her speak, I would reflect upon every word, chiseling her tale into my memory, down to the last detail. The next morning, after making certain that I was alone, I would furiously record everything and would then run and post it at the village mailbox."

Though Osaki could not read (nor sew, nor cook, having been sent out of the country so young) she never asked about these manuscripts, nor did she ever ask why Yamazaki was living with her. Others in the community decided that the younger woman was probably Osaki's illegitimate daughter, but Osaki herself never asked any questions and was grateful for the company.

Later, she introduced Yamazaki to other returned *karayuki-san* in the neighborhood, and the remainder of the book is composed of their various stories. All are buttressed by the writer's further research. She checked all the family registers in the neighborhood and all the "authorities" on what had become of her subject.

In all of this, there is a winning artlessness that doubtless contributes to the book's popularity and certainly makes the account so valuable. This is no sociological work. Rather, it is a personal document about two people. One lived a tragic and exploited life that she recounts with dignity and a complete lack of sentimentality. The other records it with honesty and diligence. The older woman never asks the younger why she is there, and the younger never asks this question of herself.

At the same time, however, she sees these lives within a larger context. "Those who were once sold into overseas prostitution are the embodiment of the suffering experienced by all Japanese women who have long been oppressed under the dual yoke of class and gender … these *karayuki-san* represent the quintessence of woman's existence in Japan."

Sandakan Brothel No. 8: An Episode in the History of Lower-class Japanese Women, by Yamazaki Tomoko, translated with an introduction by Karen. F. Colligan-Taylor. Armonk: M.E. Sharpe, 1998.

Ariyoshi Sawako

Ariyoshi Sawako (1931–1984) remains one of Japan's most popular writers, mostly due to her interest in various social problems. The bestselling *Hanaoka Seishu no Tsuma* (translated as *The Doctor's Wife*) is about the plight of women in the traditional household; her *Fukugo-osen* concerns itself with pollution in Japan; and her *Kokotsu no Hito* is about the problems of old people in modern Japanese society. Unlike many *mondai-mono* authors, however, she is not a propagandist. Instead, she is a perceptive observer whose interest is not in the problems themselves but in the people experiencing them.

Ki no Kawa (*The River Ki*), originally published in 1959, is about three generations in a provincial landowning family in Wakayama. It begins around 1897 and ends in the mid-1950s. This half-century, and the enormous changes it encompassed in Japan, is seen through three women (grandmother, mother, grandchild) and their lives.

At the opening of the book, Hana is going off to be married. It is the middle of the Meiji Period. The old ways are still alive, and she goes by boat downstream to the town of her husband—a whole procession floating along the Ki River. Though she has her moments of rebellion, she eventually becomes a model Japanese wife.

Her daughter, Fumio, is more openly rebellious. She refuses any arranged marriages, chooses life in Tokyo for herself, and eventually, with her chosen husband, is transferred abroad. Her rebellion takes the form of a feminism then thought extreme, but with World War II and its miseries, she retreats into a conventionality which her mother finds pleasingly orthodox.

The granddaughter, Hanako, born abroad, brought back before the war, is scarcely Japanese at all. She cannot even tell the difference between cherry and peach blossoms. Yet, she is docile to a degree, and as she grows older it becomes apparent that the feminine "virtues" are again to be represented.

At the end of the book, Hana, now quite old, dies. The much reduced fortunes of the family are left with Hanako. There are indications that she—so much more like her grandmother than her mother—will continue the line and what little is left of the traditional virtues of Japan.

Précised in this manner, the novel sounds as though it is about feminism and its failure in Japan. And so it is to a degree, but, while reading, one never detects the tract or even a theme this grossly stated. The characters do not conform to a thesis—rather it is characters who naturally create what passes for one. As in any good novel people are much more important than ideas. Fumio is not a feminist because that is what the novelist is interested in; the novelist becomes interested in feminism because Fumio is.

The novel is a *roman à fleuve* in both figurative and literal senses. It is about the flow of time, and the passing of the generations; it is also about the Ki River itself, along whose banks the story leisurely unfolds. This Wakayama river becomes more than a setting: it becomes a symbol for the flow of life itself—a perfectly conventional symbol treated so sensitively that some of its original power is retained. In the same way quite ordinary metaphors (mainly natural, mostly floral) are used in a way, which returns to them something of their original pathos; and, likewise, characters which are also paradigms of a situation are presented fully and fairly, with just enough left out so that one begins to believe.

Ariyoshi's methods are so classical (and so Japanese) that it is interesting to inquire a bit further into how she gets what Henry James would have called her effects. Below is an example—a description of Hana's wedding night:

"What transpired afterward remained but a fragmented memory.... For the first time in her life she had been left alone with a member of the opposite sex. Her upbringing had been such that this in itself was a traumatic experience. Toyono [her mother] had handed her a wallet into which she had slipped an Utamaro print, referring to it as a charm. Not having enough presence of mind at that moment to recall the print, Hana remained rigid as her husband swept her up into his arms. In her pain she pressed her head against the wooden pillow but took care not to ruin her elaborate coiffure. The prenuptial instructions she had received has been very sketchy indeed. Hana did as best as she could to cope."

On analyzing this passage, one is struck first by how much is left out; second, by the nature of what is included. There is no "scene," no dramatization, yet there is a full, if oblique, description.

The past (and in English past-perfect) tense endistances events: what is very much present is already informed by meditation. Those events described (the *shunga*) are not central to the experience (since unused) and yet are not peripheral since the unseen *shunga* also describes the actions recollected. Rather, described events are central to the character. The trauma of being in a room alone with a man is described (and not the trauma of the ensuing rape) because it is this former (lesser) which most traumatizes.

Yet for me to say this is obviously to belie the passage. The legal rape does not prevent our heroine's remembering not to muss up her hair. Her character (i.e., her attitude) is already formed and present, and her actions are all reactions:

this is already in our minds as we read. In fact, this is why we read. "Hana did her best to cope,"—this is a description of character in the face of new experience and the rightness of the final word (in English and, I presume in Japanese as well) lies precisely in its single syllable of delineation: this is what Hana (even, especially) is about.

Note also with what art the *mondai mono* is played down. The girl has been criminally uninformed, she is tossed to a man whose cultural role insists upon rape, she is made into chattel and object. All of this is true enough and yet—not a word about it. Instead, just enough description to make us realize that this is true but that Hana does not know it. This, in the paradox of art, makes us believe (to understand is to believe) in the *mondai* and, for once, experience rather than merely hear about it.

The "Japanese" part of Ariyoshi's technique, I would guess, lies in her precise choice of evocative and telling details, her ability to live with "emptiness" i.e., lack of all "psychological" description, how she "truly" feels, etc.), and an unwillingness to confront the reader—knowing (as an artist as well as a Japanese—and to this extent all artists are Japanese) that the whisper is louder than the shout, the unseen more powerful than the viewed.

It is this sensitivity to the facts of communication which makes the book so good and which allows us eventually to look upward (we are never told to look upward) and view, in Tolstoy's words, the great rim, the wheel of life itself turning. I am not comparing this slight and beautiful work to *War and Peace*, but I am saying that a human concern obliquely and distantly viewed allows for the apprehension of something more important than words.

The River Ki, by Ariyoshi Sawako, translated by Mildred Tahara. Tokyo: Kodansha International, 1988.

Many Japanese have an intensely pragmatic, and I think admirable, attitude toward life—and toward death as well. The compassionate dispatch of the Japanese funeral, the lack of cant, the open grief and the honest getting on with life after it is over—these qualities are certainly not lacking in other cultures, but they are here decidedly marked.

Nonetheless, like most countries, Japan also has an alternate attitude. This is for the neighbors, for society at large. So far as death is concerned it is weepy, sentimental, filled with cant. It is seen on the screen and the tube, is encountered in magazines and newspapers. It has less to do with the fact of death than with keeping up a fictive front in the face of it and doing so mainly for social reasons. One of its manifestations in Japan is the care and concern supposedly shown the old, those nearest death.

Here actuality and attitude are particularly far apart and when, in 1972, a new novel by Ariyoshi Sawako appeared and with skill and grace pointed out this discrepancy; the book became a sudden bestseller. The thrill of honesty and the ring of truth accounted for *Kokotsu no Hito* (*The Twilight Years*), selling one million copies in the first year of its publication.

It is about a working housewife who must do something about the growing senility of her father-in-law. He wanders away from home, he has to wear diapers, he fails to recognize his own family. Inquiring, the wife discovers that many families are so afflicted.

"My father," says one, "gave us a terrible time … in the end he fell off the veranda." "Was he killed?" "No, he broke his legs and was completely incapacitated. Things were infinitely easier for all of us after that." Another says: "Grandma will be around for some time … they do exercises at the Center to make them live longer. I was so disappointed when I heard that." Later, when her father-in-law has become even worse than incontinent, the heroine is talking to yet another neighbor, one who has an incontinent mother. "I'm sure it's not so much bother to clean up after a woman. It's very messy in the case of a man." "I suppose so," says the neighbor, laughing merrily, "all those additional parts to clean."

Before long she finds herself looking at her father-in-law in a special way. "He certainly did have a fine physique for his age. It suddenly occurred to [her] that his bones might not fit into an urn. An instant later, she reproached herself for having such a thought."

She begins to understand the attitude of her husband's sister who is called home for what turns out to be a false alarm. Father gets better. "But I brought my funeral outfit with me, and my mother-in-law even gave me an obituary gift. This is such a disappointment."

The state—welfare—does very little for the old, and the various centers can do only so much. She talks to the doctor, and he is philosophical (senility is "an illness of civilization, very much like tooth decay") but of little actual assistance. She must cope all by herself.

It is then that she begins to realize that "everyone had to die one day, but when she was younger she had never dreamed that such a hellish fate awaited the elderly ... old age was a far more cruel fate than death. If [her husband] were to die, she would join him in death—even if they weren't on speaking terms at the present moment."

Akiko, her name, is a heroine in more senses than one. Though she does not know that she is being funny and also intensely human in the honesty of her reactions; she does see that she has a duty to do. She rightly resents it, she knows she does not deserve it. But her husband and son will do nothing. It is left to her.

It is while doing this unwanted duty that Akiko comes to see through the cant of the official Japanese attitude toward the old. The official version of extreme old age as a time of rest and pleasure is clearly a social construct of some kind. Yet, seeing through this, she continues to do what she feels is only right. When he fouls the tatami and spreads it carefully all around, it is she who cleans him up and scrubs the mats. When he wanders out to urinate in the garden during the night, it is she who must leave her bed and rush to hold him up while he performs his functions. Otherwise, he would fall over.

One such encounter is described with a rare beauty, one typical of the insight of this novel. He totters into the garden in the middle of the night because he cannot make it to the bathroom. She rushes out to hold him up. He looks up. "'Oh, Akiko. The moon is so lovely!' Akiko looked up at the sky and saw the pale moon shining brightly. It was a cloudless night and the moon was nearly full. Akiko stood there at her father-in-law's side and gazed at it in silence."

This little scene has resonances. This, too, is moon-viewing. And this is also perhaps a modern equivalent for that ancient aesthetic enjoyment. And this also comments upon the difference between the way things are supposed to be and the way that they actually are.

The resonances continue. The husband in a later scene watches his wife hold his father upright as he urinates. "The scene reminded him of a poem by Basho. As the snow continued to fall, the small hole resembled a dark abyss." He tried to remember which Basho poem. He cannot. Isn't this proof that he himself is getting old? Then he recalls it. It is the one about the horse staling near his bed.

Ariyoshi's is what we might call a very Japanese aesthetic sensibility—one which sees the difference between real and the assumed and then finds reasons (good ones) for continuing the assumption. At the end Akiko is truly sorry when her father-in-law dies.

The Twilight Years, by Ariyoshi Sawako, translated by Mildred Tahara. Tokyo: Kodansha International, 1984.

Tomioka Taeko

One of Japan's foremost poets, Tomioka Taeko (1935-) has been translated before only in magazines and in anthologies. This is her first collection in English, the poems having been taken from her work of the last twenty years.

Her poetry is characterized by a directness and a degree of specificity (she even uses pronouns—lots of them) rare in Japanese poetry. Also, her tone is unexpected: it is dry, witty, fairly disillusioned. Burton Watson, in his introduction, considers comparing her to Dorothy Parker, which is close, but she never strives for and is not satisfied with a merely humorous point. I might compare her to some poetry-writing Jean Rhys or someone like the now neglected Kay Boyle.

Like these three women, she is urban, knows the worst, and yet continues to somehow cope. If I compare her only to other women it is because she, like they, accepts the woman's persona, that culturally determined role, and works out her freedom within its somewhat limited framework. As in one of her "Two Small Love Songs":

> The morning after our stories were over,/you lit a match./you smoked a cigarette,/you put sugar in two cups/little by little./Then you struck a match,/I smoked a cigarette,/two of us. a cheap breakfast in between./Then, you, to me,/for the first time you called me love./Then I/for the first time wept.

One does not assume that this love affair was a happy

one; indeed that it turned out not to be is one of the reasons for writing about it. Yet it is within the limits of such affairs that one determines oneself —not that this precludes talking back, as in "Please Say Something":

> To a man eating a pear/you pose a question/like/why the hell/is he turning the light./on and off/only when/you're sitting like an insect/on a chair/in the dark of/an autumn house/and revenge and such crap/doesn't count.

And not that this precludes getting hooked again and again—as in "How Are You":

> And oh yes/today too/you had an apple for a snack./and dangling your Michelangelo phallus/and angel breasts,/you walked around,/and at night/you sipped oyster stew./Like a Westerner/you tried to roar./Like a Chinese/you tried to meditate./For all this,/after taking off your meaning/along with your coat,/and with a toothpick in your mouth,/you were there.

Something smallish, hard on the outside but soft in the center, like a sour caramel, and something entirely itself—this is the impression I have of Tomioka's persona in these poems. They are touching, familiar and yet themselves.

See You Soon, by Tomioka Taeko, translated by Sato Hiroaki, with an introduction by Burton Watson. Chicago: Chicago Review Press, 1979.

Tomioka Taeko turned to fiction later in her career, after the breakup of a long-term relationship and a return to her native Osaka. Here she again moved in with her mother, from whom she had originally run away, reviewed her life, and began writing fiction. (Film scripts as well. The first time I heard of her was as scenarist for Shinoda

Masuhiro's 1968 *Double Suicide.*) And among the first post-poetry works to appear was this 1975 volume of short stories, *Dobutsu no Sorei* (*The Funeral of a Giraffe*).

In an interview included in this collection, Tomioka says that what she was writing now called for the descriptive prose of narration rather than poetry. The lyrical style was not sufficient for the critical, analytic voice which was becoming hers. The themes changed as well. No longer was she singing the song of herself, rather she was expressing the need for what she has called "a quasi-family."

(This in part explains her interest in movies. Each is made by a unit of people grouped about the director—"in the manner of yakuza organizations." They live together and "there is a strong sense of family." Tomioka liked this experience well enough to make another film with Shinoda: *Gonza, the Spearman*.)

Both of the films are based on plays by Chikamatsu and Tomioka had been familiar with the Osaka Bunraku since childhood, could read the scripts and knew the music as well. As she has said, "this Kamigata dialect is my mother tongue and it is also the basis for my sense of language."

In addition to being familiar with the rhythms and rhetoric of Bunraku, she is also able to see the conventions of the puppet play as something very near her conception of what life now was. Those who have seen *Double Suicide* will remember the black figures of the puppeteers watching the actors with unnerving neutrality, themselves unable to interfere, there only to direct ordained movements.

The characters in Tomioka's later fiction are just this controlled by forces which neither we nor they comprehend. In the short story "Time Table," which concludes this collection, the narrator compares herself to the Bunraku puppeteer. In managing a fashion show, "I had to work behind the scenes as a *kuroko*, an anonymous puppeteer in black. I had to work out the arrangements for the hall, the master of ceremonies, and the entertainment of the guests."

As an author, she regards her characters with a similar neutrality. *The Funeral of a Giraffe* is about a mother and daughter who are confronted with the body of the man who gives his name to the story. "The Days of Dear Death" is about another mother, this one getting old. Other stories are about other family members, real, false, imagined. And all endure the unnerving, implacable and neutral gaze of the author.

There is no sentimentality in these stories, and there is very little sentiment either, if by that we mean a thought or view or attitude based on feeling or emotion rather than reason. Tomioka's world is one where cause leads to effect, and there is no mitigation.

She herself has said: "I have an admiration for those who have the ability to do away with the ego and live as animals," and yet at the same time "the basis of my thinking has always been that people should be able to experience life more deeply."

These aims are not antithetical, but animals do not (or do not seem to) reflect—nor do Tomioka's characters. Rather, they experience a fruitful tension between the aims of a contemplated existence and one which is simply existed. This dynamic is one which creates the viability of the Tomioka story. It is manifestly true, and the truth lies partially in the unwillingness of the author to placate. We are shown the bars of our cage, and it is a rare author who can do this.

This she apparently does with a certain style. Her translators speak of her interest in modernist prose, of the influence of Bunraku rhetoric, but their work contains no indication of this—it is in workaday modern, colloquial language.

The Funeral of a Giraffe, by Tomioka Taeko, translated by Kyoko Selden and Mizuta Noriko. Armonk: M.E. Sharpe, 1999.

Atoda Takashi

One of Japan's more popular writers is Atoda Takashi (1935-). Specializing in the short story (he has written over forty collections), his work may be seen as defining something like Japanese popular taste.

He himself has said that the three elements important to his style are point of view, a sense of realism and judicious editing. His translator, Millicent Horton, says that she finds him particularly Japanese in his sense of nature, the choice of an aesthetic theme rather than one philosophical, a lyrical "as opposed to a symphonic" development, and his stressing "the insignificance of time" as demonstrated "by the continual juxtaposition of past and present."

In the title story, "The Square Persimmon," as in many of the best in this eleven-story collection, time plays a major narrative function. Reminded of a childhood incident involving an unknown woman and a cake in the shape of a persimmon, the protagonist retraces his steps, remembering.

Atoda's teacake, like Proust's, returns the flavor of time past, and both narrators are inspired to begin their searches. It is perhaps indicative that the Japanese searches in a much more pragmatic manner and actually returns the past to the present. It is also indicative that this is an easier answer to the problem posed than that provided by Proust. Which is perhaps why Atoda is a popular author, and Proustian parallels are inappropriate.

Nonetheless, a real concern for the meaning of the past is evidenced in many of these stories. "Floating Lanterns" is a beautiful study of death apprehended in a man's searching his memories. "Paper Doll" is the story of a man returning to the house in which he spent his childhood and finding a lost toy. "The Mongolian Spot" is a moving account of a "new" past sprung on the protagonist who learns, finally, about his parents. "The Honey Flower" shows a boy remembering earlier boyhood, a parallel with a now-dead girl, and natural connection between corruption and life.

These stories are distinguished by the sense of realism of which Atoda has spoken, one which seems quite ordinary until it is seen that its precision creates an ambivalence. This is contrasted with the everyday ordinariness of life, the meaningless things we do because we wouldn't know what to do if we didn't—the vacant rites of existence. A knowing acceptance of these is, I would suggest, Japanese.

At the same time there is some very human squirming to get out of what is also perceived as a predicament. One of the ways is through a kind of patness, a kind of falsification. "Night Flight" begins well as an evocation of past passion but then turns into a mere ghost story. Both "Of Gold and Its Beginnings" and "A Treatise on Count St. Germain" are obvious and to that extent cheap.

The expected pattern, the trick ending, the complacent isn't-life-like-that-though—these are all attempts to reassure and are false since there can be, faced with life, no assurance. Much more honest would be an attempt to disturb, because this suggests true complexity.

I cannot pretend to know whether it is Atoda's command of the poignant past or his tendency toward the facile pattern that accounts for his popularity. Probably both. Certainly, however, forty collections of short stories are too many. Like all successful Japanese authors he is caught up in a continual demand which works against the "judicious editing" of which he hopefully speaks.

He might look at the example of Raymond Carver, who refused the demands of popularity and devoted himself to pruning published stories, to sternly editing new ones before releasing them. Maybe literature (as opposed to popular writing) is truly what is left after everything else is edited away.

The Square Persimmon, by Atoda Takashi, translated by Millicent M. Horton. Tokyo: Charles E. Tuttle Company, 1991.

Yamamoto Michiko

Though she has been well known to Japanese readers these past ten years, having won both the 1973 Shincho New Writers' Prize and the Akutagawa Prize, Yamamoto Michiko (1936-) is only just now being translated.

She writes about what she knows, and she writes with feeling and with tact. Her restraint, rare in modern Japanese fiction results in the reader's willingness to more fully feel, since nothing is ostensibly asked. The surface, as in the finest Japanese narrative, is still—but, just beneath, all is living turbulence.

In the title story. "Betty-san" (the work which won the author the Akutagawa Prize, appearing in 1973 as *Betty-san no Niwa*), "Betty" herself is a Japanese woman who married an Australian and lives in Darwin. The sons are grown, the husband has changed, perhaps found himself a mistress, and Betty is all alone. She is tired of her foreign name (Elizabeth) and wants back her Japanese name (Yuko). She is indeed tired of being an expatriate but can do nothing about it.

This somewhat unpromising material is turned in a moving, beautiful lament for all that is lost simply through having had the bravery to be different. At the same time, there is no false pity, nothing maudlin about this account of Betty's empty days. Rather, there is a kind of indifference, unstudied but philosophic, which suggests that all life is like this, that little Betty, unhappy in provincial Darwin, is only an example of this—and that the unspoken "this" is the true theme of this moving story.

In "Powers" (*Maho*, the work which won the author the

Shincho Prize), Asako is another Japanese wife in Australia. Her life, while not perhaps as desolate as that of Yuko, is just as empty, just as boring. The story is made of very little: Asako, her thoughts, the neighbors; some tenuous connections, particularly with the youth Sean, a connection which will come to nothing. And yet, from these slight materials, grows a work richly moving, one which is actually about something large and important: the bravery necessary to remain alone, the heroism necessary to face life as it is.

None of this is, of course, stated—to state it would be to falsify it. Yet it is there, through the medium of the writing, through the art of inference, and through the author's tact and depth.

Why is it, I wonder, that women write so much better than men do. This is not true only of Japan (Lady Murasaki is still number one) but of the West as well (Jane Austen is still number one). And to take as example just American literature, women writers are better. Willa Cather, Sarah Jewett, Katharine Anne Porter, Eudora Welty, Jean Stafford, Carson McCullers, Flannery O'Conner—it is to these we turn if we want to know the meaning of life in America. We do not, I think, turn to, say, Hemingway or Fitzgerald. If we do, we then discover only the meaning of Hemingway or Fitzgerald—life traduced by ego.

Perhaps women write so much better because they have so much less to write about. Jane Austen never mentioned the Napoleonic wars in her novels and the novels are the better for it. By writing about less, one (if one is a good writer) always implies more. Or perhaps it is because women seem less impelled to vindicate themselves (Hemingway again and, way out in left field, Thomas Wolfe), and this being so can pay attention to the world as it is, not as it looks, nor as it should be.

Whatever the reason, women's writings are distinguished

by this attention to mundane detail, this reflection of quotidian reality, which makes possible that inner illumination, that transcendental shift, without which fiction is not literature, nor are stories, novels, worth the reading.

Yamamoto Michiko shares with the finest writers this ability to shape truth out of nothing—being perhaps able to do so because nothing is so much more typical of life than something is. In the two remaining stories in this volume, "Father Goose" and "Chair in the Rain," bored women are again the ostensible subjects, people caught in the narrow confines of prescribed feminine life, persons who want more and do not know how to get it. The woman in the former story turns cruel out of boredom, and the woman in the latter turns to a cat—but she is not Colette-like enough to see through her own interest, though Yamamoto Michiko is.

Betty-san, by Yamamoto Michiko, translated by Geraldine Harcourt. Tokyo: Kodansha International, 1983.

Tsushima Yuko

"He certainly wasn't bad as a partner for obtaining physical pleasure. Thinking herself lucky in that, at least, Izumi put her arms around Takashi's clean-smelling body. [He] always performed sex quietly, like a ceremony, never requiring of her more excitement than necessary."

Thus one of Tsushima Yuko's typical women, this one from the story "The Chrysanthemum Beetle." Content with little ("lucky in that, at least"), they are, however, usually bilked of even that. In this story, Takashi turns out to be having another affair and leaving hints for each woman to find.

The Tsushima woman has long come to realize that her life as a Japanese woman cannot amount to much. "The mother felt a growing pity for the sister who'd only succeeded in becoming the parent of three grubby children before she died ... [As] for the bereaved husband ... he'd gotten himself a young wife from somewhere, impregnated her without delay, and was the picture of fond contentment."

Thus the mother in "Missing," a story about a woman who invests her whole life in another, her daughter, and what happens when she is suddenly deserted. There are no resources upon which to fall back, there is no alternative, it would seem, to awful dependency.

At the same time, however, these women are shrewd, strong and have developed a resiliency. In "The Silent Traders," a story which won the 1983 Kawabata Prize, a woman living near the Rikugien garden discovers how full it is of cast-off pets—fish and turtles, dogs and cats as well—and admires the resilience they display. She herself has been deserted by the father of her children, and her feeling of dependency for them is matched by her near-admiration for these other abandoned—these animals returning to their feral state.

Returning to the feral—this is what Tsushima's women often experience. Such is the case in "Clearing the Thickets," where a heavily pregnant woman is working outdoors with her mother, scything a field. The scythe, a severed snake, a crushed grasshopper, the unborn already stirring—these built an extended metaphor in which a return to nature is seen as a genuine alternative.

With it comes an impatience with this man-made world. "Hawkmoths used to stray into our house, even when I was in my teens. These days, with all these concrete buildings, there's not an ant to be seen." In this sterile and unnatural world, the women of these stories turn more and more to the nature inside and outside them. But sometimes they do not find even this.

In "The Shooting Gallery," a hopeless mother wants to show her two small kids the sea, but what they find—a dirty local beach—is not at all the sparkling spectacle the kids have seen on the tube. They grow restive, and she becomes more and more passive and as the story ends is perhaps about to passively undergo yet another affair which will not and cannot lead anywhere.

Often anything is better than nothing, as the girl who invests a chance meeting with an old man with enormous significance finds in "South Wind." As also with the woman in "An Embrace," who finds herself approached by the widower of a suicide she slightly knew, only to find eventually that it was not what she had thought—he was drawn to her only because he knew that she, like his wife, had been the child of a suicide.

Tsushima Yuko knows all about what it feels like in Japan to be the child of a suicide. She is the daughter of Dazai Osamu (real name, Tsushima Shuji) who killed himself in 1948, when his daughter was just one year old.

Perhaps the reason that her heroines never once think of suicide for themselves (certainly one alternative to a fairly meaningless existence) is that the author knows suicide too well, having long suffered its effects, though experienced none of its benefits.

Knowing the worst, as the Tsushima women do, gives them a kind of freedom, however. This is a freedom from the society which seeks to maim them and also from all the cant that must accompany such an existence. These women are very outspoken, and they are quite honest. For example, one of them on Christmas says: "... all it amounts to is the birthday of some complete stranger called Christ."

This freedom is their glory. Like the tough-tender women of the admirable Jean Rhys, they know the worst, and they keep right on going. It is this which makes these Tsushima stories so interesting, so energizing—eventually even inspirational. The display of spirit is enormous—and right in the teeth of an apparent defeat.

These eight stories (originally published between 1973 and 1984) are all about different women but each shares a persona. The hopeless, level gaze which sees everything, the ability (in spite of having seen everything) to go ahead, eyes on the road—it takes a very special and very personal talent to so convincingly display this.

And a special talent, too, to construct that alternate structure, different but identical, which is the English version. Here Tsushima has finally found something like perfection in this imperfect world—Geraldine Harcourt's translation. Its tone so completely coincides with what this would be were this author writing in English that there is no "translation" at all. All is direct, immediate.

Here is an example: "She picked up the baby, stripped off his wet things, and let him stay bare." Context explains that this mother is somewhat ruefully finding solace in her child. The language explains how she feels about it. Note the laconic rhythm, the heightened colloquial tone—as though the everyday has been illuminated—and the carefully faint echo of archaic, that is, the timeless, in this use of "bare" rather than, say, "naked," which prepares us for the tiny epiphany that follows. These are admirable stories, admirably translated.

The Shooting Gallery, by Tsushima Yuko, translated and compiled by Geraldine Harcourt. New York: Pantheon Books, 1988.

Takiko was a full six months pregnant by the time her family noticed. Then "her mother at once launched into an endless stream of angry questions, demanding to know why hadn't she gotten an abortion, how had it happened, who was the man, did she want his child because she loved him, was he a married man, did he know, did she plan to bring it up herself, did she think she knew how, was she doing this to get back at her parents, did she have such a grudge against her father, did she realize what this would do to her life, and just what was the big idea?"

What follows is an account of the pregnancy, the birth, the life back home with an abusive father, the loneliness of the twenty-year-old mother, her attempts to support herself, the awful clutter of kids, and the hopelessness tempting those who stray.

Except that Takiko is not hopeless. Her story is thus neither sentimental romance on the one hand nor case history on the other. And what might have been a soap opera turns into a moving chronicle of the spirit of a single woman.

She is aware and sees things as they are. The baby is loved, but, at the same time, she knows it as "a living thing, covered in heat rash, that cried and strained and yawned." In her hospital bed, she fixes her eyes on the ceiling and "could almost see the women who must had laid under this same ceiling decades ago."

"Hundreds, no, thousands … of women had laid here, staring up at the same ceiling. And one of them was her." Here we might expect—in any conventional recounting—sadness or resignation, or the horror of existence. But Takiko is not conventional and what she experiences is surprising and right. "Takiko felt a sense of sufficiency she'd never known before, a contentment that took her by surprise."

It is not that she is anything as facile as optimistic but that she is able to observe and to analyze. She thinks of the father of her baby, the husband of the young wife in the next bed, of her own father. "Each of these men had a child and was thus a father. She could think of nothing else they had in common." Analysis for its own beautiful sake.

And she can look at herself in the same dispassionate way that she regards others. When with a boyfriend, "it was always she who sought his body first, and she who attempted greedily to bury herself in pleasure as if in a great hole she was digging with all her might."

She knows this, mentions it, but does not falsify it with feelings of regret or blame or guilt. Life to Takiko is a series of facts, including the fact of her illegitimate son. She is not even tempted to moralize. This is one of her strengths, this honesty, this freedom from social cant. Her individuality is pitted against the hypocrisy among which she lives, and it is this dialectic—one that she herself seems barely to notice—which makes her story interesting and memorable.

Takiko may not know her own worth, but her author knows it. Yet Tsushima Yuko's heroine is never presented as the paragon she truly is. A quite ordinary girl, she is toughened by her experiences. Honest from the first, she attains real understanding.

Rendering this unstated theme palpable is something that only a fine writer could accomplish. Under the realist surface and the everyday detail of this book, the lucid observation of the author knits together the entire fabric of her story. This is seen in a series of parallels so understated that the reader feels rather than notices. Takiko has an illegitimate son; the man to whom she feels closest has a boy with Down's Syndrome. She often dreams of her mother's mountain hometown; she finds her own new "hometown" in a mountain greenery. She, who spent so much time in a hospital, now works in a greenhouse, a hospital for sick plants.

These parallels do nothing so vulgar as to suggest a "meaning" in life, but they do suggest a pattern, and it is the unfolding of shape of Takiko's life, and the trueness of its delineation, that makes this book so rewarding.

That and the quality of the translation, which seems to perfectly parallel in its taut sparseness the author's text.

Look again at the opening quotation of this review and you will discover in it the entire story of the book, rendered with all of its observant humor ("just what was the big idea?"), mirrored in precisely weighted English.

Woman Running in the Mountains, by Tsushima Yuko, translated by Geraldine Harcourt. New York: Pantheon Books, 1991.

Oe Kenzaburo

In 1961 Oe (1935) wrote two novellas, *Sebutiin* (*Seventeen*) and *Seiji Shonen Shisu* (*A Political Youth Dies*), both about the right-wing student who assassinated Asanuma Inejiro, the chairman of the Japan Socialist Party. The former is about how the young man becomes a rightist, and the latter is about the murder and its consequences.

Both are concerned with how an identity is chosen, a subject which Oe first encountered in the works of Sartre. The work of the French philosopher was his specific field in university, and it is not surprising that a work such as "The Childhood of a Leader," which shows a young man choosing fascism over nothingness, should have so strongly influenced these two works.

The seventeen-year-old is in need of strong, central idea of identity since he cannot tolerate his being merely human. A chronic masturbator (much detail here), vacillatory to a degree (he began on the far left), he wants to make a hard, unfeeling shell to call his own, and so he makes one in that home of such ambitions—the far right.

No sooner were these books out than Oe was paying for his insight. As Miyoshi Masao says in his introduction, "the right-wing reaction was instantaneous. Oe received threatening letters ... some hurled rocks at his study; a dozen right-wing thugs screamed menacing threats in front of his house, and the midnight phone calls never ceased."

The author's own thoughts on the matter are recorded in the 1987 *Letters to the Memorable Year*, a work which shows both the bravery of the author and his honesty with himself. "I lost all prospects of publishing in the face of the rightist threats, while having to receive letters from the left-wing every day that charged me with cowardice ..."

And all of this because of a work which bared a political truth. One can trace it in the first of the two novels. "It seems like I'm always having erections. I like erections. I like them because of the sensation of energy boiling up through my body." Later: "Should I become a left-winger and join the Communist party? Would that solve my loneliness?" Then he attends a rightist rally: "A feeling of superiority flits past me like a bird. I catch it and don't let it go."

He later joins the rightist party and gets to wear the uniform. "It gives me strength when I walk the streets ... my body is covered with an unyielding armor, like the carapace of a beetle." And later, before the assassination, "It's the armor of the Right. I have an enormous erection. I will keep this erection through my entire life ... My body, my soul, all of me will continue to stand erect."

This traces only one thread through the fabric of this rich work, but it becomes apparent that Sartre's is not the only influence. Through Joseph Kleinman's very interesting *Japanese Writing Today* (completed in 1993 and unfortunately yet to find a publisher), I learned that *Huckleberry Finn* was the favorite work of the young Oe and that he was the very first to discover *Catcher in the Rye* at the Matsuyama American Culture Center.

His seventeen-year-old's voice shares much with those of both Twain's and Salinger's youngsters—someone disturbed by the world as it is, someone painful unsure of self. Oe's young rightist might, indeed, be read as Huck Finn or

Holden Caulfield gone wrong. (Interesting in that both boys have been targets of library book-banning rightist attacks in America itself.)

In Japan one consequence of such a direct accounting for political inclination was that the two novellas were not republished, due in part to the craven publishers but also because Oe, who after all has to live here, refused permission.

Now the first of them has been translated and published in the U.S.A. The second, however, is not included. Instead, an interesting (and equally sex-obsessed) story, the 1963 *Seiteki Ningen* (unaccountably translated as *J.* in English) about the political basis of *chikan* activities in the public transportation system, is offered.

Yet, though *Seventeen* is published, it seems not to have been distributed in any conventional way—adding yet another odd page to the strange publishing career of this novella. The American edition is the work of Blue Moon Books but was "especially created" for the Book of the Month Club. Perhaps it was never for sale. This would account for its never having come to Japan and for its absence from lists of translations of Oe's work.

J & Seventeen, by Oe Kenzaburo, translated by Luk Van Haute, introduction by Miyoshi Masao. New York: Book of the Month Club, 1996.

Here is a collection of four long stories (in what seems to be a splendidly adept translation) by the leading author of *A Personal Matter*. One of them, the title story, "Teach Us to Outgrow Our Madness," continues the theme of this novel—the relationship between the fat father and the defective son. Another, "Aghwee, The Sky Monster," shares a similar subject—a man haunted by a child.

The longest, "The Day He Himself Shall Wipe My Tears Away," is the most disturbing—the narrator, waiting to die in hospital, his thoughts compulsively returning to the day the war ended and "to the current administration of his own country, a nation controlled by men who were clearly war criminals who had survived."

The best story (previously translated by John Bester) is the famous *Shiiku*, here called "Prize Stock," about a black American flyer captured during the War in a backward Japanese village, his death and how a small Japanese boy feels about this. This is one of the finest of modern Japanese novellas and reveals Oe's stature more immediately perhaps than do the two novels already translated the one mentioned above and the one called *The Silent Cry* and published by Kodansha.

Teach Us to Outgrow Our Madness, by Oe Kenzaburo, translated with an introduction by John Nathan. New York: Grove Press, 1977.

This admirable publication—*Japan, the Ambiguous and Myself: The Nobel Prize Speech and Other Lectures*—is a collection of four speeches delivered by Oe. The translations are by various hands including those of Yanagishita Kunioki and Yamanouchi Hisaaki.

Oe early gave a talk at Duke University in 1986 on "Japan's Dual Identity: A Writer's Dilemma." It begins with a surprising but accurate statement that one of the reasons for the decay of Japanese literature was because of "that element in the Japanese nation and its people that makes them unwilling to accept the fact that they are members of the third world and reluctant to play their role accordingly."

Japan, he says, has been blatantly hostile to its fellow third-world nations in Asia—and he quotes examples. "We have been aggressors toward those nations among which we should count ourselves. The burden of that knowledge weighs heavily on me." The reasons were the avid pursuit of modernization for its own sake and the consequent competition with "the colonial powers of the West."

After World War II, all this and its consequences became quite clear. In 1945 "the Japanese, in losing the Pacific War, saw for the first time the entire picture of the modernization of a nation called Japan; and it was postwar literature that most sensitively and sincerely painted that picture of Japan and its people."

This kind of literature, Oe says, stopped appearing after 1970. The rage for modernization again erupted and with it any feelings of equality with the other nations of Asia evaporated. The emblems of difference were not those of wartime Japan but are just as much in evidence. And among these is precisely a lack of that sensitivity and sincerity so evident in postwar Japanese writings.

Nowadays studies of cultural theory have taken the place of observation and these have come the West. Derrida, Lacan, Barthes, all the others—theoretically applicable to Japan or not—are treated as though their works were literature rather than literary theory. In Japan littérateurs now think that "an intellectual effort has been made merely by transplanting and translating the new foreign concepts into Japanese." Idea-mongering has taken the place of writing—and the kinship with Asia is once again forgotten.

This early lecture is the longest and the most diffuse, perhaps because of an inclusive earnestness and an unwillingness to leave anything out. This admirable trait also means that the talks quite frequently overlap, but in this age of bite-size ideas, such expansion is welcome.

The second talk, "On Modern and Contemporary Japanese Literature," given at the San Francisco Wheatland Conference in 1990, takes up, as it were, where the earlier talk left off.

"The years between 1945 and the economic growth of the 1960s was a period marked by the fact that, while people had the greatest difficulty satisfying their material needs, the moral issues they found addressed in the literature of the time were at their highest tide." This is no longer the case.

Rather, moral issues—now that material needs have been met—are scarcely being addressed at all. Oe finds the phenomenon initially an economic one and points to the singular and sobering fact that the sales of Murakami Haruki and Yoshimoto Banana alone are "greater than of all other living [Japanese] novelists combined."

This is not envy (after all, Murakami and Banana have not much chance of a Nobel Prize)—this is concern. The very popularity indicates the problem. Yet, though nothing like a solution is at hand, there are counter-signs. Other writers, just as young though not nearly so hyped, have begun to find an inspiration in Asia. Examples are given, and Oe ends this talk on a cautiously hopeful note: "This would lead us directly away from a narrow, aggressive nationalism, toward a more open future."

In the 1992 "Speaking of Japanese Culture before a Scandinavian Audience," Oe goes even further in defining the dilemma. Comparing early Heisei with middle Meiji and the world of Natsume Soseki, he finds those fierce appetites of which the earlier novelist complained are "now in the 1990s manifested in every aspect of our greedy consumerism ... status-conferring brand-name products from Europe fill the shelves of Japanese stores ... and the anonymous mass of Japanese consumers line up to buy them, eager to satisfy this strange craving of theirs."

One might expect that such examples of conspicuous consumption as the purchases of Rockefeller Center and the Van Gogh "Sunflowers" would "come under attack from the Japanese public, but they haven't, in large part because people realize that the corporate giants are only doing on a grand scale what each of them is doing privately."

In such accepted views, where members so easily

meld, Oe finds room for concern. Typically, and bravely, he finds other examples as well, ones usually ignored. "There is a wide range of opinion regarding the emperor system in Japan today, but it is alarming to see it regaining any degree of popular support, for it has the kind of power that tends to override differing views."

Among the many things that I admire in Oe, it is this rectitude, that which impels him to state an unpopular truth and to unmask an all but universally condoned evasion. In his Nobel Prize 1994 acceptance speech, he continued the moral themes which have illuminated all of his writings—including the earlier talks.

Here he finds contemporary Japan split between two opposite poles—poles illustrating the ambiguity referred to in the title of his talk. There is the fact that "the modernization of Japan was oriented toward learning from and imitating the West;" yet the country is situated in Asia. This ambiguous orientation made possible Japan's choice of role as "an invader in Asia, and resulted in its isolation from other Asian nations, not only politically but also socially and culturally." A further ambiguity is that "in the West, to which its culture is supposedly quite open, [Japan] has long remained inscrutable or only partially understood."

"What I call Japan's 'ambiguity' in this lecture is a kind of chronic disease that has been prevalent throughout the modern age." And he finds everywhere that this ambiguity is accelerating. Yet, just as "at the nadir of postwar poverty, we found a resilience to endure it, never losing our hope of recovery." So now, though "it may sounds curious to say so ... we seem to have no less resilience in enduring our anxiety about the future of the present tremendous prosperity."

Oe's voice is recognizable one because it is the voice of reason—one which is divorced from merely personal concerns and which seeks to describe and to understand. He can see quite well this "uncontrolled development of inhuman technology"—and he is the only one to warn us against it.

I cannot imagine another person of equivalent stature making the brave and even personally dangerous observations which Oe freely states here and in other of his writings. That he chose a ceremonial occasion to make them is equally admirable. The Nobel Prize is, after all, given those who make what it would define as a humanistic contribution, and this is precisely what Oe does.

As a person, he says, "with a peripheral, marginal and off-center existence in the world," he would still seek "to be of some use in the cure and reconciliation of mankind." This is what he does in this brave, reasoned and passionately honest book.

Japan, the Ambiguous and Myself: The Nobel Prize Speech and Other Lectures, by Oe Kenzaburo, Tokyo: Kodansha International, 1994.

Togawa Masako

The Japanese are just as taken with murder mysteries as that other *shimaguni* people, the English. And, like them, the Japanese turn out mysteries of all sorts, sizes and shapes. From the very first, an 1887 adaptation of Edgar Allan Poe's "The Murders in the Rue Morgue," the murder mystery has been endemic.

There were, to be sure, mystery stories before that. Following the Chinese example there had been a number of stories about wise sages deducing guilt—the sort of thing that Sherlock Holmes was to exemplify for the West.

Arthur Conan Doyle's famous creation was not introduced into Japan until 1889, however, and by that time such writers as Kuroiwa Ruiko had begun writing

Japanese-style mysteries. These owed much to Poe—a fact which will be apparent if you repeat aloud to yourself the name of the most famous of the group: Edogawa Rampo.

Though the Japanese mystery story was almost always of the riddle type—a problem surrounded by pieces of evidence not all of which fit together—the sage or sleuth was not invariable. Some writers of mysteries (Yokomizo Seishi and his insufferable Kindaichi) depended upon the master deducer, while others (Tanizaki Jun'ichiro, among them) did not.

Scholars have noted two major trends in the Japanese murder mystery. One is the tale of logical deduction which finally reached the point of readers growing tired of—in the words of Nakajima Kawataro—"the so-called great detectives who solved mysteries only for the sake of the mystery." The other is the fantastic and "decadent" tale which eventually descended into s/m violence of the sort in the West associated with the Mike Hammer mysteries and worse.

There have been, at the same time, however, other murder mystery manifestations. One of these is the very popular Matsumoto Seicho whose many books offer original combinations of mystery solving and social concern, i.e. the symphony conductor may have done it all right, but he only did it because he was trying to conceal his leprosy, the sufferings from which are wrongly considered a crime by society itself.

Such mysteries as these may seem a bit fantastic to the West, used to more sober fare, but even the "logical" Edogawa went in for human "furniture" (always female) and the like. Be that as it may, a logical extension of the Japanese murder mystery has been the attempt to combine orthodox detective fiction with social consciousness.

One can now detect a further development—the highly sophisticated murder mystery which dispenses with great detectives and attempts to show how people really react around a crime, one which attempts to account for that crime using only ordinary social values.

An example of this later is Togawa Masako's excellent *Oi Naru Genei*, winner of the 1962 Edogawa Rampo prize, which has now just been translated as *The Master Key*. Here we have a 1951 murder which is gradually, twelve years later, coming to light. The "detectives" are all non-professional (most of them unprofessional as well) each working without knowledge of the others.

They are in fact, a number of retired and/or unmarried women who all live together in a large for-women-only apartment. They have little to occupy their minds and their time except new religions, gossip, back-biting and whatever mysteries they can dream up. Society's treatment of the unmarried female here accounts not only for the crime but for the solving of it as well.

With logic and panache—two highly noticeable qualities often denied the Japanese writer by foreign commentators—Togawa Masako presents the riddle and then displays all of the pieces which are going to be used to complete the puzzle.

The result is a mystery novel in a most unusual and interesting shape. Mildly modernist, full of varying first-person reflections, and lots of shifting viewpoints, the book—moving backward and forward in time—weaves a story consistently surprising and consistently credible.

Also, and this I take to be a sign of maturity in the mystery novel, this book seems to be about much more than merely who done it. With its restricted locale and its unusual psychological depth, it tells us more than the history of a murder; it tells us something about the nature of suspicion, of belief. With its emphasis upon new religions, it indicates that, though the religion is phony the belief, that which sustains us, may not be.

In this larger sense, the book is about belief—its necessity and its consequences. Not that anyone would stop to consider it while reading this fascinating murder mystery. It is only later that this occurs.

The Master Key, by Togawa Masako, translated by Simon Grove. London: Century Publishing Company, 1985.

Yoshimasu Gozo

Yoshimasu, born in 1939, is a poet quite outside the contemporary Japanese tradition. Influenced by epic and the native tradition of other countries (that of the American Indian, in particular), he is a bard who sings of ancient beginnings.

He literally sings, standing on the stage and putting himself in an apparent trance, "voicing his lines as if possessed, as if in delirium," it has been said, "as if echoing the snatches of words and sentences heard in his and other people's dreams."

A latter-day shaman, he is also a sophisticated poet whose works may be chanted but are also intended to be silently read. I have been told that this experience is almost equally startling because Yoshimasu's poetry is very "visual." The three types of Japanese writing (*kanji* and the two *kana* syllabaries) are used with apparently dramatic effect, and their sharp visual contrasts are a part of the poem.

This could potentially discourage translation, but in fact, Yoshimasu is translated more than many modern poets. In English he has appeared in the Penguin *Postwar Japanese Poetry* (1972), in *The Poetry of Postwar Japan* (Iowa University, 1975) and in the collection *A Thousand Steps ... and More* (Katydid Books, Oakland, University, 1987). Sato's, however, is the first collection entirely devoted to the poet.

The choice of translator could scarcely have been more to Yoshimasu's advantage. Sato Hiroaki is one of the most distinguished translators of Japanese. His anthology of poetry, *From the Country of Eight Islands*, which he completed with Burton Watson, won the American PEN translation prize for 1982. Sato is also the author of many collections, including the delightful *One Hundred Frogs*. Still, translating Yoshimasu must have been a major labor. It is precisely those qualities for which the poet is known ("visual" poetry, tone) that are most intractable.

W.H. Auden, writing of the splendors and miseries of translation, said "I have always believed the essential difference between prose and poetry to be that prose can be translated into another tongue but poetry cannot." Yet at the same time he is moved and influenced by poems in translation (the subject is Cavafy) and reasons that since he is moved then "this belief must be qualified." The degree of qualification must, however, be determined by the translator.

Auden believed that when "a poet 'sings' rather than 'speaks' he is rarely translatable." The "meaning" of a lyric by Campion is inseparable from the sound and rhythmical values of the actual words he employs. Sato would, I think, disagree on this point, and his major argument would be the success of this Yoshimasu collection.

In his interesting and revealing terminal essay, Sato discusses the whole vexed question of translation and indicates the varied advantages and liabilities of the two approaches: strict and free. In business translations (the way poetry translators usually make their livings) he finds the free translation essential and gives some amusing examples.

A letter asking for Japanese funding came to him in the typically pretentious Americanese of the '80s. The Japanese sponsor would, if it gave money, accrue "special opportunities for client cultivation while fulfilling a number of marketing and public relations goals," which would "add a new dimension to your corporate image" and "invest in the community's quality of life."

Sato properly found this to be so puerile as to be insulting and so his translation was very free. The single Japanese sentence selected to replace most of the declamation was amorphous, in very acceptable Japanese, and perfectly served its purpose, though it might have sounded too spartan to the debauched ears of the original writers. "It went something like: 'Your cooperation will greatly help promote a better U.S.-Japanese friendship'," he says.

For lyric poetry, however, Sato is strict. He has attempted to be "slavishly faithful" to the original, right down to the punctuation. This is severe but right: the Yoshimasu is not just a collection, it is a book in its own right.

And it is a book which is not only "visual" (a quality which even the utmost strictness will not render visible in English) but which is deliberately difficult to skim. Everything is used to slow down the reader: commas after each word, italics strewn about, small caps, parenthesis, brackets. Reading it is not a comfortable affair, but then it is not supposed to be.

Rather, it is a translation into English of the experience of hearing Yoshimasu's voice. This voice is the full style of the poetry and, while never having heard Yoshimasu in person, I can image that what Sato is capturing is the tone itself.

Osiris, The God of Stone, by Yoshimasu Gozo, translated with an essay by Sato Hiroaki. Laurinburg, North Carolina: St. Andrews Press, 1987.

Ikezawa Natsuki

Born in 1945 in Hokkaido, Ikezawa Natsuki here makes

his debut in English translation. Although he majored in physics in university, he also translated Gerald Durrell and lived in Greece for a number of years before returning to Japan.

His first novel, the title of which might be translated as *The Stratosphere of a Summer's Morning* (1984), is about a young man who drifts to a deserted island and discovers his relationship with nature, a theme which recurs in the author's work.

Islands also appear in such later works as *Mariko/ Mariquita* (1990), *Singing in Babylon* (1990) and *The Failure of the Mathias Girl* (1993), which won the Tanizaki Prize. So, perhaps consequently, are natural societies contrasted to constructed ones.

Those who believe in psychology may make what they will of the fact that Ikezawa is the (illegitimate) son of Fukunaga Takehiko, another well known writer. Surely more important, however, is that the younger author has created a parallel world—one which lies alongside our own but is quite different.

This is the theme of *Still Life* (1988), a two-story collection (three more have been added for this English edition) which won both the Akutagawa Prize and the Chuo Koron Newcomer's Award. Though the acumen of Japanese literary prizes is as open to doubt as that of other countries, one feels that Ikezawa is truly original.

The parallel worlds in his work serve to comment upon our own. "You shouldn't think that this world exists for your benefit.... You and the world are like two trees standing together. Neither approaches the other, both grow erect ... but it may be that the [other] world is scarcely concerned with you at all."

There are other divisions as well. "You know the world is not really divided into East and West, but into the illusory world of the military and the actual world of ordinary people. You could describe it as an illusory purgatory or a potentially real hell."

Sometimes, the dichotomy is of more recent vintage. While sleepily driving (and shortly before perhaps being set up by a maybe Russian agent—the military purgatory again) the protagonist "struggled with the illusion that he was only playing a game.... He couldn't believe that was an actual road outside. It had to be a booth he was playing in, designed to make it seem that way."

The opposed worlds occasionally collide, as in "Revenant," the final story in this collection, a very fine allegorical adventure tale about the discovery of an ancient world, one that insists upon an apprehension of the essentially dual. For example, "when someone eats, he puts a piece of the outside world inside him."

The food chain is examined. Plankton eat the algae, and small fish eat the plankton; larger fish eat the smaller, and even larger fish eat them. "Finally, I eat them. But nobody eats me." Though someone just might take a bite in this strangely parallel place we all know but rarely get to.

Having won the 1992 Shogakukan Literary Prize for "Tio of the South Island," Ikezawa now lives on another island—Okinawa—in proximity to a military purgatory. This is his debut in English, and he is fortunate in his translator—the work reads as forward, as laconic and as mysterious as the author probably intended it to.

If literature means imaginative writing that gives a shape to our lives, intensifies our understanding and (courtesy of Dr. Johnson) "enables the reader better to enjoy life or better to endure it," then Ikezawa is a true littérateur.

Still Lives, by Ikezawa Natsuki, translated by Dennis Keene. Tokyo: Kodansha International, 1997.

Nakagami Kenji

Nakagami Kenji (1946–92) was one of Japan's most important writers. His significance lay within the life that he so honestly lived and powerfully proclaimed.

He was born in Kumano, a region that even now remains mysterious. Filled with forests and Shintoistic religions, it has been called Japan's home of the gods. Nakagami called it "the crotch of Japan."

The author was also born into Japan's most stigmatized class, an officially unrecognized and deeply repressed group which only now, well over a century since anti-discriminatory laws went into effect, is achieving anything like parity.

Nakagami was no political spokesman. Rather, he was an artist who described this life with directness, honesty, anger and an utter lack of self-pity. For him, the ghettos of Kumano and the wilderness surrounding them were the homes of demons as well as gods, and the animistic world was still very much alive.

The West knows his work mainly through Yanagimachi Mitsuo's extraordinary 1985 film, *Himatsuri*, for which Nakagami wrote the script. Here the gods of the forest are truly felt, and the work that demons do is experienced at its bloody conclusion.

That script, however, remains untranslated. Indeed, there have been few editions of his work in English. (There are more in French, including the 1994 novel *Sanka*.) The only other English translations that I know of are Mark Harbison's version of "The Immortal" (included in Kodansha's *The Showa Anthology*) and Sato Hiroaki's edition of *The City of Gravity* (which is unpublished). Like that other observer of the underside of modern Japan, Yoshiyuki Junnosuke, Nakagami remains untranslated, while every new plastic effusion of Yoshimoto Banana and both Murakamis get translated.

Finally, however, here are seven of the shorter works. These stories, written between 1974 and 1981, indicate Nakagami's achievement: All of them illustrate his powerful directness, a quality that is built upon his specificity.

"His life seemed more fragile than the cicadas sawing in the wind." "There is the sound of water, like someone wading through a mountain stream." "The pure blue sky was so perfectly clear that day you could have pricked it with a needle."

A distrust of generalization (that bane of most modern Japanese fiction) gives Nakagami's prose its crisp authenticity—it that feels right the way a haiku feels right, although the author is otherwise distant from the genteel world that produces official Japanese arts.

But then, in that sense, Nakagami is not "Japanese" at all, if this means repeating the comfortable anodynes of much modern fiction. In another sense, however, he is the most Japanese of modern authors—if this means uncovering the true nature of a people who have had centuries of Tokugawa-type "guidance" laid on them.

Like the film director Imamura Shohei, Nakagami is interested in the lower part of the body politic. Just as the film director said that it was in this portion (both politically and individually) that Japanese authenticity was to be found, so the writer concerns himself entirely with this sub-world that is actually the sphere of divinities.

In the "crotch of Japan" of which Nakagami writes, the old gods are always present—especially in the extraordinary historical stories, and particularly in the superb "Tale of a Demon" (*Oni no Hanashi*, 1981), where celestial diabolism truly works itself out.

All the stories reflect the miraculous that is always there if you pay enough attention. Ghosts roam these pages—usually the same one, a brother who killed himself and whom Nakagami could never forget. Folk tales are repeated and acted out—in one particular story a dog being fed to a falcon gives birth. And yet, these are everyday horrors and wonders. In the most death-drenched prose, life erupts: "His erection stiffens until it is too big for her fist."

For a publication of this importance, there is a singular lack of presentation in this edition: no introduction, no bibliography, nothing but a few facts on the jacket. As with most highly original authors, it is necessary to know something about Nakagami in order to appreciate his accomplishment and to respect his achievement. I have attempted this here.

Snakelust, by Nakagami Kenji, translated by Andrew Rankin. Tokyo: Kodansha International, 1998.

Slowly, the West is discovering the work of Kenji Nakagami. Now comes a new collection. It consists of three early works: the 1975 novella "The Cape" (*Misaki*), and two short stories from 1978, "House on Fire" (*Kataku*) and "Red Hair" (*Akagami*). It also helpfully comes with a translator's preface and afterward, a full biographical note and informative essays on the three works.

Despite his being born into Japan's stigmatized class, a deeply marginalized group, Nakagami was no political spokesman, however. Rather, he was an artist who described life in Kumano, where he was born, with honesty, anger and a complete lack of self-pity. Much of his work was closely based upon his own life and, indeed, the central patterns of his fiction were the patterns of those facts. Both "The Cape" and "House on Fire" share the same characters, the same archetypes: the missing father, the brother who killed himself. Behind these loom the myths that so resonate in his work.

The father assumes something like divine status when Nakagami draws upon the Japanese myth of the noble exile, the destroyer of the mother's "nest," the matriarchal retreat. In the distance, one discerns these ancient figures enacting their rituals. "By equating low and high, outcast and noble," says translator Eve Zimmerman, Nakagami demonstrates how "the need to keep such categories distinct results in discrimination (*sabetsu*), the oppression of one group by another."

Not that this is apparent to the casual reader—or even to the interested scholar. Critic Eto Jun wrote: "I couldn't help feeling that after seventy years, Japanese naturalism had finally fulfilled its promise." And one of the qualities of Nakagami is that he can be read as though he is the equivalent of Erskine Caldwell, that his Kumano ghetto is Japan's God's Little Acre.

The jacket compares Nakagami to William Faulkner. A resemblance might be the author's suggestion of forces in the distance, of an ancient epic being repeated. The protagonist of "The Cape" sleeps with his half-sister and so allies himself with that pair from the *Kojiki*, Izanagi and Izanami, who created Japan by having sex. When the modern hero feels the body of his sister beneath him, "a vision came to him of the cape protruding into the sea. Swell up, rise up, he thought. Tear the sea to pieces."

Despite the blood, the pain, the overpowering sexual detail of much of Nakagami's writing, one would be right, I feel, to see him as detached and thoughtful and (to make use of a polarity that would not have occurred to him) objective about his subjectivity.

This is the view of Yomota Inuhiko who, in his fine 1987 study, urges that Nakagami be seen as a practiced writer of fiction, who in each new work is bent on criticizing and deconstructing the previous one. Certainly, we are not here concerned with any nature-boy sort of writer, nor are we presented with a novelist for whom sex represented freedom. It is said that D. H. Lawrence concluded penning *Lady Chatterly's Lover* with his fly open. It is impossible to imagine Nakagami writing in this fashion.

For Nakagami, nothing represented freedom except for the search that was his work, one which continually asked him the same question: Who are you? Forced by the accident of his birth to doubt, he strove to affirm, whatever the cost.

"I'll give you separation," says the protagonist of "House on Fire," "but just one thing, when the time comes, I'll kill you, your parents and the kids." He says this "stroking his daughter's head as she sat with the book open on her lap." He then continues, "I'm not joking. If everything's gonna fall apart, at least I'll do that."

When the wife stares at him and asks how he could do something like that, without any reason, he answers: "A reason? I'll just make one up afterward. It's six of one, half a dozen of another." In such a manner, at such atrocious cost, does a man invent himself.

This process has rarely been so painfully achieved as it is in the work of Nakagami and if this record were truly naturalistic it would be unreadable. But it is not. It is the chronicle of a progress, the record of a person's passing through scorn and shame to achieve a self. This is honest metaphysical fiction.

The Cape and Other Stories from the Japanese Ghetto, by Nakagami Kenji, translated with a preface and afterword by Eve Zimmerman. Berkeley: Stone Bridge Press, 1999.

Furui Yoshikichi

Until now, only three stories by Furui Yoshikichi have been translated: "Crab under the Snow" by Mark Harbison "Night Fragrance" by Kathy Merken and "Wedlock" by Howard Hibbett. Interest in this author has so grown, however, that appearing simultaneously are two new collections.

That of Meredith McKinney contains "Grief Field," "The Bellwether" and "On Nakayama Hill," in addition to the title story; that of Donna Storey contains "The Plain of Sorrows" and "The Doll," in addition to the title story. None of this material overlaps, and all is necessary to appreciate this important but until now neglected author.

Neglected abroad, that is. In Japan, Furui's reputation is assured; he has won most of the major literary prizes and is known as an important and innovative stylist. He is even considered "the most representative writer" of one of those categories that Japanese critics are forever inventing.

This one is called the *naikono sedai*, which might be translated as the "inverted generation." I cannot pretend to know what is meant by this and can only find it odd that this most independent and individual of writers should be forced into a group to make life easier for critics.

It is true, however, as Storey writes, that Furui has stated that "in his writing he was interested in portraying how the external influences one's internal reactions."

Furui's writing is introspective in that he is interested in the contemplation of thought, and his characters tend to be found in fraught situations. Yoko, for example, in the earliest of these stories (1970), is found in the first sentence "sitting alone at the bottom of a deep ravine."

She is ill, something mental though never diagnosed. This illness is a metaphor—but it is dramatized, not identified. We learn from it, as she does. Yoko's illness sets her apart from the ordinary. She is beyond social concepts. She is consequently an individual—her illness has made her one—and her inquiry is into the formation of the concept of self in Japanese society. When someone asks her what it means to get well, she answers: "It means that I'd make the people around me feel more comfortable."

We also learn something about places of isolation. Standing in for Japan itself are a series of narrow valleys and gorges. There is not only Yoko's ravine, there is also the ravine in the title story of the McKinney collection, and others as well—peaks, precipices, cliffs. Japan's mountains, as Storey says, are appropriate places to dramatize the Japanese psyche. They are places of danger but also places of discovery and transformation.

Yoko, like the schizoid heroine of Shinozaki Makoto's remarkable film *Okaeri*, is not only defined by disease, she discovers herself through it. Illness reunites her with her husband; it fulfills her life. Furui would agree with both Susan Sontag and Emiko Ohnuki-Tierney who have, in their separate seminal studies, indicated that illness is an affirmative metaphor in that it leads to the creation of self.

It is for this reason that the ending of "Yoko" is so ambiguous. She goes to the hospital, and she agrees to get well, but what is well? Sick, she was herself. The happy ending deprives her of this. When you are well, you are once again only a social being.

Yoko's disease is undiagnosed, but that in "The Plain of Sorrow" is one of Japan's most taboo-ridden: cancer, the illness which, in Japanese hospitals, cannot even now speak its name. Through it, however, as in Kurosawa's film *Ikiru*, one may address the deepest of society's fears. Here, it enables formation of the individual and is by its nature immune to permanent cure. In the Furui story, cancer is transformed from constant crisis to tranquil contemplation.

One may profitably read these stories as "Japanese"—

that is, as essays into the particular nature of the local society. One of the most brilliant is the 1974 story, "The Bellwether." In it the narrator remarks that it might be "possible for us to awaken at some point from ... mass existence and return to our individual selves. More frightening is the possibility that we might dissociate ourselves from the scream that spontaneously rises up within us and instead take off at a thunderous run, preserving chill and intact the discipline of the stampede."

Miyoshi Masao has argued that, because of society's hostility toward personality and the inner consciousness, unless one imports or invents a new literary form, its expression in the Japanese language becomes nearly impossible.

In this light, and illuminating further the quality of Furui's writing, it is interesting that he is also the translator of two of Europe's most respected expressionist writers: Robert Musil and Hermann Broch. The protagonists of Furui's stories, no less than those of *A Man Without Qualities* and *The Sleepwalkers*, permit us to view action through introspective consideration—which is a kind of expressionism: originally an art term in which painters sought to avoid the presentation of an external reality and, instead, to project themselves and their own personal vision.

While it would be too much to call Furui an expressionist, since there are also Japanese antecedents (the *shishosetsu* transcribes mental states as well), it is useful to think of Musil while reading him. Both writers are concerned with the problem of conceptualizing the individual under circumstances which would hinder it, and both are believers in the worth of the single, distinctive person—one who cannot or will not become a mere social cipher.

The nuances of Furui's thick and layered prose are enlightening, rewarding and here well-captured by these sensitive translations. As to which collection to acquire—both, of course.

Ravine and Other Stories, by Furui Yoshikichi, translated by Meredith McKinney. Berkeley: Stone Bridge Press, 1997. *Child of Darkness: Yoko and Other Stries*, by Furui Yoshikichi, translated with an introduction and critical commentaries by Donna George Storey. Ann Arbor: Center for Japanese Studies, University of Michigan, 1997.

Nakayama Chinatsu

"TV's rotten, it's hopelessly corrupt." Yet, "it ought to be ethical. We know that popular support doesn't necessarily make a thing right—look at Imperial Japan, or Hitler. We oughtn't be pandering to mass tastes. The makers of the programs, the people who stoke up that proto-Fascist machine, ought to have a firm ethical basis for what they do."

Right on—but then we stop and realize that the man who says this is among the sleaziest, one who was parlayed himself to the top of the corrupt world of the tube, who is himself in charge of perhaps the worst example—the highly popular daytime panel show: "Good Afternoon, Ladies."

The format of this highly-rated program is to find someone who wants his wife back and makes a public TV plea. Shortly, "with the cooperation of our viewers," the runaway's whereabouts are traced. TV crews barge in, preferably when she is in bed with the man she ran off with.

Then the guilty couple is forced back to the studio where they confront the irate husband and a panel of "experts" who advise the participants of this true-life drama. Almost invariably, the wife is given a hard time. "If she is holding out to save her pride," says one of them, "all I can say is grow up."

The panel is composed of *sensei* and "talents," those

show-biz types who can be counted upon to deliver moral judgments on those unfortunate enough to be caught on the program. The viewing public, of course, sides with the panel. "The public aren't interested in other people's rights. Except while they're enjoying the sight of them being violated."

This is the observation of one of the people who sees through the "entertainment"—but then, in a way, all of those involved see through it, and go right on. Only one—a pretty young assistant chosen as "Mascot Girl" in order to liven up the proceedings—wants out. She is unable to stand the cruelty, the terrible irresponsibility of the program. And she is simply shown her contract and told that: "No one ever leaves."

This is the story of the novella which concludes Nakayama Chinatsu's brilliant collection, originally published in 1980 and now available in a fine translation by Geraldine Harcourt. Nakayama knows what she is talking about. She was herself a TV "personality" and before that a child actor—and later a Diet member and a leading feminist. Her TV world has the hollow ring of complete authenticity.

Her panel is just as repulsive as such truly are; the producer is a man who did pop lyrics until he started writing essays in "a light satirical style that breathed freedom and democracy to the delight of a public sated and disenchanted with the 'happiness' of economic growth"; and one segment of the script, given complete, is a masterly recapturing of the self-serving, frivolous and unminding cruelty to be seen on such real TV programs.

At the end, one "guilty" pair is simply dropped, husband paid off, because these sad lives threatened to turn dull. A new "appeal" is made. Sure enough, another deserted husband is found and shortly, "with the cooperation of our viewers" (that is, public treachery), the errant spouse will be found.

One of the strengths of this novella is that the author settles for no easy answers. Nothing is plain back and white, everything is ambivalent, and people who speak the truth are often bad at heart.

The ambivalence of life, the impossibility of simple right and wrong is again demonstrated in "The Sound of Wings," a story about a happily married woman who falls in love with another man. She wants both, knows that "their ménage would have lasted as long as her husband allowed. It was Toshio and her husband who had not permitted life to be the beautiful thing she had conceived."

The understanding husband only appears indulgent. Actually, he has her all figured out and proceeds to make her feel as guilty as possible. She, imprinted since childhood, feels that a woman is usually somehow wrong. And his apparent forbearance makes her question her lover's real ardor. A girlfriend finds this Toshio of her's unsuitable. "The word struck [her] with the strangeness of some new piece of slang."

And in the end, she is talked out of the lover. Yet the wily male victory is not complete. She still has the pride to walk out on her husband, too. Having wanted both, she learns to live without either.

Nakayama's refusal to avail herself of the solaces of an agreed upon morality may mean loneliness for her characters, but they enjoy a kind of integrity rarer in all fiction and perhaps even rare in Japanese.

This is what the child star learns in "Star Time" (the piece which gave the 1980 collection its title *Koyaku no jikan*) when she feels that she has "a much firmer grip on the fantasy of the play than on the real world in all its strangeness and complexity . . . ." But she does not know that "roles continue offstage" and is often thrown upon her own resources.

But they are there to be used. As Nakayama, a sometimes aphorist, writes: "Children are egotists who think only of themselves, while adults are egotists who tend to think they're thinking of others." So, in the end, the child actress, growing up alone, turns to the audience—"She sensed their responsiveness as they were drawn to her and pushed away, caressed and hurt by every word and gesture." She slowly comes to rest in "the solid world of plywood and paint ... in the sun of spotlights."

Last December this translation won the "Independent" Award for Foreign Fiction, and it deserves it. It is perhaps not *jun bungaku* but, for me it is the most exciting Japanese fiction to have recently come out in translation.

Behind the Waterfall, by Nakayama Chinatsu, translated by Geraldine Harcourt. New York: Athenum, 1990.